"I DON'T INTEND TAE GO QUIETLY."

"Fire at will, my girl. I've survived worse things than you could throw at me," Gray replied.

Bonnie tilted her head slightly, her expression articulating her doubt. "Funny, Shamus Gordon said almost the exact same thing tae me when we were children after I warned him tae apologize tae my friend for splattering mud on her best dress."

Gray had to bite the inside of his mouth to keep from grinning, figuring an ill fate had befallen poor Shamus. "So what happened? Did he apologize?"

"After a wee bit of coaxing."

This time, Gray couldn't help smiling, envisioning the lad strapped to a rack, a gleaming, razor-edged pendulum swinging ominously above him and a pixie-faced Bonnie chortling with glee. "What kind of coaxing, dare I ask?"

"Let's just say a person with only one good eye and a limping gait has more important things tae concern himself with than bullying others. Tyrants usually get their comeuppance." She leveled him with a pointed look. "Just a word tae the wise."

And with that veiled threat hanging in the air, Bonnie gave a toss of her wild mane and ascended the rope ladder, leaving Gray to laugh so hard he nearly drowned.

THE DEVIL'S DUE

Melanie George

ZEBRA BOOKS
KENSINGTON PUBLISHING CORP.

http://www.zebrabooks.com

ZEBRA BOOKS are published by

Kensington Publishing Corp.
850 Third Avenue
New York, NY 10022

All Kensington titles, imprints and distributed lines are available at special quantity discounts for bulk purchases for sales promotion, premiums, fund-raising, educational or institutional use.

Special book excerpts or customized printings can also be created to fit specific needs. For details, write or phone the office of the Kensington Special Sales Manager: Kensington Publishing Corp., 850 Third Avenue, New York, NY 10022. Attn. Special Sales Department. Phone: 1-800-221-2647.

Zebra and the Z logo Reg. U.S. Pat. & TM Off.

First Printing: November 2001
10 9 8 7 6 5 4 3 2 1

Printed in the United States of America

To a very special friend . . . You know who you are.

They look'd up to the sky, whose floating glow
Spread like a rosy ocean, vast and bright;
They gazed upon the glittering sea below,
Whence the broad moon rose circling into sight;
They heard the wave's splash, and the wind so low,
And saw each other's dark eyes darting light
Into each other—and, beholding this,
Their lips drew near, and clung into a kiss;

A long, long kiss, a kiss of youth, and love,
And beauty, all concentrating like rays
Into one focus, kindled from above;
Such kisses as belong to early days,
Where heart, and soul, and sense, in concert move
And the blood's lava, and the pulse a blaze,
Each kiss a heart-quake—for a kiss's strength,
I think, it must be reckon'd by its length.

—Lord Byron

Prologue

Christmas Eve, 1910

"Tell us a story, Grandpa!"

Gray winced as two youthful voices raised in unison blared in his ear, jarring him from a bliss-filled moment of sniffing the air, the aroma of a plump goose with all the trimmings making his mouth water.

His granddaughter, Maggie, perched daintily on his right knee, the molten glow from the fire in the hearth behind her burnishing her mahogany curls and tinting her smooth, cherubic cheeks with gold.

Liam, Maggie's twin brother, bounced exuberantly on Gray's left knee, prepared to vanquish imaginary foes with his small, wooden sword, several of his thrusts coming precariously close to his sibling's head.

Gray took hold of Liam's wrist before he snagged a ringlet and screams ensued, which would then cause Gray's darling wife to hasten from the kitchen, soothe the child and glare at Gray as if he were the sole cause of the fracas, her expression saying: "I only gave ye one job tae do, husband."

Yes, one job. Occupy the children. A momentous task indeed.

Gray suspected he was the one his wife wanted to keep occupied. She claimed he was more underfoot than the children, always sampling the dinner fare and endeavoring to steal a kiss, which was true, but certainly not worthy of banishment from the kitchen in his opinion. Neither of his brothers had been exiled, for which they gloated unrepentantly as he was being ushered from the room.

"A story, hmm?" Gray scratched his chin.

"Grandma says you tell the best ones," Maggie asserted, her breath scented with the peppermint candy that same grandmother had given her.

"Well, I do have a knack for a good yarn, I suppose," he returned, his injured pride bolstered.

"Grandma says it's 'cause you're full of wind and bluster," Liam felt inclined to point out, deflating Gray as effectively as a hairpin in a balloon.

Gray harumphed. Wind and bluster indeed. No Sinclair who had ever lived had to make things up. Excitement and adventure thrummed through their veins.

"Like that story you told us about them short people who blew darts at you," Maggie said.

"They weren't just 'short people,' " Gray corrected in a somewhat disgruntled tone. "They were cannibalistic pygmies attempting to kill me with poison arrows while I wrestled a crocodile, which they considered sacred."

Maggie giggled. "That's a funny one, Grandpa!"

"Oh, oh!" Liam resumed his bouncing. "What about the fat lady who squeezed you until you turned blue?"

Gray frowned. "If she had squeezed me any harder, you two disbelievers wouldn't be here right now."

Maggie entwined her fingers with his and blinked up at him with eyes full of faith and love. "I believe you, Grandpa. Even if it isn't true."

Gray threw back his head and laughed. "Thank you, moppet. Even if you don't believe me." Then he tucked both imps close to his sides, an arm around each. "All right. Which story shall it be tonight? The one about how I bested One-eyed Jack, the meanest pirate ever to sail the seven seas? Or how I survived in an underground cave for five days with no food or water in the company of rats as big as Grandma's favorite cast-iron pan?"

Both children shook their heads.

Clearly some people were hard to impress. They were like their grandmother in that.

"Hmm. Perhaps those stories are a bit too rough-and-tumble. How about a Christmas tale, then? I can tell you about a snowy night long, long ago when a jolly old elf visited my house. He landed on the roof in a red sleigh pulled by eight flying reindeer." Flying reindeer. That was a good touch. Perhaps he was a better story-teller than he thought.

"Oh, Grandpa," Maggie giggled. "That's 'Twas the Night Before Christmas!"

Gray gave her a sheepish grin. "I knew that. I was just testing you."

Liam chimed in, "We want to hear the other story."

Gray's brows drew together. "What other story?"

Maggie said in a hushed voice, "The one about the jewel beyond price."

Ah, the jewel beyond price. Gray smiled to himself. That was indeed a tale.

"You promised, Gramps," Liam persisted. "You said when we was old enough, you'd tell us. Well, Mags and me are eight now—and that's old, I vow!"

Gray chuckled. "Well . . . I don't know. That story is really meant for grown-ups."

"Please, please, please!" they begged in unison, fully prepared not to let up unless Gray relented.

Maggie tugged on his shirt in earnest until Gray leaned down. "We won't tell Grandma if you say cuss words," she whispered in his ear. "Cross our hearts." Then she peered at her brother. "Right, Liam?"

"Right!"

Who could resist that added bonus? Gray thought, kissing both their foreheads. Besides, the mature parts of the story he could gloss over, replaying those scenes only in his mind.

"All right. The jewel beyond price it is."

Resounding cheers and exuberant declarations that he was the most wonderful grandpa in all the world lilted into the air. Then the noise began to fade, growing dimmer by the moment as his thoughts traveled to another time.

Gray's gaze slid to the window, his mind's eye skimming over the crystalline waters of the ocean, going back . . . back . . . to the day all those years ago when he had forged the mighty seas, a determined man on an uncertain voyage.

And as the night wind swirled around the house and a magical hush fell over the snow-covered hills, he began to tell the story of how a treasure hunter found himself a jewel beyond price.

"Once upon a time . . ."

Chapter 1

Thirty years earlier

Gray had the mother of all hangovers.

Or a hell of a headache at the very least.

His entire being was one lethargic throb after the next and he possessed the telltale floating equilibrium of the sublimely intoxicated. His brain rapped persistently against his skull, clearly hoping someone would answer the summons and release the bilious mass before it expanded and found other orifices from which to escape.

The remainder of his body, otherwise known as the Unwitting Vessel of his Foolish Overindulgence, fared no better. Gray now understood what two hundred pounds of potatoes jammed into a fifty-pound sack felt like.

Even if his tongue didn't lie like dead weight in the sweltering cave that was his mouth, the possibility of verbalizing in multisyllabic words would overshoot his capabilities at that moment. A groan was the best he could muster, to which he applied himself with all the enthusiasm of a man in his unstable and unhappy condition.

Gray aspired to rid the fog from the twisted wreckage of his mind and recall what had transpired over the last twenty-four hours to serve him up on a silver platter in his current ignoble state.

Clearly he had been poisoned—or under the iniquitous spell of some form of voodoo, hoodoo, the evil eye, or an apocalyptic hex that rendered his mental faculties and assorted limbs virtually useless, which, if one followed that thread, seemed to lead, albeit circuitously, back to his initial assumption.

Inebriated to the point of head-hanging shame.

Although—he could simply be dead.

Yet logic seemed to dictate that if he were dead, he wouldn't be feeling poorly enough to *wish* he were dead.

Ergo, that ruled out posthumous suffering—and perhaps voodoo, though he could envision some misbegotten, lonely-hearted female with a doll likened in his image, large pins, an egregious smile and far too much time on her lily-white hands.

Which, again, looped him back to square one.

Think! Damn it!

A polluted stream of conscious thought back-paddled against the remnants of the alcohol, memories flitting around like milkweed in a spring breeze, a few disquieting images flashing through his mind, which Gray attributed to downing one too many glasses of that bottled lightning, a dim recollection of untold refills of scotch and water pinging heretofore benumbed nerve endings.

Jesus Christ, what heinous form of misery had been unleashed from that alcohol? A liquid mallet with the paralyzing effects of a thunderbolt? The back of his blasted skull hurt like hell squared, which was odd considering the fact he was facedown in the dirt—if the squalid grit coating his parched lips was any indication and his taste buds were still in working order.

Bloody hell, he was getting too damn old for this—

and since the sands of time had yet to flow upward, he wouldn't be getting any younger. Time, he decided, to take up less vigorous activities—like napping.

With some effort, and a rather piteous moan, Gray rolled to his side in search of elusive comfort, to be rewarded by a sharp rock digging into his flesh. "Have mercy, O Lord," he muttered, his eyelids fluttering open, or attempting to do so at least; they felt weighted down by the sins of the universe.

Nearly a full minute ticked past before his eyes ceased spinning and he could focus. Clarity, however, was not always a good thing, especially when one awoke in a medieval nightmare.

Four dank stone walls surrounded Gray, a rank and cloying stench permeating the air, and there was the small fact that he was shackled, handcuffed like a common thug, a rather compelling turn of events to say the least.

With a jerk, he sat up, a purely reactionary move and one his ill-used body didn't appreciate. As the world began to swim merrily before his eyes, he concluded an upright position was not a good idea if he enjoyed consciousness.

With creaking protest from his aching limbs, Gray reassumed his horizontal posture and stared blankly at the dilapidated roof, filled with the same mind-numbing lethargy abstract art engendered in him. Tiny prisms of light shined through slivers and a steady drop of water targeted his forehead as if this additional form of torture was necessary.

Drip, drip, drip . . . squeak, squeak, squeak.

Squeak?

At last, an interesting development.

Gray's newly refocused gaze slid sideways and his head followed suit, the water now drip, drip, dripping on his throbbing temple, to discover that he didn't have this little slice of heaven to himself. Two substantial-sized rats peered at him from beneath a cot, darkness engulfing all but their beady, demonic black orbs. Gray figured they were just waiting for the pall of death to weaken his ability to fight.

But he'd be damned if this was the way his perfectly amoral and joyously truant life would end, as the main course for disease-infested rodents in this abysmal nexus of the universe. Disappearing without a trace, not a single soft female to wail over the untimely passing of the man they called the Magician because of the finesse with which he used his wand. His tombstone reading: HERE LIES A CONGENITAL IDIOT GONE TO THE GREAT BEYOND ON THE RED-NOSE EXPRESS.

Not bloody likely. He was a Sinclair, after all. If he had to die, he would go out nobly, like impaling himself on his own sword or something.

Gray bit back an oath at the snap of pain that corkscrewed down his spine, out his toes, into the ground, and back up his spine again as he hefted himself to his feet.

Taking hold of his chin, he jerked his head left, then right, to crack the kinks from his neck, an orchestral event that had every vertebrae unscrambling in tones ranging from alto to soprano. Then he glanced down to assess the rest of his person.

Mother of Christ, he was a sinister-looking mess. A creature revived from the depths of a four-day bender. A jagged tear ruined his once pristine white shirt, exposing his left shoulder and half his arm. His black leather pants—for which three prime bovines had sacrificed their lives—had a layer of grime on them. And his new boots were scraped, as if he had been dragged across rock-strewn ground.

"Note to self," Gray muttered in a raspy voice that had the quality of the sun-scorched Sahara. "Stop drinking."

Tentatively, he touched the back of his head, wincing as his fingers probed a substantial lump, which seemed to refute his hangover theory but solidify the origins of his headache.

What the hell had happened to him? And where in God's name was he? Scotland came to mind. Then again, so did purgatory.

Gray stopped grumbling his litany of four-letter words when he heard the sound of voices, loud voices, drawing nearer to his cell. Lynch mob? Could be. But lynching for what was the question.

Stiff-limbed, Gray hobbled to the small square opening in the stone wall, four solid iron bars imparting that he was not an honored guest, as if his shackled state hadn't conveyed that adequately enough. He squinted into the distance, a single blinding ray of sun beaming directly into his eyes.

Something was coming.

The next instant, four huge figures burst around the corner of an overgrown Hawthorne bush, throwing glances over their shoulders and practically tripping over each other in their wild flight.

"Get out of the way, ye clumsy oaf!" one bellowed.

"Watch where ye're goin', ye stupid buffoon!" another shouted back.

"Shut up, ye two, and step aside!" the third tossed in, barreling between the first two men.

"Oh, no, ye don't," the fourth one yelled. "Ye'll no' leave me back here with me arse hangin' in the wind. Make way!"

All four men dove in different directions, yet somehow ended up behind the same cluster of vegetation near the inhospitable cube Gray was locked in.

Well, he thought, leaning his shoulder against the wall, at least there was a somewhat entertaining aspect to his stay in this pit of despair. But what, he wondered, could have frightened men such as these?

The smile slipped from his face as yet another body appeared, silhouetted for a heartbeat within the sun's golden rays, obscuring the face of the beast that had made four brawny Highlanders run as if the hounds of hell had been unleashed.

The figure moved out of the glare of the sun, eyes transfused with rage. Gray swallowed, finally understanding what had the ability to start a male stampede, eight hundred pounds, collectively, barreling through the woods like a runaway freight train.

Oh, yes, Gray recognized this beast, had glimpsed it once or twice, and knew it made men world round quake with dread.

Its name: Angry Female.

"Duck, man! Here comes another one!"

Cautiously, the men straightened and peered over the top of the shrub at the irate woman lofting whatever she could lay her hands on at them—and with a vegetable garden and a chicken coop, she had ample supplies.

"Sweet mother in Heaven, what did ye say tae the lass, brother?" one demanded in an accusatory voice. They all possessed similar builds, the same shoulder-length black hair, and scruffy, unshaven faces.

"Nothin', I tell ye!"

"You're lyin', Ian," another growled, spitting the dirt out of his mouth, which he had gotten from diving onto the ground too fast in an attempt to avoid an expertly wielded knife spiraling toward his head. "Damn it, man! What in God's name did ye do tae rile her this time?"

Ian, the man being berated, who appeared to be the youngest of the group, shrugged, his expression chagrined. "Well, I said the lass shouldn't ignore her womanly duties tae her husband-tae-be."

Three groans followed this statement.

"Will ye never learn tae keep your mouth shut on that front, ye imbecile? Ye know how the lass feels about her 'womanly duties.' When will ye ken that the girl isn't like regular women?"

"And whose fault is that?" Ian shot back. "I told ye we should've gotten a nursemaid for her after Mother died. But, nay, ye convinced Father we didn't need one. Ye said we could take care of her on our own." He pointed over the top of the shrub in the girl's general direction and nearly got his finger taken off. "Ye see what all your smart plans have wrought, Aidan?"

Gray squinted into the distance, hoping to get a better look at the female causing all this commotion. She was too busy scurrying around trying to find other wound-inflicting implements to hurl at the men for Gray to distinguish any of her features.

Every time he thought he'd get a glimpse of her face, her long banner of mahogany hair whipped around, obscuring his view, hair that cascaded well beyond her buttocks and gleamed with streaks of red fire and a hundred other elusive tints distilled from the sun.

"Come out from behind there, ye rotten curs!" she shouted. "I'll show ye my 'womanly duty' with a knock upside your empty skulls!"

Aidan sighed and shook his head. "I knew it was a bad sign when the lass didn't cry when she was baptized. The devil's still in her, I tell ye."

"Aye," the other three muttered in unison.

Then Aidan scowled at his brothers. "Whose idea was it tae teach the lass how tae throw a knife? Robbie?"

"Don't look at me! Fergus is the one."

"I didn't! That was Ian!"

Once more, all eyes were on Ian. "Well, er, the lass needed tae be able tae defend herself." He quickly added, "But it was Aidan who taught her how tae shoot a gun."

Aidan shook his head vigorously. "Not I, lad. I taught her how tae fight. 'Twas Robbie, the dolt, who showed the lass how tae use a gun."

Robbie shrugged. "I taught her for the same reason that ye taught her how tae fight and Ian showed her how tae use a knife. 'Tis a dangerous world we live in."

The brothers all elevated their gazes over the edge of the bush, cautiously eyeing the girl. "Aye," Ian murmured, "a dangerous world indeed."

"I wonder how long she'll stay angry this time."

" 'Twas nearly a whole week the girl glared at us the last time."

"Aye, and I still swear she spiked me food with that herb she gives to old man Cheevers when his bowels are in an uproar," Fergus muttered. "Couldn't find me way out of the privy for nigh on three days." He scratched his head in stupefaction. "And all I did was tell the girl she might want tae consider wearin' her hair up once in a while instead of in a witch's tangle down her back. 'Tis indecent, I tell ye."

Aidan heaved a heartfelt sigh. "Can we blame the lass for being as tough as the rest of us with no female tae teach her the way of it?" He nudged Robbie in the side. "Talk tae her, man. She'll listen tae ye. I think she likes ye the best."

Robbie scowled at his brother. "Oh, no, ye don't! The last time ye gave me the job of speakin' tae her, she came at me with a scythe. I'll no' have me head lopped off—or any other body part, thank ye. Ye do it, Ian."

"Not me!" Ian quickly negated that plan. "Ye do it, Fergus."

"I'm not doin' it. Let Aidan do it. He's the oldest."

Aidan eyed each of his brothers in turn. "Cowards, the lot of ye. All right, I'll do it." He took a deep breath, swallowed, and then hesitated.

"Well, what are ye waitin' for? Saint Ninian tae come swoopin' down on a bolt of lightnin'? Get to it, man!"

Aidan waved a dismissive hand at them. "I'm goin'! Don't rush me now!" He gradually rose, his body half in and half out of the line of fire. "Now, Bonnie, let's end this madness. What do ye say?" A substantial-looking apple bulleted toward his head. Aidan ducked just in time. "Your turn, Ian."

Ian glared at his brother and then inhaled a fortifying breath. "Bonnie? Lass?" He inched his way upward. "Now, ye know I didn't mean what I said before. At least not the way I said it. 'Tis just that I think it's best if ye try tae behave a bit more—'' His words were aborted as Fergus yanked him to the ground.

"Are ye daft, man? Are ye trying tae get us all killed? The object here is tae soothe the girl's temper, no' tae rile it again. Bah!'' He waved him away. "You're hopeless.'' He squared his shoulders. "I guess there's nothing for it but for me tae give it a go. Cover me, lads.'' He eased only his head and shoulders above the bush. "Bonnie, girl, it's me. Your favorite brother Fergus. Now is a good time for us tae recall what the Good Book says about vengeance. 'Let not the sun go down on thy wrath.' I think—''

The girl's response was to lob a rotten egg at him, smacking him squarely in the face, yolk running down one red cheek and dribbling onto his tunic. So much for being the favorite brother.

Gray could no longer contain himself. He threw back his head and roared with mirth, bringing all eyes swerving to him. "Good God, throw a tent on that circus already,'' he said when he could breathe, endeavoring not to laugh as it only hurt his aching sides. "A bigger bunch of piffling buffoons I've never seen.''

"Ah, look! Our guest is up!'' Aidan commented sardonically. "How's your head, English dog? Hurtin' much?'' He smirked, and Gray longed to reach through the bars, ram a hand down the chucklehead's throat, and rip out his windpipe.

"Unlock the door, you kilted sod, and we'll see who has the last laugh.''

The man cocked a mocking brow and folded his arms across his chest. "Challengin' me, are ye, Sassenach?''

"How about I cut off your hand and punch you in the jaw with it?''

That wiped the smile from Aidan's face, a flush scorching up his neck. "That's a mighty brave attitude for a man in your position,'' he said through clenched teeth. "Considerin' there are four of us tae one of ye.''

"Four men who can't handle one slip of a girl. I'm not worried."

"I think he's talkin' about our fair sister, brothers."

Sister? These four dim-witted mountains had a sister barely taller than a thimble? It seemed impossible. "I hate to tell you this, but your sister is not exactly sunshine personified; rays of light do not radiate out her belly button. In fact, she needs her backside blistered. Maybe that will temper her sour disposition."

The men all exchanged looks, and then the one called Robbie said, "Ye hear that, brothers? The man thinks all the lass needs is a spankin'."

"I would be more than happy to administer it," Gray offered. "The girl is a willful brat."

"I see. And may I ask, do ye know how ye got tae be in there?"

"Obviously one of you malignant bastards bashed me over the head when my back was turned."

A secret smile curved the corners of Aidan's lips. "And there ye'd be wrong, English. 'Twasn't any of us who got the better of ye."

"Then who was it?"

A small body shoved its way between two of the towering giants, the heat of the girl's sulfurous glare enough to wither a man to ashes as the egg-throwing spitfire said defiantly, "Me."

Gray's casual demeanor quickly evaporated as he glowered at the female who claimed to have bested him, a Sinclair, a man who had never been bested by any woman—since his mother.

"How does it feel tae know a lowly female knocked ye out, English?" one of the men taunted.

"Now, what were ye sayin' about a spankin'? Seems tae me the lass has the upper hand."

Gray ignored the pack of accursed idiots and narrowed his eyes on the woman glaring at him. He just couldn't believe it. This tiny, albeit bellicose female was the cause of his pounding skull and subsequent incarceration? How could it be?

She must weigh all of one hundred pounds; though well-shaped, her figure delineated not in a dress but in a form-fitting white shirt, knotted at the waist, giving him glimpses of a tantalizing belly button.

Her lower half was encased in a pair of buff-colored breeches that hugged the small expanse of her waist and accentuated short but slender legs. Supple brown boots completed the ensemble.

But it was her eyes that truly captured his attention. They were bluer than an azure sea and deep enough to drown in, turbulent with belligerence at that moment, though no less stunning for it. In that single glance, Gray could tell this woman didn't give a tinker's damn what anyone thought of her. She was ruled entirely by her passions.

"You hit me from behind," he drawled. "That's not very sporting of you."

"And I'd do it again if I had tae." Her coolly acerbic expression purveyed her lack of remorse over her actions, reducing him, quite effectively, to less than a grain of sand.

Clearly, he had not engendered an impression. "May I ask, does your jaw unhinge when you capture prey?"

To which she retorted, "Do ye make an effort tae be stupid or does it just come naturally?"

A begrudging respect burgeoned inside Gray. Few people could amply match wits with him, yet this girl held her own. However, he had yet to bring out the heavy guns. "So what's the matter, sweetheart? Did I pass you over for another woman? Is that the reason for all the venom? Or is clubbing unsuspecting men over the head merely a part of your nature? A mating ritual, perhaps?"

"I wouldn't lend ye a cup of air, ye craven swine, let alone let ye touch me."

Moderately piercing blow. Ego suffering a mild setback. *Regroup and retaliate with a simple yet effective male tactic.* A leer with a healthy dose of sexual innuendo, the kind that implied he was looking for a refresher course in getting his face slapped. "I bet you're a wildcat in bed."

Instead of anger, the girl slanted an intrigued brow, perhaps recognizing an equal in this wicked game of verbal sparring. The men, however, didn't see it that way. The two apes closest to her took a menacing step toward Gray's cell.

She grabbed both their arms. "Leave him." Then she moved toward his cell, halting in front of the iron bars, only the strength of the stone wall separating them.

Unafraid that she was close enough that he could reach out and throttle her should he choose to do so, she stared at him, her small hands lifting and wrapping around the metal.

Gray faced her, curling his fingers around the bars— directly beneath her hands. His ire began to melt as he gazed into those captivating eyes, musing over whether he had ever seen such a blue in all his vast travels— irises sprinkled with shades of wisteria and gold dust— and concluding that he hadn't. Those eyes were unique.

She leaned closer, rising on tiptoe. She was glorious, the rise and fall of her breasts mesmerizing him, the soft mounds pushing against the fabric of her shirt. His grip tightened on the bars, his entire body tautening, the world fading into a peripheral blur as she pursed her lips . . .

And spat in his face.

Gray's reaction was swift, so swift, in fact, that the girl gaped at him in shock as she found herself his captive, her wrists shackled by his unrelenting grip. No matter how hard she struggled, she could not break free.

"Stay where you are!" Gray ordered through clenched teeth when he saw her bodyguards rush forward. "I can break her wrists before you take another step."

The men hesitated; then the one called Aidan said tersely, "Keep digging, English, and ye'll be digging your own grave."

"Oh, now, that's original," Gray returned sardonically. "Don't you have anything better?"

"Let her go and we'll consider sparin' your miserable life."

Gray barked with laughter. "What are you going to do to me, I wonder? Have this little girl throw stones at me?" The little girl in question hissed at him, striving rather industriously to dig her nails into his forearms. He hauled her forward against the rough stones, delving deep into her eyes and saying with soft menace, "I don't cower quite as easily as these men do. Bear that in mind, my dear, before you act rashly again."

"I'll tear your tongue out and roast it over a fire!" she vowed furiously, her eyes like two poison darts of nightshade.

A half grin curved Gray's lips. "You are quite a handful, and once I'm quit of this place I will enjoy taming you."

"Ye'll not be tamin' anyone, ye braying ass," she spat. "I'll see ye boiled in a vat of oil and your bones fed tae mongrels before I let ye touch me!"

"You are a violent one, aren't you? But we shall see about your claims." Gray yanked her closer, so that her face pressed against the bars, bringing them eye to eye. "In fact, my sweet, I look forward to your attempts."

"I'll make ye sorrier than ye've ever been in your whole rotten life if ye come near me."

Gray watched her mouth, the way she formed her words, and was jarred quite ardently by an urge to taste those lush, tantalizing lips. "I'm already sorry, my girl," he murmured.

"Do ye know what ye are?" she asked tightly, waiting for him to lift his gaze and meet her blazing blue eyes.

"No, what am I?"

"A blowhard . . . a bully . . . and a coward."

With practiced ease, the girl managed to land a devastating uppercut, skillfully chosen words her weapon. A coward. The last person who had called him a coward and lived to recite the tale was his mother.

Gray released the girl so abruptly, she would have fallen had one of the men not grabbed her. He tried to catch hold of the threads of his anger as visions of a confused, hurt eleven-year-old boy assaulted him, a boy gazing up into the cold, uncaring face of his mother.

"*You always were a little coward,*" she jeered, staring down her formidable nose at him. "*Always letting Damien fight your battles for you. You're useless.*"

Gray had spent every day since then trying to prove he was no coward, that he wasn't useless, and that he could help his older brother instead of it always being the other way around. But Damien never needed help.

Until now.

Now, when time was of the essence.

Gray's jaw tightened, delayed anger layered with frustrated impatience at his incarceration flowing through him as his senses returned in full. "I want to know why you have me locked up," he demanded. "What am I being accused of?"

The answer was quickly forthcoming, gut-wrenchingly simple and rife with infinite condemnation.

"Murder."

Chapter 2

The word reverberated through the dank walls of Gray's living tomb, striking a chord within him that most people probably never confronted unless they were the ones accused of such a heinous crime.

"Murder? You've got to be kidding." Silence met his remark. Silence as edifying as it was surreal, thundering in his ears with sickening force. Gray drove a hand through his hair, visions flashing through his mind, the same mental pictures he had dismissed as being particularly disturbing figments of an alcohol-sodden imagination, too unbelievable to be real. "This is crazy. I didn't kill anyone."

"Aye, ye did," Fergus retorted with a snarl. "And for that ye will be tried by the counsel, and if found guilty, ye shall swing from the hangman's noose."

Gray had been catapulted into a nightmare and couldn't remember when or where it had begun. He searched his mind, attempting to string together the sequence of events that had led up to the moment he'd been bashed on the head.

He had been sailing from Ballycastle at the tip of

Northern Ireland after retrieving his first mate, Prophet, who hadn't been expecting Gray, since barely a week earlier he had given the man time off to visit his brother.

Shortly after departing Ireland, they had collided with a squall that had come up out of nowhere. By the time the storm ended nearly a day later, they had been blown off course and one of the ship's sails was badly damaged.

Gray located a concealed inlet and dropped anchor, vainly endeavoring not to view the mishap as a bad omen on a journey so recently embarked upon. The dismal interpretation stayed with him nonetheless.

The delay chafed at Gray's already raw nerves, a growing demand for action dogging his heels. Prophet, who understood him as well as Gray's own brothers, who recognized the need that drove him to make this trip, suggested going ashore to see what they could find.

What they found was a tavern.

And one drink to dull the edge of Gray's harrowed impatience digressed into several.

At some point, Gray had stumbled outside, vaguely recalling a need to relieve himself. He made his way to a shadowed corner of the building and nearly fell over something.

That's when he saw her.

A young girl, no more than seventeen, prone at his feet, her unblinking eyes staring up at him, the horror of her death still reflected in their lifeless brown depths, asking him why he had been too late to save her.

A gaping slash exposed her neck, the wound stretching ear to ear, manifesting in a macabre smile, speaking far too eloquently of the agony she had suffered. Her crimson blood seeped onto the ground, the warm pulse of life a puddle around her.

Gray knew her, remembered her face, could picture the way she had looked when color had tinted her cheeks. She had been one of the women crowded around the table with him and Prophet, full of bright laughter, a ready smile, and a saucy attitude. Yet something pensive had shone in her eyes as the night wore on.

Gray knelt beside the girl, pressing his hands gently over her eyelids to close them, saying a silent prayer for her soul. A glimmer of something caught his eye then, a runnel of silver light. He tilted his head to the side and noticed the savage tip of a bloody knife under a dilapidated box.

With a sense of displacement, Gray retrieved the razor-edged dagger and held it aloft. The light from a shard of the moon reflected wickedly off the blade, casting an enlarged shadow of his hand and the knife superimposed on the wall next to them.

A bead of bright blood cascaded gradually downward toward Gray's hand, immobilizing him as he monitored its descent, bile rising in his throat to choke him.

A horrified gasp sounded behind him. Through a queer distortion of time, he began to turn, catching a glimpse of a booted foot before something hard crashed with deadening force against the back of his skull, pitching him into darkness until he woke up in this cell to find his deepest nightmare had become a stark reality.

With a sickening lump in his stomach, Gray glanced at his stony-faced captors. "I didn't kill that girl," he said, his voice a pained rasp. "She was dead when I found her."

"What a convenient story," Aidan mocked, his tone accusing.

"It's the truth, damn it!"

"We have a witness who saw ye kneeling beside Sarah's body, a bloody knife in your hand."

A witness.

In that moment, the final piece of the puzzle slipped soundlessly yet explosively into place as Gray's gaze clashed with the malevolent blue eyes of the witness, the one he had taunted, had pushed.

The one who now held the key to his freedom in the palm of her hostile, capricious hand.

He knew then he was doomed.

Gray lay on his crapped-out cot, hands clasped behind his head, staring with mute violence at the same shitty crack in the ceiling for God knows how long, the turbulence inside him escalating as the night dragged on, his mood vacillating between disbelief, disgust, confusion, and anger.

Anger eventually won out.

Beneath his cot, the benighted rats scurried. Gray felt just volatile enough to give them a bludgeoning taste of his boot heel. But then who would keep him company in the endless hours before dawn? Unguarded moments when insidious thoughts seeped through like fissures in a dike, a slow-burning pain fueling a fire that he allowed no one to see, impotent rage at finding himself stuck with another label to stack on top of all the others. Murderer. Coward. Useless.

Bastard.

And within the realm of the latter there existed a whole repertoire of creative variations, most of which Gray had been called at one time or the other during the course of the murky downward spiral that had become his life.

But, in truth, he was just a plain old genuine bastard, stamped with that auspicious title the day he was born. He was an ugly secret. A skeleton in the closet. A family disgrace.

Gray threw his forearm over his eyes, as if this might block out memories better left buried, galling reminders that burned at the bottom of his brain.

But the mind could be a vicious enemy when abandoned to its own devices, shepherding a man down roads he'd prefer not to travel, shattered visions of a painful childhood reminding him why many people shouldn't have children, didn't deserve them, that some papal edict should be instituted that restricted men and women who were emotionally inept, incapable of warmth, compassion. Love.

Reminding him that his blood was tainted by deception—forever ruined by his mother's infidelity, leaving him teetering on the very rim of civility, adrift in moral obscurity.

The sins of the mother had been visited upon the son—in stiletto fashion.

Over the years, the reality of his illegitimacy slowly eroded Gray's insides until there was nothing left of him to give a damn. After too many years of hurting, he was finally able to block out the whispers about his mother and her lover.

His envy, however, never quite dissipated the certain knowledge that his brothers were true Sinclairs, bound by blood to each other, while he was the illicit product of one of his mother's scandalous affairs.

Neither Damien nor Nicholas knew the truth. Gray had never told them, and his mother seemed to revel in lording the ugliness over him alone. Gray wondered if his father suspected the real point of his origin—that the gentle-hearted Earl of Blackstone had housed the bitter fruit of another man's loins. If his father had known, he kept the knowledge to himself. But that didn't surprise Gray. Niles Sinclair had been the antithesis of his wife. Unfortunately, he was no match for her.

With each passing year, Gray had seen the vital force ebb that much more from his father's body, sucked away little by little over the years because he had cared too much and loved unwisely, a ghost eventually consumed by shadows.

Gray still remembered the fleeting touch of his father's hand, frail fingers curling over his, flesh suffused with the pallor of an inevitable death. "My son," he had whispered, then breathed his last.

Son. So small a word, but what import it carried.

And with his father's passing went the last of an era, the last of a breed of nobility. Now only three hard, unforgiving men were left. Men who were raised to believe kindness meant weakness, caring could bring destruction, and a woman was only as faithful as her options.

With a low growl, Gray shoved off his makeshift bed and stalked to his single window on the outside world, seeking only to forget, to lock away the pain for another hour, another day, another year.

Like a misplaced lifeline, he gripped the cell bars and breathed, concentrating on each inhalation until he had stilled the rumbling unease within him and banished the grim specters to the netherworld one more time.

Beneath the window, his less-than-vigilant guard slouched on a squat wooden bench, fast asleep, a half mug of ale next to him, his nose emitting a fluttering whistle on each exhale.

Gray raked an agitated hand through his hair. What a bloody mess. If only his brothers could see him now, witness the depths to which he had been brought by a petite Scottish lass with a temper more volatile than a pit viper.

Just thinking about the girl—Bonnie, her brothers had called her, which clearly didn't apply to her disposition—made Gray's blood begin to percolate.

A sudden movement caught the corner of Gray's eye then. Something or someone stalked beyond the tree line, just outside his range of vision. A cloud obscured the moon as a figure nudged aside the foliage and crept toward Gray's cell; the guard slumbered on, unaware of the threat.

The person halted beside the bench, raised one arm over his head . . . and used his other hand to poke the guard in the arm. Like a tumbleweed, the man draped forward and plopped unceremoniously onto the ground, his wheezing snores uninterrupted.

"Well, I'll be damned, that stuff really worked."

Gray recognized the voice immediately. "Prophet?"

The man's head jerked up as the moon drifted from behind the cloud, a ray of white light slanting across a familiar weather-beaten countenance. "Aye, lad, it's me. Old Prophet, come to save your miserable hide." A work-roughened hand reached out to clasp Gray's through the bars, attached to a portly body that Prophet claimed was merely the end result of his height being too low for his width.

"Damn, but you're a sight for sore eyes." Gray nodded toward the unconscious guard. "What did you do to him?"

"Slipped an old sailor's potion into his ale. He should slumber peacefully until the cock crows in the morn."

"A simple clubbing over the head would have worked just as effectively." Gray should know, after all. His head still thumped two beats faster than his heart.

"Now, lad, you know I abstain from bloodshed whenever possible."

Gray rolled his eyes. An ex-pirate who shrank from violence. That was one for the record books—as was the fact that the man had the sex drive of a crusty barnacle. "Whatever your methods, I appreciate it."

Prophet mumbled something, clearly uncomfortable with the gratitude. "I need to tie a rope around you to keep you out of trouble," he said gruffly. "Between that face of yours and that chip on your shoulder you're always daring someone to knock off, I'm either saving you from lovesick women or men looking to take a swing at you."

For reasons Gray had yet to discern, Prophet had taken it upon himself to be his keeper as if he were still a green lad. God bless the sentimental old muttonchop. "Need I remind you that this side trip to the seventh circle of hell was your idea?"

Prophet harumphed. "I see incarceration has not sweetened your disposition."

"Did you come here with the express purpose of lecturing me?"

"Well, the idea did cross my mind. I mean, what better opportunity will I have—considering the scuttlebutt on this sheep-infested wilderness is that you are to be hanged."

Gray snorted with disgust. "Tried and convicted all before breakfast. These people are bloody unbelievable."

"They have it out for you, lad."

Gray didn't need that patently obvious fact pointed out to him. His sharing quarters with rats spoke volumes for how these people felt about him.

"They intend to see justice meted out at any expense," Prophet added solemnly.

"At my expense, you mean."

"Aye, I believe so," he replied with a nod. "But that's why I'm here. I'll have you out of there in a wink and then you can put this all behind you." And while Prophet hustled to unbolt the cell door, he left his words behind to echo in Gray's mind.

Put this all behind him. Could he do that? Would he ever forget that young girl's bloodless face? Her empty eyes? The bright red puddle spreading out beneath her?

If he left now, he would be branded for life as a murderer. Prevent a victim from finding justice. Never prove himself innocent. There'd be a cloud looming over him, staining whatever future he hoped to create for himself. He'd be running away, accepting the easy way out, and the knowledge would cauterize a hole in his gut.

By leaving now, he'd be precisely what Bonnie had called him: a coward.

The bolt sliding back on the door roused Gray from his musings. Prophet stepped into the cell, a grimace on his face. "Cozy," he mumbled. "Well, come on, lad. Time's a-wasting."

Gray remained where he was. "I can't go," he said quietly.

Prophet's bushy brows drew together. "What do you mean you can't go?"

"I have to stay here and clear my name." His name was all he had left, his only link to his family, and he'd be damned if he'd let these apple-cheeked Philistines take it away from him.

Concern replaced Prophet's frown. "You know they are looking for someone to crucify."

"I know. But I have to try. I don't want to be glancing over my shoulder for the rest of my life."

"And I don't want you being hanged for a murder you didn't commit."

Gray smiled inwardly, not realizing until that moment how important it was to him that at least one person believed he was innocent, knew he wasn't capable of committing such a horrific crime.

"Don't worry. I have no intentions of staying here long enough for them to hang me, should it come to that."

Prophet nodded, appearing vastly relieved. Then he said, "Does your desire to stay have anything to do with that girl who got the better of you?"

Gray's appreciation back-flipped to annoyance. "She didn't get the better of me," he returned tersely, but he didn't hear himself deny that part of his reason for staying was because of Bonnie.

She believed him to be a murderer and a coward. He would prove to her that he was neither. And no stone walls, four mammoth brothers, or mortal effort this side of hell would stand in his way.

"No?" Prophet cocked a bushy gray brow. "Things look different from where I'm standing."

"Don't worry about the girl," Gray returned, his gaze drifting out the window and into the windless night to the isolated castle looming on a crag a short distance away, knowing that somewhere within Bonnie slept, sound and content—and blissfully unaware that she had taunted the wrong man. "I can handle her."

"Leave her alone, lad," Prophet warned, as if reading Gray's mind and discerning what he had in store for the sharp-tongued firebrand. "That way trouble lies."

Chapter 3

The girl was a minion of the Antichrist.

A pint-sized virago in league with forces from the dark side.

In fact, she just might *be* the Antichrist, Gray concluded the next day, after he was summarily jolted from sleep when something loud clanged in his ear, causing him to bang his forehead into the wall, fall out of his cot, and hit the rock-strewn dirt with a bone-jarring thud, a cloud of dust rising up like an earthen hand to choke him.

When he'd hacked the last lungful of dirt from his throat and blinked the grit from his eyes, he discovered a pair of petite, black-booted feet in his line of vision. He knew exactly who they belonged to.

Clenching his teeth, he glanced up. "You."

The girl cocked a sleek brow. "Sleep well, did ye?" The sarcasm in her words was exceeded only by the mockery in her smile. Now if only her face matched her attitude, Gray thought grimly. Unfortunately for him, she was pretty. Too damn pretty, in fact.

Worse, she sported another one of those knotted

shirts that hugged her breasts like a lover's hands and mercilessly taunted him with intriguing glimpses of her smooth, flat stomach and that peekaboo belly button, effectuating a surge of wanton rebellion in his mind—and an itch for carnal love at all points below, a fact that, if not unique, was singularly vexing in this particular instance.

Gray ignored the tray of food in the girl's hands, knowing the only sustenance he required at that moment was the kind that appeased the fire of anger sizzling in his gut.

He had never knelt at any woman's feet and he'd be damned if today would be any different. In fact, now that the girl was standing so boldly in front of him, the time seemed ripe to commit mayhem. Then her brothers would really have suitable cause to hang him.

Gray had barely risen two inches when a strong hand clamped menacingly down on his shoulder, thrusting him back to his knees. A quick sidelong glance revealed sausage-sized fingers and hairy knuckles.

His gaze traveled up an arm that appeared to be the circumference of a small tree trunk to a chest that he estimated was about fifty-four inches around, the shape bearing an uncanny resemblance to a potbellied stove.

Finally, Gray's appraisal halted at the man's face. Ugly did not describe his appearance. Nor did grotesque. Hideously unique was perhaps more apt. Every feature seemed to cave inward, as if a heavy object had lain squarely over the brute's face until the front part of his skull was sufficiently flattened. Here, Gray thought with a foreboding of bodily injury to his already battered person, was a man at ease biting the heads off chickens.

"I've brought your breakfast, prisoner," the girl said in that homogenous tone of mockery, obviously reveling in her role as warden.

"I guess I don't have to eat my left foot, then, huh?" Gray wasn't sure what demon incited him to provoke the girl, especially when he should seek to curry her favor, strive to get on her good side—if she had one, that was.

Perhaps the desire to nettle her arose from the fact that he still stung rather grievously from her loaded comments of the day before, and being spat on, and rudely awoken from the whole five minutes of slumber he had managed to get in between questioning his sanity for not decamping with all due haste, listening to the night creatures that had pined away for hours on end, and speculating if the bastardly rats would mistake him as dinner.

The girl's narrowed eyes informed Gray that he had once more stepped over her invisible line and entered the realm of her formidable pique. "By all means, eat your left foot!" she huffed defensively. "Rot for all I care!" With military crispness, she spun on her heel.

Gray wasn't exactly sure how events transpired next. All he had wanted to do was keep the girl from leaving. He hadn't been aiming for her breast, but somehow that's where his hand ended up.

More surprising, however, was the fact that he was not immediately slapped into oblivion. He expected a wallop that would have him seeing stars. Even the brute seemed temporarily immobile, as if shock held everyone in thrall—everyone but Gray, that was. He figured he'd hang on until the ax fell. An opportunity like this didn't trot along every day, and for reasons unknown—addled wits, perhaps?—he was experiencing a die-hard case of lust for the little head basher. His groin flamed hotter than hellfire.

For such a petite girl, she had amazing breasts, full, weighty in his hand. An added bonus was the feel of her nipple hardening beneath his palm. His body, for all the extraneous abuse and neglect it had taken of late, responded instantly.

Then a ham-sized fist burst out of nowhere and smashed into his jaw with punishing force, ending the idyllic moment as the floor raced up to meet him.

Gray jiggled his head to return the focus to his eyes and tested his aching jaw, rotating it back and forth to make sure it was still attached. A few of his teeth felt as if they'd been loosened.

He glanced up at the girl and detected her ever-present anger. Yet he glimpsed another emotion as well. Concern? He'd be damned if that wasn't what it looked like.

He contemplated playing up his injuries, going for the wounded and helpless trump card to see where that got him. Unfortunately, he didn't formulate that plan soon enough as the all-too-familiar expression of scorn clouded her face.

Disgruntled, Gray nodded toward the hulking man. "Tell your friend he hits like a girl."

The giant took a menacing step toward Gray, but Bonnie hastened in front of the man. "Leave him," she ordered. Then she leaned down, face to face with Gray, and said in a muted voice, "Are ye anxious tae meet your Maker?"

Gray's gaze skimmed over her delicately sloped nose, her high cheekbones, paused appreciatively at her full, red lips before colliding with those killer eyes. "Why? Would you miss me, sweetness?"

She straightened so fast that Gray swore he heard her spine crack. "Keep your comments behind your teeth, prisoner, or Selwyn will make ye sorry!"

"Selwyn? Who the hell—?" Gray noticed the uncomfortable expression on the big man's face and made the connection. *"Selwyn?"*

The giant bared his teeth and growled in reply.

Gray threw his head back and roared with laughter, nearly falling over in his amusement.

His warden shot him a glare. "Selwyn will be helping me, so if ye don't want any trouble, I'd advise ye tae watch what ye say."

Still chuckling, Gray rose to his knees. "Helping you with what? Pound stones into dust? Lift up North

America so you can sweep underneath it? Hold back
the ocean so you can pluck shells from the sea floor?''

Selwyn made an odd noise. It was either a laugh or
the first warning sign that he was about to erupt into a
berserker rage.

"Just consider him a little reminder that it's best not
tae press the extent of my good nature," she retorted
in a tight voice.

A subtle challenge danced invitingly in that statement,
inducing the rogue in Gray to test her supposed good
nature. "You mean I can't stick my tongue in your belly
button even though you are offering it up so sweetly?''

The girl's gaze shot downward, noticing where his
head was and realizing that her partially exposed stomach was directly in his path. Snapping blue eyes jerked
to wicked silver. Now it was Gray's turn to repay her
mocking smile—then he leaned forward.

Mere inches from his target, he was thwarted by the
giant, hoisted into the air and tossed backward onto the
cot with the driving force of a gale wind. Pain radiated
down his left side as he waved yet another dust cloud
away.

No concern etched the girl's face this time. Only ire,
pure and simple. "Ye'll keep your tongue in your mouth
if ye ken what's good for ye, English."

Gray kneaded his left shoulder where it had slammed
against the wall, feeling decidedly put out. "My name's
not English—or prisoner or swine, for that matter. It's
Gray. Can you say that? Gray? It's really not that difficult."

She harumphed, but for a hairbreadth, the harshness
left her face. Then she gave a slight shake of her head,
jutted that stubborn jaw forward, and marched over to
his cot with cool efficiency. "Here's your food." She
plunked the tray down beside him.

A length of silken hair tumbled forward, sweeping
over Gray's leg and hand, jarring him like the flick of
a whip. Without conscious thought, he lifted the cool,

lustrous strands, fanning them through his fingers, reveling in the satiny texture, and wondering what it was about this gamine-faced shrew that made him feel like some smitten adolescent half-wit whenever she was near.

"Stop that!" she fumed when she saw what he was doing, ripping her hair from his grasp.

He graced her with the cool, appraising glance of the highly insulted. "You touched me first."

"I didn't do it on purpose!"

"That is up for debate. Perhaps you might consider wearing your hair up so such a heinous thing doesn't happen again. I may be your prisoner, but I deserve to be left unmolested."

"I didn't—I wasn't—" Bonnie stammered, hating the horrible wretch for flustering her, knowing that was exactly what he intended.

What really angered her, though, was that his grin more than his words caught her off guard, his expression so full of lazy sensuality, she had to remind herself to breathe. Bonnie had known from the first moment her eyes locked with his that he would be an adversary far more subtle than any she had ever dealt with before.

Why had she stubbornly maintained that she would take his meal to him? Claiming that as the laird's sister the prisoner was her responsibility when she'd never personally seen to any other prisoners.

Because, were she honest with herself, she'd admit the brute intrigued her. How shameful to find a murderer altogether too interesting as a man.

From the first moment she'd laid eyes on him, a maelstrom had been set off inside her. When he looked at her, something delicious and frightening fluttered to life in the pit of her belly.

He was a handsome devil, inhumanly perfect, heedlessly indecent, possessed of a sinful dimple and a doubly wicked grin, not at all what she expected a murderer to look like. Why couldn't he be wart-nosed and pockmarked? Or wear a patch over one eye and have a few teeth missing?

Did he have to be so broad shouldered? Be blessed with such sleek bronze skin? Have hair that reminded her of a moon-drenched night, wild and gleaming, brushing his shoulders in reckless abandon? And a face so heavenly to look upon it was almost hypnotic?

Even in his dirty clothes, he reminded her of a warrior. The knowledge scared and thrilled her. No man had ever intimidated her. No man had ever challenged her. This man did both.

Why did he have to be a murderer?

Worse, why did he have to be English?

She pivoted on her heel and tried not to run for the door.

"Wait!" he called out.

Bonnie stopped, though why she wasn't sure. She should be slamming the door on him instead of standing there half in and half out of the cell, unable to go another step forward yet unable to turn around.

"Please," he murmured. "Stay."

What was it about the man that made him so hard to resist?

Taking a fortifying breath, Bonnie faced him, silently praying he would not look at her in that devouring way, his gaze drifting over her with suggestive intimacy, eyes that bespoke a long familiarity with creature pleasures, making her feel as if he touched her physically.

"Aye, Sassenach. What is it?" she demanded, thankful her voice didn't waver.

"The name is Gray," he reminded her.

Gray. Bonnie silently tested the name. It suited him. He had eyes the color of a winter's dawn, clear and compelling one moment, dark and dangerous the next. And charm—charm he had in abundance. But Bonnie vowed she would not succumb. She was too strong for such a thing.

She hardened her resolve. "What do ye want, English? And don't mess me about."

He smiled a silky-sweet smile that Bonnie imagined had melted many a female heart and clearly marked him as a seasoned rake from a hundred paces. "Mess you about? I wouldn't dream of it, Scottish."

"If ye have nothing of import tae say, then I'll bid ye farewell." She began to turn away.

"I didn't kill that girl."

His words stopped her yet again, but for an entirely different reason this time.

The conviction in his voice.

The same conviction she had heard the night before, causing her a moment of hesitation, wondering, if only for a heartbeat, if he spoke the truth.

But she had seen him hunkered down next to Sarah's body, seen him holding the bloody knife . . . seen the horrific gaping wound on Sarah's neck. Bonnie paled at the memory.

What secret had Sarah wanted to impart that made her beg Bonnie to come to that secluded spot behind her father's tavern? Had Sarah felt safe there? Unsuspecting of the evil that lurked as she waited in familiar surroundings?

Bonnie would never know what her friend had wanted to tell her. Yet she couldn't shake the feeling that Sarah had died because of it.

But if that was true, then how could the man sitting across from her be responsible? He was a stranger to their small part of the world. From all accounts, he had been enjoying some drinks in the tavern, carousing with the women, neither of which Bonnie had a hard time picturing.

"I didn't kill her," he repeated, those eyes, darkened now with determination, boring into her.

"I saw ye," she murmured, hating the tremulous quality of her voice.

"What you saw was a man kneeling next to an injured woman, nothing more."

Even though she had not seen him inflict the death-blow, his presence had been damning. Now she was the only person who could right a wrong and give her friend a modicum of justice. The responsibility seemed almost too heavy to bear.

"The counsel will be discussing your fate tonight."

A slight tic worked in his jaw. "Discussing my fate. I see. Why do I feel as if my fate has already been decided?"

"Ye will be given the opportunity tae speak in your own behalf." But even as the words left her mouth, Bonnie knew he recognized her assurance as mere evasion. How could she admit that she didn't know if he would be treated justly?

After witnessing what she had the day before, villagers angrily clamoring for swift retribution and never once speaking of justice or fairness, caused doubts to settle in her mind. Tension hung heavy in the air. They expected a hanging, and nothing less would suffice.

"You do realize that if you convict the wrong man, you will still have a murderer on your hands." He posed the concern that had haunted Bonnie from the moment she had looked into his eyes as he professed his innocence.

"Aye," she murmured. "I understand." All too well.

Chapter 4

"I say hangin' is too good for the bastard!"

"Aye! Let him suffer the way poor Sarah did!"

"Filthy murderer!"

"English dog!"

Gray stared dispassionately at the people around him spewing hatred: men with clenched fists and eyes promising vengeance, pale-faced women denouncing him as a fiend of satanic proportion, children sneaking wide-eyed glances at him from behind their mothers' skirts, as if he were some bugaboo newly arisen from a swirling eddy of despair in a black universe.

Gray had hoped for a fair trial, but he wouldn't get one here. He had already been convicted in the eyes of public opinion, a court of emotions versus logic, bias versus open-mindedness. But being accused of something he didn't do should be secondhand by now.

God, if he wasn't getting maudlin, wallowing in a bout of pathetic self-pity. Damien had never complained about his lot in life, and if anyone deserved to bitch it was his brother. He, too, understood the stigma of being labeled.

Society called Damien the Devil, but he was one of
the best men Gray knew. He had protected his younger
brother from their mother's wrath, taking the brunt of
her abuse on himself. And now, when Damien needed
his help, Gray found himself in the middle of another
mess.

His brother had never requested any help, nor would
he. Had it not been for Hugh Lennox, Earl of Myddleton, a man who had always been a great blight on
humanity, and the Sinclairs in general, Gray would have
been none the wiser about Damien's dire circumstances.

He would have never known his family was about to
lose everything—including their beloved family home,
Silver Hills.

Silver Hills was a stronghold for Gray—real, solid,
indomitable. The happiest days of his childhood had
been spent there, in part because his mother hated
the place, found the history boring, the handcrafted
Flemish tapestries and suits of armor distasteful, country
living loathsome; the air was too chill at night, the morn-
ings too damp, the people too provincial. She preferred
the endless gaiety and inanity of London. And that
suited Gray. The summers were his to enjoy.

His father came alive during those months, basking
in a freedom he never got under his wife's barrage of
demands and nagging. The days were spent in a variety
of idyllic pursuits: fishing, riding, hunting. At night,
Gray and his brothers took turns beating their father
at chess—who always lost very strategically.

Like Gray and his brothers, his father had grown up
at Silver Hills, and his father's father, and six more
generations of Sinclairs, and every male had left a piece
of themselves within those hallowed halls.

Though Gray didn't deserve to be a part of that legacy,
Damien and Nicholas did. This was his chance to do
something for his father, as well as repay Damien for
all he'd done over the years—and exorcise bloody Myddleton from their lives forever.

Myddleton, the man who knew so much about their business because he held the banknote to Silver Hills, waving it over their heads like a sword of Damocles.

If it was the last thing Gray did, he would save his home from falling into Hugh's hands—even if he had to kill the condescending son of a bitch himself.

Half brother or not.

Gray realized he was rubbing his finger raw twisting his gold ring, a habit he had taken to whenever deep in thought or troubled.

The ring had belonged to his father, who had bequeathed it to Gray on his deathbed, placing it in Gray's palm and closing his fingers around the cool metal, telling him that someday he'd find what he was searching for.

Gray loved his father, but the man had always been a bloody dreamer, and now, with the bestowal of an old ring and a map yellowed with age, he had decreed Gray the keeper of that dream. That had been Gray's legacy, his inheritance. Fairy tales, myths, and legends without substance.

He did not want the burden, the responsibility. The heartache. But if ever there was a time he needed to believe in a dream, it was now.

He gazed hard at the insignia etched deeply into the gold: an eagle with wings outstretched, a shield, and a crown. The royal emblem of a once mighty king of Spain, Ferdinand II, the ring purported to be a gift from his one true love, his wife, Isabella, presented to him shortly before her death in 1504.

A pretty story, but certainly no more, heralded by troubadours and still believed centuries later by people like Gray's father, who had never been blessed with the Midas touch. Things Niles Sinclair touched did not turn to gold, and no king's ransom would be his at a favorable hand of cards, whose rare occurrence was the reason his family was about to lose everything. No, his father had been duped, as usual. That was his special gift.

Now it seemed that liability would become Gray's as well.

"Everyone take a seat!"

The announcement, barked out by one of Bonnie's brothers, snapped Gray back to the present. It appeared the moment of truth had arrived. Truth, what an interesting anomaly it was—and what a damnably awkward inconvenience he must appear to actually want to find it.

With much grumbling, the men and women took their seats. Gray stared straight ahead, as he had when they had brought him into the hall, wrists and ankles shackled.

Nevertheless, he knew the exact moment Bonnie arrived, entering through a door somewhere behind him. He could feel her steady regard, her gaze questioning, wondering if he was guilty, attempting to discern if some evil lurked within him that could have driven him to murder.

"We are here today tae decide the fate of this man." Gray knew without looking that Aidan pointed a finger at him, his tone branding him with guilt in those few words. "He is charged with the crime of murdering Sarah Douglass." The crowd stirred angrily at the reminder of the death of one of their own. "What say ye, prisoner, on these charges?"

Gray slowly turned his head, eyeing the people assembled at the long table behind him, his gaze sliding over each member of the panel before coming to rest on Bonnie, who scrupulously avoided looking at him.

He waited. Finally, she cast troubled blue eyes his way, an expression in their depths that he would not mistake as sadness for him. She believed him a murderer. Why he cared what she thought, he couldn't fathom.

"What is your answer, prisoner?" Aidan demanded, his voice harsh with restrained anger.

Gray took his time but finally deigned to regard the man now gnashing his teeth because Gray had had the

nerve to look upon his sister. "I didn't kill that girl,"
he replied, wondering how many times he had repeated
those words, even though they garnered the same reaction every time he spoke them. Outright disbelief. "She
was dead when I found her."

Unwavering hostility reflected in Aidan's gaze, his
mind, like that of his clan, already made up. "And why
should we believe ye? Anyone could say such a thing
hoping tae save their life."

"Because I had no reason to murder her."

"Why were ye in the alleyway, then?"

"I was answering the call of nature," Gray replied
bluntly, noting several of the men nodding their heads,
confirming he wasn't the only one who had used the
alley for that purpose. He had merely been unlucky
enough to be the first one to come upon the girl.

"And ye were drinking, were ye not?"

"I had a few glasses of scotch." Gray recalled his
erroneous assumption that he had suffered from a hangover, roundly cursing himself for his zealous binge,
never expecting a time would come when he actually
wished his problem would have simply ended in heaving
instead of hanging.

"So ye were drunk."

"A bit impaired perhaps, but not so bad that I
didn't—"

"And ye were carousing with a group of women, from
what I understand."

Gray deduced where the man was going with his questions, merrily leading him down a primrose path toward
a sturdy length of hemp. "I was talking to a few women.
Since when is that a crime?"

Aidan came from behind the table, long strides eating
up the distance until he stood beside Gray's chair. Leaning forward, he hissed, " 'Tis a crime if ye raped that
girl."

A roar of voices soared through the vaulted chamber,
but Gray heard none of it as he leapt from his chair

and lunged at Aidan, his shackled hands getting enough hold around the man's throat to squeeze.

They crashed to the floor, impotent rage coursing through Gray's veins, Aidan's one word—rape—causing him to snap, unable to withstand another lie, another label. Another lethal blow to the only thing he had left. His pride.

Many hands tried to pry him off Aidan, voices swearing in his ear. Only one voice registered through the haze of his consuming anger, however. Bonnie's.

"Gray, please! He's my brother!"

And Gray just let go.

Then Bonnie's brothers descended, grabbing his arms, roughly hauling him back as Aidan's right hook slammed into his jaw, his punishing left into Gray's midsection.

"Stop it!" Bonnie cried.

"Bastard," Aidan hissed, glaring at Gray as he swiped the blood from the corner of his mouth with the back of his hand. "Get him back in the chair and tie him down tae the bloody thing this time!"

"No!" Bonnie jumped in front of her brother. "I won't stand for it! He's a human being and deserves tae be treated as such." A rippling of voices swept through the room at her vehement declaration.

Bonnie didn't know where her ardent stance had come from, considering she had treated Gray just as horribly as her brother now treated him. Perhaps worse.

But Aidan's vicious accusation had been unwarranted and only served to incite the crowd. But more than that, Bonnie had witnessed the toll that one hideous word had taken on Gray. She wouldn't allow his dignity to be further abused.

"I'm laird here, Bonnie," Aidan said in a growling voice that might have intimidated someone else, but not her. She had grown up with him, knew him when he wore short pants, could still see the boy in him striving to live up to a man's job.

She leaned forward and said only loud enough for him to hear, "Then act like it." Then she pivoted on her heel and retook her seat, praying no one could tell how shaken she was.

A tense moment passed before Aidan ground out, "Leave off with the bindings and let's get back tae this damn thing."

Bonnie breathed a sigh of relief, but she didn't dare look at Gray to gauge his reaction. She saw too much when she gazed into his eyes, perhaps more than was truly there.

"Bonnie."

Bonnie started, realizing her brother was speaking to her. His slightly narrowed gaze made her wonder if he knew where her mind had been. "Aye?"

"I think it's time ye addressed the crowd. They want tae hear from ye."

Bonnie had known this moment was coming, had dreaded it, and no matter how she had prepared, she still wasn't ready. She understood the impact of the next few minutes, how lives could be forever altered. On one side was Gray's fate, the other side a clan's pain. She very nearly buckled under the weight of her burden, cognizant that every word had to be carefully measured.

All eyes fastened on her as she stood. She drew a deep breath to ease the knot that had settled in the pit of her stomach—and then began. "My heart, like all of yours, bleeds from the pain of Sarah's loss, and I want what everyone here wants. Justice. Yet justice tempered with conviction, with certainty. I won't deny that I found this man"—she gestured toward Gray—"leaning over Sarah's body, a bloody knife in his hands. But I can't speak of what brought him tae that place, at that time, whether his intent was tae harm or tae help. He says he's innocent—"

"Ye canna believe anything that comes from an Englishman's mouth!" a voice rang out from the crowd.

"Aye! We had no problems here until *he* came along!" someone else snarled.

Bonnie recognized the man as Sarah's cousin.

"Ye know that's not true, Gavin. We've had our share of problems. Do ye forget so soon the sheep that were stolen from ye only three weeks ago?"

"That's different," he retorted, gaining the nods of the people around him. "They were only sheep."

"And is the stealing of them not a crime, then?"

"Aye, but—"

"There are no buts. A crime is a crime, and each is punishable tae different degrees."

Another man rose to his feet. A hush descended over the crowd as they looked upon the person who had suffered the most from Sarah's death. Her father.

His face was a mask of agony, his hat clutched in his hand, knuckles white as a lone tear coursed down his cheek. "I don't want any man tae die for a crime he didn't commit. That wouldn't avenge the death of me sweet Sarah." His voice caught on his daughter's name. "But this man"—he pointed a bent finger that shook with emotion at Gray—"was found beside me daughter's lifeless body. This stranger tae our quiet hamlet. And even if he didn't kill her as he claims, he didn't save me darling girl either, didn't call out for help. He did nothing."

His voice broke. "Isn't that a crime? Didn't Sarah deserve better than that?" His old eyes beseeched and accused Gray in the same glance. "Why? Why did it have tae be my girl? She was a sweet lass . . . the only precious thing I had left in this world. Why?" he sobbed.

The woman seated next to Sarah's father stood and wrapped her arms around his thin, quaking shoulders. He appeared to have aged twenty years before Bonnie's eyes. She feared the frail old man might not see the passing of another year. His daughter's death had sapped the vital essence from him and left him little more than a shell of his former self.

He was escorted from the room, too defeated to fight another battle, too soul-weary to remain. When the eyes of her clan fell upon Bonnie once more, the determination to see someone punished for Sarah's death etched each face; Gray, the object of their wrath.

Then someone asked the question Bonnie had prayed no one would pose. "Do ye think the man is guilty?"

She had spent the day wondering about that very thing, drifting in a state of confusion, hearing Gray's voice in her head as he claimed his innocence, seeing the haunted expression in his eyes, pieces just not fitting together. She remembered her initial reaction, which was to believe him—and that had yet to change. The man might be many things, arrogant, hardheaded, irritating, cocky . . . but a murderer?

Yet, as Bonnie gazed around at the sea of faces waiting expectantly for her response, she felt conflicted. "I . . . I don't know."

"Then why did ye hit him over the head? Why not give him the chance tae explain?"

"Because the lass believes in action first and questions later," came a voice from the back of the room, loud and distinct. "I pity any man who finds himself at the receiving end of Bonnie MacTavish's ire."

Bonnie briefly closed her eyes, not needing to see the face of the man who spoke to know who it was. Ewan Cameron.

The man she was to marry.

Chapter 5

Ewan was laird of Clan Cameron, a man known for getting what he wanted—and what he had wanted since Bonnie was thirteen . . . was her.

Her father, God rest his soul, had agreed to the union in the hopes of bringing peace to the clans, a dying man's last wish.

Bonnie would have done anything for her father, even if it meant marrying Ewan, a man she didn't much like. But love was not a factor in marriages such as theirs. The future happiness and prosperity of her clan had to come first.

For years, the two families had been rivals, sworn enemies, a long-standing feud bringing bloodshed to her Highland home—a feud that had begun over a piece of land.

The Camerons claimed the MacTavishes had unfairly won two hundred acres of property in a card game between Bonnie's grandfather and Ewan's grandfather.

What made the discord all the worse was that the land in question possessed the main water source for miles around, meaning the owner could charge money for its use, any amount he chose since demand outweighed supply.

As well, the land was rich with peat moss—a key ingredient in the production of whiskey—and producing whiskey was how they made their money.

Ewan sauntered toward her down the center aisle, broad shouldered, tall, with a face some women might call handsome. His measured stride conveyed his lack of concern for interrupting counsel business. He acted as if he were already a member of the family. Bonnie didn't appreciate his unwarranted encroachment or his unabashed arrogance.

He stopped before her. When he reached out to take her hands in his, Bonnie held them back. The slight narrowing of his eyes told her that he didn't appreciate the public rebuff. She didn't care.

"May I help ye, Laird Cameron? As ye can see, we are in the middle of clan business."

"My apologies for the interruption," he intoned, not looking the least contrite. "I just found out about the terrible tragedy that has taken place. I was surprised that I didn't hear about it directly from the lips of my betrothed." The cloaked rebuke was said just loud enough for everyone to hear. Then Ewan faced the crowd. "I came tae offer my condolences and express my heartfelt sorrow over the death of young Sarah. Though I didn't know her well, I thought her a fine woman, one who didn't deserve tae die in such a manner."

Bonnie could see her clan approved of Ewan, which sometimes made her wonder if she had judged him unfairly—or if it was merely that their memories were not as long as hers. Perhaps they simply wanted peace at any cost.

"Thank ye for your sympathies," she said with as much patience as she could muster. "Now, if ye'll excuse us?"

Ewan ignored her and headed toward Gray. "Is this the animal who stands accused?"

Bonnie hastened to step in front of Ewan, but not because she was afraid of what he might do—but of what Gray might do. Gray's eyes had darkened to a dangerous degree, his taut body emanating a menace that Ewan was either too blind or too stupid to see.

"Look at him," Ewan spat. "The man has no remorse."

A rumbling murmur of assent went through the crowd, escalating an already volatile situation and setting the spark to Bonnie's short fuse.

"If ye plan tae stay, Laird Cameron," she said tightly, "then I'll bid ye tae take a seat."

Ewan's frosty gaze snapped to her, a muscle working in his jaw. "I only came here tae help ye, lend my support as your future husband."

Ewan's idea of support was Bonnie's idea of control. He always treated her as if she was incapable of taking care of herself, preferring her in a more submissive role, a part she would never play.

Perhaps that was why Bonnie so enjoyed sharpening her skill with her dirk, to tweak his patronizing nose, especially since her aim tended to be truer than his.

"I appreciate your concern, but I don't need any help."

"Ye always were a headstrong lass."

" 'Tis a fact, and would be unwise of ye tae think that might ever change."

His large hand encircled her upper arm. "Ye are going tae be my wife, Bonnie. Don't forget that."

"How can I forget when ye remind me every day?" Bonnie bit out, flicking a glance at the hand holding her, then at Ewan's face.

With a muttered oath, he released her. "I remind ye because ye seem intent on forever putting me off."

That Bonnie would not deny. She should care for him, seek friendship if nothing else. But the ability to do so eluded her. Perhaps time would bring understanding.

Unfortunately, time was not on her side. Ewan had become more and more persistent about setting a wedding date. Soon she'd either have to commit or break the betrothal. Should she choose the latter, the peace the clans sought would be a distant memory. But she did not have to make her decision just then.

"This is not the time tae be discussing our relationship," she told him in a low voice.

"Or lack thereof," was his pointed retort. "Ye know how I feel about ye Bonnie."

Gray cleared his throat then, bringing their gazes swinging to him. A look of boredom wreathed his face, but his eyes communicated something else entirely.

"Do you mind having this little lovers' quarrel another time? I'm in the middle of being tried for a crime I didn't commit and I'd like to get on with it."

Ewan took a threatening step toward Gray, and Bonnie found herself squarely in the middle of the two men. She placed her hands against Ewan's chest. "Please . . . just go." When he didn't budge, she gave him a slight push. "I want ye tae leave, I said!"

Slitted black eyes snapped to hers, and Bonnie feared he would not comply. Ewan was not a man who took well to being told what to do. To her relief, he stepped back.

"Fine," he said in a clipped undertone. "I'll go. But we have tae talk Bonnie. Ye can't avoid me any longer."

With a final glare at Gray, Ewan pivoted on his heel and strode down the aisle, throwing open the double doors at the back of the hall with a force that rebounded through the room, telling Bonnie their discussion was far from over.

"Is he always so pleasant?"

Gray's droll comment snapped Bonnie's gaze from Ewan's retreating form to her antagonist. She expected to see amusement at her expense etched on his handsome face. Instead, Gray's regard was so intense, she had to catch herself before taking a step back.

Maddened by her reaction, she rounded on him. " 'Tis none of your concern, so ı'll thank ye tae keep out of it!"

"I see you and your lover both possess that same unique charm."

"He's not my lover!" Bonnie snapped before she could stop herself, silently cursing her rash tongue. The man had an extraordinary talent for flustering her.

A hint of a smile curved his lips. "Is it all right for the condemned to give his blessing to this most auspicious union? Perhaps a kiss for the bride-to-be?" His gaze dropped to her mouth, and Bonnie hated the tingle that centered there.

Why did this man whom she didn't know, who was brash and brazen and prodding, make her want . . . Bonnie cut off the thought. Clearly the stress was causing her to think irrationally. Once this situation was behind her, she would be herself again, even though a small voice whispered that this moment, this man, would not soon be forgotten.

"Ye'll mind your behavior, prisoner, or ye'll find yourself gagged." Wonderful, now she sounded no better than Aidan.

The amusement vanished from Gray's face and was replaced by banked hostility. "Someday, Scottish, you might very well regret pushing me."

The fact that she felt even the slightest shiver run down her spine, or the smallest dose of intimidation, escalated Bonnie's anger at herself, which she directed at the man responsible for it.

Heart thundering away, she leaned down, met his rapier-edged glare, and said with more control than she felt, " 'Tis a feat ye won't live long enough tae witness— even should ye live tae be a hundred, *English*."

Then she straightened and spun away from him, heading back to the counsel table to resume the trial that had been abruptly interrupted, silently praying for the strength to get through this day—whatever the outcome.

Aidan rose from his seat, regarding her for a long, tense moment before facing the assembly. "We'll waste no more time mincin' words. These are the facts and they are undisputed. The prisoner was kneelin' beside Sarah's body, a bloody knife in his hand. He had spent the night drinking and confessed to having overindulged."

"The hell I did!" Gray said fiercely.

Aidan's jaw tightened. "Keep your thoughts tae yourself, prisoner. Ye had your chance tae speak."

"Did you even question any of these people?" Gray demanded. "Ask a single one where he was or what he had been doing on the night of Sarah's death?"

"I told ye tae keep quiet!"

"Or did you figure you had a convenient scapegoat, so why bother looking any further?"

Fury blazed in Aidan's eyes, his hands clenched at his sides, fighting for control as he reeled around to address the members of the counsel. "How do ye vote? Guilty or no'?" His gaze swung to the end of the table.

"Guilty," the first person replied, then the second.

Bonnie saw something building, a decision that once made could not be undone. She jumped up from her chair. "How can ye sentence a man tae death when ye can't say conclusively if he committed the deed?"

"Sit down, Bonnie!" her brother commanded.

"All I am asking is that ye think with your minds and not with your hearts, tae ask yourself why this man would murder Sarah. If ye cannot reasonably answer it, then how can ye sentence him tae death?"

"He wanted Sarah and she refused him!" someone offered as a reason.

Before Bonnie could think of how the words sounded, she pointed at Gray and said, "Look at him. Do ye see his face? Do ye think a man as comely as this one has to force a woman intae his bed?'' She groaned inwardly at what her words had revealed, not only to her kinsmen, but also to the man whose gaze she could feel boring into her.

Her unorthodox point appeared to have made an impact on at least a few people. They mumbled among themselves while casting surreptitious glances at Gray, trying to discern something on his face that could not be read, something that either was or wasn't. And that was all this trial amounted to in the end. Variables. Variables of the mind, the heart, a decision made from inference and gut feeling.

Gut feeling. Simple, yet so complex, mixed up as it was with emotion. How much emotion was she basing her convictions on? On that singular moment when she had heard sincerity in Gray's voice as he professed his innocence, glimpsing something in his eyes that bolstered that claim?

Bonnie well understood that Gray's denial of guilt could be as gossamer as the shadowed reality that existed at the moment of Sarah's death, whether he was sinner or sinned against, as he crouched beside her body.

''I have something tae say!'' a voice called out then.

Bonnie glimpsed the top of a dark head as a man shouldered his way through the crowd, yet she knew him well, considering he was often her betrothed's shadow.

Sean Cameron, Ewan's cousin, and the man who had once held Sarah's heart.

Aidan came forward. ''Aye, Sean. What is it?''

Sean wrung his hands nervously, his gaze darting about as people crowded around to hear what he'd come to say, the future hanging in the balance as precious seconds ticked by.

''There was another witness tae Sarah's murder,'' he finally said. ''A person who saw everything that night.'' The news sent a ripple of shock through the crowd.

''Another witness?'' Bonnie couldn't believe what she was hearing.

"And who is this witness?" Aidan demanded.

Sean swallowed hard and then replied, "Me."

"Ye were at the tavern that night?"

He nodded and dropped his head. "I wanted tae speak tae Sarah about . . . us. I came intae the tavern just as she was goin' out the side door, the one that opens up tae the alleyway. I waited for her tae return. When she didn't come back, I went tae look for her." Sean glanced up, his eyes glossy with unshed tears as he added in a barely audible voice, "I was too late tae save her."

Bonnie wanted to ask him why he hadn't come forth with this information immediately and what had brought him here at the eleventh hour, and how she could have missed running into him in the alleyway, and why he hadn't made an attempt to capture Sarah's assailant or even shout a single alarm, and how he felt about slinking away like a coward while the woman he claimed to have loved lay dead or dying on the ground.

However, her moment of hesitation was filled by her brother. "So what did ye see?" An eerie hush descended as everyone waited to hear Sean's reply.

Sean's gaze shifted, his arm shaking slightly as he raised it and pointed a finger at Gray. "I saw that man kill my Sarah."

Chapter 6

The moon was a full, bright disk making its ascent into the night sky, a white globe of luminous light whose rays cut a swath straight to Gray's cell.

Home of the condemned.

On the words of one scrawny, lying sack of sheep shit, Gray had been found guilty of the murder of Sarah Douglass and sentenced to hang come the morning. Little did his accusers know he wouldn't be there in the morning.

He had had enough of this farce, this mockery of justice. He should have left with Prophet, ended something that never should have begun, said the hell with trying to do the right thing for a dead girl and hoping to clear his name.

Why had he cared so much about proving his innocence anyway? He thought he had eradicated the part of himself that gave a damn a long time ago, after waging similar battles as a child, screaming into the wind and never having a single soul hear him. Why had he expected his luck to change?

And why had he allowed himself to think for one

moment that Bonnie had believed he was innocent rather than discovering the hard way that she was really just making sure he was guilty?

Once she was no longer the sole witness to his supposed crime, what Gray had thought was her defense of him reverted to capitulation, the burden of his imminent death no longer hers alone.

And for that reason, he waited for her. She would be arriving any minute with his last meal, and whether she came alone or with the giant, nothing would change the fact that she would be his ticket to freedom.

Gray stepped away from the window, slipping back into the darkness to await her arrival. Soon now. Shortly fate would swing once more.

This time in his favor.

Bonnie set Gray's supper down on a side table so that she could retrieve the key to his shackles. She stared hard at the key, recalling the harsh words she had exchanged with her brother, trying to get him to pay heed to her concerns, to question Sean further instead of treating the man like some conquering hero when, if his story was true, he was a sniveling poltroon.

But her brother wouldn't listen, and Bonnie suspected anger was the reason. Gray had gotten the better of Aidan, even in his handcuffed state, and her brother felt publicly humiliated.

Of course, Gray's explosion had worked against him as well. That was all the counsel members had needed to see to brand him guilty, instead of realizing that he had lashed out because his honor had been impugned. He had behaved exactly the way her brothers would have under similar circumstances.

Bonnie had tried her best to make Aidan see reason, but she had failed, and now there was nothing else she could do.

But to let Gray go.

Her brother had left her with no other choice. Gray was to be executed come morning, and she couldn't stand by and watch a man be put to death when she still had doubts about his guilt. If she only had some time. But she didn't. And the little bit she did have she was wasting.

Bonnie swiped the tray from the table, grabbed a lantern, and headed out the door, determined to follow through on her plan, no matter what the backlash of her actions.

Trepidation prickled her skin as she neared Gray's cell. She wondered why the lantern she had left him was not lit—and why Gray was not standing at the cell window glaring at her, as he did every time she came with his food. He seemed to possess an uncanny ability to anticipate when she would be arriving.

Bonnie held her lantern aloft, shining the light through the cell window, a thread of panic sluicing through her when she didn't see Gray. Could he have escaped? But how? The cell door was locked from the outside, the bolt still in place.

Hurriedly, she laid his tray on the ground next to the door, her hands shaking as she wrenched the bolt back, thrusting the lantern in front of her as she hastened into the cell.

Her breath expelled in a whoosh when she saw Gray lying on the cot, his shackled hands behind his head, his ankles crossed, a hint of a smirk on his handsome face, a smirk that said he had purposely baited her.

"In a hurry to see me tonight, are you?"

A shiver ran down Bonnie's spine as wave after wave of Gray's barely checked rage washed over her. She chided herself to stand firm even though the small cell suddenly felt no bigger than a thimble. "I thought ye might be hurt," she said lamely.

He rolled his head to the side to regard her more closely, staring at her with the full power of those penetrating silver eyes imbued with a frosty shadow, stark and cold as moonlight on ice, tousled hair spilling across his forehead, making him look like a fallen angel brooding on some secret rebellion. "And would it matter if I had been hurt, considering I'll be dead tomorrow?"

Even though she had come on an honorable mission, his words affected her. *He* affected her. What was it about him that managed to rattle her when she was usually so composed? Or make her tremble when she had never trembled before any man? Dear God, did she even know what she was doing?

Doubts suddenly assailed Bonnie. Seeing Gray like this, the coldness in his eyes, feeling the threat that emanated from him, she began to wonder if she had made the right decision. The man now studying her with preternatural intensity was not the same man she had come to know. This man looked ruthless.

This man looked dangerous.

"I-I've brought your dinner," she stammered, heat prickling her skin though the evening was cool.

"Really?" He cocked a brow. "Where is it?"

Bonnie flushed, realizing she had left the tray outside in her rush to get into the cell. It was only beside the door, but she'd have to turn her back on Gray to get it.

"Stay there," she told him sternly.

"And where might I go, do you think?" he mocked with a patronizing air, rattling his shackles.

Feeling somewhat secure that she could reach the tray quickly, Bonnie lunged for it and was back in less than a second . . . to find her prisoner sitting up, his back propped negligently against the wall, appearing as if he'd never been lying down at all.

Her heart leapt to her throat, her ears full with the reverberating sound of her blood. Was he playing with her? Subtly letting her know that she had underestimated him? That he could have made it to the door if he had felt so inclined?

Bonnie had the sudden sensation that he was the

cat . . . and she the mouse. Barely contained animosity resonated beneath his show of outward calm. And when he slowly rose to his feet, the threat became very real.

"I have a dirk and I know how tae use it," she warned.

"I have no doubt of your sincerity. But would you really kill an unarmed man?"

"Aye, if ye push me." She prayed he wouldn't push her; then he'd see her claim for the fabrication it was.

"Fine." Leisurely, he began to undo the buttons of the borrowed shirt he wore, his own having been discarded, though her brother had wanted to make Gray sit in front of the assembly in his torn, blood-speckled garment.

"W-what are ye doing?" Bonnie's eyes widened as he peeled back the shirt, exposing his chest, all hard planes and bronze, chiseled perfection.

"Go ahead," he said.

The heat of embarrassment seared her cheeks as her gaze snapped to his face. "What?"

"Kill me," he replied. "I won't stop you."

Bonnie gaped at him. "Kill ye? Are ye daft?"

"You've already sentenced me to death. Why not turn the knife yourself?"

This was complete madness, insanity at the highest rung. "Because I'll not take another person's life, that's why!"

"But you don't mind watching someone else take my life. Interesting. You surprise me, you know. I didn't think you were such a sniveling coward."

His taunt stung like a backhanded slap, painful and unexpected, and when she spoke, she couldn't quite withhold the hurt from her voice. "Why do ye blame me for your predicament?"

"Oh, I don't blame you," he returned in a tone of barely repressed animosity. "I blame myself for stepping foot in this barbaric, backward country."

"Why did ye come here then, if ye hate it so much?"

He edged nearer to her, his gaze intent on her face.

"I think the better question is why did you come here . . . to my cell. Alone," he added in a whiskey-dark voice, trying to frighten her—and succeeding. "Could it be some lust burns beneath that icy exterior?"

Bonnie suddenly felt cornered. She needed to get out, to think. She stared down at the supper tray she still clutched. "If ye don't want tae eat—"

"Food is the last thing on my mind at this moment." He was close enough now that only the tray separated them, which he tugged from her hands and carelessly tossed behind him, breaking dishware and scattering food.

The jarring noise snapped Bonnie from the daze she was in, awakening her to the very real danger now facing her, and the need to defend herself.

She wrenched the dirk from her boot, thrusting the weapon toward Gray, the tip a scant inch from his chest. "Stay back, ye devil's spawn, or I swear I'll kill ye!"

Her threat only made him smile. "We've already been through that, my girl. I gave you the chance to do away with me, but you didn't take it."

"I'll do it now. Make no mistake."

"So do it." He advanced a half step, the lethal point of the blade pressing against his chest, just below his rib cage, a tiny drop of blood appearing and then drifting slowly downward to disappear behind his waistband. "Go ahead," he softly prodded, leaning forward. "Kill me, Bonnie." His warm breath against her ear sent delicious waves through her body.

Bonnie's hand began to tremble. "Why are ye doing this?"

"Why not?" he murmured, his lips whispering along her jaw, making her want to tilt her head back and know the sweet press of his mouth against her throat.

"Just leave me alone," she breathed.

He straightened, a muscle working in his jaw. "I'm not your betrothed, my girl. I'll not be so easily dismissed." Then, without warning, his hand clamped around her wrist, holding her hand immobile and keeping the dirk at bay.

Bonnie gasped, reeling from the speed with which he had struck. She struggled wildly, trying to wrench free, but his hold was viselike, escalating her panic. She beat her single fist against his chest until he captured that hand as well, pinning her roughly against the wall, her arms above her head, his massive frame enveloping her.

Her fear redoubled when she could not budge him, his male heat overwhelming her, allowing her no quarter. He made not a single attempt to stop her fruitless, one-sided skirmish. Instead he waited for her to reach the conclusion he had known from the onset.

There would be no escape.

Bonnie ceased struggling, her chest heaving with exertion as they stood there suspended in time, the look in Gray's eyes compelling as still waters—and just as lethal.

"Why won't ye leave me alone?" she asked in a tremulous voice.

"Because I can't," he said gruffly, his gaze hardening, his expression grim, as if the admission was something he didn't want to divulge but was torn from him anyway. "Lord knows I've tried not to think about you, want you. Hate you." His anger blasted her, coiled around her as effectively as his hand imprisoned her. "But I could think of nothing else but this moment ... the moment the tables turned and you became my prisoner."

His words hit her like cold water. "I won't let ye take your anger out on me."

"You have no choice." His head dipped toward hers, his silky hair tumbling forward, the lantern casting shadows, sharpening angles. "I'm about to have my first taste of freedom, and I will savor it and make it last for as long as I can."

"Ye'll get nothing from me!" Bonnie vowed, trying to yank free of his unrelenting grasp.

"No?" His slow descent halted, his lips so very close to hers, his voice an exquisitely sensual rasp that summoned a reckless hunger in Bonnie. Every fiber of her being reacted to his nearness; he enveloped her, leaving her nowhere to go, no place to hide, only focusing her attention acutely on the solid six-plus feet of beautifully savage reality in front of her. She prayed for strength even as her gaze floated to his lips.

"No," she returned defiantly.

A hint of a satyr's grin tilted up the corners of his mouth, its effect singularly devastating. "Still full of spirit, I see. Good. I don't intend to crush that spirit, but to fulfill its potential."

"And how do ye plan tae do that?" she asked, sounding breathless and wondering what compelled her to say anything, to delve into his eyes and get lost, to want to find a reason, any reason, to end the battle and surrender on his terms.

"The kiss," he replied in a husky voice.

"What kiss?"

"This one." He hauled her tight against his long, hard frame, his lips capturing hers, fusing their mouths in heated intercourse, sending Bonnie headlong in a world where nothing existed but sensation, intoxicating and addictive, leaving her weak, trapped inside a body that had suddenly turned traitorous.

His lips molded hers, his tongue exploring, teasing, tasting. Bonnie had never experienced anything like this, never had a man kiss her in such a way, never had she wanted one to—until now.

Her nails tested his flesh, muscles flexing beneath her fingertips, hot rivulets of desire running through her veins as his tongue dipped inside her mouth, coaxing her into a response. Her tongue battled with his, their contact as fierce in the kiss as it was in the war they waged.

Gray's visceral groan mingled with a mewling sound Bonnie suddenly recognized as coming from herself, communicating more eloquently than words that she was drowning in the moment, the man, and she wanted more.

The realization rattled her, shaking her from the euphoric web Gray had spun around her, his recent boast ringing in her ears.

I don't intend to crush that spirit, but to fulfill its potential.

She had given him exactly what he wanted, what he so arrogantly claimed he could get.

With a cry of despair, Bonnie shoved him away, an overwhelming need to lash out blinding her to the consequences as she swung her dirk, the blade slicing across his stomach, a dark line of crimson blood blossoming in its wake.

Chapter 7

Too late, Bonnie discovered the cost of her rage, staring in horror at the injury she had inflicted, unable to believe she had used her dagger to hurt anyone. That the wound appeared to be superficial didn't matter, nor did the fact that she was sorry. She had stepped over the line, lost control. She had come to help and had only succeeded in making things worse.

If only she could believe she had been defending herself against a real threat, some physical harm, but the only threat Gray had truly posed was to her senses, her emotions, perhaps even her heart—and the realization had scared her like nothing she had ever known.

Gray could have hurt her in so many ways, but his punishment had been a kiss, and he couldn't have chosen anything worse. For in that one glorious moment when his lips melded with hers, Bonnie felt as if her life had just begun only to realize the life she envisioned could never be hers. Another path had already been chosen for her—and another man.

Bonnie waited for Gray to make a move, to say something, do something. Yet he remained motionless, blood trickling slowly down his stomach.

When she dared to glance up at his face, what she saw was more horrible than the damage she had caused his body. Something imminently threatening had tarnished his eyes, making them appear almost black in the muted, dying light of the lantern.

Bonnie wanted to tell him that she had come to his cell with the intention of helping, to confess the reason she was there alone and why the guard was not standing watch, but running a fool's errand instead.

But Gray certainly would not believe anything she said now. She could almost hear him mocking that she had a funny way of helping. Or perhaps that mild rebuke was merely a product of her own mind, because looking now at Gray's granite-hewn countenance, she suspected he would have much more to say than that—and much worse.

"I didn't mean—"

"Yes, you did," he interjected brusquely. "I simply made the mistake of forgetting you had claws. I won't make such a mistake again." He lifted his shackled hands. "Unlock them." His tone, though low, was as dangerous as newly honed steel. "The time for games has come to an end." He thrust his hands closer. "Unlock them. *Now!*"

Like a deer ensnared in the light, Bonnie stood immobile, unable to bolt out of trouble's way, her fate sealed even as her mind screamed danger.

Her hand trembled as she delved into her pocket, her fingers brushing cool metal, familiar notches and grooves, a tangible element that brought home the seriousness of the situation with unequivocal clarity. She withdrew the key, hesitated slightly, and then slid it into the lock . . . freeing her prisoner.

Bonnie edged away from Gray, pressing into the hard, cold stone wall as if she could become one with it, mutely observing him as he rubbed his wrists, his scrutiny never wavering from her face as he eyed her with the same intense concentration a lion eyes a gazelle.

What was he waiting for?

Bonnie's mouth went bone dry as he took the four steps separating them, an efficient grace to his movements that put her in mind of a predatory cat. He raised a hand toward her face.

Bonnie's palms flattened against the gritty stone, but she refused to give him the satisfaction of seeing her cower. She lifted her chin, defiance blazing in her eyes as she glared at Gray, daring him to strike her.

No blow landed. Yet his touch upon her cheek was just as startling, just as devastating. His thumb stroked feathery light back and forth, mesmerizing her as swiftly and as surely as he had only moments earlier.

The clamp of cold steel closing around her wrist brought the moment to a jarring halt. Bonnie's gaze snapped downward to find that Gray had shackled one of her wrists.

Her head jerked up. "What are ye doing?" She struggled against her bond. "Take this off!"

"How does it feel to be my prisoner?" Gray queried in a silky voice.

Panic overwhelmed Bonnie, her blood racing through her veins as she wrenched harder and harder in a fruitless effort to free herself. "Let me go!"

"I think not." Then he linked the other end of the cuffs on his wrist, binding them together. Bonnie's alarm redoubled. She lunged for the key in his hand. He held it out of reach. "Not so fast, my girl. You and I have a little journey to take."

"I won't go anywhere with ye!"

"Regrettably, you have no say in the matter. Terrible thing about freedom is that it's rather hard to swallow when the privilege has been taken from you." His smug, hateful expression told Bonnie he reveled in her defenselessness. Captive had become captor, leaving her at Gray's mercy as surely as he had been at her brother's.

"Ye'll never get away."

"Ye of little faith," he mocked, an ironic slant to his lips. "With you at my side, I feel my chances of escaping this demented masquerade are excellent."

"My brothers will come after ye. They'll hunt ye down like the beast ye are."

Gray raised a sleek, dark brow. "Beast, am I? How interesting. Do you kiss all the beasts you know with such fervor?"

Heat scored Bonnie's cheeks. "You're the only one!"

"You mean I'm the only man you've kissed?"

"Of course not!" she retorted indignantly. "I've been kissed plenty!"

"Plenty, huh? I thought you kissed like an untried virgin myself. Shall we give it another go? I could have been wrong."

What she wouldn't give to clobber his arrogant head! "You're loathsome," she hissed, and thought she saw his lips twitch with a grin. The wretch!

"And what about your betrothed? Is he a beast, Bonnie?" The sound of her name on his lips was an invisible caress that made her tremble.

Bonnie strengthened her resolve and fought back in the only way open to her. "At least Ewan wouldn't use me tae sneak away like a coward!"

Any hint of softness evaporated from Gray's face. The fire that flared to life in his eyes nearly scorched her, his jaw clenching and unclenching as he leaned his head down. "I'll only warn you one last time to watch what you say."

Bonnie's own temper had risen right along with his. "Or what? Ye'll beat me? Break me? Bend me tae your will? I'm not afraid of ye."

"Oh, but you should be afraid," he murmured, his tone as black as the night. "Very afraid." The solid expanse of his chest was so close to hers that Bonnie dared not breathe.

A voice inside her warned Bonnie to cease provoking

him, that such foolhardy behavior could only lead her down a path it best not to trod. But no man had ever cowed her, and this man would not be any different.

However, any retort she might have made was aborted when he tugged her toward the door. Bonnie dug in her heels with a vengeance, but her efforts were ineffectual. His strength far outweighed hers. He yanked her forward so forcefully, she slammed into his broad back.

With a final glance into the darkness, he exited the cell, dragging her along behind him. A quick scan of the area revealed they were utterly alone. Bonnie's heart sank—but her determination to be free did not ebb.

She kicked, punched, and scratched her antagonist at every opportunity. At one point, she even tried to sit down—all to no avail.

"Stop or I'll scream!" she then threatened, which succeeded in getting his attention.

He halted abruptly, and once more Bonnie barreled into his back. He tossed a wry glance over his shoulder. "If you don't behave, I will have to gag you. I promise you won't appreciate the methods I employ, so it's best to keep on my good side."

Bonnie's chest heaved from anger and exertion. "Ye have no good side, ye overbearing lout!"

"If I wasn't so stouthearted, my dear, your biting comments might wound my pride."

Oh, that was it! Bonnie had suffered all the abuse she was going to take. She opened her mouth, intent on blasting out the scream of her life, but before she could utter a sound, Gray's hand clamped over her mouth.

"Why do you never heed a warning?" he growled tersely in her ear, sending chills along her arms, his mouth so close to her neck she could feel his warm breath.

Bonnie stood suspended, waiting for him to either move back—or press his lips to that spot behind her ear where his mouth lurked temptingly. Her eyes wid-

ened with the realization that she actually wanted this
. . . kidnapper to touch her!

Rage burgeoned forth, and she bit down on his finger
as hard as she could.

"Goddamn it!" he swore fiercely, shaking the injured
appendage.

Bonnie knew supreme satisfaction—and it lasted all
of a second before she was hoisted into the air and
tossed over Gray's shoulder.

"Put me down!" She squirmed in vain, her hair nearly
sweeping the ground as he started down the incline—
a rather steep incline. Her indignation was momentarily
forgotten. "Stop! Ye'll fall!"

"We certainly will if you keep wriggling, but you never
take the things I say to heart, so I imagine the outcome
is anyone's guess."

Fear of tumbling down the craggy hill made Bonnie
wild. "Let me go! Let me go!"

The arm slung over her back lifted and a mighty hand
thwacked her bottom. "Be still!" he commanded.

Bonnie blinked, more stunned by the fact that Gray
had spanked her than hurt. Her astonishment quickly
passed, however, and her anger returned in spades. She
would scratch his eyes out! No man laid a finger on her
and remained male for long! But since she wanted to
live long enough to exact her revenge, she choked back
her rage and stilled her limbs—until they reached the
bottom of the hill.

Then she called Gray every name she could think of,
and when she could come up with no more, she made
some up. Her nemesis merely trudge along, ignoring
her.

Bonnie didn't realize they had reached the water until
Gray tipped sideways . . . and released her, sending her
tumbling into the frigid ocean, her irate scream muffled
by little salty bubbles.

She burst to the surface spewing water, her hair plastered to her face like a clump of seaweed. She swiped

the wet, heavy tresses away and glared at her antagonist. "Ye . . . animal!"

She expected his usual drollery, or at least that glower he had so perfected. Instead, he surprised her and unlocked the handcuffs, saying simply, "Treat people like animals and they act like animals."

With barely a second glance, Gray swished past her, disappearing into the murky gloom like a Pagan god merging with earth and midnight and unknown realms. Bonnie wondered if this was the end of the line, and the sight of his broad back was the last she would see of him.

Good! She hoped he choked on a blowfish!

So why was she just standing there instead of running away as fast as she could?

Bonnie peered into the all-consuming darkness, trying to catch a glimpse of Gray as gentle waves lapped at her waist. She waited. A minute ticked past, then two . . . and three. Was he gone? Could it be . . . over?

The question had no more than entered her mind when he reappeared, towing something behind him. An unexpected spurt of relief washed over Bonnie—and some other emotion she couldn't adequately define, a stirring inside her at the sight of him mantled in midnight shadows, an Adonis sculpted from the sea.

His black leather pants, long ruined, gleamed with water, molding his flesh in provocative ways. His silky blue-black hair was now wet, tossed carelessly back, slick against his neck and the top of his shoulders. Moonlight danced erotically over the taut planes of his chest— and slanted golden paths across the nasty gash on his stomach.

Bonnie longed to touch the wound, wipe away the last traces of blood, apologize for hurting him, which was utterly ludicrous in light of her current situation. Yet the desire was there nonetheless.

The remembrance of his big body encompassing hers as he backed her into the stone wall made her heart beat just a little bit faster. Not a single part of him had touched her physically, yet his heat had seared her clean through, his presence overwhelming.

Bonnie wrapped her arms around herself, a sudden chill overtaking her, shaking her from her reverie as Gray came ever nearer—and her chance for escape grew ever more distant.

Even as her mind railed that it was too late to make a bid for freedom, Bonnie still wheeled around and stumbled toward the shore, her sodden pants hampering her movements as she splashed through the water, certain she need only get dry land beneath her feet to give herself a fighting chance.

Bonnie could hear Gray splashing behind her, coming up swiftly. She knew she had lost, but she would not give up that easily. She pushed through the water as fast as she could, falling, sputtering, the sandy bottom tripping her up. Just another three feet . . . two feet . . .

The air whooshed from her lungs as a steel band snaked around her waist. She and Gray tumbled toward the shore. He rolled at the last instant so that she landed on top of him.

The press of his body against hers, the immediate quickening of her blood, and her freedom now lost, made Bonnie go wild, thrashing as he sought to manacle her wrists with his hands, their tempers flaring even as a sultry breeze threatened to fan the flames of anger into something far more dangerous.

Bonnie elbowed Gray's stomach and heard him grunt and hated herself for suffering even a second of guilt at hurting him again. He momentarily loosened his grip, and she attempted to use the reprieve to her advantage, yet that blasted ironlike arm twined about her, slamming her back against his body.

She fought with desperation but seemed to do no more than situate herself further between his rock-hewn thighs. It was then that she caught a glimpse of her shirt, gaping open—her breasts pressed intimately against his chest.

Bonnie went stock-still, squeezing her eyes shut and praying he didn't notice her state of undress, even though she knew that was a pointless hope. Her flesh suddenly felt extraordinarily sensitive, every nuance of wet skin against wet skin, hardness against softness, conspiring against her. She dared not move, even breathe.

Beneath her palms, she sensed the restless, barely contained energy flowing through Gray, his body as tense as a coiled spring. When his hands tenderly combed her hair from her face, Bonnie thought she would surely die. Anger she could take from this man. Mockery she could defend. Tenderness she was completely helpless against.

Don't look at him, her mind warned.

But as Gray had once accused, she could never heed a warning. Her eyelids fluttered open and his silvery gaze impaled her, unfurling the warmth deep inside.

His gaze skimmed down her nose, across her cheekbones, along her jaw, and paused at her lips. Inevitably, that heated regard descended to where her breasts met his chest. Bonnie's breath arrested in her throat, a sweet ache culminating at the juncture of her thighs.

She remained motionless as he lifted clinging strands of her hair from her shoulders, her neck . . . the tops of her breasts. Perhaps instinct or some hidden need induced her to stir against him, cuddling the hardness straining the buttons of his trousers.

Gray clenched his teeth, a muscle in his jaw working as if he fought for control. A tiny thrill shot through Bonnie. Had she brought the mighty warrior down? Gained the control that he had wrested from her with the force of his superior strength? The thought was heady.

He made her long to test her theory, explore at length, capture his wrists as he had done to her and do as she pleased. She felt wanton and wicked and desirable. It was pure madness.

A large, slightly callused hand glided over her shoulder, his fingers stroking through her wet tresses to cradle the back of her head, drawing her down, the kiss fated.

The touch of Gray's lips against hers made the world tilt and everything cease to exist beside this moment. The kiss was not gentle, not a tender exploration, but wild and fierce and all-encompassing, a consummation of their combined tempers, the heat of the battle, the soaring heights of a victory hard won.

Gray's free hand skimmed along her side, easing underneath the edge of her shirt, his fingers dipping into the indentation of her spine . . . and moving downward. His hand molded her buttocks, tested her flesh, made her feel his tempting hardness more fully.

Bonnie barely noticed that he rolled with her until cool, wet sand and lapping water touched her back, Gray's hard frame pressed against her, half over her, his lips having never left hers. Her nipples hardened painfully as his wet chest rubbed sinuously against her.

Bonnie did not understand what was happening to her, how she could hate this man yet not hate him at the same time. A look drugged her. A kiss annihilated her.

He drew back, his direct, heated regard making no apologies. Bonnie swallowed as his gaze lowered, inch by excruciating inch, coming to rest on her fully exposed breasts. She had never experienced such conflict, wanting to cover herself one moment and wanting to let him look, let him touch, the next.

He cupped one globe, molding it, pushing the peak upward. "Beautiful," he murmured, his voice thick, his one word sending another rush of liquid heat to pool at the core of her.

Then his head dipped, his hair teasing her flesh as his mouth closed with purpose around the aching nub. Bonnie arched her back as a pleasure so sweet, so heavenly, coursed through her, bringing with it a need so strong, the yearning frightened her.

"Don't," she begged in a whisper. "Please."

Gray's head rose, but he did not look at her. Instead he closed his eyes. The tautness about his lips bespoke a struggle to rein in his rampant desire, a desire Bonnie understood but had to deny.

His unquestioning capitulation had surprised her. What she had expected him to do, she was not sure. Perhaps ignore her as he had far too often? Try to bend her to his will as he was wont to do? Or perhaps take her body whether she allowed him to or not?

With unexpected tenderness, he pulled her shirt together, trying to fix it properly but finding buttons missing, the result of their struggle. He surged to his feet and held out his hand for her. Bonnie hesitated and then placed her palm in his.

When at last she stood before him, only inches separated them. A gentleness lingered in his eyes as he stared down at her. Then he shrugged out of his shirt and slipped it on her, no words passing between them as Bonnie allowed him to dress her as if she were a child. Even though his shirt was four times too big and as wet as hers, simply wearing it warmed her, made her feel strangely comforted.

The moon peaked from behind a cloud, cascading across his face, highlighting his strong profile and the determination in his jaw, imprinting the memory in her brain.

He turned then. But he did not head for the shore. Instead, he waded farther out into the ocean—tugging her along with him.

"What are ye doing?"

"Leaving," he replied gruffly.

It was then Bonnie noticed what he had been pulling behind him before she had tried to flee. A rowboat. He had known exactly where to find it. But how?

The question was forgotten when his one word sunk in. *Leaving.* "And what do ye plan tae do with me?"

Gray grabbed the rope tied to the front of the boat from the water before facing her, his voice without inflection as he replied, "Take you with me."

Chapter 8

Through hooded eyes, Gray watched the expression of shock etch Bonnie's lovely, treacherous visage at his blunt declaration, an admission that stupefied him as well, unexpected as it was—rash and incredible and bloody surreal. The words had sprung to his lips and nothing had held them in check.

He should be laughing heartily right now, telling her it was all a joke, that the last thing he wanted was a reluctant, waspish, rattle-him-to-the-brink-of-endurance female coming along on what might very well be the most important journey of his life.

But no laughter was forthcoming. He remained entirely closemouthed.

The only tangible evidence that conveyed he wasn't dreaming was the dull twang ferrying back and forth across his stomach, courtesy of Bonnie's dirk.

Though he was still angry about that little fiasco, truth was, his lack of attention to the knife had caused the incident. Seducing Bonnie had been his sole focus, her nearness easing inside him like a slow-building heat, his mind consumed by a desire to ravage the warm satin of her lips and drown by degrees in the hot, dark flood of his need. Perhaps, if he looked closely, the concept that he had gotten exactly what he deserved might rear its ugly head.

Though Bonnie was one of the most fearless women he knew, she must have been frightened having a convicted murderer kissing her, caressing her, and who had wanted to go on doing both, whose rage and pain at craving someone he could never have was even now barely concealed.

He should let her go, he knew. He had gained his freedom and was in the final lap. Very shortly now he would be putting this nightmare behind him. He didn't need her. But when she had started to run, common sense dropped away, and all he knew was that he had to chase after her—and hold on for dear life.

Damn her.

Damn him even more.

Strangely, she didn't resist when he lifted her from the water and sat her down inside the boat. Shock, he suspected, still held her in thrall. The daze would not last long. Best to hasten on his way.

Gray climbed into the boat and began to row in earnest. Bonnie spoke not a word, and he cursed himself for recognizing a moment of concern on her behalf— and worse, guilt.

He shouldn't feel anything close to guilt. She was the one at fault, after all. She and her rotten brothers had planned to have him executed, hanged by the neck until dead. So why should he feel sorry for her? His reaction made not a bloody bit of sense. But neither did his wild attraction to her.

Gray rowed with fevered strokes, seeking a vent for his unabated desire, which had been on slow burn from the second he had clapped eyes on Bonnie. What had he been thinking to kiss his enemy, the person who had, not so long ago, spat in his face?

He hazarded a glance at her, seated across from him,

wet and angry, two things that only increased her allure. His shirt clung to her every curve, cradling the swell of those lush breasts, her rigid nipples straining against the fabric.

Gray's groin contracted painfully as he mentally re-lived the feel of her, the taste of her, his body still ensnared in her passion, a hunger that rivaled his and had consumed his every sense. He had meant to get his revenge on her, but she had gained the upper hand.

Gray forced the thought aside, gearing himself for her inevitable attack, unsure whether her eruption would be verbal, physical—or both. Only knowing whatever direction her ire took, the recoil would not be long in coming.

She didn't disappoint him.

"You're so low they'll have tae dig up when they bury ye," she hissed.

Relief coursed through Gray. Even though Bonnie's comments could cut clean through the marrow of a man's bones, he was still glad she hadn't simply fore-gone her stinging taunts and lunged straight for his jugular instead.

He'd almost welcome **hanging** to toppling overboard with a slippery Bonnie to contend with. The girl rarely incited his rage but always incited his passion. He'd sink to the ocean floor in under a minute.

Knowing that, he should have made a point of keep-ing his remarks behind his teeth instead of prodding the girl. But he finally understood what it was the devil made people do. "And you, my girl, are a pain in the arse with more bravado than brains and about as much charm as a toothless smile."

Her spine stiffened. "If I'm so horrible, why didn't ye leave me back on shore?"

Hell, Gray thought, she would have to pose the one question for which he didn't have a plausible answer. "Collateral," he replied. Now, if he only knew what the hell he meant.

Bonnie narrowed glacial blue eyes at him. "Ye intend tae use me tae ward off my own kin when they come after ye. Is that it?"

Gray hadn't really thought of it that way, but since she had so kindly offered something workable, he might as well use it. "Exactly."

She folded slender arms beneath lush, send-him-to-an-early-grave breasts, her entire aspect radiating mutiny. "I think you're forgetting something, English."

"Oh? And what's that, Scottish?"

She leaned forward and replied, "Ye'll have me tae deal with, and if it's war ye want . . . it's war ye'll get."

Why the idea of a full-scale hostile encounter with this fork-tongued sprite was an intriguing prospect, Gray preferred not to examine too closely. "Is that a promise?"

"Aye—'tis a promise."

And it was one promise Bonnie planned to fulfill if it was the last thing she did. She'd make the smug, silver-eyed scoundrel the sorriest man alive for kidnapping her, sorrier still for pressing his mouth to hers in a kiss that had seared her all the way to her soul, and for bringing something to life inside her, sensations she'd never felt before.

But it was hard to concentrate on retaliation when Gray sat before her naked to the waist, glorious and unabashed. The spray off the water glistened on his skin, a sliver of moon making golden paths across his rippling stomach, his wound no longer bleeding, the saltwater having cleansed and staunched its flow, leaving only a mean red line as a reminder of her folly.

Bonnie tried not to stare at the flexing bands of muscles across his chest, or the broad, straining expanse of his shoulders, or admire the large hills and taut valleys of his corded arms.

She was so absorbed in trying not to stare that she nearly leapt from her seat when a shrill whistle pierced the air. Her eyes widened as over the crest of a breaking wave a vessel loomed, rising out of the water like a mammoth black bird of prey.

"Sweet Mary . . . what's that?"

Without breaking from his rowing, Gray replied, "It would appear to be a ship."

His sarcasm grated Bonnie's already frayed nerves. "And do ye think I don't know a ship when I see one?"

"You asked—"

"I know what I asked!" she snapped. "Are they friend or foe, is what worries me."

"Friend—to me at least. You, I'm not so sure about. They don't take kindly to spitting, kicking, punching, and, most assuredly, stabbing."

Bonnie refused to rise to the bait and instead eyed Gray suspiciously. "And how would ye know?"

"Because that, my girl, is the good ship *Revenge*. Rather apropos name considering the circumstances, wouldn't you say?"

"And ye know the captain of that ship, I suspect?"

"That I do. Very well, in fact—considering I'm the captain."

Bonnie gaped at him, waiting for some hint of mockery to give him away. But his expression was completely serious. "That ship . . . is yours?"

"I believe I answered that question."

"Ye never said ye had a ship."

"I never said I didn't either."

Bonnie hadn't taken into considered how Gray had arrived in Scotland. Such information hadn't seemed relevant at the time, considering the circumstances and his subsequent incarceration.

"Has it been here all this time?"

He nodded. "My crew has been awaiting my return far more eagerly than you have been planning my demise."

Bonnie tried to make sense of his sudden revelation. "If they were here all along, why did no one come forward tae help ye?"

"Because I told my first mate to have the men stand fast."

"But when did ye speak—"

"Every night."

Every night? A stranger had been crawling about beneath their noses and they hadn't known? No. Not possible. He had to be lying. "If ye spoke tae him every night, then why didn't he try tae release ye?"

"He did try."

"So he failed then?"

"No."

A slow-moving chill crept over Bonnie's skin as the import of Gray's startling revelation sunk in. While she had been tormented by the idea of her brother taking the life of a man who might very well be innocent, Gray had been silently mocking her, mocking all of them. He hadn't needed her help—but he had used her weakness to his advantage.

A voice called out from the darkness. "Welcome back, lad. You had us worried. We thought maybe you didn't free yourself and we'd find you swinging from the gibbet come morning."

Gray chuckled and glanced up at the man speaking. "Perish the thought, old boy. I'm far more resourceful than you give me credit for."

Bonnie heard nothing more of the exchange between Gray and his man. She had been duped, and the only thought consuming her mind at that moment was of escape. It was now or never. Vaulting from her seat, she plunged headlong into the frigid black sea.

Gray wheeled around just in time to see Bonnie's feet disappearing beneath the murky depths of the water, her body surfacing a good twenty feet away.

"Bloody hell!" he swore before diving in after her. She was a strong swimmer, but he had longer arms. He swiftly overtook her. She retaliated by slamming her foot into his privates and paddling away, leaving him to gargle the Atlantic and be thankful that the deadening weight of the water kept him from suffering the full force of the anger behind her actions.

Getting behind Bonnie, Gray twined his arms tightly around her waist, but she continued to fight vigorously against her fate, her squirming working on Gray in the wrong way.

"Leave off, woman, or we'll both drown!"

"Ye'll drown, ye bloated clod! And I'll be glad for it!"

Between the heaviness in his groin and his stinging stomach, Gray thought her prediction might very well be an accurate one. "If I go, you go. And just in case you weren't aware, these are shark-infested waters, so we're likely to be eaten alive instead of drowning. With the scent of my blood, I estimate we have about five minutes before we're surrounded."

That stopped her endless contorting. "Sharks?" Her gaze darted around, perhaps searching for a fin cutting through the rolling swells.

"Yes, sharks. But I imagine you aren't afraid of them either."

She snorted. "Of course not." Yet she couldn't contain the shiver that ran through her.

"Everything all right out there, Cap'n?"

"Fine," Gray returned tersely, wondering how loud his lie rang in that single word. One thing he wasn't feeling at that moment was fine. He had a sinking sensation that Bonnie's explosive temper wouldn't be what did him in, but his unyielding desire for the mean little spitfire.

Her long hair flowed out over the water, winding around him, the mahogany tresses dark as midnight, warming every part of him that they touched. His arm clasped bare skin as her shirt ends floated upward, his thumb skimming the underside of her breast.

Gray gritted his teeth, struggling to control the urge to cup that sweet mound, remembering the tempting weight so vividly the recollection bordered on painful.

Bonnie stiffened, perhaps realizing where his hand

was—or perhaps remembering their encounter on the beach. He wondered if she had felt anything when he'd kissed her, anything more than that first rush of heat. But how could she? She hated him, after all.

The thought was like a valve, effectively closing off Gray's ardor. "Let's go," he said gruffly.

Whether she comprehended that he had won this battle or the threat of sharks was the impetus for her ready compliance, Gray wasn't sure. Either way, he was relieved when she paddled toward the ship. Each fight with Bonnie only made him that much more determined to tame her and to sip once more from the well of her passion.

At the Jacob's ladder, she hesitated, gnawing that lush lower lip, perhaps contemplating another attempt at liberation. Gray eased up beside her to deter such thinking, trying not to be drawn in by those indigo eyes that had captured him from the first, tempting him to unravel the mysteries that simmered within their depths.

She scowled at him, brimming with her usual defiance. "I advise ye tae keep your distance if ye ken what's good for ye."

Gray held up his hands in supplication, deciding now was not the proper time to tell her that she'd be sharing his quarters, which should prove an interesting arrangement—if he lived long enough to enjoy it.

But he had his reasons for bunking with a woman who would probably plunge a knife in his back at the earliest opportunity. Damien taught him long ago that a smart man kept his friends close—but his enemies even closer. Unfortunately, Damien never enlightened Gray on how close he should keep the enemies he was attracted to.

Even closer came to mind.

As if reading his thoughts, she added, "Be warned: I don't intend tae go quietly."

"Fire at will, my girl. I've survived worse things than you can throw at me."

She tilted her head slightly, her expression articulating her doubt. "Funny; Shamus Gordon said almost the same thing tae me when we were children after I warned him tae apologize tae my friend for splattering mud on her best dress."

Gray had to bite the inside of his mouth to keep from grinning, figuring an ill fate had befallen poor Shamus. "So what happened? Did he apologize?"

"After a wee bit of coaxing."

This time, Gray couldn't help smiling, envisioning the lad strapped to a rack, a gleaming, razor-edged pendulum swinging ominously above him and a pixie-faced Bonnie chortling with glee. "What kind of coaxing, dare I ask?"

"Let's just say a person with only one good eye and a limping gait has more important things tae concern himself with than bullying others. Tyrants usually get their comeuppance." She leveled him with a pointed look. "Just a word tae the wise."

And with that veiled threat hanging in the air, Bonnie gave a toss of her wild mane and ascended the rope ladder, leaving Gray to laugh so hard he nearly drowned.

Chapter 9

Gray wasn't laughing anymore.

In fact, he was ready to devise a mutiny, walk his own plank, and pray mightily for sharks.

After less than seventy-two hours at sea, the balance of power had shifted and Bonnie was putting him quite strenuously through his paces.

The first day on board she had dumped salt in his coffee—pepper in it the next, and bloody benighted rube that he was, he didn't learn from his initiation, so she got over on him two more times before he wised up.

Then the spiteful harridan had located a needle and thread in one of the drawers in his cabin and sewn up the armholes on three of favorite shirts—and his silk dressing gown!

If that wasn't bad enough, he'd been turfed out of his own quarters, relegated to a hammock, which the vicious piece of work tied into an unrecognizable lump the first night, leaving the cold floor as his only option.

And lest he forget the blood-curdling screams . . .

Gray never knew when the girl would let loose with

one of her random shrieks that were so piercing the reverberation threatened to crack the timbers, bringing everyone running, expecting to see her bleeding to death on the floor, his letter opener thrust in her chest.

Knowing his blasted luck, Gray would be kneeling beside her body, endeavoring to extract the letter opener when everyone rushed in. Then he'd find himself on trial for another murder he didn't commit—not to say this particular transgression hadn't crossed his mind, tempting him on an almost hourly basis.

Bonnie was a dancing flame on a ship full of dynamite, one needing only to come in contact with the other to blast the entire eastern seaboard into oblivion. The capillaries at the base of Gray's skull were beginning to pulsate in anticipatory dread, and he felt like he'd swallowed a burning rock that had lodged dead center in his chest.

Well, Bonnie had promised to make his life miserable and she was amply fulfilling her threat. Gray need only stare at the bits of egg clinging to his bos'n mate's hair and the strawberry jam meandering down one ruddy, embarrassed cheek to dissect that another day had dawned bright and sunny in hell.

Ye gods, was there no end to his torment?

"What now?" Gray asked, noting the dread in his voice.

"The girl refused tae eat again," the man replied, and then added sheepishly, "I didn't duck fast enough."

Gray pinched the bridge of his nose, his nerves at a wisp-thin frazzle. Bonnie had attacked one well-meaning sailor after the next—food her weapon of choice, preferring the messier edibles like pudding or oatmeal over a rasher of bacon or a slab of beef.

Gray had naively thought he might have more luck sending his bos'n mate into the lion's den this time around since the man was Scottish, he and Bonnie kindred spirits—or so Gray presumed. One would think he'd know better by now.

Another plan shot to almighty hell.

"I told you to strap her down and feed her if she refused again," Gray said, a dull throbbing centering between his eyes.

"I tried tae, mind ye. But, well, she bit me." He erected the injured digit for inspection. Gray's own finger ached in sympathy, vividly remembering Bonnie's sharp teeth digging into his flesh. "She don't make it easy for a man tae do his job, Cap'n."

Gray didn't need to be told that. He was living the nightmare. "She's a vicious piece of work, I know."

" 'T'ain't that, sir. 'Tis just that the lass looks so . . ."

"Innocent?" Gray inserted. "Incapable of malice? Like butter would melt in her mouth?"

"Aye," he replied, a hint of a sigh in his voice. "When she smiles, you think—"

Gray held up his hand, not needing to hear the rest of the man's words to divine what he was going to say. "When she smiles you think you are the only person in the world upon whom she has bestowed that smile—and how could a smile so winsome harbor such grievous intent?"

Chagrined, the man nodded and bowed his head.

Gray understood how his bos'n mate felt. He well knew that smile. He had almost been fooled by its winsome charm on a few occasions. Fooled into thinking the girl didn't hate him as much as he thought. Fooled into believing he might not appear a murderer in her eyes.

Gray dismissed the man and numbly watched him hasten away to get cleaned up, the snickers of the crew following him. Gray, however, felt no amusement.

Instead, he brooded. An uncommon happenstance for a man who, as a general rule, did not let things bother him, and if something should trouble him, he certainly didn't allow anyone to see it. But Bonnie had a way of peeling away that veneer, or perhaps wearing away was more appropriate.

Gray stalked to the railing, fighting the urge to check on Bonnie, to see what mischief she created, for certainly that fertile mind was conjuring up some new mayhem to inflict upon him. She was a bag of tricks, never giving any indication of when she might strike—only that she would.

He should just release her and end this madness. There were one or two ports where he could drop her off, give her money for passage home. What would a few hours veering off course mean in the scheme of things? The jewel would still be out there, taunting him just like Bonnie did, challenging Gray to find it, to fulfill his father's dream and save his family from ruin.

Christ, he had to be insane hunting down a treasure that was probably as ethereal as a myth, a fruitless endeavor that would leave him with a goose egg in the end.

Yet . . . if there was even a possibility the gem existed, he had to try to find it. What Damien needed—what they all needed—was to create a new legacy and rebuild what had been lost. And simply winning some blunt in a card game or selling something to help pay off a few of Damien's debts would not solve the problem.

One time. One search. And then no more.

Gray perceived a presence beside him. He didn't need to look to know it was Prophet, come to dole out his daily dose of I-told-you-so. Gray sighed, figuring he either had to take his lumps now or merely prolong the inevitable.

"All right, spit it out."

"Spit what out, my boy?" Prophet regarded him with feigned innocence. "I've merely stopped to enjoy a moment of this glorious day"—then came the plug—"even if I do worry that the girl's stomping about will produce a hole in the ship's hull and we will all sink to the bottom of the ocean. Other than that, I'm perfectly content."

"Leave off," Gray growled. "I'm not in the mood."

"I imagine you wouldn't be. A lack of sleep tends to

bring out your bad humor. And you, lad, have not been the same since you brought that girl on board. You can't blame a body for being curious as to what would possess you to do such a thing." Then he shrugged. "But you're the captain, and I certainly wouldn't dare question your motives, no matter how odd."

Gray snorted. "You've questioned everything I've done since I first met you. Why should now be any different?"

"Perhaps because there is a woman involved, and in the past, you never mixed business and pleasure."

"You think having that razor-tongued harpy on board is a pleasure? Think again, my friend."

"Oh, I don't know. Seems like what you two have is a case of impassioned fury."

Gray glowered, fairly certain he wasn't going to like the avenue Prophet intended to traverse. "What the hell are you talking about?"

"Simply put, you want Bonnie and you will use whatever means necessary to get her. Hence, dragging her along when you could easily have left her behind."

"Want her?" Gray gaped at his friend. "Are you crazy? The only feelings I have for her are homicidal. I'd prefer to twist rusty nails through the soles of my feet." That was what Gray got for hiring a first mate who was not only smart, as well as a smart aleck, but who believed that because he had once attended a seminary he was now all-knowing. "The only thing I wanted her for was to make sure I got away."

"Hmm. So you couldn't have parted ways on the beach? Or left her in the rowboat once you made it safely back to the ship? It was necessary to bring her along even *after* you had made good your escape?"

Gray's scowl deepened—in the hopes of deterring Prophet from leveling any more accusations that hit too close to home. Unfortunately, black looks and threats of bodily injury never worked on Prophet.

"I have my reasons," Gray finally muttered.

Prophet quirked a brow but made no further remarks on that front, but that didn't prevent him from returning to his original topic. "Regardless of the whys and what-fors of your actions, I suspect Bonnie wants you, too—though why she would after you kidnapped her and locked her in your cabin is an endless mystery to me."

Gray narrowed his eyes at his friend. "Have you jumped ship, perchance?"

Prophet ignored him. "You must admit that you are not possessed of the most delicate touch when it comes to women."

"Are you implying I was rough with the girl?"

"I'm merely saying that because you have gone through life with that face and that build, women didn't care so much about your lack of social skills—like charm, for example."

Gray couldn't believe what he was hearing. Now he lacked charm? Worse, he was being tutored in the ways of women by a weather-beaten ex-pirate whose smile showed a gap where a tooth should be. What next?

"If you will recall, I was the one about to be hanged for a crime I didn't commit *and*"—Gray pointed to his stomach—"she stabbed me."

Prophet spared him a glance that said, "You survived, didn't you? Buck up, man." Out loud, he remarked in his usual astute way, "Making a pass at her, were you?" The man had the uncanny ability to see what others could not. Such insight could be damnably unnerving. "You do enjoy using the inopportune moments, my boy."

"So I kissed her. I've kissed lots of women."

Prophet nodded, donning his worldly-and-wise expression. "This is true, but you have never dragged the reluctant ones with you."

"There have never been any reluctant ones."

"Ah . . . so the lass is a challenge, then? You didn't

care for her rebuff; therefore, you plan on keeping her your prisoner until she relents."

Gray didn't like the direction the conversation was taking. "I don't know what I'm going to do with her," he bit out.

"But you don't intend to let her go. At least not any time soon. Can we agree that is an undisputed fact?"

Gray thought to refute Prophet's blunt appraisal but knew that, like spitting in the wind, the backlash would only end up on his face. "Yes."

"I see," Prophet murmured. "And what about the jewel?"

"What about it?"

"Well, I'm curious to know whether you plan to tell the lass about your quest."

His quest. It sounded so official. So . . . real. And for no particular reason Gray could pin down, he wanted to confide in Bonnie, to garner her reaction and find out if she believed he was as crazy as Gray was beginning to suspect he was.

Gray couldn't quite figure it out, but Bonnie had the power to make him want to divulge secrets he never intended to tell. But doling out such information would be akin to handing her an ax and asking her to hack him into small pieces.

And yet . . . what if she didn't think him madder than a March hare?

What if she believed him?

"I don't know yet," he replied gruffly, averting his gaze to stare out over the glittering expanse of the sea.

In less than two week's time, barring unforeseen trouble, which seemed somehow inevitable, considering the vexing Scottish cargo he carried, Gray would have the answer he sought. He'd know if he was simply a gullible sap who had been duped into believing this golden-tinted paradise existed—or an undeserving son who had realized his father's dream.

Prophet's intense regard bore into Gray. "For a man

who normally reeks of decisiveness, you are awfully inde-
cisive lately."

"I've got a lot on my mind."

"Aye," Prophet intoned gravely, "taking the world's
troubles onto your shoulders again."

"Not the world's," Gray corrected.

"Only your family's." Prophet hesitated and then
said, "Not everything terrible that has happened to your
brothers and father is your fault, my boy. You've got to
stop blaming yourself."

Gray stiffened, feeling too volatile, too on edge to
discuss his family, to hear Prophet lecture him once
again about letting old wounds heal. Prophet didn't
understand that some wounds would never heal, that
when one picks at a scab long enough it festers, leaving
a permanent scar.

"I'm not having this discussion."

"Fine," Prophet capitulated, but Gray heard the frus-
tration in his friend's voice directed at him. "Then let
me readdress the issue of our high-spirited guest."

"I wish you wouldn't," Gray muttered.

"You know the girl's brothers will come after her,
don't you?"

"I do."

"And what do you intend to do then?"

Good question. "I'll figure that out when the time
comes. In the meanwhile, we will continue on as usual
and ignore the girl's machinations."

"Ignore her, hmm?"

Gray noted that his comment seemed to amuse
Prophet. "It's not a hard thing to do if you apply yourself
to it. The girl is just trying to get a reaction out of us.
If we don't give her one, she will eventually desist."

"You think so?"

"I know so." In fact, Gray felt more confident about
his plan the more he ruminated on it. "I'm going to
remain calm, let the girl's childish attempts to annoy
me roll off my back."

"Roll off your back, eh?"

"Like water."

"I see. Then it wouldn't bother you if she was flinging your belongings out of the porthole in your cabin, for example?"

Gray rested a hip against the bulwark and crossed his ankles. "Not in the lea—" The words died on his lips as the significance of what Prophet was relaying hit home.

Gray spun around just in time to see a pair of his new boots go overboard, bobbing in the water like a buoy next to at least ten books, an expensive Chinese vase he'd won in a poker game, and a gold-topped mahogany walking stick his brother Nicholas had given Gray when he had fractured his ankle the year before.

But it was when the first of Gray's maps arced through the air and into the briny blue that he felt compelled to act, Prophet's booming laugh following him as he flew across the deck.

Bonnie smiled to herself as she watched Gray's belongings riding the waves, looking like little orphans as the ship sailed farther and farther away.

He would call her actions childish, and perhaps they were, but she had to strike at her captor in any way possible. She couldn't allow the rotten man to succeed in making her a victim or to think she would sit meekly by while he did his worst. She was Scottish, after all— and in the words of Scotland's truest patriot, Sir William Wallace of Elerslie, "Pro libertate!"

"For freedom!" Bonnie resounded, her spirit fortified as she plucked another map off Gray's desk.

She was about to pitch the chart into the water to join his other woebegone belongings when the cabin door crashed against the wall and a massive frame filled the space, a face and a body as rigid and perfectly formed as a Greek statue.

Her adversary had arrived.

Took him long enough.

Bonnie had thought the man might just allow her to toss out everything he owned and do nothing about it. He was a difficult person to get a rise out of.

Even when she had poured the contents of a two-hundred-year-old bottle of cognac in the chamber pot and then thrown the empty bottle at him when he returned to the cabin—just missing his head—he had done nothing more than regard her in that superior way of his. Then he did an about-face and departed—and didn't come back that night.

Bonnie was glad to be rid of him. His presence was unsettling. He had a way of looking at her as if seeing clear through her—or making her stomach flutter in the oddest fashion.

When he was there—he was *there*.

At last she had done something to warrant his full attention. Although the look on his face didn't bode well for her. His expression was as dark as an approaching thunderstorm. An enraged Adonis come to earth to deliver his wrath. Bonnie couldn't help the slight shiver that coursed through her.

"Put that down," he said with silky menace, his gaze flicking to the map she held.

Bonnie's nervousness evaporated as soon as he barked out another one of his imperious commands. "And if I don't?" she challenged. "What will ye do? Lock me in your closet? Throw me in the hold? Make me walk the plank? Give me ten lashes with a cat-o'-nine?"

"Too easy," he returned in a voice that was frightening in its calmness. "I'll throttle your supple white neck and your body will go the same way as my boots. Now"—he measured the word—"give me that map."

A tiny voice cautioned Bonnie not to push any further, that she had amply succeeded in annoying him, which was what she'd set out to do, since he hadn't left her much choice. But she never did heed that inner voice when she should.

"And what will I get if I give it tae ye?"

"You will get to stay alive, that's what."

Bonnie wasn't overly concerned by his threat. He had made such statements before and never followed through, even though she had goaded him past what most men would tolerate. He could have killed her ten times over. He had a perfect opportunity and ample reason after she slashed his stomach. Yet he'd done nothing.

Perhaps that was when Bonnie knew conclusively that Gray hadn't murdered Sarah. He might look fierce and talk fierce, but that was where the threat ended.

"What's so important about this map?" she taunted, intrigued by how intently Gray scrutinized her movements as she waved the paper lightly between her fingertips.

"Just put it down and I may let you out of my cabin," he said through gritted teeth.

The idea of seeing anything other than the four walls of Gray's cabin nearly swayed Bonnie into dropping the dusty scroll and bolting for the door. But her curiosity to know why an old map had been the key to getting her captor's unwavering attention was far greater.

"Could it be this yellowed piece of paper means something tae ye, English?"

"I would not tempt the fates if I were you, my girl," he warned ominously.

Bonnie took that as a yes. "What is this a map of?" When seconds ticked by with no reply, she thrust the paper out the porthole, dangling it from her fingertips as incentive. "Well?"

His jaw clenched and unclenched, his eyes promising hell should he get his hands on her. "It's to a lost island," he said through gritted teeth.

Her interest was immediately riveted. "And what's on this lost island?"

"Nothing, for all I know."

Bonnie couldn't distinguish whether he was telling the truth or not; his gaze was hooded, his expression inscrutable. "Are ye a pirate, then? Out searching for hidden treasure?"

A strange look passed over his face before his features hardened, telling her that he had said all he was going to say. His belligerence just increased her desire to find out more.

She noticed a few words in a foreign language near the middle of the paper. She pointed to them. "What does this say?"

Stone-faced, he regarded her. Bonnie figured she would have to ladle out another dose of incentive if she desired a reply, but he surprised her.

"O coração sagrado."

The way he spoke the words caused a slight tremor to run through her. "What does that mean?"

He glanced out the porthole behind her, as if seeing something on the horizon. "It's Portuguese for 'the sacred heart.' "

"What is the sacred heart?" she asked, unable to quell the interest in her voice.

"A legend," he replied cryptically. "Or perhaps nothing more than a myth believed in by fools and dreamers."

A legend. How mysterious and wonderful that sounded. "And do ye believe in this legend?"

His gaze slid her way, and for the first time since Bonnie had met Gray, she could see utter clarity in his eyes. No deception or mockery or bitterness marred their beauty—only a trace of the pain that seemed to always linger on the fringes, a pain Bonnie tried not to see. She didn't want to feel anything for this man, least of all a need to discover what tormented him, for surely something did.

"I don't know what I believe." His words, for all they didn't say, spoke volumes to her.

"Are ye headed tae this island?"

"Perhaps."

"Will I get tae see it?" Bonnie wasn't sure where that question came from. The last things she should be thinking about were lost islands and legends. But in all her twenty-two years she had never left Scotland, and suddenly the idea of an adventure seemed exciting.

Gray regarded her for a long moment and then murmured, "Do you want to see it, Bonnie?"

Why did he have to say her name like that? His voice so deep it rumbled? So smooth warmth washed over her? Just looking at him, raw masculinity in his every move, made the strangest thoughts pop into her head, imagining he was a present just waiting to be unwrapped.

Those heated moments on the beach came back to Bonnie in a rush, memories so poignant they deposited an indelible imprint in her mind, coaxing her senses to life. She could almost hear the rippling of the wind through the trees, feel the cool, gritty sand beneath her—and the enveloping heat of Gray above her. She despised him, yet he haunted her. He was forbidden, yet he tempted her to be reckless.

Bonnie waited motionless as Gray moved toward her, powerless to stop him. She closed her eyes, knowing she stood a chance of resisting his potent allure if she didn't look at him, didn't see him stare at her lips in a way that made her heart turn over in her chest.

The touch of his finger beneath her chin startled her; the map, no longer as important as the flesh-and-blood man standing before her, fluttered to the ground.

Slowly, Bonnie opened her eyes, Gray's sultry gaze branding her, as if he knew every secret in her heart. The silky soft tumble of his hair swept his shoulders, luring Bonnie to sift her fingers through that wild mane, the need so intense her hand ached from restraint.

The finger beneath her chin glided along the delicate underside of her jaw, wreaking havoc with her balance.

"I'm going to kiss you," he rumbled in a husky voice, his tone not asking nor demanding, only stating his intentions, clearly, precisely, and with unfailing purpose.

Bonnie opened her mouth, not sure what she intended to say, but no words would come anyway. They simply weren't there. Her breath hitched in her throat as Gray's head descended.

The first press of his lips upon hers was as gossamer as feather down but no less powerful, no less engrossing, weakening her knees and shattering her resolve. Heaven help her, she was disintegrating.

That kiss, how it encompassed her, his mouth drawing everything from her and demanding more, asking for something she didn't know how to give—or perhaps she was too afraid to relinquish whatever it was.

He smelled of spice and the sea, his tongue a treat to savor as she crowded closer to him, feeling as if she couldn't get near enough. She wanted to wrap her arms around him and hold on for dear life, and it was that realization, that truth, that restored reality.

She placed trembling hands against Gray's chest, his heart pounding in thick strokes beneath her palms as she pushed him away.

His head lifted, his gaze questioning. How she understood his confusion. Her own was just as great. She still tasted him on her lips and hungered for more, even as she denied herself. And him. "Why do ye make it so hard tae resist?" she murmured in a shaky voice.

"Why do you make it so hard to stay away?" he returned in a devastatingly sensual tone. He leaned down, his lips brushing along her ear. "Give in, Bonnie. Surrender to me. I promise I won't hurt you."

Surrender. Never had Bonnie imagined that submitting to another person could be such a heady prospect. Never had she given the idea an instant of consideration. Until now. Until Gray. She knew he wouldn't purposely hurt her. But he didn't realize that he would hurt her no matter his best intentions.

"I can't," she replied with what little resistance she had left. "Ye know the reasons as well as I."

He slowly straightened, his eyes narrowing on her face. "Because you and your kin think I'm a murderer."

Bonnie wanted to confess that she knew he wasn't a murderer. But that would only make matters more difficult. Yet, she couldn't bring herself to agree with him, as would be best to put distance between them. "It's more than that."

"No," he bit out, "I think it's exactly that." He stepped back, drawing his warmth away and leaving only a bone-chilling cold in its stead.

He bent down and swept the map from the floor. Then he turned on his heel and headed for the door.

Swinging the portal open, he hesitated on the threshold. Without looking at her, he said over his shoulder, "Though you may think me a murderer, I'm not entirely devoid of human compassion. You are free to leave my cabin."

"What about leaving the ship?" Bonnie forced herself to ask.

"That, I'm afraid, I can't allow." And then he was gone, leaving his words to echo in her ears, and hollowness to take up residence in her heart.

Chapter 10

Brilliant sunlight as sweet as any nectar hit Bonnie full in the face as she exited the companionway the next morning and stepped out onto the main deck, momentarily shielding her eyes as they adjusted to the sudden wealth of light, its warmth a silent splendor.

Before her, a breathtaking vista of blue and green coalesced into a vivid tapestry, spreading out in all directions as far as the eye could see. The Atlantic shimmered with golden prisms, exploding white crests, windswept surfaces, and wild grandeur, the silver line of the horizon beckoning like a mystery she longed to explore.

As Bonnie stood there amid the bustle of her captors, idly watching a lacy cloud roll past, the ship thrumming with an unexpected vitality, a sense of anticipation awakened inside her. The day seemed pregnant with possibilities, an adventure waiting to be taken, carrying her along as surely as the tide.

She closed her eyes and tipped her head back, inhaling deeply of the sea's salt tang, listening to the simple sounds of the ship slicing cleanly through the waves, breaking water splashing against the bow, the barest hint of mist moistening her skin.

That subliminal voice she loved to hate prodded that she should be searching for new ways to vex her captors and free herself, but another voice, one that reveled in her newfound freedom, quelled that urging, if only for a short while.

"Beautiful day, isn't it?"

Startled, Bonnie's eyes snapped open to find a salty-looking sailor standing next to her. The man's face was browned by years in the sun and pruned by the weather, deep grooves around his mouth lending character. He gave her a hesitant smile, as if wondering about the reception he would receive. His kindly green eyes told Bonnie she had nothing to fear.

"Aye," she replied tentatively, "a lovely day indeed."

"I'm glad to finally get the opportunity to meet you, my girl."

Bonnie told herself to remain aloof, keep her distance from anyone associated with the sap-headed captain, but the older man's broad grin was so infectious, she couldn't help but return it, foiling her best intentions.

"Are ye sure about that?" she asked. "Most people on board this ship wouldn't share your enthusiasm."

"Most people on board this ship haven't witnessed the full effect of your smile either. Besides"—he shrugged—"captivity can sour even the mildest disposition. Our own captain was a shining example of that," he added with a wink.

Talk of the captain whisked the smile from Bonnie's face, reminding her of her plea to be released and his cool response: *That, I'm afraid, I can't allow.* Ha! He could have allowed it. He was just a bully—who was far too handsome for her peace of mind.

That realization, of his physical presence, was what bothered Bonnie the most, the way her traitorous body responded to him whenever he was near. And for that reason, she had to keep her distance.

But how easy would that be when she was trapped on board his ship and sharing his quarters? The latter discovery had catapulted her into such a pique of temper that Bonnie suspected the crew, and its revered captain, thought her a candidate for Bedlam.

Well, that was fine with her. Best to keep them wondering what she would do next. In fact, their reactions—eyeing her warily and keeping well out of her way—were rather ironic, and she relished her role of tormentor.

"So ye mean he wasn't born a big lout?" she said, voicing her feelings for her captor on the off chance there might be one person in the entire world who didn't already know how she felt about him.

The man chuckled. "Don't let that gruff exterior fool you, my girl. The lad is a pussycat at heart."

Bonnie snorted, preparing to enlighten the old fellow on what she thought of his captain—the barbarian who had kidnapped her, hauled her around like a sack of grain, tossed her into the frigid ocean as if she were a rejected mackerel . . . kissed her tenderly, allowed her to throw things at him, and released her from his cabin even after she had pitched his belongings out the porthole and threatened his precious map.

Bonnie decided she could set Gray's crewman straight later. At the moment, something else tugged at the back of her mind. "You're the one, aren't ye?"

"The one?"

"His first mate. Ye came tae free him."

"The lad told you, did he?" The man scratched his head, appearing a bit chagrined. "Well, yes, I did come to release him. He is my captain, after all—and my friend. I feel a certain responsibility toward the boy."

The boy. Bonnie found that amusing. Gray might be many things, none of which was a boy. "He said he didn't leave with ye when he had the chance. Is that true?"

"Aye, that's true."

"That makes no sense. Why would he stay?"

"To clear his name, of course." The comment was made in such a way that it sounded as if she should have surmised the answer.

"But he could have been hanged."

"The captain's no coward."

Bonnie recalled a time not long ago when she had accused Gray of being just that. What she remembered most was his response to her accusation. He had looked at her in the same way a person who has been mortally wounded looks at his killer. The expression had chilled her straight through.

She hadn't meant what she'd said. She had been striking back. Words had always been her weapon when no other avenues were left open to her. Any man who would stay to clear his name, face an angry mob and her brother at his provoking best, was no coward.

But her stubborn pride would not allow her to confess that. "He's reckless," she said, the criticism sounding somewhat odd coming from her, considering she, too, possessed that flaw.

"Aye," the man conceded, "the lad does have a tendency to be a bit rash."

"A bit?"

Green eyes twinkled with mirth. "All right, a lot. But his intentions are good."

Bonnie crossed her arms, her expression dubious. "And what might ye say his intentions were when he brought me on board?"

"Ah, now that's a tricky question." The man scraped a hand across his stubbled chin. "If I had to guess, I'd say that you must have something he wants—something only you can give him."

That statement rattled Bonnie more than she would have expected. She quickly brushed off the first mate's words and their odd allure. "I know what I can give him—a wallop tae his thick skull!"

Her vehement reply garnered her a chuckle. "I don't

think a pair of harder-headed people exist. You two are perfect for each other."

"Perfect? Ha! Your captain is stubborn tae a fault, wants everything his way, and never backs down."

"Much like you, I suspect," the man returned, his smile never wavering. He went on before Bonnie could formulate a stinging comeback. "But I've been remiss. I've yet to properly introduce myself." He held out his hand. "The name's O'Brien—Prophet O'Brien."

Bonnie hesitated a hairsbreadth and then took his hand. "Bonnie MacTavish."

"Bonnie . . . the name fits you."

Another charmer, Bonnie thought. Just like his vexing captain. "Prophet is a rather unusual first name."

"My first name is actually Joseph, but people have been calling me Prophet since I was a young man. Everyone has a theory for how I came about the nickname. Not a one of them have been right so far."

"Even the illustrious captain?" Bonnie queried, her gaze straying to Gray.

He stood at the helm, his thick black hair gleaming like a sable pelt, his darkly tanned face a study in serious deliberation as he conversed with a member of his crew, oblivious to her presence.

She should be happy he was ignoring her, that he assumed a stony countenance of frozen courtesy whenever their paths crossed, looking at her as if he saw the ruination of mankind etched in her forehead.

The gulf between them had grown to nearly unbreachable proportions, but it was better this way. Kept her focused on her goal: escape. Whenever Gray was around, she could scarcely concentrate. So why, then, did his disregard annoy her? Her reaction made no sense.

"Not even him," Prophet replied. "But I will confide the truth to you." He leaned close and said in a conspiratorial tone, "I once intended to become a priest."

Bonnie blinked in surprise. "A priest?" She could

see why people had never made that guess. Prophet was
the last person, besides the captain, she could picture
as a man of the cloth. He looked as if he'd been born
to the sea.

"Aye." He nodded. "I studied at a seminary in Montalegre, a quaint town nestled in the hills of Portugal,
near Spain. Then one day I woke up and realized that
my family's desire, more than my own, was what pushed
me to become a priest."

Bonnie heard nothing beyond the word *Portugal,*
recalling the words Gray had recited to her the day
before. *O coração sagrado.* She wondered how much
Prophet knew about this mysterious sacred heart.

Bonnie intended to gently probe the topic with
Prophet, but a bone-chilling screech filled the air, nearly
jolting her over the railing.

Shading her eyes with her hand, she glanced upward
to search for the source of the rasping caw in time to
see a large bird of prey swooping down from the crow's
nest—and bearing straight for her.

With a gasp of alarm, Bonnie ducked as the feathered
behemoth glided smoothly over her head, executing a
large circle above the deck before landing with an ele-
gant flourish near the bow, directly behind Gray, perch-
ing on the capstan as if just waiting for someone to die
so it could pluck the meat from his bones.

"Sweet Saint Catherine . . . that's a—"

"Vulture?" Prophet finished for her. "Ugly spud,
isn't she?"

Ugly seemed almost complimentary, considering the
bird's naked yellow head, white breast feathers, black
wings, hooked bill, feather ruff of scarlet, and several
hideous, fleshy orange-colored growths.

"What does it want?"

Prophet shrugged. "Food, I suppose. The thing is
always hungry."

Bonnie's stunned gaze snapped to Prophet. "Ye feed
that creature?"

"The captain feeds her mostly."

"He keeps a vulture as a pet?"

Prophet's bushy brows drew together in contemplation. "Lady Beatrice isn't really a pet as much as an indulged companion. Gray found the bird half dead on a swarming dock in India and nursed it back to health. She's been with him ever since. But Lady B earns her keep. She can spot land and other ships better than most men. Damn odd, it is."

He thought that was odd? The fact that a vulture was not only a member of Gray's crew but kept vigil in the crow's nest was unbelievable.

The bird sidled up next to Gray, nudging him in the back with her beak. Without the slightest worry that the animal's strong jaws might excise one of his fingers, Gray stroked her neck.

"What kind of name is Lady Beatrice for a vulture?" Bonnie asked, although naming a vulture at all seemed beyond comprehension.

"The bird's namesake is a vulture, too—of the human variety. So it's fitting."

Bonnie hadn't been expecting such a thought-provoking revelation. "Who is Lady Beatrice?"

"The captain's mother," Prophet replied, looking as if he has just taken a bite of something sour.

Bonnie gaped in a rather unflattering fashion, but she was that floored by the admission. The dislike Gray must feel for his mother to name a vulture after her! What could have caused such a rift?

She darted a glance at Gray, wondering once more about the things that had shaped his life, made him the man he was today—fiercely proud, often haunted, movingly vulnerable at times.

Shifting her gaze back to Prophet, Bonnie said, "She's that bad?"

"Worse," he fairly spat. "The only difference between Gray's mother and that vulture is that the real Lady Beatrice doesn't wait for her victims to die before she tears into them. That woman treated the lad and his brothers like they weren't good enough to lick her shoes. I don't know how a mother could be so cruel to her children. The lad laughs it off. That's how he deals with things, to pretend they either don't exist or they don't bother him."

Bonnie had witnessed firsthand how unemotional, and almost detached Gray could be. During his trial, for example, and the way he dealt with her when she was at her provoking best.

"How do ye know so much about his mother?" she asked.

Prophet laced his fingers through the shroud channel above him as the ship dipped into a trough. "Gray's father hired me as a deck hand more than three decades ago when few people, let alone an English noble, would give an Irishman a job, never mind if I was born in America. That's the kind of man Niles Sinclair was, bighearted, generous, a real gentleman. Loved those boys like no father ever has. Tried to protect 'em the best he could."

"What happened to him?"

Prophet shook his head sadly. "He died a few months ago, and not a one of those boys has been the same since. Nearly tore 'em apart. Sometimes I think the captain took it the hardest of the three. He's hurting, lost, and I can't seem to do a damn thing about it. Boy won't let anyone past the barricade he's built around himself. I don't think even Damien or Nicholas realize the extent of their brother's despair."

Bonnie was beginning to understand the pain she glimpsed in Gray's eyes in those brief moments when he let his guard down. She was struck by a strange relief now that she knew someone had been there for Gray at such a low point in his life.

"There's something he's not saying," Prophet went on, "and I can't get it from him. The lad needs someone to help mend the wound that's festering inside him. He doesn't think he needs anyone, that he's fireproof and nothing can touch him, but I know that's not so." Prophet surprised her then by clasping her hand; his words were even more of a shock. "You can help him, my girl. I feel it in my bones. He responds to you."

Bonnie felt as if she'd been blind-sided by a rogue wave. "He kidnapped me, Prophet. I think you're forgetting that."

Prophet waved a dismissive hand. "He merely borrowed you."

"Borrowed me?"

"He'll let you go."

"When?

"Eventually." Then he muttered something that sounded suspiciously like, "I think."

Bonnie had every intention of telling Prophet that his suggestion was pure madness, that whatever the outcome of this journey, there would be nothing salvageable between her and the man who had forced her from her home and family, but Prophet forestalled her.

"Just think about what I've said." He gently squeezed her hands before drifting away to resume his duties, denying Bonnie the opportunity to level another protest.

With a frustrated sigh, she turned toward the railing, ruminating over Prophet's request though she tried not to. She couldn't help Gray, couldn't make his healing her responsibility—even if for one crazy moment she'd wanted to. Why Prophet thought she could mend whatever scars lingered within Gray, Bonnie didn't know.

Yet she couldn't stop her heart from aching for a young boy who had been cursed by such a hard-hearted mother and who had so recently lost the single most important person in his life.

Bonnie forced herself to shut out the thought, closing her eyes and lifting her face to the wind, seeking to dismiss Prophet's words as the sweet breeze caressed her hair, whispering through her tresses like fingers, evoking images of Gray no matter how desperately she endeavored to block him out.

She sensed him beside her then. It was strange, this uncanny ability she had to intuit his movements, know when he was near, feel the warmth in his regard even at a distance. She suspected that even if they stood on opposite ends of a crowded room, she'd know exactly where to find him. Bonnie had never experienced anything like this with another person.

Gradually, she opened her eyes, and as her gaze locked with Gray's, Prophet's entreaty echoed in her ears. *You can help him, my girl. I feel it in my bones. He responds to you.*

And Lord help her, she responded to him.

"Are you feeling all right?" he quietly asked.

"I'm fine," she replied, her chest suddenly tight, his regard so intense that she had to force herself to look away—or get lost within the magic he so easily cast over her, a spell that could rebound into a devastating force of destruction if she let it.

"I saw you talking to Prophet."

"He's a nice man," she said quietly. "I like him."

"But you don't like me, do you?"

His question caught her off guard, but she suspected he preferred it that way. It allowed him to remain in control, and she knew that was important to him.

Gray was a mystery she couldn't unravel. He was difficult yet soothing, unfathomable yet sincere, abounding with an inner violence and outward restraint, his world taut with dark, tormented passions. Sometimes he seemed on the verge of anarchy.

"I don't know ye really," she murmured.

"Would you like to know me? Or don't I have a right to ask, considering I'm a murderer and a kidnapper?"

Bonnie hated when he did this to her, when he let her glimpse that susceptibility in him, and all she could do was reject what he offered, ignore whatever peace he strove to make, stiffen her resolve another notch and pray she didn't splinter into a thousand shards under the weight of her burden.

"All I'd like tae know is where we're going."

Those beautiful full lips that had kissed her with such heat, such fierce tenderness, thinned. "You'll know soon enough." Then he turned on his heel, intending to walk away. This time, Bonnie couldn't let him go; she grabbed hold of his arm and swung around in front of him, blocking his path.

"I want tae know now. Ye can't continue tae put me off."

"Don't press me, Bonnie," Gray warned, staring at the small hand on his arm, thinking how easily he could crush those delicate bones, how it might be worth suffering his own personal hell to earn her fear and loathing rather than have those emotions foisted upon him unjustly.

But, fool that he was, he wanted only to take her hand in his and hold her palm against his heart and ask her what she felt—and what she was doing to him.

Why did he need so desperately for her to believe in him? To see him as a man and not a monster? The desire all but consumed him. She had created a wound inside him, one of passion instead of pain. Her indomitable spirit routed him; somewhere along the way, she had become an incandescent flame in the frozen chaos of his life, inexorably tugging him from his self-imposed exile.

He stepped away from her, gripping the wood railing instead of her. What demon had compelled him to bring this beautiful, maddening girl along with him on a quest whose outcome might be as sustaining as a wisp of smoke? The answer eluded him time and again.

"Why do ye ask more from me than I can give?" she asked, her voice a soft plea, those blue eyes boring into him, seeking in a way that made hiding impossible.

Gray recognized the truth in her words and realized that he wanted something from her. A yearning pulsed inside him, a wish for peace, a serenity that somehow he knew this girl could provide, pulling him back from the brink of an all-consuming emptiness. He could lose himself in her.

Foolish dreams. Just like his father. Bloody cursed.

"Is that what I do?"

"Aye," she whispered. "Ye know I have no other choice but tae fight. I don't belong here."

His jaw clenched. "Are you so desperate to return to your future husband, then?"

Bonnie recoiled at the question. Desperate to return to Ewan? The answer came quickly, silently, and without hesitation: no. She wasn't eager to return to him. She hadn't even thought about him.

"This is wrong," she said, not wanting to speak about that part of her life. "Ye know that."

"Do you love him?"

"That's none—"

"Do you, Bonnie?"

How did he manage to twist her so easily into knots? To send her mind spinning down paths it had never traveled, with nothing to stop its dizzying spiral.

Anger at Gray for his demands and with herself for feeling anything other than loathing for him made her lash out. "Aye! I love him," she lied. "Are ye satisfied? Is that what ye wanted tae hear? I love him, I love him, I love him! And I hate you!"

His face turned thunderous, his jaw working. For a second, Bonnie thought he was going to strike her; his fingers curled into his palms.

Instead, he wheeled around and stalked toward the helm, leaving her to watch the rigid line of his back and wonder why the day had suddenly grown dim though the sun still shined so brightly.

Chapter 11

Bonnie woke the next morning feeling as if she hadn't slept more than four minutes, having tossed fitfully all night. The way Gray had looked at her on the deck the day before hounded her dreams.

Could that be why she wanted to admit the truth now? Confess that she had no feelings for Ewan, that she had just told Gray that lie to . . . what? Push him away? Block out the emotions he evoked in her? Deny whatever intangible thing flared between them when they were together?

What good was speculation? He hadn't given her the chance to retract her words because he had never returned to the cabin, and the emptiness had been vast.

Odd that she should be comforted by his presence when he was there. Yet night after night, her restlessness grew as she tried not to glance his way, to muse over what he was doing as he lay in his makeshift bed on the floor, if perhaps he might be thinking of her—as she thought of him.

A few times, late at night, she had dreamed that he stood beside the bed and watched her sleep, even lifting her hair and sifting the strands through his fingers, whispering her name in a way that made her heart take flight.

And when those dreams had filtered into the morning, a blanket of contentment still enfolded her, a sense of peace she had never experienced before. But she had lost that tenuous thread now that she had thrown down a barrier with Ewan's name on it.

Bonnie rolled to her back and plunked the pillow over her head, desiring nothing more at that moment than to hide out for the rest of the journey. But an unfamiliar noise caught her attention, a scraping next to the bed, like claws scratching the wood.

Claws.

Beneath the pillow, Bonnie's eyes widened and her throat went dry as she recalled the only thing on the ship that had claws.

Lady Beatrice. The vulture.

With an economy of movement, Bonnie slid the pillow from her face, one eye peering about the room, her heart hammering in her ears as she waited for something to spring out at her. Nothing did, yet the noise continued unabated.

Afraid to breathe, Bonnie eased to her side, then to her stomach. Gripping the edge of the bed with the tips of her fingers, she pulled herself parallel with her hands and peered cautiously over the side . . .

Then she blinked.

The culprit was not Lady Beatrice or anything remotely despicable. In fact, the sight that greeted her made Bonnie smile broadly and her heart swell as the sweetest, most precious puppy yapped in her face.

"Well, hello there, my wee darling. And where did ye come from, may I ask?"

The puppy hopped excitedly on its back legs and then wrapped its furry white front paws around Bonnie's hand when she reached out to pet its head, a raspy pink tongue vigorously licking her palm and fingers.

She ruffled the fur between the dog's ears, its small body an onslaught of wriggling, its tail batting back and forth, blinking at her with large, dark chocolate eyes— one ringed in black. Bonnie fell instantly and hopelessly in love.

Scooting farther over the edge of the bed, she scooped up the puppy with minimal effort, its weight not yet proportionate to the paws it had to grow into. Warm puppy smell reached her nostrils: a hint of fish, a whiff of the sea, a dollop of earth, and all those indefinable scents that belong solely in the canine realm.

The pup plopped down on her chest, limbs spreading everywhere as it promptly set about bathing her face as it had her palm. Bonnie's heart felt lighter than it had in a long while. "Do ye have a name, my fine laddie?"

"Jack."

The reply came out of nowhere, startling Bonnie, even though the masculine timbre of the voice she would recognize all the days of her life.

Lifting herself only enough to see over the puppy's head, Bonnie discovered Gray lounging in the threshold, a shoulder propped against the doorjamb, those large, muscular arms that she well remembered folded across his chest.

The puppy, having detected his master's voice, scrambled off her lap and raced loose-limbed across the floor toward him, skidding the last three feet and twirling into Gray's ankles.

With a deep chuckle that had a certain male beauty to it, he hunkered down and scratched the dog behind its floppy ears. "Getting in trouble, are you? I thought I told you to stay put?"

Bonnie began to rise but remembered she wore no more than one of Gray's shirts, which she had pilfered from his closet even though she suspected he wouldn't have balked if she had asked to borrow it. With only one set of clothes to wear, she had to try to keep them in some semblance of repair, and Gray's shirt fit her like a nightrail, the ends almost reaching her knees.

Sitting back, Bonnie draped the bedsheets around her. "Don't scold him on my part. I'm sure he meant no harm."

Gray peered up at her, a single lock of sleek dark hair slanting rakishly across his brow, making him look utterly endearing and unmistakably virile.

The sun had bronzed him to warm mocha, the color set off to perfection by his linen shirt, the deep *V* exposing his neck and a good portion of his chest, his sleeves rolled back, allowing her a glimpse of corded forearms.

A rush of heat sluiced through Bonnie, a memory of Gray with his shirt off, water spraying across his chest. Absorbed in the moment, she barely heard his reply.

". . . spoiled pup with a voracious appetite. Reminds me of a brisket with teeth. He lurks in the galley, waiting for the cook to drop scraps. He'll soon outweigh us all, I fear."

A heart-melting half grin curled the corner of his lips as he played with the pup, pushing Jack away only to have the frisky dog dive after his one hand while Gray caught Jack's back paw in the other hand and twirled him around, leaving the dog to nip at whatever hand was closest—and getting neither.

Bonnie was content to watch the byplay, languid and oddly at peace. Then Gray suddenly glanced up and caught her staring. She scrambled for something to say.

"Where did ye get the name Jack from?"

"I started off calling him Pup. Then, when he found his sea legs along with a renewed enthusiasm for seeking out whatever trouble he could find, I changed his moniker to Nuisance. It became readily apparent that he didn't appreciate that name because he refused to respond to it. So I dubbed him Jack because with that black ring around his eye he reminded me of a crusty old sailor I once knew who wore a black patch over his right eye.''

The dog cocked its head, as if knowing his master was speaking about him.

"What kind of dog is he?''

Gray shrugged. "Mutt, I guess. I found him wandering around the London wharves before we departed. That place is unfit for humans, let alone animals.'' He gave the pup a hearty pat on his tummy and then stood up. "He's one hell of a sailor, though. I'll give him that much.''

This new side of Gray—sweet, solicitous, and compassionate to needy animals—took Bonnie aback, perhaps because she had only seen the worst of him thus far and was now just glimpsing the man beneath the facade of indifference, at ease in his natural environment.

"Why are you looking at me like that?'' he asked.

Bonnie was appalled to discover that she was staring at him again. "I guess I'm just surprised.''

"And why is that?''

"Well, I didn't picture ye as the type of man who would take in stray animals.''

His body stiffened almost imperceptibly, but Bonnie knew the signs. She had insulted him and she hadn't intended to. "I imagine you think I'd use Jack for shark bait or something equally malicious?''

"That isn't what I meant,'' she retorted, but the moment was lost. His features returned to the cool mask of a polite, distant stranger.

"I left something for you.'' He gestured to a spot next to her.

Grateful for the distraction, Bonnie turned to see what he pointed at. And there, draped over a chair beside the bed, was a lovely blue day dress trimmed in lace.

A soft sigh escaped her parted lips, a sound of delight, full of feminine appreciation that would have surprised her had she even heard it, having so long denied that side of herself, trapped as she was in a world of men who dared her to be as strong as they, compelling her to be all the tougher in the process, her true self disappearing bit by bit.

Bonnie tossed her legs over the side of the berth, completely forgetting her scanty attire as she fingered the material, the plush cotton as soft as kitten fur.

Closing her eyes, she tried to imagine herself in the outfit, transformed from a bedraggled caterpillar to a glorious butterfly and wondering what Gray would think of such a metamorphosis.

When she opened her eyes, she found him standing beside her, his eyes dark and smoldering as he watched her. "Do you like it?" he asked, a note of hopeful expectancy in his voice.

"It's . . ." Beautiful, wonderful, the nicest gift anyone had ever given her. "It's very nice."

His expression changed, growing shuttered once more, and Bonnie regretted being so cheap in her response, for not saying what she truly felt.

"You don't have to wear it. I just thought . . ." His voice trailed off and he glanced away.

"I'd love tae wear it."

His gaze swung back to her, a half grin tugging at his lips. The sight affected her so acutely that she almost forgot what she had been about to say. It took her a moment to remember.

"When did ye leave the dress?"

"Late last night," he admitted, gently tucking a tendril of her hair behind her ear, lingering for a moment before curling his fingers into his palm and lowering his arm. "I couldn't sleep."

The space between them seemed to radiate with pure energy, and her dreams of him standing beside the bed and touching her hair in a similar fashion no longer seemed quite so improbable. She wondered if his inability to sleep had anything to do with her. Perhaps he was experiencing the same restlessness she felt?

Almost reluctantly, Bonnie took a step back, needing to put some space between them. "Where did ye get the dress?"

"My cousin Jules used to travel with me and my brothers—until she fell in love and got married. Then we weren't quite as interesting as her new husband."

Bonnie wondered at the relief she felt at discovering the dress did not belong to a mistress. "Prophet mentioned ye had two brothers."

Gray nodded. "Damien and Nicholas."

A renewed bout of curiosity sprung up inside Bonnie, a desire to know more about this man who was such an enigma, distant and hard one moment, sweet and strangely gentle the next.

"And where are they now?"

"Back home in England." A parody of a smile touched his lips. "Probably stirring up trouble."

"Like you do?"

"Not quite like I do, I'm afraid. They tend to stay away from outright murder and kidnapping as it puts a damper on their social life." Though his words were mild, Bonnie could tell he did not take the accusations leveled against him lightly.

"So why aren't ye in England, too?"

"As opposed to enjoying the hospitality of your brothers and Mr. Hangman?"

Bonnie frowned. "Why must ye twist my words so?"

He glanced away, raking long, lean fingers through his wind-tousled hair. "Overdeveloped cynicism, I suppose. Always searching for hidden meanings. Force of habit. Or perhaps none of the three. As to why I'm not in England, other interests await my attention."

As usual, he was vague. "And do these other interests have tae do with the map?" she asked pointedly, not feeling inclined to subject herself to any more of his cryptic responses.

She expected another cleverly worded riddle instead

of the truth, but that was not what she got. "Yes . . . they do," he said.

In a small way, he had let her in, allowed her a tentative exploration that might vanish as quickly as it arrived.

As if venturing across a carpet of feathers with no form or substance beneath, she said, "I'd like tae hear about this place that holds your attention."

"It doesn't hold all my attention," he murmured. "At least not at this moment."

Bonnie's breath locked in her throat as his gaze drifted to her lips.

"Do you think that if things had been different between us, if events hadn't transpired in this way, that we could have been friends?"

The question rocked Bonnie back on her heels. To be Gray's friend; what might that entail? Would it mean he wouldn't stare hungrily at her mouth as he was doing now? Or that she couldn't bask in his heat as she was at that moment?

Would her lips not tingle so much if they were just friends? Would she not feel the delicious shiver course through her body whenever he cast those smoky eyes her way?

With an abrupt jolt, Bonnie found herself at the brink of a precipice, about to fling herself into the unknown—and never more ready to close her eyes and rejoice in the free fall, her mind drifting in a dream world, envisioning things that, in real life, could never be.

"Bonnie?" Gray softly prompted. "What do you say?"

"I . . ." She caught her lip between her teeth, trapped between wanting to say one thing and needing to say another.

"What if I said I was sorry?" he asked. "Would that change things?"

Sorry. How could one small word hold so much impact, mean so much that Bonnie wondered how things might have been between her and Gray had she not found him beside Sarah's body. What would have happened if only a moment had ticked by and he had glanced over his shoulder? What might she have seen in his eyes? The same thing she heard in his voice? Sorrow. Sincerity. Pain.

If only . . .

He cupped her chin and lifted her head, forcing her to look into his eyes, allowing her a brief glimpse into his very soul, to shiver at something that could not be weighed or measured . . . only understood in the mind, like a second in time that encapsulated an eternity, a force of human nature that could only be reckoned by a nuance, a gesture.

"Would an apology make a difference, Bonnie?"

Could she allow it to make a difference? There were things that would not change no matter if she wanted them to or not. Yet, even knowing all that, she still murmured, "Yes . . . it would."

He gently brushed his knuckles across her cheek. "I'm sorry, Bonnie." His words were as sweet a caress as his fingers on her face. "Please . . . forgive me."

At that moment, Bonnie would forgive him anything, but she could not tell him so. For with all the strange and foreign weakness she possessed when it came to Gray, her sense of self-preservation would not permit her to take that next step, to venture over that invisible line she now trod so closely. So dangerously.

His head dipped toward hers, seeming to take an eternity in the descent, as if the world held its breath, waiting to exhale when their lips met. Or perhaps he was leaving her the opportunity to push him away, to deny a kiss she had thought about since the first time he'd brushed his lips against hers.

Then those lips, warm and full, melted into her in an onslaught so tender, so poignant, no moment before or in the future would ever quite capture the seductive essence. The sweet exploration ended all too soon.

Bonnie's eyelids fluttered open, and she pressed trembling fingers to her mouth. Gray stepped back, watching her with an inscrutable expression, his chest rising in the same uneven rhythm as hers, conveying that he was not as in control as he would have her believe.

"Have dinner with me tonight," he said.

Dinner. An entire evening to look across the table at him, to have him so threateningly close that a mere smile could assault her senses. She should say no, inform him that his kiss changed nothing, that whatever spell he so easily cast over her would not stop her from fighting, from doing whatever it took to be free.

And yet Bonnie nodded, her female heart unable to deny him.

Chapter 12

Gray hung back in the doorway of his quarters, awash in a sense of unexpected contentment as he covertly observed Bonnie playing a game of tug-of-war with Jack, her sweet laughter the kind that could haunt a body, as intoxicating as any siren and quite able to imperil many a man intent on discovering its source—or one man, like him—to ruin, reaching in vain for something that had eluded him all his life.

Dangerous ground, Sinclair, his mind warned, backing off the subject and taking note of the contorted object Bonnie and Jack fought over, the victor awarded the prize of something that looked remarkably like one of his shoes.

He should be irked, Gray thought. Between his belongings becoming the dog's toys and Bonnie heaving a number of his things out the porthole, he might soon be without anything to wear, read, or sleep in.

Fact was, though, he didn't give a good damn. He'd happily forfeit just about anything to enjoy a moment like this one, seeing Bonnie's face lit with delight, sitting on the floor as demurely as one could in a dress, an exuberant Jack dancing around her.

God, she was magnificent, this woman, his nemesis. The Lord was playing one hell of a cruel joke on him to have thrown this rare pearl in his path, an impossible female who didn't recognize the depths of her beauty, while he couldn't ignore it. Her lush body tempted him more with each passing day, causing him to stay away or risk losing the silent struggle he waged.

So why was he here, then? What lunacy had prompted him to share a meal with Bonnie when he had steadfastly avoided any intimacies? Walking around with blinders on instead of taking the chance she would kill him softly with ardor-raising glimpses of her adorned in his shirt, as she had been that morning. Never had the garment looked that good on him.

Perhaps, Gray reflected, she had hit upon a more apt way of striking back at him, below the belt, literally. He wouldn't put such machinations past her. She was that eager to be rid of him—a fact that effectively doused his flames.

So the question remained . . . why was he here?

Because, that other part of him replied, *he had a damnable need to confide his secret.*

All day he had rationalized that he wouldn't be confessing so much as deigning to enlighten his hostage on the length of her stay. Bloody unnerving, though, when one's conscience laughed at one's reasoning.

The pup's excited yapping gave Gray away. But he was thankful for the distraction to take his mind off Bonnie as he knelt down to pet his loyal companion. "Hello, Nuisance."

Bonnie stiffened, hearing Gray's voice, her nerves suddenly on edge. All day anticipation had been building as she waited for this moment, time seeming to tick backward during the interminable hours.

Taking a steadying breath, she rose to her feet, grateful that the dress covered her shaking legs. She busied herself fluffing out her skirt, pretending indifference and a false calm as she geared herself for Gray's reaction to her new appearance.

She had spent nearly an hour brushing her hair, needing to give her hands something to quiet their uncharacteristic fidgeting. Now the tresses crackled with renewed life. She knotted the mass high on the back of her head and left a long length hanging from the middle of the knot in an intricate ponytail, a few wisps framing her face. The style was surprisingly liberating—and made her feel feminine.

Knowing she could no longer delay, Bonnie steadied herself and faced Gray. Nothing could have prepared her for the staggering male beauty of him. He filled the doorway like a glorious titan, his gleaming ebony mane tied back in a queue, emphasizing a rugged jaw and chiseled cheekbones.

The light from the sconce closest to him painted his hair with golden fire. He had donned a pristine white shirt and snug-fitting biscuit-colored trousers, which only served to highlight his muscular physique.

"Hello," he murmured, his voice washing over her like a breeze on a sultry night.

"Hello."

"This is for you." He held out his hand, and Bonnie gasped at the huge conch shell he presented, multihued with luminescent color. "I know most men would bring flowers or sweets, but—"

"It's magnificent." Gently, she lifted the conch shell from his hand. When she glanced up, his intense silvery gaze arrested her, the warm, rich scent of him a heady delight.

He gave her a hesitant, boyish smile. "They say if you ask a question and then hold the shell up to your ear, you will hear the answer."

A smile tugged at the corners of Bonnie's mouth at his preposterous claim. "I've never heard such a thing."

"Here . . . let me show you." He cupped his hands

beneath hers and held the shell close to his mouth, whispering something she strained to hear. Then he titled his head to the side, pressing his ear to the opening of the shell and nodding.

"Well . . . what did ye ask?" Bonnie prompted when he said nothing, trying to ignore the tingling where their hands met.

Smoldering slate-colored eyes lifted to hers as he straightened. "I asked if you believed that I wouldn't do anything to hurt you."

Bonnie's heart clenched at the sweet sincerity of his words and the expectant look in his eyes. The desire to confess that she knew he would not harm her, at least not physically, nearly spilled forth.

But such a declaration might give too much away, reveal things better left unsaid, knowing the tenuousness of their situation.

So she kept the truth bottled up. "What was the reply?" she asked.

Gray took the shell from her hands and sat it on the wood chair next to them. Then he coiled a muscular arm around her waist, bringing her close to him. "It said that with gentle persuasion all things are possible." Lowering his voice, he asked, "Will you give me the chance to persuade you, Bonnie?" His gaze dropped to her lips and her drowsy mind thought how lovely his persuasion would be.

A throat being cleared behind them jolted Bonnie from the sensual haze Gray had woven around her, tearing her from that gauzy world, her cheeks burning with guilt as she jumped back.

With a low growl, Gray swung around to find his cook loitering in the companionway, his round cheeks ruddy with embarrassment, a large tray bearing their meal in his hands, and an excited Jack leaping at his feet. Yet, for some reason, nothing other than the fact that the man's presence had thrown ice water on his fire registered in Gray's mind.

"What do you want?" he snapped.

The cook hefted the tray. "I've brought your supper, Cap'n."

Gray could have laughed at the irony that another tray of food had come between him and Bonnie. Then again, something always seemed to be standing in their way.

With a frustrated mutter, Gray took the tray and dismissed the cook. Jack, on the other hand, could only be persuaded to decamp when Gray plucked a slab of meat from his plate and placed it strategically outside the door. Nothing, however, could retrieve the lost moment, as evidenced by the fact that Bonnie was now halfway across the room, her gaze wary.

Gray sighed inwardly. So close! So damn close! He could practically taste her lips, which left him little appetite for mere food. Best, then, to get to the subject at hand.

He put the tray down on a small, round table set off in the corner and then pulled out her chair, his gaze riveted to the silken column of her neck, barely holding in check the need to nuzzle that sweet length.

He set a plate of steaming food in front of her—what was on the plate he didn't know, or care. Expectation crackled in the air. Whether it was his or hers, Gray wasn't sure.

"Do you remember the map?" he asked as soon as he took his seat, not feeling particularly inclined to bother with a lot of preamble as he uncorked a bottle of wine and poured them both a glass. "You know, the one you threatened to throw out the porthole?"

She glanced up sharply, appearing startled by the question. "I remember it. 'Twas to a lost island, ye said. And when I asked if we were headed there, ye acted as if I'd just demanded that ye tell me your darkest secret."

His darkest secret. If only she knew what it was. What would she think of him then? To discover that he was the illicit spawn of an adulterous mother.

"Not my darkest secret, surely," he said, the words wrapped in bitterness. "That would no doubt bore you."

"How would ye know?" Her gaze was surprisingly intent, her remark unexpected and jarring.

And for one dark, insane moment Gray almost confided, the black void yawning in front of him like an invitation to divulge, to blurt out the ugliness, shock her, see that beautiful face pale, those eyes viewing him differently.

But he reeled in the uncomfortable thought and stilled the barely perceptible trembling that always came over him when he unleashed that particular beast.

"I think you'd much prefer to find out where we're going, wouldn't you?" A new light came into her eyes that told Gray his sordid, dirty secrets no longer held quite so much appeal. He didn't give her time to reply one way or the other. "Have you ever heard of the Azores?"

She shook her head.

Gray realized belatedly that Bonnie probably didn't know much about the world outside her small section of Scotland. In a way, he envied that. He had seen far too much of the uglier side of life in his travels—poverty, homelessness, endless cruelty.

Christ, he was beginning to hate himself and the sickeningly sentimental bend of his thoughts.

He reached behind him and grabbed a map of the North Atlantic region. He slapped the chart down on the table between them. "The Azores is an archipelago, a group of islands, about fifteen hundred kilometers to the west of the Iberian Peninsula, roughly between latitudes thirty-seven and thirty-nine degrees north. Here." He tapped the map. "The islands evolved from a series of volcanic eruptions, some of which are still active today.

"For all intents and purposes, the islands were discovered back in the early fourteen hundreds, though there are some writings that suggest scholars knew about the

Azores thousands of years before that, perhaps going back as far as the Phoenicians in five-ninety B.C. Navigators noted only seven islands at first and then came across two more some thirty years later.

"The lands, however, were not really explored until Christopher Columbus came along toward the end of the century, though his arrival was quite unintentional. His caravel ran against a fierce storm as he approached a section of unexplored and treacherous ocean near the Azores known locally as the *misterios,* the mysteries, a vast, eerie-looking wasteland.

"He anchored off the largest island, now known as Santa Maria, but from all accounts he never set foot on land because he believed he'd be imprisoned and returned to Portugal for treasonably shifting his services to the Spanish crown.

"The basic story that circulated was that Columbus's quest was to discover if the earth was flat or round, but in truth, most people at that time knew the earth was round. He embarked upon his voyage to seek out new lands—and hopefully return with a fortune in gold and precious gems. Some theorize the potential riches were the real motivating component. Columbus had a benefactor, after all, a Spanish queen who was quite powerful, for one. The last thing a government who had spent untold amounts to outfit this journey wanted was some dirt and rocks."

Gray reached a hand inside his shirt then, extracting a familiar rolled-up parchment. Opening the map Bonnie once threatened to toss in the ocean, he smoothed the chart over the top of the other map, superimposing the images. "This map is the key to my search. I doubt it's the original, but rather a very accurate duplicate. The markings appear similar to the type of cartography that was done back in that time, when latitude could be ascertained with a fair amount of accuracy, but longitude was still a mystery. Captains relied heavily on charting their courses by dead reckoning—guesswork, basically.''

Bonnie gasped, incredulous. "Are ye trying to say that this map dates back nearly four hundred years?''

"As I said, the map itself may be a copy. Even so, I believe it is a fairly accurate depiction, or at least that's what I'm banking on.'' He slid the yellowed map to the side of the chart of the Atlantic region and said, "Do you see anything different on my map as opposed to this one?'' He pointed to the newer chart.

Bonnie pushed her untouched food to the side and studied the maps. Gray's chart was a bit cruder-looking and lacked all the intersecting lines, but other than that, they appeared the same. Except . . . She glanced up, frowning. "Here, between these black markings . . .''

"Yes?''

"Well, ye said there were nine islands and I counted ten on your map.''

"Precisely.'' He smiled and scraped his chair closer to hers. "I must have checked a hundred maps, sure there had to be a mistake. This tiny island is not charted on any of them—except mine.'' He paused for a moment and then said, "I believe this tenth island exists.'' He glanced up, scrutinizing her face. "That's where we're going.''

"But I thought ye said the waters surrounding these wastelands were dangerous.''

"For some perhaps, but I've been told I can sail through the eye of a needle. You have nothing to worry about. I won't let anything happen to you.''

His words should have reassured her, but they didn't. Just looking at the dark patch on the map made her shiver, dread settling in the pit of her stomach, an internal warning that would not be quelled.

"It's too dangerous,'' she said in a muted voice.

Either Gray didn't hear her or chose to ignore her. "This is where I was headed before my ship got caught in a squall, sustained damage that caused me to drop anchor in an inlet off the Scottish coast—and where I soon found myself accused of murder."

That brought Bonnie's head up and turned her mind from the map to a murder yet to be solved. "So that's why ye were in our village?"

He nodded.

"And the tavern . . . ?"

"Prophet's idea of killing time." Gray's lips curved in a bitter smile. "Perhaps 'killing' is not the right word."

His story of how he arrived not only made sense, but it explained away a number of the questions she had. Yet Bonnie was still a bit confused. "Why didn't ye reveal any of this information at your trial?"

"Every time I tried to talk, your brother cut me off."

Bonnie remembered that horrible day well. Aidan had barely allowed Gray a chance to speak in his own defense, and that was part of what prompted the blowup between her and her brother. That, and the issue of Ewan's cousin, Sean.

"But I doubt I would have told your brother that part of the story anyway," Gray added. "I didn't want to get my crew involved. All I needed was a lynching."

"That wouldn't have happened," Bonnie refuted, automatically coming to her clan's defense. Yet, were she honest with herself, she would admit that Gray's assessment of the situation was probably more accurate than her own. Bloodlust had shown in people's eyes, a palpable tension that could have very easily erupted into violence.

He raised a skeptical brow. "If you will recall, your clan didn't seem inclined to believe anything I had to say. I think they would have been happy to hang me there on the spot."

Bonnie couldn't bring herself to comment further on the matter of Sarah's death, as the situation had escalated beyond her control that day.

Staring absently into her wineglass, she replayed those

terrible moments in the great hall until the gentle touch of Gray's hand on hers brought her back.

He clinked his glass to hers. "Drink up." Then, taking his own advice, he downed a healthy swallow.

Bonnie hesitated and then took a sip, and another, closing her eyes and enjoying the smooth glide of the rich wine, allowing herself a moment to shut out thoughts of murder, kidnapping, and unwanted weddings as the liquor created a warm path inside her.

When she opened her eyes, she found Gray had leaned back in his chair, his face cast in semi-shadow, the flicker of the single taper in the middle of the table giving his features a saturnine cast.

"What is it you're searching for?" she asked, barely hearing the sound of her own voice as her heart beat unnaturally loud in her ears.

"What makes you think I'm searching for anything?" His words were casual, but his demeanor seemed forced. "Perhaps I'm merely trying to discern whether the island truly exists."

Bonnie didn't believe that explanation. She had seen something in his eyes before he had backed out of the light, his utter lack of an expression conveying that he hid something.

"Does your journey have anything tae do with the sacred heart?"

His brow lifted the slightest bit. "I see you remember."

"I forget very little."

"As do I." His voice held a husky note that sent a rush of warmth over her, telling her that he remembered every touch that had passed between them since they met. "And you are quite right. This trip has everything to do with *o coração sagrado.*"

"What is this sacred heart?"

He swirled the liquid in his glass and then held it aloft, candlelight filtering through it in golden shafts. "If the tale holds true, it is a spectacular jewel, a one-of-a-kind gem claimed to have a value beyond price.'' His gaze focused on her. ''The only red diamond known to exist in the entire world. Hence its name.''

Though Bonnie knew little about precious stones, the possibility this rare jewel existed seemed improbable. Yet, the *idea* of a red diamond existing filled her with a sense of wonder. ''What makes ye think it's still out there after all this time?''

''I guess I have to believe it is or else—'' He stopped abruptly, his finger tightening on the stem of the wine-glass.

''Or else?'' she gently prompted.

His lips tilted upward in a self-deprecating smile. ''Or else I would look rather stupid, now, wouldn't I?''

Bonnie frowned. ''Why would ye look stupid?''

''Because only a fool would believe such a stone not only exists but that no one else has found it in all these years.''

''But what if it is out there? If no one ever tried anything new or different, if the world hadn't a single dreamer, where would we be?''

''Dreamers,'' Gray said in a low, wry voice. ''That was my father, full of his grand fantasies. Up till the day he died, he believed the stone was out there.'' He scoffed lightly. ''Now I guess he'll never know.'' Gray finished off the liquor in his glass.

''He'll know,'' Bonnie murmured.

Gray slanted her a glance but said nothing.

''So the map originally belonged tae your father?''

He nodded. ''He gave it to me on his deathbed— along with this ring.'' He stared at the ring and then twisted it off his finger, placing the weighty piece of gold in her hand.

The ring felt warm from Gray's skin, tingling her palm. Bonnie lifted it to get a better look at the insignia etched into the gold with incredible craftsmanship. ''What is this emblem?''

''The royal seal of the King of Spain, Ferdinand the

Second. My father claimed the ring was once worn by the king himself, a gift from his wife, Isabella. I've since discovered, however, that several loyal vassals were given replicas of the ring. My father believed the ring proved the map was genuine.''

Bonnie heard the equivocation in his voice. "And what do you believe?"

He shrugged. "I don't know."

She studied him for a moment. "I don't think ye'd be out here searching for this one-of-a-kind gem if ye didn't care a wee bit about what ye might find.'' She hesitated, then quietly asked, "Did ye come on this journey for yourself . . . or for your father?"

He tensed, as if she'd hit upon a sore spot. "Maybe a bit of both," he finally admitted. "For years my father wanted to fulfill his dream, to travel beyond the restrictive confines of his title, his responsibilities . . . his wife.'' A slight grimace twisted Gray's lips at the last two words, and Bonnie remembered Prophet's remark about how cruel Gray's mother had been to him and his brothers. She wanted to ask Gray about her but decided now was not the time to probe him on such a sensitive issue.

"And what happened?"

"He was never able to fulfill his dream, or any other for that matter. Too many other things required his attention. I guess . . ." He paused. "I guess he hoped that I would take up where he left off."

"And is that what you're doing?"

Gray shoved his fingers through his thick hair. "I don't know what I'm doing. I keep waiting to figure it out, but I can never quite manage the task."

"I think ye've already figured it out or ye wouldn't be here. But I think you're a bit afraid, too."

A scowl clouded his features. "That would imply I was a coward, and I am damn well not a coward."

It all came back to that coward issue. How she wished

she had never said the word. "Being afraid isn't the same as being a coward. A coward would never have stood up tae my brothers, or faced a mob of angry people, or stayed in jail at the risk of hanging when he could have escaped. That doesn't sound like a coward tae me." Her words seemed to ease his displeasure, and yes, his hurt.

He rerouted the topic with his usual practiced ease. "And what is it that you fear, Bonnie—or don't you fear anything?"

"Oh, I have fears, all right. Sometimes they're so strong they nearly overwhelm me, but I fight back, because if I don't, the fear will take over."

"And are you afraid of me?"

"No," she replied with quiet resolution.

He took her by surprise when he suddenly leaned sideways and kissed her fully yet all too briefly on the mouth. Then he straightened in his chair, appearing for all the world as if he'd never touched her, as if their lips hadn't met and that electric spark hadn't flashed between them.

Gray plucked the roll of bread from his plate. "Would you like to hear the rest of the story now?"

"There's more?"

Gray smiled, clearly amused at the incredulity in her voice. "Yes, there's more. A piece that is perhaps even more fantastic than everything else you've heard thus far."

Bonnie couldn't believe anything would top what had been revealed this night. "And what could possibly be more fantastic than a lost isle and a rare red diamond?"

"Perhaps the part about the island being a gateway to another land, one that dwells entirely below the sea, a civilization that disappeared into the Atlantic Basin hundreds of thousands of years ago."

Bonnie gaped at Gray as if he had begun spouting some dark, ancient language no one had heard since before the crucifixion of Christ. "A land beneath the sea?"

"Certain philosophers claim that the land above the water developed into continents that were eventually colonized, such as England and America. Plato called the land below the water . . . Atlantis. The eighth continent." Gray plucked a book from the shelf, the cover dulled with time and handling, and flipped to a passage and began to read, " 'There is an island opposite the straits which you call . . . the Pillars of Heracles, an island larger than Libya and Asia combined. From it travelers could, in those days, reach the other islands, and from them the whole opposite continent which surrounds what can truly be called an ocean.

" 'For the sea within the strait we are talking about is a lake with a narrow entrance; the other ocean is the real ocean, and the land that entirely surrounds it is properly termed a continent. On this island of Atlantis had arisen a powerful and remarkable dynasty of kings . . .' " He closed the book and stared down at it.

A land below the sea, a sort of parallel universe beneath the waves. It was simply too fantastic to fathom. Bonnie shook her head. "Such a place could not possibly exist."

"Who am I to say what does and doesn't exist—or even what is or isn't anymore? Whether the lost island is a gateway is not my concern. My goal is to find the jewel."

Bonnie rose from her chair and moved to the porthole to stare out at the dark beauty of the ocean, wondering what mysteries might lie beneath its glassy surface. "Atlantis."

"I know, it's rather hard to fathom—more so since my father won the fabled map in a card game, a feat more incredible than stumbling across lost islands and priceless gems, I assure you."

Something inexplicable twisted inside Bonnie at

Gray's comment, something that seemed uncannily familiar. "A card game?"

"Unbelievable but true. Rather amazing to think how many things are won and lost because of a hand of cards."

Bonnie knew only too well. "Like finding yourself betrothed," she mused aloud, her eyes suddenly widening as she realized what she had inadvertently divulged.

Gray sat up straighter in his chair, far too much interest now gleaming in his eyes. "You're getting married because of a card game?"

Bonnie frowned at him, not appreciating the amusement in his eyes. "Forget I said anything."

"Forget? That is a statement too provocative to be forgotten."

"Well, I'm not telling ye anything so ye'd best try!" She sounded petulant, but she didn't care. Drat the horrid man for having such uncanny hearing!

"Now don't pout, my girl. It won't get you a reprieve, if that's what you're thinking. I'll simply hound you until you've confessed the story. So do tell. I'm overflowing with curiosity."

Bonnie maintained her glare for another moment and then realized he would not relent. The expression on his face told her that he was utterly determined to know the truth, his threat to hound her not an idle one.

She heaved a sigh and confessed. "About thirty years ago a terrible feud broke out between my family and Ewan's. His grandfather claimed my grandfather cheated in a game of cards, which, if ye knew my grandfather, ye'd know that was ridiculous. He was one of the most honest men I knew."

Gray slanted her a skeptical look. "Honest enough to bet you away at the turn of a hand?"

"I wasn't bet away!" she huffed, even though she had thought the same thing on occasion.

"So what was your bride price? An ace-high straight, perhaps? Or a simple pair of fours?"

Bonnie glared at Gray and folded her arms mutinously across her chest. "Go tae the devil."

"Come now, love, let's not act peevish."

Bonnie itched to slap the amused grin from Gray's face even as his endearment warmed her. Nevertheless, she remained closemouthed.

"So was anything else, er, lost in this card game?" he asked.

Bonnie hesitated, doubtful that she wanted to impart more information for Gray to tease her with. But what was the point of holding back now? He already knew the worst, which was her role in this story.

"On the last hand of cards, Geordie Cameron, Ewan's grandfather, bet a large tract of land; he was that certain he would win."

"I presume he didn't?"

Bonnie shook her head solemnly. "What made the loss all the worse was that the land contained the main water source for miles around."

"I see," Gray murmured, the light of understanding dawning in his eyes.

"My grandfather wanted tae end the feud, tae know he had brought peace tae his people before he died. So it was agreed I'd wed Ewan tae bring that peace." Before Gray could interject with another taunt, she quickly added, "I'll make the best of the arrangement, of course. A MacTavish always does."

He regarded her for a long moment. "Does your beloved know the fierce bride he's getting?"

Bonnie's cheeks suffused with heat at his remark— and her body responded to the penetrating look in his eyes.

"Does he see the passion in you?" he went on. "Does he even recognize it?" He came out of the chair then and advanced toward her. "Because I recognize it, Bonnie." He stopped a few inches in front of her. "There's a fire in you that any man would kill to possess."

Bonnie told herself to breathe. "I'm no man's possession."

"No," Gray murmured, "You're not, are you?" He stepped closer, his gaze moving to her lips, telling her clearly that he intended to kiss her. "But right now, this moment . . . you're mine."

Chapter 13

You're mine.

Two words that caused everything inside Bonnie to liquefy into a hot pool of desire. Gray gave her little time to ponder the implications of his sensual declaration or even issue a protest, should she want to—but she didn't want to.

One of Gray's large hands planted firmly on the wall to the left side of her head, the other hand, on the right side, effectively trapping her. His head descended; her breath suspended . . . the world stopped.

The first touch of his lips was a gentle sweeping across hers, a feathery caress. The second assault robbed her of thought as he coaxed her mouth open, lips slanting across lips, breath intermingling, heat rising.

Her arms lifted and twined around his neck, pressing her body closer, wanting to feel all of him. His one hand skimmed along her side, the other cupped her buttocks, bringing her tighter against his hips.

Then his mouth left hers and scored a path of heat down her neck, her head tipping back to give him access to that sensitive spot at the base of her throat.

A low keening noise broke from her lips as he began to tease her nipples through her dress, the incredible ache building, inexorably transporting her to a precipice from which her body longed to plummet.

With deft fingers, he undid the row of buttons at the back of her bodice, the material whispering off her shoulders and down her arms, exposing her to his hungry gaze, a hint of a red flush tinting her chest.

Slowly he slid to his knees, stopping to lave each nipple as he lowered himself and then leaving his hands to take up where his mouth left off.

"Ah, that sweet, sweet belly button," he said in a husky rasp, leaning forward to taste her with his tongue, Bonnie's fingers digging into the silky mass of his hair as he explored.

He tugged the dress from her hips. From somewhere inside her daze, Bonnie once more had the fleeting thought to protest, to beg him to stop. But she didn't want him to stop, and when his fingers and mouth began to explore the nest of curls at the apex of her thighs, Bonnie didn't think her legs would support her. She felt liquid, as if her body, mind, and soul were slowly seeping into a dream where only light existed.

"Gray . . ." she whimpered.

"Don't be afraid." He rose just as Bonnie's limbs gave way, carrying her to the bed and laying her back, her legs dangling over the side and Gray above her. "I'm going to love you, Bonnie, but I will leave you a virgin. I won't take what belongs to another man, but I must have you. If you don't want me, tell me now, or by God, I will touch and taste every part of you that has haunted my dreams."

He was giving her a choice, telling her to either turn him away now or grant him permission to do every seductive, erotic thing that glittered in his eyes.

"I . . . I want you, too."

His eyes closed briefly and he expelled a shuddering breath, as if she'd just taken a mighty weight off his shoulders. When he opened his eyes, Bonnie gasped at the intensity captured in the quicksilver depths.

And then his mouth and tongue were everywhere, skimming along her collarbone, tasting the tender inside of her elbow, making sweet paths along her stomach, and then tracing the underside of her breasts before, inevitably, capturing one distended peak.

Bonnie arched off the bed as hot bliss raced through her. When Gray eased his finger between her slick petals, sliding back and forth across the engorged nub, the last vestige of any reality other than Gray and what he was doing to her body dropped away. She felt on the brink of heaven, the pleasure culminating inside her seeking an outlet. Bonnie almost died when Gray ceased the heady torture.

Like a wild thing, she grabbed his shoulders when he began to straighten. He chuckled and dropped a kiss on her lips. "Don't worry, my wanton dove. I'm not through with you yet. I promise."

Then he lowered himself to his knees once more, spread her legs, and fulfilled his vow as his warm, wet tongue replaced his finger. A rainbow of color burst behind Bonnie's eyes.

He tormented her for what seemed like forever, taking her to the edge of the precipice time and again and then pulling back just enough to make her cry out, her head tossing back and forth, her body completely in his possession.

She watched him through hazy eyes as he stood up between her spread legs, her body sprawled across his bed, every part of her throbbing for him.

He peeled off his shirt, and Bonnie was staggered by the male beauty of him, the sinful raw masculinity. She wanted to feel that hard flesh touching hers, but every time she tried, he pushed her hands away.

She gasped when he unbuttoned his pants, freeing the velvet and steel length of him that she had felt pressing so intimately into her hips. Captivated, Bonnie couldn't resist the urge to stroke him there. He flinched almost violently at her first tentative exploration.

He took hold of her wrist, stopping her infatuated enjoyment of this new part of him. "Don't," he said in a raw voice. "I'm holding on by the barest thread, love."

Like a beautiful, golden god, he lowered himself to the bed, corded arms placed on either side of her body, holding his weight back, a sheen of sweat on his brow, his face a study in control, telling her he waged an internal battle.

"I won't enter you, I promise," he said, panting slightly as the first glide of his manhood spread her slick folds and caressed her sensitive nub.

Bonnie had to bite her lip to keep from moaning, her arms flung wide, her fingers digging into the bedsheets as hot silk rubbed over wet satin, the pace gradually increasing, that sweet fire burgeoning again as Gray's rocking became faster, his long sweeps more intense, building into a primal fervor.

He coiled his arm beneath her when she arched her back, feeling as tightly strung as a bow as he took her nipple into his mouth, suckling deeply, drawing every ounce of passion from her.

Then the world dissolved, her blood roaring in her ears, muting the sound of her cry as she threw her head back and found the pinnacle of the sun, rays of pleasures radiating through every limb as the first intense contraction hit her, long and deep, holding her suspended between heaven and earth before the next pulse came, sending her spiraling downward in a spent heap, drowsy as the throbbing continued.

Gray rolled to his side, and Bonnie snuggled contentedly against his chest, feeling oddly safe in his arms and almost loved as he gently stroked her hair.

And as sleep began to overtake her, she thought she heard him speak, though the whispered words seemed to come to her from a dream.

"Sweet Bonnie ... how easily you could break my heart."

Chapter 14

A week later, an opportunity to have the one thing Bonnie had been so certain she wanted presented itself. Freedom, in the form of a bustling Lisbon port.

Standing at the porthole in Gray's cabin, she could hear the men topside shouting directions back and forth as the ship jockeyed for quay space. They were stopping to retrieve additional food supplies for the last leg of their journey.

She shouldn't feel guilty now knowing what she had to do, yet a sense of sadness settled over her. Her action would irrevocably sever the tenuous bond that had formed between herself and Gray, the fragile trust she doubted came easily to him. Never again would she experience the sweetness of his touch, communicating to her the only way he knew how—with his body.

The past few days he hadn't even waited until night descended to tutor her in the ways of physical love between a man and a woman. The urge hit him at various times and with more frequency, and she hadn't the will to stop him.

One day, he had hauled her off the deck, in front

of everyone. He had been standing behind the helm plotting their course one minute, and the next he had taken her boldly by the hand, saying nothing as he tugged her to their cabin, slammed the door shut with a booted heel, and loved her with a reckless, almost frenzied abandon.

But each time they came together, he made her want him just a little bit more, touched her soul that much deeper, tore down the walls she had to keep erected so she wouldn't fall into a terrible trap . . . one that might ensnare her heart.

Gray had kept his vow to leave her a virgin. No matter how she pressed her body to his, writhed beneath his magical touch, yearning for something she did not wholly understand, he refused.

But one night, the silken glide of his manhood had eased into the part of her that pulsed after she reached her climax, the tip of him sliding in just a fraction, filling her in a way she'd never been filled before, and Bonnie had sighed into him, welcoming that new intrusion as she arched her hips to take him in more fully. To her dismay, he had withdrawn immediately.

"I won't do it," he had said in a harsh rasp, more to himself than to her, mumbling something about pregnancies and children and then another word, spoken fiercely and very low, but which sounded suspiciously like *bastard.*

From that moment forward, they both pretended nothing was missing, loving each other with their bodies and allowing themselves to forget the different paths they were destined to take during those sweet, languid hours.

Now everything seemed to have come to such an abrupt end, reality crashing in on their idyllic existence. And Bonnie realized in one of the most honest moments of her life that she wasn't running away from Gray to return to Scotland. She was running away from the feelings he evoked in her. Feelings she doubted he would ever return. And that, more than anything, was why she had to go.

Jack's whimper roused Bonnie from her musing. She knelt down beside him and felt tears build behind her eyes as he stared at her with big, forlorn brown eyes.

She stroked that special spot behind his ears, which always made him collapse in a puddle of blissful obedience at her feet. This time, however, it didn't work. He continued to whine and press himself tight against her leg. Bonnie wondered if he sensed things weren't the same, if he understood that they would never see each other again after today.

The tears she'd been trying to keep in check rolled down her cheeks as she picked Jack up and hugged him close. "I'm going tae miss ye. But I'll never forget ye. Never."

She put him down and then abruptly pushed to her feet, forcing back the tears. She had to concentrate on the task at hand. Her window of opportunity would be very small.

Swimming to the dock would be her only method of getting to shore because she couldn't simply walk down the gangway. Leaving the ship would be the easy part. The hard part would be convincing someone to return her to Scotland.

Bonnie didn't know how long it would be before Gray realized she was missing. She could only hope to have a few hours head start, perhaps even be out to sea on another vessel homeward bound before he was the wiser.

Her heart felt heavy thinking about the pain her duplicity would cause him, the rage he would feel when he discovered what she had done, how deeply her betrayal truly went . . .

That she had used his map as her ticket to freedom.

It was the only item she could lay her hands on that might convince a ship's captain to take on an extra passenger, especially one who didn't have the money to pay for her trip, an item only a seaman would recognize as valuable.

With leaden feet, Bonnie turned toward Gray's desk where the map had lain for the last few days as he poured over other maps, charted courses, endeavoring to deduce the mystic riddles embedded in centuries' old cartography.

With shaky fingers, she picked up the map, telling herself that Gray had to have memorized it by now, that its disappearance would not mean the end of his voyage.

Yet that same voice told her the map was more than simply a means of finding a lost island; it was a piece of Gray's legacy, handed down to him by his father.

Bonnie almost faltered, thinking to leave the map and hope for the best. But without an offering, she might very well find herself stranded.

Tears threatening, she rolled the map up tightly and stuffed it into an empty wine bottle, plugging the top with the cork to keep the map dry while she was in the water.

Tucking the bottle beneath her arm, she cautiously opened the cabin door. Confirming that no one was in the companionway, she exited the room, the puppy at her heels.

"Stay here, Jack," she told him, but it appeared he had no intention of listening to her. Bonnie tried to shoo him back into the room. "Go on, now. I've got things tae do and ye aren't invited." He cocked his head but continued to ignore her. "Ye stay right here, do ye understand? I'm not playing with ye. Stay here." Bonnie gave the pup a stern look that she prayed he would heed and turned on her heel. When she glanced down, she found Jack trotting beside her.

Bonnie heaved a sigh. She had no more time to argue. Jack wouldn't be able to follow her once she got to the stern, where she would take her plunge into the ocean. Even if he wanted to jump in after her, he was too small to do so.

Her nerves jangling, Bonnie made her way down the corridor as quickly as possible. She had almost reached the end when a door suddenly swung open and she barreled smack into Prophet.

She gasped and almost lost her hold on the wine bottle. With lightning speed, she thrust her stolen booty behind her back, hoping against hope that Prophet hadn't seen it.

"My apologies, lass," he said in his usual jovial manner, righting Bonnie with infinite care, his eyes like those of a kindly father as he stared down at her. "I wasn't watching where I was going."

Bonnie tried to find her voice, panic having closed off her throat. She prayed she didn't look as guilty as she felt.

"Are you all right?" he asked, scrutinizing her, which caused perspiration to prickle her upper lip.

"Fine," she lied, thankful her voice didn't quaver.

He didn't look as if he completely believed her, but he let the matter drop. "Well, then, can I escort you to the deck? There's nothing quite like watching a crew as well oiled as this one pulling together in a mastery of seamanship." He held out his arm. "What do you say, lass? I'd be the envy of every man with such a pretty woman on my arm."

Bonnie's palms grew clammy and she feared the wine bottle might plummet from her hands at any moment if she didn't get away soon. She hoped the look she gave Prophet was sufficiently flattered. "I'd love tae go on deck in the company of such a handsome man, but I . . ." She searched for a plausible excuse and couldn't come up with anything very convincing. Then she noticed the pup sitting at her feet and was now glad he had followed her. "But I promised Jack a few minutes of play."

Prophet sighed his disappointment. "All right, then. I'll see you topside."

Bonnie remained rooted to the spot until Prophet

disappeared up the stairs at the end of the companion-way. Once he was out of sight, her shoulders sagged as she released the breath she had been holding.

"Too close," she murmured, and then proceeded in the opposite direction, pushing the hatchway open, grateful for the cool breeze. She had felt suffocated.

Quickly she moved to the stern and looked over. The sea was relatively calm and the drop to the water wasn't far. She glanced around. All was quiet. Most of the crew were either at the bow or helping to secure the ship's ropes on the dock.

"I guess this is it." Bonnie knew Jack was still beside her, but she could not look at him for fear of losing her nerve.

Trembling, she hooked one leg over the railing, then the other, until she clung to the edge of the ship. She glanced down at the water and wondered why the drop now seemed so much farther than it had before.

She closed her eyes briefly to still a wave of dizziness, inhaled a steadying breath . . . and then jumped from the ship.

The distant sound of Jack's barking made Gray smile to himself as his crew tied off the last of the lee lines and got ready to go ashore.

Bonnie and the rapidly growing pup had become fast friends over the past few weeks. Wherever Bonnie was, Jack was not far behind. Gray felt almost jealous at the attention she lavished on the dog.

If only he could allow himself to enjoy such freedom with her, to bask in the simple moments they shared. But she was his hostage and he was her kidnapper, and he couldn't allow himself to forget that. He hadn't brought her along on this journey for his pleasure, though she had given him more than he deserved, and he hadn't brought her so that he could dwell on her laughter or feel warmed by her smile as he did far too often.

But why he had brought her at all was a question, as yet, still unanswered.

Gray wondered what kind of reaction he would get from Bonnie when he told her that she could come ashore with him, that he had made plans to treat her to a traditional Portuguese dinner. He imagined she'd be happy to eat anything other than ship's fare for one night.

Maybe, he thought, he'd buy her another dress. She should have more than one. A woman like Bonnie should have a closet full of pretty fripperies. All the things he couldn't give her—unless he found *o coração sagrado*.

Gray shook his head. What was he thinking? When this journey was over, he would return Bonnie to her family . . . and to her betrothed. Though Gray knew taking Bonnie home was the right thing to do—the only thing to do—he couldn't quite keep the thought from souring his mood.

Jack's persistent barking shook Gray from his musings. He glanced over his shoulder and tried to catch a glimpse of Bonnie at the stern, but he didn't see her. A sudden chill swept down his spine, an unexpected feeling of dread.

He shoved away from the railing in the middle of bellowing an order and went to search for Bonnie. He had barely taken a dozen steps when Jack came racing across the deck and began jumping on him.

Gray's concern was mounting by the second. Where was Bonnie?

Jack wheeled around, heading back the way he had come and Gray immediately charged after him.

When they reached the stern, Jack started spinning in circles and barking wildly. Bonnie was not there. In a moment of panic, Gray thought she might have fallen overboard. He dashed to the rail, terrified of what he might see when he looked over. Nothing but calm waters greeted his eyes.

Gray's desperation to find Bonnie redoubled. He prayed he was overreacting and that he would find her in his cabin as he raced toward the stairs leading to the lower deck. A hand on his arm stopped him. Wild-eyed, Gray swung around.

"What's the matter, lad?" Prophet asked, worry etching his brow.

"Bonnie," Gray said disjointedly. "Where is she? Have you seen her?"

"Aye, just a few minutes ago. She was coming out here to play with Jack." Then the dawning light of understanding spread across Prophet's brow. "You haven't seen her?"

Gray's frenzied gaze slashed back to the spot where Jack yet remained. "Oh, God." The blood drain from his face. "She must have fallen overboard. Oh, Christ . . ."

He flew to the railing and was climbing up on it to dive into the ocean when Prophet forcibly drew him back.

"Think, lad," he said harshly, restraining Gray with a strength that belied his age. "The lass is a competent swimmer. If she fell overboard, she would be able to make it to the docks or call out for help."

"She could have hit her head on the way down or . . . I don't know." Gray wrenched his arm from Prophet and swung a leg over the railing.

Prophet grabbed the back of his shirt. "Stop and think, will you!"

"Goddamn it, man! Let me go! We're wasting time."

"I saw Bonnie in the companionway a short while ago. She was acting strangely. I didn't think much of it at the time. Now I believe I understand why she was behaving that way."

"Spit it out, man! What are you saying?

"I'm saying that Bonnie didn't fall overboard. She jumped."

"Jumped? No. You're wrong. She wouldn't—"

"God, lad, how obtuse can you be? Are you so blinded by your feelings for her that you can't see what's happening here?" Prophet shook his head. "What is the one thing she wanted more than anything else? That she vowed she would have since the moment she set foot on this ship?"

Understanding came on Gray with the impact of a tidal wave. "Her freedom."

"Aye, her freedom. The lass saw her chance for escape and took it."

Gray squeezed his eyes shut, feeling the blackness descending, the ugly darkness that crept over him each time another person managed to tear out a piece of his soul.

He had given Bonnie everything he could, done all that was in his power to make her happy . . . confided things that dwelt within the deepest recesses of his heart, and this was how she repaid him? By stabbing him in the back at the first opportunity?

Fool. What a bloody damn fool he was to trust her for even a moment. She was no better than his mother, another conniving bitch full of fucking platitudes.

Then a thought brought Gray's head up, sending him racing for the hatchway and throwing it open with resounding force; Prophet, close behind him, was saying something that Gray's numbed mind didn't catch.

He crashed open the door to his quarters and came to a dead stop. For one brief moment he expected to find Bonnie laying in bed waiting for him, or propped up on one of his pillows absorbed in a book. But the cabin was deserted and he knew she was gone.

Prophet stumbled up beside him in the doorway, breathing heavily. As if in a daze, Gray walked over to his desk, knowing what he'd find when he got there.

The map was gone.

He roared Bonnie's name with all the black rage that eclipsed his rational mind.

* * *

Bonnie stood on the docks, hidden behind a bunch of tall wooden crates, shivering from head to foot; the sun's warmth tempered by an unexpected breeze made her clinging clothes feel that much damper.

Her hands were numb and she had to keep checking to make sure she still held the wine bottle. Inside, the map was unharmed. She hoped for the same luck for herself.

She slid down the side of the crate and wrapped her arms around her knees, hoping to generate some body warmth. How much time passed with her sitting in that position, she wasn't quite sure, but eventually the stiffness and some of the chill left her limbs.

She had purposely avoided looking in the direction of Gray's ship for fear of what she'd see—and fear of the need pounding inside her to forget all about running away and go back to the safety of Gray's cabin, Gray's bed . . . Gray's arms.

But he had his own path to follow—and so did she. Her family was sure to be worried. That was all Bonnie could allow herself to think about. Dwelling on "what ifs" would do her no good.

Inhaling a deep breath, she forced herself to rise. She had barely straightened when the most horrible sound pierced the air. Utter dread roiled in the pit of her belly, for she knew the anger and anguish that had caused such a bellow.

Gray had discovered she was gone—and realized the extent of her treachery.

Bonnie felt frantic with the knowledge. She had thought she would have more time, longer to plan, perhaps find some dry clothing so she wasn't walking the docks like some half-drowned washerwoman. But good fortune was not with her. Nor was time.

All the way down the pier various crates were stacked. If she could just keep behind them, then hopefully no one would see her and therefore be able to give any clues as to her direction or whereabouts when Gray came looking for her—and he would look for her. She had no illusions about that.

Bonnie eyed her quarry at the end of the dock: a ship called the *Scotch Mist*, which, from the name, she hoped might have a Scottish captain who would help a stranded kinswoman—armed with a golden map.

Keeping to the shadows, Bonnie hastened down the wharf, her heart pounding in her ears, fearing that any moment Gray would jump out in front of her and snatch her up.

Her heart sank when she noticed how empty the deck of the *Scotch Mist* was. It appeared all hands had gone ashore, leaving her no one to speak to about her plight—or to hide her from the man soon to be tracking her.

The thought of sneaking on board and stowing away crossed her mind, but if the ship wasn't heading anywhere near Scotland, she'd be worse off than she was before.

Bonnie nearly cried at her misfortune. But worse was the realization that suddenly dawned on her. What if she couldn't find anyone to take her home and Gray didn't come after her? Then she'd be left in this town and might not ever see Scotland again.

Just as utter panic was taking hold, Bonnie spotted a crewman on the deck. A relieved breath exploded from her lungs. Now she had to move quickly.

Darting anxious glances left and right and finding no one about, Bonnie broke from the cover of the crates, hastening up the gangway and onto the ship.

The solitary crewman spun around upon hearing her, his look fierce enough to shatter stone, effectively stopping Bonnie in her tracks. His expression quickly changed as he assessed her, and the first words out of his mouth told Bonnie she had made the right choice in picking this ship.

"Are ye lookin' for someone, lass?"

"Oh, thank God!" Without thinking how she must look, Bonnie rushed forward, nearly falling into the man's arms as her legs suddenly gave way from the stress of her mad flight. Huge hands gripped her arms, holding her steady. "Y-Ye must help me," she begged, her teeth beginning to chatter as the clamminess of her clothing seeped further into her bones. "I've been k-kidnapped."

"Kidnapped?" The man regarded her speculatively. "What are ye talkin' about?"

"Men . . . they took me from my home against my will."

"Men, ye say? What kind o' men?" His gaze was no longer on her face, but instead roamed freely down her body and slowly back up again.

Bonnie tried to quell the thread of worry that coiled through her. The man had the right to wonder about a girl who must look like a creature from the sea, all soaking wet and raving. She refused to believe a fellow Scot would behave ignobly, even if his gaze lingered on her breasts, where Bonnie could feel her shirt plastered to her body with excruciating clarity.

"I have no time tae explain. They're coming for me," she rushed out, trying to make him comprehend the urgency of her situation. "Please let me speak tae your captain."

"The cap'n isn't here. The whole crew's out carousin'. We've been at sea for nigh on three months now." He eyed her once more, and this time Bonnie didn't mistake the gleam in his eyes. " 'Tis sorely put out I am tae have been the one ordered tae stand watch. I could use a bit o' pleasurin' m'self, sweet. Seems the Lord has seen fit tae send me some sport."

Bonnie's mind, hampered by fear and cold, took a moment to fully understand what the man was saying to her. She shook her head. "No . . . that's not . . . I need your help. Don't ye understand?"

"Aye," he said, licking the corner of his cracked lips, "I understand." He grasped her upper arm and began tugging her across the deck. "No one will be back for hours. It'll just be the two of us."

"What are ye doing?" Bonnie tried to yank her arm free, alarm rifling through her. The sailor's fingers tightened with a punishing force that made her wince. "You're hurting me!"

"Be a good lass and I will not be too rough with ye." An evil smile curled the corners of his lips. "Though I like it rough, mind ye. I like tae hear me women moan and beg."

Growing excitement glimmered in his black eyes. Bonnie knew her strength would be no match for his. Yet she would not go without a fight. She swung around to scratch him, but her wrist was immediately clamped in his viselike hold.

"Don't try nothin' or I swear ye'll regret it." Then he gave her a shove. The black hole of the companionway loomed before her. Bonnie knew that if the man got her down those steps, she would be doomed.

At the last minute, she spun on her heel, stomped hard on his foot, and then kneed him in the groin.

"Bitch!" he exploded, doubling over.

Bonnie wasted no time dashing for the gangway. Large, rough hands reached for her, missing the first time, but not the second, hurtful fingers tangling in her hair and yanking her back, her scalp burning as if every strand had been pulled from her head.

She screamed, reaching behind her to grab her hair and ease the punishing force of his hold. She grappled with her attacker, managing to rake her nails down his face.

Cursing viciously, his hand exploded across her face, sending Bonnie sprawling sidelong to the hard deck, the air nearly knocked from her as darkness threatened to engulf her, spirals of light flashing behind her eyes.

She rolled to her back just as the brute stomped

toward her, the wine bottle digging into her side. The next instant, the bottle became a weapon as she smashed the thick glass as hard as she could against his head, driving him to his knees, blood pouring out of a gash in his temple, covering his left eye and half his face.

One black orb, filled with deadly savagery, jerked in Bonnie's direction. She screamed again as the man lunged for her. She scrambled backward, kicking his hands away with her feet as he closed in on her, knowing she was now in a deadly race for her life instead of her virtue.

He trapped her against the bulwark, looming menacingly over her. And as he reached for her, Bonnie was sure his blood-streaked face would be the last thing she ever saw.

Gray wasn't sure why he felt so uneasy as he stood with his crew in the middle of the wharf, thundering orders for them to fan out and find his recalcitrant runaway.

The rage at Bonnie's deception was still there, but the emotion was eclipsed by an unnerving sense of worry. The docks were filled with sailors who hadn't seen a woman in weeks, perhaps months.

Gray tried to ease his concern by reminding himself that Bonnie could take care of herself, the barely healed scar on his stomach proved that fact.

Still . . .

He started down the docks, not hearing any of the merchants hawking their wares or the prostitutes plying their trade or even cognizant of the general bustle around him. His mind was focused on only one thing: finding Bonnie.

A sudden piercing scream snapped his head up, the frightened, wild sound slicing straight through his gut and scaring him like nothing every had.

"Bonnie," he said in a raw whisper, and then took

off running, barreling several people over who didn't get out of his way fast enough and shoving others to the side.

The sound of his heavy breathing and the roaring of his blood were all Gray could hear, his eyes madly searching the docks. Dear God, where was she?

Then the second scream rang out, bringing his head whipping around and riveting his attention to the ship docked at the end of the quay. The *Scotch Mist.* Of course! It made sense. Bonnie would attempt to get away on a ship she hoped was bound for Scotland.

A figure emerged suddenly, rising from the deck, a burly man nearly Gray's size but almost twice his bulk— his face covered in blood.

His focus tunneling on the ship, Gray ran toward it, crates and baskets and carts flying as he took the fastest route, barreling up the gangway just as the man leaned forward, fists clenched.

Gray's gaze jerked to the figure huddled in a corner, one side of her face swollen. A black rage engulfed him, propelling him across the distance, his body slamming into the hulking bastard with the crippling sound of bone against bone.

Gray was on his feet before the man knew what had hit him, grabbing the scum by his collar and hefting him forward to plant a devastating blow to his jaw, sending blood spewing from a jagged cut in his lip. Gray's fist repeated the same motion over and over again, wanting to annihilate the man for touching Bonnie.

He barely registered the hands grabbing wildly at his shoulders, voices shouting in his ear to stop or he would kill the man. Didn't they know that's what he wanted?

Then he was tackled by several bodies, his fist connecting with someone's midsection before he realized it was one of his own men; Prophet was standing just outside the ring of bodies swearing at him, saying something about getting the hell back to the ship before the law threw them all in jail.

"Bonnie," Gray rasped, suddenly frantic again, throwing all four men off him as panic flooded his senses once more.

Then she was before him and pain twisted in his gut, seeing the cut on her lip and her swollen cheek beginning to turn black and blue from the force of a blow that must have sent her reeling.

"Goddamn it, I'll kill the whoreson!" Gray raged, surging to his feet; Bonnie's jumping in front of him was the only thing that stopped his advance on the man now bloodied, both eyes swollen shut, his face barely recognizable as anything but pulp.

"Stop it!" she pleaded.

Gray's gaze snapped to her face, bloodlust simmering just below the surface of his skin.

"I didn't want this. None of it." She shook her head, her hair a tangled jumble around her face. "I didn't mean . . ." She dropped her head into her hands.

Gray couldn't think. He couldn't speak. He barely felt Prophet tugging at his arm.

"Jesus, man! Let's be away or we'll all be tossed in the gaol!"

Gray was dimly aware of a crowd gathering at the base of the gangway and some sense of urgency, but the red haze of anger still hung over him, and he could articulate none of what he was feeling.

With a growl, he grabbed Bonnie and swung her up into his arms, shouldering his way through the gawking crowd, seeking any reason to slug someone. Never had he felt so out of control. He hoped, for Bonnie's sake, that some semblance of calm had returned to him by the time they reached the ship.

Chapter 15

Bonnie pressed her cheek closer to Gray's chest, quaking inside from the nightmare that had so recently clutched her in its grasp. She tried to concentrate on the steady thump of his heart, knowing that if she thought about anything else, she might just fall apart.

But images of the sailor's cruel face crept in behind her closed eyelids. Visions of what might have happened to her had Gray not come along flashed through her mind despite her best efforts to keep them locked away.

She shivered, and Gray instictively pulled her tighter against his chest. Bonnie stared up at the rigid line of his jaw and knew he was still in the grips of the demon that had caused him to beat her attacker until the man's face was a bloody mess. He had been her avenging angel, wreaking destruction on mere mortals with diabolical grace.

His gaze suddenly levered down, catching her unaware, and it was as if Thor had hurled two mighty thunderbolts; the effect of that solitary glare was that devastating . . . and that frightening.

Those eyes loudly communicated that she'd get no

quarter. Clearly Gray had no intention of allowing her to escape him again, and Bonnie couldn't help but tremble at the prospect that he might not be the lesser of the two evils she encountered that day.

Her only hope lay in getting him to put her down once they were on the deck of the *Revenge* and then making a run for it. She would lock herself inside his cabin, at least until he had calmed down, which, from the look of him, would be in about ten years.

Well, he had once told her that the name he had given his ship was apropos. How true that statement would turn out to be today.

Bonnie didn't expect Gray to grant her wish and let her down simply by asking him to do so, but he surprised her, though his methods were not all that was gentleness. Yet, for the briefest second, when they stood facing each other and his gaze drifted to her cheek, his anger seemed to dissipate, something almost sad lingering in his expression.

Bonnie didn't want to be affected by that look, to yearn to lean forward and drop her head onto his chest, hoping he'd put his arms around her and pull her close, stroking her hair and whispering that everything would be all right.

He raised his hand toward her face as if he wanted to touch her, then clenched his jaw and lowered his arm, appearing even angrier, if that was possible.

Bonnie shook herself from the languor Gray always managed to curl so easily about her, a voice of self-preservation prodding her to flee while she had a chance.

That thought in mind, she wheeled around to make a dash for the companionway, hoping to get to Gray's quarters before he did and then find anything she could use to block the door. The slide bolt would not be enough to keep this man out.

Her plan was foiled when an ironlike hand clamped around her wrist, halting her dead in her tracks.

Gray's silky soft words, however, almost stopped her breathing.

"Going somewhere, my dear?" The ominous tone of his voice didn't bode well for her.

Swallowing, Bonnie slowly swiveled around to face him. The first thing she noticed was the look in his eyes. His pupils had expanded to such an extent that his eyes appeared more black than gray. Rage radiated from him like an unholy aura.

The next second she was swept off her feet like a funnel of wind had sucked her up. This time, however, she found herself over Gray's shoulder instead of gently cradled against it, the resounding cheers of his crew furthering her humiliation.

Bonnie used one hand to lever herself against Gray's back and the other to hold her unruly hair off her face. She sought a friendly mien, one savior in the crowd who would come to her aid.

She spied the man she'd pitched her breakfast at her first day on board, and next to him was the sailor she threw her lunch at the day after that. Beside him was the man who came to check on her the following afternoon and got her shoe in the back of his head. Each sailor wore an identical expression that proclaimed she deserved exactly what she got.

Then Bonnie glimpsed one kind visage. "Prophet!" she called out in desperation as Gray trudged determinedly across the deck.

Prophet gave her a sympathetic look and shook his head, his expression telling Bonnie she was on her own this time.

Then the dimness of the companionway swallowed her and Gray. A thought flitted across her mind as to when she would see the sun again—or rather *if* she would see the sun again. Gray was so mad, who knew what would happen to her?

"What do ye plan tae do?" she asked, hating the

tremulous quality of her voice as she posed the question nagging her.

Gray made no response. Instead he kicked open his cabin door with a booted foot and slammed it shut with resounding finality.

In the next beat, Bonnie was flung into the air, wincing in expectation of the pain, but having the soft bounce of Gray's bed to cushion her blow.

Her head whipped up. Gray loomed over her like a threatening bird of prey. Quickly, she scrambled to her knees, but he was too damn tall for her to meet him eye to eye. "Don't touch me!"

"You have nothing to fear on that account. I wouldn't touch you if you begged me." His words struck her like a whiplash, meant to wound and succeeding quite admirably.

"I want tae go home!" she demanded. "Ye can't keep me here against my will!"

"You forget, I'm the captain of this ship. I can do whatever the bloody hell I please."

"I refuse tae be treated me like this!"

"Treated like what? I've given you my food, my cabin . . . my very bed." His voice dropped as he said the last few words, his gaze raking her form, making Bonnie acutely aware of how her damp clothes molded her body. Those steel-colored eyes lifted to hers, a hint of self-mockery in them. "What else do you want, my love?"

Bonnie ached to throw something at him. She knew what he was saying, what his taunting, seductive words hinted at. "I'd ask for your heart on a silver platter, but ye'd have tae possess a heart first!"

Her jibe hit its mark with unerring accuracy. A muscle worked in his jaw. "Life's a bitch, my girl. That's best gotten used to."

"Aye, and you're a bastard!"

His gaze narrowed almost imperceptibly, but his coolly distant words belied the fact that she had struck a nerve. "I never claimed to be otherwise."

"How could I have ever thought ye didn't kill Sarah?"

Bonnie cursed her foolish, rash tongue, now having given him further ammunition to use against her.

"Well, this is certainly a revelation," he remarked in a sardonic voice. "What brought on this sudden faith in my innocence, I wonder?

"Does it matter now?" she retored angrily. "It's over anyway. Ye've made good on your escape."

"Over?" He laughed bitterly. "Sarah's murderer is still on the loose . . . and I've never been officially cleared of the crime."

"Whoever killed Sarah will be found," Bonnie vowed vehemently. "I'll never give up looking for her murderer."

"As well you shouldn't." He regarded her closely, making Bonnie want to fidget under that intense scrutiny. Then he took her off guard by saying, "You weren't going to let me hang, were you?"

Bonnie remembered how many times she had wanted to tell him how she felt, that she didn't believe him guilty of Sarah's death—more so after they became intimate—but there never seemed to be a good opportunity. Now her stubbornness wouldn't let her confess.

"I don't know what you're talking about."

"You came to my cell that night without Selwyn. Why?"

"He was busy." The lie sounded lame even to her ears.

"He had been your shadow every other time."

She shrugged. "So I left without him? I'm capable enough tae handle ye on my own."

"My recollection on that matter is a bit different."

Bonnie's recollection was different as well, but she had no intention of agreeing with him, even though he'd had the upper hand since the moment she had stepped through his cell door on a mission to free him— perhaps even before then.

"Well, maybe your brains are still scrambled from

that blow ye took tae the head," she returned with a smirk, not giving an inch.

He scowled at the reminder. "One more grievance against you to add to all the others."

"All the more reason tae let me go."

"No," he said in a low, purposeful voice, sinking down onto the bed next to her. "All the more reason to make you stay."

Bonnie had to remind herself to breathe as Gray's leg came within a half inch of hers. The man had a way of enveloping her without even touching her.

Then he surprised her by brushing his knuckles across her swollen cheek. "Does it hurt?" he asked, but without his earlier rancor.

Bonnie almost allowed herself to lean into Gray's hand, to let him soothe the ache, but that was a sweet trap she had fallen into far too many times already. So she lied and pulled away. "I'm fine."

She wished he would leave. She didn't want him probing, to see more than she wanted him to. But if there was one thing she had learned about Gray, it was that he could be utterly relentless.

"Why did you run away from me?" he asked, sounding as if he took her defection personally. "I treated you well, gave you everything you wanted. I told you about the stone . . . about my father."

Bonnie longed to rail at him for doing this to her, for striking a chord that she didn't want to acknowledge, for making her heart constrict at the loss of the tenuous bond they had shared.

"What did ye expect me tae do?" she snapped, needing the defense of anger to keep him at an emotional distance. "I told ye I would fight, that ye had no business bringing me, that I had tae get back tae my family."

"Back to Ewan, you mean." His expression hardened. "Do you think of him when I'm touching you, Bonnie? Do you picture him above you instead of me?"

No, she wanted to confess, she could think of nothing

but Gray during those heated hours when he loved her. More and more often he was on her mind even when he was not with her. "Why does it matter?"

He grabbed her arms and shook her. "Tell me, damn it!"

"No!" she shouted. "I don't think of him! No man has ever touched me the way ye have."

With a snort halfway between doubt and disgust, he released her. "Why did I ever believe you were any different than the others of your sex? Not a faithful, trustworthy bone in your body."

Bonnie leapt from the bed. "Don't ye dare lump me intae a category with the rest of your women!"

"You, my little witch, are in a category all your own. At least other women were obvious in their desires, some wanting a man to provide for them, lavish gifts upon them, and some just looking for a hard and fast tumble. I could read the deception in their eyes; it was as crystalline as the ice running through their veins. But you . . ." He made a harsh sound low in this throat. "You managed to put one over on me—and nobody has done that since . . ." He stopped abruptly and looked away.

"Since your mother?" Bonnie inserted, feeling petty and cruel and hating herself for it. But Gray had a way of crumbling her guard and sneaking up on her senses.

His gaze snapped up, as if she had pointed a pistol at his head. "What the hell do you know about my mother?"

She glimpsed that residue of pain in his eyes. She didn't understand the need she had to discovery the origin of his hurt. Yet, there it was, and no amount of wishing she didn't care would make it otherwise.

"I know ye hate her."

"Hate," he bit out, "is such a mild word when speaking of my mother. Then again, a word has yet to be invented that accurately describes how I feel about her. But that is neither here nor there, and this is where I tell you to mind your own bloody business. You know nothing about my mother.''

"Why don't ye tell me, then?"

"Leave off," he growled, his eyes blazing fire.

"Why is it ye demand everything from people yet you're not willing tae give anything back?"

"Don't analyze me."

"Ye enjoy pitying yourself, don't ye?"

"Yes, I enjoy it. Is that what you want to hear?"

"I want tae hear the truth."

"Bastards do not understand the truth."

"Ye mock me."

"Who's mocking you? Do you think you're the first person to call me a bastard?"

"Is that what your mother called ye?"

"Among other things. Are you satisfied now?"

"So was she cruel tae ye? Did she lock ye in a closet? Beat ye with a belt? Tell ye her life would have been better without ye?"

A muscle worked in his jaw. "Let it go."

"Or were ye the bad one?" she kept up, ignoring the silent warning. "Were ye a nasty child? Did ye stomp about and glare at her when she didn't let ye have your way?"

"End it, Bonnie," he cautioned.

His expression was so menacing, she nearly faltered, but if she stopped now she might never get the answers she sought.

"Maybe there was nothing ye could do tae make her any different, so why do ye blame yourself for her lack of love?"

"Enough!" he roared, coming off the bed like a shot.

With the force of a freight train, he backed her into the wall, two hundred pounds of pure rage, his heat blasting her, his body pinned against her, and all Bonnie wanted to do was wrap herself around him and take away the hurt her words had caused. God, this was madness. Insanity. But she couldn't stop it.

"What did she do tae ye?"

"Goddamn it! Stop pushing me!" He slammed his hand against the wall behind her head, and the entire cabin shook from the force.

"Tell me!"

"No!"

"Tell me!"

He raised his hand sharply, as if he might hit her, the tortured look in his eyes breaking her heart. A low moan issued from his throat as he stumbled back and then spun away from her. In that moment, Bonnie realized that he was not the bully, as she had once taunted.

She was.

Reaching out, Bonnie laid a hand on his shoulder. "Gray . . ."

As if burned, he flung her hand from him and stalked away. "Don't," he bit out.

She deserved his scorn. She had treated him far worse than he had ever treated her. "I shouldn't have brought up your mother. Ye were right. I know nothing about her—but maybe I'd like tae know . . . maybe I'd like tae know more about ye, tae understand what drives ye." The muscles in his shoulders tensed, yet he said nothing. "Ye overwhelm me sometimes—and no one has ever done that."

A moment passed in silence, and Bonnie thought he would keep up the pretense, but then he said in a barely audible voice, "Perhaps you overwhelm me."

That was an admission Bonnie thought she'd never hear from this man. He was too strong, too proud to admit any shortcoming. But in her eyes, his confession was not a weakness but one more of his strengths, one more quality she begrudgingly admired.

Hesitantly, she moved to stand in front of him, unlocking a memory inside her that she had kept buried away for a long time, one she was willing to reveal if it would make Gray open up to her.

"My mother died giving birth tae me," she said, feeling the old familiar tightness in her chest at rehashing the past. "Complications of labor—at least that's what I was told when I was old enough tae understand why other people had a mother and I didn't. No one blamed me outright for her death, yet I felt as if I was tae blame. And I felt such a loss at having never known her, only hearing the tales my brothers told me of the type of person she was. I envied them, the fact they had been lucky enough tae have memories, that they had shared something with her that I would never have the opportunity tae experience."

Bonnie didn't expect any compassion from Gray, not after what she had done, yet he said softly, "Life couldn't have been easy for you."

Bonnie shrugged. "It wasn't so bad. I learned things most girls wouldn't. How tae survive, how tae fight for what I wanted." Though sometimes it seemed as if the fight never ended nor the daily struggle for acceptance.

Growing up in the sole company of men—Highland men, who lived by the law of the land, rugged men, who thought to indulge her and treat her differently because she was female—made Bonnie want to prove she was as good or better than they were. In the bargain, however, she had lost a piece of herself, perhaps the only connection she had with her mother.

"The point I'm making is that it took me a long time tae realize it wasn't my fault that my mother died and it wasn't my fault I grew up tae look exactly like her or that I was a constant reminder tae my father of his loss. I didn't mean tae cause him pain, and yet I blamed myself, cursing my hair, my eyes—whatever it was that kept my father from loving me. I would have done anything tae change that." And she had. To earn a place in her father's heart, she had agreed to marry Ewan Cameron.

"He was a foolish man if he never appreciated the woman you became," Gray murmured.

Bonnie's heart flipped over in her chest. Gray had a

way of making her feel as if she were the most special thing in the world, even when she didn't deserve it. That was his gift, what drew her to him. And in that moment his sins no longer seemed quite so big, the gap between them not so wide ... her desire for him not so wrong.

"And I don't think your mother appreciated the man ye've become."

Instead of her words bringing comfort, they brought the strain back to his eyes and the tautness to his lips, putting space between them once more.

He took a step back. "You need to get out of those wet clothes before you get sick." Then he pivoted on his heel and quit the room. And like that, it was over. The talk, the need, the discovery.

The healing.

Chapter 16

Four days later, the silent anticipation of what would happen next on the voyage was shattered by the words booming across the deck with the force of a cannon blast.

"Ship off the starboard bow!"

Gray was drummed from his daze at the bellow, realizing he had been staring at Bonnie who stood at the port rail with Prophet. He had been wholly absorbed in her every gesture, watching the way her lips moved, how her eyelashes lowered when she was embarrassed or how her laughter sounded sweeter than any nightingale.

Gray wondered when the ominous prediction of his downfall had fused into reality, when his desire for Bonnie had changed into a yearning that had little to do with the lushness of her body, but rather Bonnie herself.

Since snatching her back from the clutches of the sailor he had happily bloodied, Gray had done his best to ignore her, even bunking with Prophet instead of staying in his own cabin, where the sight and smell of her might tempt him too much, entice him into making revelations that he had barely managed to escape divulging when Bonnie had probed him about his mother. He had allowed himself to get too close, to forget the purpose of this journey.

He couldn't be distracted. Any diversion or muddling of his sense could cost people their lives. They were in treacherous waters where pirating was still alive and well, and killing captives was a sport.

With a growl, Gray snatched up the spyglass beside him and glanced in the direction of the ship that had appeared out of the strange mist they had been encountering for most of the day.

He couldn't make out much about the ship at this distance, so he couldn't discern if the vessel was simply a passing brig, renegades intent on robbery . . .

Or Bonnie's brothers.

Why the last possibility rocked Gray more than the first two, he didn't want to examine too closely. Whatever the ship's purpose, Bonnie was staying with him until he was damn good and ready to give her back.

Gray felt her come up beside him then. Prophet shadowed her as if the girl needed protection, as if she wasn't fully capable of disarming a man in a variety of ways. The realization annoyed Gray to no end.

"Who is it, lad?" Prophet asked, positioning himself squarely between Gray and Bonnie, his intention more than obvious.

"What do I look like," Gray snapped, "a bloody mystic?" Christ, that sounded like the answer of a reasonable man. Now both Prophet and Bonnie were staring at him as if he'd lost what little was left of his sanity. Maybe he had. "Let's just hope they sail on without incident."

He could tell Bonnie wanted to know if it was her brothers, come to rescue her. But he'd be damned if he would give her up without a fight.

God, he thought feeling half crazed, she would leave him if given the chance. Just because she had allowed him to touch her intimately didn't mean she wanted to stay with him, didn't mean she could change who she was—or that he could.

Stay with him? Good Lord, what was he thinking? Theirs was a temporary arrangement borne out of necessity, too much desire on his part, and nothing more. He had been momentarily bewitched by her eyes, those lips . . . the way she saw into him. The way she could soothe him even when he tried to fight it.

Dangerous. That's what the girl was. Too damn dangerous.

Gray forced the thought aside, ignoring Bonnie's unspoken question far better than he ignored her presence, peering harder at the ship now that the mist had lifted entirely. What he saw nearly brought him to his knees.

"Holy shit . . . it can't be."

"What is it?" Prophet urged.

Instead of answering, Gray took another look through the spyglass, feeling the astonished gape on his face but unable to do a damn thing about it.

Without removing his gaze from the distant ship, he handed the spyglass to Prophet, who put it to his eye only to jerk it back a second later. "Good God." He rubbed his eyes as if something hindered his vision and then, like Gray, he held the spyglass to his eye again.

Bonnie glanced at Prophet then Gray, an edge of alarm creeping down her spine at their expressions. "What is it?" she asked when utter silence reigned.

With mechanical movements, Prophet handed her the spyglass. Hesitantly, Bonnie lifted it to her eye and searched for the source of the men's shock.

She noticed nothing unusual about the two-masted brigantine in the distance, the white sails raised and blowing briskly in the breeze. All appeared normal, except . . .

"Where's the crew?" Not a single person was anywhere to be seen, which was more than passingly strange and brought forth a sense of disquiet in Bonnie. She glanced at Prophet and Gray, who still wore identical expressions of amazement and confusion. "Well?" she prompted on a rising note.

Gray's gaze was oddly vacant when he looked at her. "I imagine they're dead."

"Dead?" Bonnie felt the blood drain from her face. "I don't understand. What's going on?"

"That's the *Mary Celeste.*"

"And?" she prompted when Gray said no more.

"And the *Mary Celeste* was last seen sailing eastbound from New York . . . eight years ago."

Bonnie blinked. "Eight years ago?"

"She never returned. She simply . . . vanished. The ship was believed lost at sea and all hands drowned."

Bonnie couldn't fathom what Gray was trying to tell her, but he didn't need to say more as the rumblings among his crew began to grow, their words seeping into Bonnie with the same numbing affect as a death-inducing chill.

"Ghost ship . . ."

"Haunted . . ."

"A bad omen . . ."

The last remark thrust a shiver down Bonnie's spine, a strange premonition that did not bode well.

Bonnie had the oddest sensation that they were being watched—that perhaps the *Mary Celeste* herself was observing them, tempting them to come closer, like the beckoning spider to a wary fly.

"The curse," Prophet mumbled in a muted and unfamiliar tone.

"Curse?" Bonnie's alarm redoubled. "What curse?"

Gray sank down onto the capstan next to him, raking a hand through his windblown hair. "I thought it was all rubbish," he said, more to himself than her. "But the mist . . . the ship . . . all here."

"Will someone please tell me what's going on?" Bonnie demanded, trying to tap down her rising fear.

Gray glanced up at her, as if finally remembering she was there. "I didn't think it was true."

"Ye didn't think what was true?"

"My father was not the first one to know about the lost island," he said, his words sounding vaguely like a confession brought on by a purposeful omission of facts. "There have been stories circulating for centuries, though most people never believed them, discounting the tales as just another myth."

"Portuguese folklore," Prophet took up where Gray left off. "Stories not known to everyone. I knew them because of all the years I lived in Montalegre. When I told you about meeting Gray's father, there was part of the story I left out. You see, he had come to Portugal all those years ago to better understand the legend behind the mythical stone know as—"

"The sacred heart?" Bonnie filled in.

Prophet appeared a bit startled by her declaration, as if surprised she knew about the gem. He slanted a glance at Gray, who, looking a bit chagrined, turned away.

"Aye," Prophet said. "The sacred heart. At first, I found it a little hard to believe that this gentle, non-assuming man had a map that led to the legendary lost isle of the Azores. But the earl would not be deterred. He was sure he held the key to an amazing discovery."

"A dreamer," Gray muttered, reminding Bonnie of their conversation, when he had said the same thing.

"No, not a dreamer, lad," Prophet corrected. "A man with a purpose, with convictions."

Bonnie had no intention of asking what had stopped Gray's father from completing his quest. She already knew. His wife. That was a Pandora's box she would not open. And even should she want to, Gray was no longer paying attention. Instead, he stared out across the water, appearing leagues away, beyond her, beyond all of them.

"Part of the story behind the legend," Prophet continued, "is the curse. Perhaps that's why the tale yet lives. The island mariners, being a rather suspicious lot and deeply religious, tend to blame any mishap near the Azores on the curse."

"And what does the curse entail?" Bonnie asked, wondering if she truly wanted to know.

"It's rather simple. All who attempt to find the lost isle will die."

Ensconced in Gray's cabin, Bonnie stared up at the ceiling, thoughts tumbling one on top of the next as she lay in a tub of bathwater that had grown cool, her wet hair dangling over the rim of the tub and brushing the ground.

As hard as she tried not to, she couldn't help replaying the events that had transpired that afternoon on the deck, seeing the eerie presence of the *Mary Celeste* in her mind's eye.

She remembered vividly the way the wind had suddenly changed, blowing a cover of mist over the water once more, blanketing the ship entirely, leaving the crew to speculate in hushed voices over what they'd seen.

Goose bumps not entirely related to the cool water prickled Bonnie's skin. She rose from the bath. Closing her eyes, she stood there, enjoying the last drops of water rolling off her body, allowing the sound of creaking timbers to fill her ears and lull her into a state of deep relaxation, which might explain why she never heard the cabin door open.

Gray wondered if he was awake or if he dwelt within the fantasy realm that had tormented him nearly every night since he had deserted his own quarters, thinking, foolishly, that if he didn't see Bonnie, he wouldn't dream of her.

He had been so wrong.

As he softly closed the door, afraid to break the spell

that ensorceled Bonnie, he realized no dream could be as perfectly real as this.

Like a nymph arisen from the open petals of a dewy rose, she stood in the middle of the tub, her body glistening with water, her skin glowing like a pearl lit from within. She was all supple curves and delectable valleys, her body firm and ripe.

Gray's ardor slammed into him like a fist and the only thought that crossed his mind was not turning around and leaving while muttering an apology for not knocking first. It was that he just might kill anyone who interrupted this fantasy.

A sharp gasp brought Gray's head up, his gaze locking with Bonnie's. He waited for her to leap from the tub and grab something to cover herself, then promptly regale him with obscenities that would convey exactly what kind of lecherous swine she believed him to be. If he were a gentleman, he'd at least turn his back and allow her a moment of privacy.

But he had never claimed to be a gentleman.

"I thought you might want to talk," he said, surprised he could speak coherently considering his current state of arousal.

Conversation had been his intention when he sought Bonnie out, thinking to assuage any fears she might have about the voyage, especially now that they were so near the island—if his calculations proved accurate. However, that plan slipped to the background at this new and most remarkable turn of events.

"May I have my towel, please?" That's all she said. No screeching. No blushing. No maidenly attempts to cover herself.

Instead, she stood before him like a pagan goddess, unabashed in her loveliness, beads of water peaking at the tips of her breasts, his tongue longing to taste her ethereal fire, reminding him vividly, and with no small degree of physical discomfort, of the passion they had shared—before she ran away from him.

He hadn't touched her since . . . and he wondered if she had missed him as he had missed her. All his smart plans and machinations to make her suffer for her trickery had wrought only one thing.

To make him suffer.

Avoiding Bonnie hadn't kept him from recalling every delectable inch of her flesh when he closed his eyes at night. The memory had been seared into his brain with the force of a white-hot blade.

Gray plucked the linen towel from the top of the chair it was draped over. He faltered on the first step he took toward Bonnie. And the second step as well. A sudden shocking realization came over him.

He was shaking. Trembling. He. The magician. The master of finesse. A charter member of the famed Triple Threat. Bastard or not.

"May I have the towel?" she asked again.

"Huh?"

She pointed. "The towel."

"Oh—the towel." *Suave, Sinclair. Very suave. Nothing like standing there and gaping like a lecher.*

Swallowing hard, Gray headed toward the tub—and Bonnie. He couldn't look at her—that face, those breasts, that belly button, the dark nest of wet curls at the juncture of her thighs.

He groaned inwardly and forced the vision of her beauty from his mind, vowing not to think about the little beads of liquid caressing her skin, sliding temptingly over her body.

Bonnie smiled to herself at Gray's uncharacteristic fumbling. His nervousness lessened hers, though his presence caused warm butterflies to unfurl in her stomach.

The thought of running for cover upon seeing him had crossed her mind but had evaporated just as quickly. Gray had seen every inch of her body—and in the most intimate of ways. How she had missed his touch, ached for him each night as she lay alone in his bed—as she ached for him at that moment.

Little beads of sweat moistened his brow as he walked toward her, looking like a man who was about to meet his executioner. He thrust the towel at her, a spot on the floor encompassing all of his attention.

Bonnie felt wicked, her blood racing with reckless longing for this beautiful, endearing, boyishly vulnerable man. She wanted him to touch her.

"Could ye dry me, please?"

At first, she thought he hadn't heard her, though he was barely two feet away. Then his gaze slowly and somewhat reluctantly elevated to meet hers.

"Dry you?" His voice was no more than a brittle rasp.

"Please."

When he made no move, doubts began to assail Bonnie. Perhaps he no longer wanted her. He had scrupulously avoided her since that fateful day he had hauled her bodily from the Lisbon dock. She had thought his aloofness merely anger at her defection.

But maybe her attempted escape had caused a far bigger rift. She knew all too well how a woman's treachery had affected Gray, how her actions would be a betrayal to him, perhaps a fatal blow to whatever had been growing between them. The thought brought with it a bone-deep sadness that banished her butterflies and left only a heavy emptiness.

Ashamed and embarrassed by her boldness, Bonnie stepped from the tub and reached for the towel. Gray held it away from her. Then he dropped to his knees before her, his head bent, his posture almost reverent, whisking away the emptiness in Bonnie and filling her with the sweet strains of life.

The first touch of the soft linen on her calf sent a spike of liquid heat spiraling through her. She closed her eyes and reveled in each sweeping contact, sometimes feeling the barest caress from Gray's hand instead of the towel.

She shivered when his lingering, methodical preoccupation with his task brought him to a sensitive spot behind her knee, a spot she never expected to cause her to react so strongly when Gray had pressed his lips to it the first night they were together.

Bonnie held her breath in anticipation as he patted down her thighs, making sure not to miss a single piece of flesh, working his way upward with a thoroughness she found maddening.

She nearly leapt out of her skin when his fingertips brushed her downy curls, her body tensing, leaning into him, hoping . . . wanting . . .

Yet he continued drying her, making not a single advance to further the intimacy. Why wouldn't he touch her? Could he really no longer desire her? Despair crept over Bonnie, a vicious inner voice advancing her fears.

Yet when Gray rose to his full height and she could finally see his face, Bonnie knew she had been wrong. Lines of tension and restraint bracketed his mouth, the rigid way he held himself telling her that he sought desperately for control. The relief she felt, she wanted to laugh with it.

His expression was of such concentration that she longed to cup his check, to dust back the silky length of hair falling across his forehead. But then the towel swept across her nipple and she had to bite her lip to keep from gasping with raw pleasure. She yearned for him to taste her, suckle her as he had on those nights that now seemed so long ago.

"Gray," she murmured, the room alive with the husky sound of her voice.

He glanced up, the smoldering heat in his eyes burning the breath from her lungs. His head lowered, anticipation building inside her—only to be dashed when a persistent rapping sounded at the door.

Gray swore fiercely beneath his breath. "What is it, damn it?"

"Come quick, Cap'n! The island . . . it's there. We've found it!"

Gray stiffened, the expression of mild shock on his face conveying he had harbored doubts about the island's existence. "We found it," he murmured, as if needing to hear the words from his own mouth to believe what had already been confirmed. Abruptly, he glanced at her. "Bonnie, I—"

She pressed a finger to his lips. "Go on. I'll be right there."

He gifted her with that boyish smile, gave her a brief kiss on the lips, and then broke for the door. Bonnie watched the door close after him with a certain wistfulness, a sensation of things ending. Gray had found his island.

She padded to the porthole, staring out into the horizon as dusk fell, a vibrant array of watercolor on the ocean, dusting the waves in pink and blue and gold.

Then she caught sight of a tiny speck in the distance, a dark peak rising majestically from the water, appearing out of the same clinging mist that had enshrouded the ghost ship that afternoon, renewing Bonnie's concern, a shiver of foreboding slithering along her spine.

And as she turned to get dressed, the silence seemed to whisper to her, the single word an eerie lament.

Cursed.

Chapter 17

The first wave slammed into the ship's leeward hull at three A.M.

The ship's bell had chimed the hour only moment's before, waking Bonnie from a troubled dream, her body prickled with cold sweat, a sense of dread hanging over her.

The sheer force of the wave nearly flung her out of bed. She managed to grab hold of a post as the ship pitched wildly to one side, throwing anything that wasn't secured about the cabin.

Lightning fractured the sky, and through the port-hole Bonnie saw the barrage of rain slashing sideways like thousands of watery knifes, the wind roaring with a soul of its own, so strong the sound was almost tangible.

A muffled scream erupted from her lips when a shad-owy figure moved across the room, like a wraith disen-gaged from the wall paneling. Bonnie sagged in relief as a fleeting sliver of moonlight illuminated a face: Gray.

"It's all right," he said, taking hold of her arms and pulling her close, comforting her for a moment before another wave lifted the ship up on a crest and barreled down the other side at a dizzying pitch.

"What's happening?" she asked in a terror-stricken voice, gazing sharply up into Gray's face and noting the tautness about his eyes and mouth.

"Don't worry. It will be all right." He dropped a quick kiss on her forehead and gently pried himself from her clinging hold. "Just stay here and batten down anything that moves." He grabbed up his shirt on the way to the door. In the threshold, he warned once more, "Stay here." Then he was gone, out into the dark companionway.

And Bonnie was completely alone.

She started abruptly as the wind keened with an unearthly howl, timbers creaking ominously, straining beneath the wild fury of a storm that seemed to have arisen out of nowhere. The warning of the curse echoed fatalistically in her ears.

Another wave sent Bonnie tumbling backward into the wall, nearly knocking the breath from her. Struggling against the heave of the ship, she stood, white-knuckled, grabbing the edge of the porthole, horror clogging in her throat as she witnessed the roiling ferment that tossed them about like a toy, leaving them at the mercy of a raging beast.

Rain drove hard against the glass, the weather thickening, rogue waves swelling to higher and higher dimensions with each passing moment, transposing a once calm sea into tossing desolation.

Not a single ray of moonlight lit their way. It was as if they'd been sucked into a swirling funnel, the ship pitching madly in the murky darkness. Time seemed to stop as the storm grew in its black intensity.

Rigid, Bonnie sank down on the bed, gripping the edge as if her very life depended on it. She tried to concentrate on her breathing to still the fear that escalated with each punishing jolt the ship sustained.

Terror rapidly grabbed hold of her despite her best

efforts, an inner voice convincing her that someone must need help on deck. She would do just about anything to keep her mind from the terrible anguish of the storm.

Stay here, Gray had warned.

But she could not.

Bonnie scooped up the lantern that rattled back and forth on the floor and quickly lit it, the tinder going out three times before she managed the feat, her shaking hands complicating a simple task. Then she flew to the door and flung it open. Frigid water hit her bare feet. Panic assailed her. They were sinking!

Bonnie had never been afraid of anything in her life. But, dear Lord, she was terrified of this, of dying when she'd only just begun to feel as though she was living. Her only thought was of finding Gray.

The ship rolled and dipped dizzily in the heaving sea, jostling Bonnie from wall to wall as she tried to make her way down the corridor, the sparse light from the lantern flickering crazily from the draft sweeping through the passageway, the muted sound of male voices speaking words without distinction, as if they came from nowhere and everywhere.

Abruptly, the vessel listed wildly to one side, brutally slamming her against the wall causing her grip on the lantern to loosen, sending tin and glass arcing through the air, a scream rising on her lips as the light shattered beside the forward stairwell, red hot sparks spewing in all directions. In an instant, small but hungry flames eagerly licked at the wood.

Reckless with terror, Bonnie swung away from the destruction, racing blindly down the companionway, heading for the stairs located at the stern.

A cocoon of blackness engulfed her, as if the fire had caused the night to recede from its devouring embrace and gather within the accompanying shadows.

Bonnie reached out, hands groping in front of her to feel her way along. She tripped, the forward momentum of the ship sending her sprawling toward the ground, saltwater rushing into her mouth as the Atlantic further invaded the corridor, soaking her to the bone.

Sodden and desperate, Bonnie almost gave in to the sob of hysteria rising in her throat. But thoughts of her family and Gray bolstered her strength to drag herself along.

Relief soared through her when her fingers traced something familiar: the first tread of the stern stairwell. On hands and knees, she crawled up the steps, cold, numbed fingers slipping clumsily over the latch, jiggling it free and then shoving against the closed hatch cover.

It didn't budge.

A spurt of cold fear pushed through her veins as she struggled to her feet and heaved her shoulder against the thick wood. Nothing happened. Dear God, she was trapped!

She pounded feverishly at the door, screaming for help until her voice grew raw and her hands ached, unwilling to accept the reality that she would not be heard above the ceaseless barrage taking place just beyond the portal.

A sudden burst of light caught her attention. Wild-eyed, her gaze snapped to the far end of the corridor, seeing the bright flames of a building fire, the first whiff of smoke reaching her nose, leaving her stuck between two evils—drowning or death by smoke and fire.

Driven by a fierce need to survive, Bonnie gathered up the last remnants of her strength and put the full force of her meager weight into ramming her shoulder against the portal one more time.

With a deathly moan, the hatch gave way, but she had no time for gratitude as the immense power of the driving wind hoisted her up and dragged her forward slamming the door behind her, leaving her on deck and shivering in the pelting, freezing rain, Gray's thin shirt plastered to her trembling body.

The storm was everywhere, completely surrounding

them, a tempest without center, without boundary. Just the ship and the sea—and the sea was winning.

Great gusts of charged air threatened to knock Bonnie back to her knees as she attempted to rise to her feet, the deck below her as slick as a sheet of ice.

From the corner of her eye, she caught sight of the enormous body of water gathering beneath the ship, like a liquid beast, pitching them skyward. Bonnie lunged for the door, capturing the handle in a death grip as the howling wind tugged fiercely at her, as if a mighty hand had wrapped around her midsection, intent on foiling any escape.

She lost her tentative hold and hurtled in a backward slide across the deck, her hands fumbling for a stronghold as the bow rose and the stern dipped—the sea, and death, looming just behind her.

A scream tore from her throat, her fingers clawing madly toward a broken piece of rigging, just out . . . of reach. A lurch and a rush of water shoved it within her grasp at the last moment, stopping her descent into the black abyss.

Clinging to her precarious lifeline, Bonnie's body shook uncontrollably, rain pouring over her eyes, blurring her vision.

"Help me!" The wind sucked away her words and then tossed them back in her face.

Her grip on the rigging started to slip as rain seeped between her icy fingers, her strength ebbing, her slowly numbing mind wondering how much longer she could hold on.

The ship tipped precariously to one side. She let go of the rigging, sliding sideways toward the bulwark, a sturdy brace against the storm's savagery. She gripped the railing, holding on for dear life as she found her footing and began working her way toward the helm.

Bonnie had almost made it to the bow when a piercing cry split the air. *"The mizzenmast is breaking! Watch out below!"*

The words barely registered in Bonnie's mind as the awful creaking noise of the wood splintering apart brought her head up . . . just as the huge pole began its descent straight for her.

Only moments before the mast would have crushed her, someone shoved her out of the way, saving her from certain death . . . but sending her careening across the water-slicked deck on an unstoppable slide—headlong toward the raging, angry claws of the open sea.

"Bonnie!" Gray cried out, watching in horror as her small form skidded over the planking with nothing to stop her inevitable spiral overboard.

His heart thundering away with fear, Gray dove after her, barreling toward her even as she moved farther out of his reach.

Only three feet, Goddamn it! Two feet . . . come on!

Then her legs went through the hole, her hand stretched out toward him. "Gray!" she screamed.

"*Bonnie! No!*" he roared as her body slipped over the side, the sight of her wide, terrified eyes something Gray knew he would never forget.

He slammed lengthwise into the bulwark, the rain blinding him as he thrust his hand through the opening, his fingers locking around Bonnie's wrist at the last moment, snatching her from the clutches of the monstrous sea.

Bracing his legs against the bulwark, he fought wind and rain to haul her back to safety. "Dear God," he said in an agonized voice, holding her tightly within his embrace. "I thought I had lost you."

She clung to him in desperation, sobbing against his chest. "I . . . I thought I was going to die!"

"I would never have let that happen," he vowed, knowing how close he had come to disaster. He kissed her temple, his hand smoothing over her wet hair as the storm raged around them.

"Captain!"

Gray's head snapped up and he squinted through the

nearly blinding sheet of rain. He spotted his quartermaster waving wildly at him. And that's when Gray saw what had happened. Prophet was pinned beneath the fallen mizzenmast.

Bonnie clutched Gray's shirt as he started to rise. "He pushed me out of the way when I would have been killed," she cried. "This is all my fault!"

Gray dragged Bonnie to her feet and drew her toward the companionway. "Go below and tie yourself to something and don't come back up here again!"

"But—"

"Just go!" He gave her a slight shove toward the hatchway and then took off toward his fallen friend, disappearing into the darkness and rain.

Bonnie watched Gray go, not knowing what to do, fearing now that she'd only get in the way of the crew trying to do their jobs.

She reached for the handle to the hatch, battling with the portal as the wind laid a mighty hand against it, keeping it firmly closed.

Finally, the wind shifted and she managed to fling the door back. Heavy black smoke assaulted her, angry flames shooting through the opening, needing only a single gust of air to ignite the blaze into a raging inferno.

Bonnie almost fell to her knees under the weight of guilt, knowing her shattered lantern rather than the storm's savagery might very well cause people to die this night. Then she stiffened, hearing a terrified sound. Barking.

Oh, dear God! Jack!

The puppy was trapped below. Caught somewhere amid the blaze. She had to save him. But the fire was working its way up the stairs, the rain seeming to only beat it back temporarily.

Squatting down, Bonnie tried to see through the haze of smoke, the fire chewing its way along the walls, but the floor was as yet untouched.

Knowing her luck could change any minute, she flew

down the stairs, jumping the last three steps to avoid the flames and racing down the corridor toward the galley, where Jack usually stayed.

She flung open the door and the dog nearly barreled her over in his wild flight to freedom. He raced in a disoriented fashion down the hall—going in the wrong direction.

"Jack, no! Come back!"

Bonnie charged after him, just managing to catch hold of him before he attempted to go up the stairs that were now totally engulfed in flames.

Smoke filled Bonnie's lungs, choking her as she stumbled down the hallway with a terrified Jack in her arms, once more heading toward the stairwell at the stern of the ship—and the hatch she had so recently battled, praying this time her path would not be barred.

Relief poured through her when the hatch cover opened without a fight. But once outside again, she made a startling discovery.

The rain had stopped.

Not a single drop fell from the night sky, yet the wind wailed plaintively around them, the ocean rocking them from one mammoth swell to the next. And as she stood there still as death, Bonnie realized the storm was not subsiding, but that the worst was yet to come.

They were within the eye of the beast.

She heard her name being called. It was Gray. He stood at the bow, one arm wrapped around Prophet. Relief soared through Bonnie. Yet once more, they stood at opposite ends of the ship. In between them was the fire, the flames rising up through the deck, smoke instead of rain now blurring Gray's face.

Bonnie thought she heard someone cry, "Behind you!" as a mighty roar echoed in her ears, a sound that chilled her blood, as she glanced over her shoulder and glimpsed the towering forty-foot wave arcing over the stern, a mass of water closing over her head, sweeping her off the deck and into the sea, Jack still clutched desperately in her arms.

The last thing Bonnie saw before the frothing surf dragged her under was the sight of the *Revenge* wrapped in flames.

Chapter 18

Something warm and wet tickled Bonnie's cheek.

She stirred from the bone-deep lethargy that cloaked her, her mind still ensnared in a dream of Gray dropping sweet, hedonistic kisses along her jaw, the image so vivid she could actually feel the feathery touch of his expert mouth.

She wanted to open her eyes and see him, but she felt so tired . . . her eyelids so heavy. She thought she might have spoken his name aloud, but she couldn't be sure, drowned out as her thoughts were by a rumbling noise, like the precursor of lightning.

In the foreground, a whimpering, somehow familiar, resonated a chord inside her. A small voice urged her to wake up; things were not as they seemed in her sleepy world.

A gentle nudging against her chin finally roused her to wakefulness, alerting her to the salt tang in her mouth and the gritty feel of sand beneath her cheek, a cool lapping of water against her bare toes and a not quite unpleasant heat warming the back of her legs.

The whimper she'd noted became a whine, forcing

Bonnie's eyes open, a jolt of shock darting through her as a face pressed close to hers, nose to nose. The cheerful bark that accompanied her awakening jerked Bonnie's head up.

"Jack!"

Mad licking followed her revelation, the puppy's effusive greeting whisking away the last traces of the debilitating weariness that had enshrouded her.

Bonnie rolled to her side and hugged Jack's jubilant little body to her, happily accepting the kisses he bestowed. Then, in a rush, the remnants of a nightmare fell in on her with full, dreadful force.

She sat up with a start, Jack scrambling from her abrupt movement as everything came back to her. The ship. The fire. A towering wave. A black eddy swallowing her up.

And Gray.

Standing on the deck in a paralysis of disbelief, racing to the railing moments before the ship was ingested into the mouth of the storm, calling her name, the sound echoing with heart-wrenching despair, one final glimpse of the tragic desperation etched on his face rending her soul as liquid death took her by the hand.

What had become of the crew? Prophet? Could she and Jack truly be the sole survivors? Had everyone gone down with the ship? In the fire that she had caused?

The idea of never seeing Gray again, of never having a chance to tell him how she felt about him, of the life he made her want . . . lost. All lost.

Bonnie leapt to her feet, shaking her head wildly. "He can't be dead. He can't be." She barely took notice of her surrounding, the pristine white beach, the rolling crests of the surf, as she scanned the horizon, despair filling her when she saw no ship, only the vast, endless ocean spreading out as far as the eye could see.

Down the shoreline, she glimpsed a piece of driftwood floating in the rolling froth, spiraling in the same spot, caught by a powerful undertow. Bonnie didn't know why she ran toward it, cold sea spray kicking up on her bare legs, wrapping a chill around her as she pushed out into a breaking wave to tug the hunk of wood from the water.

She didn't understand the need she had to hold that piece of timber, to stare at it as if she didn't know what it was, what it meant, her conscious mind desiring nothing more than to block out the reality in front of her, the indisputable proof her heart longed to deny.

Bonnie remained rooted to the spot, scalding tears running unbidden down her cheeks, only Gray's shirt around her to warm the chill that had settled over her, the only item she had left to remind her that he had existed.

Jack's plaintive bark finally registered in Bonnie's mind, but she felt numb, emotionless, as if the person she had once been had disappeared, leaving only a black void to mark her place.

Dazed, she turned toward Jack . . . and the sight that met her eyes hit her with an impact that nearly brought her to her knees. Scattered among the trees and brush behind her were the broken remnants of a once beautiful vessel, the sea having churned the *Revenge* into debris, reducing life and vitality and hopes into smashed bits.

Weakness overcame her, sending Bonnie sinking to the ground, lost somewhere between nightmare and reality. Jack tugged something from the wreckage and trotted toward her with it, blissfully unaware of the destruction around them, of their desolation, of the utter hopelessness of their situation.

He stopped in front of her and sat down as she had taught him to do. Then he dropped his prize in front of her, an item he recognized only as a toy, but which made the ache inside Bonnie redouble.

Gray's shoe.

Through a haze, she took hold of the shoe, a gradual

disintegration taking place inside her, a final crumbling. Buckling sideways, her sobbing became a living thing.

Jack climbed into her lap, sensing her sorrow and trying to comfort her, licking her and nudging her hand with his cold, wet nose. Bonnie burrowed her face in the puppy's warm neck, the solid, stoic little animal allowing her to expend her misery.

When nothing remained inside her except hollowness, Bonnie lifted her head and forced the pain aside, knowing that if she allowed the despair to get the better of her, thought too much about what awaited her, she might lie down and never get up, and she couldn't do that. Jack needed her.

Through glassy eyes, she glanced around, never having felt so utterly alone, trapped here in this hidden oasis, a place both tragic and beautiful, lush with vegetation. Tall trees with huge fringed palm fronds swayed in the tropical breeze and flowers bloomed in the most exotically vivid shades she had ever encountered; unseen birds trilled their songs high above. Gray would have been so pleased with this place, with realizing his father's dream. Now he'd never know.

A choked sob welled up in Bonnie's throat at the thought, threatening her tenuous calm. Jack's slight whimper reminded her of her vow, forcing her to concentrate on their survival, what they would drink, would eat.

She pushed to her feet, trying not to look at the wreckage of the ship, focusing her mind and energy on the sweet face staring up at her with such devotion, such trust.

Bonnie frowned then, noticing little puncture wounds on Jack's shoulders, small dots of blood standing red on his white fur.

"Oh . . . you're hurt." She knelt in front of him, checking to see if he was still bleeding, puzzled by the three tiny marks on the back side of each shoulder and the single bloodied spot in the front. He appeared fine otherwise, the saltwater most likely having helped cleanse the wounds. She scratched him between the ears. "Ye'll be all right," she murmured, relief flowing through her. She didn't know what she would do if anything happened to Jack.

As if understanding, Jack cocked his head and blinked up at her with round black eyes, so endearing, so sweet . . . and so painful for Bonnie to look into. She didn't know how they would survive in this isolated place, alone, completely at the mercy of the elements and whatever animals might make this island their home.

She contemplated the first problem facing them: securing food. She wondered if she could fashion some kind of spear and try to catch a few fish. But what would she cook the fish in, should she managed to snare any? She had not a single pot or pan, fork, knife, or plate. Nothing. Could she even build a fire?

She had always thought herself ready for anything, but she had been wrong. Yet what could have prepared her for this test of her faith and fortitude?

She began to look around for a suitable stick to fashion into a makeshift spear when something caught the corner of her eye, a bright flash of silver light gleaming amid the pile of ship's rubble.

She turned, curious yet hesitant to head toward the object, afraid of what she might find, of what she might see. Jack bounded off in the direction of the debris field, and Bonnie forced herself to follow, taking the puppy's lead and steeling herself for whatever discovery awaited her.

Her pace slowed as she neared the spot, her heart thumping in ever-thickening strokes with each step she took, picking her way carefully among the scattering of personal belongings and broken wood, refusing to glance too closely at the items.

Bonnie stopped and stared down at the object that had caught her eye, its steel tip wedged deeply into the wood, which would explain how it had been carried over the water instead of sinking to the ocean floor.

She bent down and yanked her dirk from the planking, holding the knife up to the light. Though she had never thought much about God and the mysterious ways in which He worked, there was no overlooking this particular miracle.

A barely audible sound brought Bonnie's head up. She tilted her ear into the wind to catch the rumbling vibrations. As she listened, the sound expanded, becoming a repetitive cadence that rippled a shiver down her spine.

The heavy beat of drums.

She was not alone.

Her heart slammed into her ribs. She called to Jack and fled toward a covering of trees to get out of the open expanse of beach where anyone might see her.

Her mind raced with the same frenzied, erratic rhythm of her heart as she realized that staying alive might not be as simple as finding food and shelter.

Hidden within the dappled woods, Bonnie listened, attempting to discern from which direction the drums had come. The air filled with the reverberating noise.

Cautiously, she made her way to the other side of the trees, opposite where she had been, making sure to maintain her cover as she came to a rise that looked directly down into another long white strip of beach, the scene before her like something out of a nightmare.

It was not the group of men she saw kneeling in the sand, familiar and bedraggled, half-dressed savages standing behind them with lethal-looking spears that pushed the fear through Bonnie's veins. It was the single man, lying facedown in the sand, shirtless, unmoving, and unforgettable, that did.

Gray heard the sound of his own moan resonating in his ears, every conceivable part of his body screaming curses at him as he began to rouse himself from the lassitude enveloping him.

Facedown and gritty, a memory tickled the back of his mind, a sense of déjà vu, the unexplained yet certain knowledge that life was repeating itself—an explosive pain on the back of his head, big satanic rats, hulking giants . . . and a glorious blue-eyed Athena.

Reality crashed in on him.

The ship, the fire, the sea . . . Bonnie being dragged under the water.

Gray's eyes snapped open. Urgency and panic sluiced through him as the memories flooded in on him in a rush. He had to find her!

With a groan, he struggled to his hands and knees, his head hanging low, needing a moment to let the dizziness pass, along with the nausea from swallowing saltwater. His stomach churned, illness threatening. He concentrated on deep breaths until the danger passed.

Then came the soul deep guilt.

After all the self-doubts and the recriminations, all the fear of failure, he had found the lost island, the famed Isle of the Mist, and he cared not a damn bit about it. Prophet had called this journey a quest. What it had become was another failure, in a long line of failures. Lives wasted. His father's dream tainted. Dear Lord, if he had lost Bonnie, too . . .

The possibility scared Gray like nothing he had ever experienced, propelling him to action regardless of his body's opposing desires. He surged to his feet, closing his eyes for a moment as he waited for the world to right itself.

When his balance resurfaced, Gray opened his eyes—only to discover a very sharp, very deadly spear pointed directly at his heart. His gaze elevated in increments and finally fastened on the face of the warrior whose eyes promised a painful death should Gray make one wrong move.

Inhabited. His island was inhabited.

Why hadn't he planned for this possibility? Not once had he considered the prospect that people might live here. Historically, many lands believed to be without human occupants had not only been settled, but the denizens had successfully made a life for themselves—until explorers came along and thought they had a better way of doing things, inevitably aiming to fix something not in need of repair.

Looking at the man standing in front of him, Gray felt as if he had truly stepped into another time, a time when those false prophets had bestowed token gestures of friendship just before usurping everything within their reach.

Though he had no intentions or interest in taking over—if he could even do such a thing in his precarious position—a token of friendship would not be remiss at this juncture. Banked anger lurked in the savage's eyes, red and black war paint smeared across his cheeks a warning sign that their intrusion was not taken lightly.

Gray lifted his hands in supplication. "I mean you no harm."

The warrior narrowed his eyes on Gray, his grip tightening on his weapon, clearly not understanding what Gray had just said.

The man reminded Gray of an Indian with his sun-blackened skin, long ebony hair that made Gray's shoulder-length hair look short in comparison, and only a loincloth covering his body.

Yet the tilt of the eyes was different, the facial features a unique heritage—one with a distinctly Spanish influence, which shouldn't surprise Gray. The inhabitants of the other Azorean islands were of Spanish and Portuguese descent. Why shouldn't these people be as well? It didn't seem beyond the scope of possibility that these natives had come from the neighboring islands and had known this tenth isle existed when no one else did.

Gray took a chance and repeated his pledge in Spanish, which earned him a curious frown from the warrior.

Yet a shade of understanding flared in the man's eyes. Gray tried again in Portuguese. That did the trick.

The man nodded, yet he didn't seem impressed by Gray's vow, remaining staunchly mute and regarding him with suspicion, his gaze taking in what remained of Gray's clothing, which consisted of only his tan breeches.

"My ship," Gray said, "it was destroyed in a storm."

The man paid him no heed. Instead he circled Gray, as if this might illuminate some mystery.

"Have you seen other people?" Gray then asked, half expecting his question to be ignored. Instead the warrior grunted and gestured to a spot behind Gray.

Making no sudden moves, Gray glanced over his shoulder and found a number of his crew lined up along the shoreline, a fierce-looking group of savages guarding them.

Gray was grateful and relieved to see that so many of his men had survived. He counted four sailors missing. And Bonnie. At the end of the row, he glimpsed one haggard face wearing a slight grimace, the man next to him keeping him upright.

"Prophet."

"Aye, lad. The good Lord has seen fit to keep me on this planet for another day. Glad to see you up and about. I was worried."

The truth of that statement was plainly written on Prophet's face, which seemed to show the signs of age it never had before. Gray had always thought Prophet invincible, that even the sands of time would not affect his friend. But now Gray knew that no one was immune to death.

Even him.

"Bonnie?" he asked, being purposely cryptic, unsure of how much these people might truly understand. If he and Prophet had lived, Gray had to believe Bonnie was alive as well. And if she was somewhere on the island, he didn't want to give anything away.

Prophet shook his head sadly, his gesture communicating his meaning more effectively than words ever could, bringing a painful stab to Gray's heart. He wouldn't believe Bonnie was dead. She was strong, a survivor.

He returned his attention to the warrior who Gray suspected was the leader, repeating his earlier vow that neither he nor his men meant any harm. Thinking about Bonnie made his tone more urgent this time. She might be lying somewhere injured or dying, alone, waiting for him to save her, and he was detained here arguing with this grunting savage.

"My men are hurt and need someone to look after them."

The leader's reply was a snort, which made something inside Gray splinter. His hands clenched at his side, his control disintegrating. He took a threatening step toward the warrior and barely ducked in time to miss the sharp stab of the spear. A corner of the weapon clipped him in his side, sending a shaft of pain rebounding through his injured ribs.

He lunged toward the man, but the two natives flanking the chieftain flew at him. Gray saw the blurry outline of something angling toward his head, the blow sinking him to the ground, loud voices of protest from his men swimming in his head, unconsciousness seeking to pull him under.

A razor-sharp spear pressed against his chest with life-threatening steadiness; one swift downward motion would kill him instantly. One thing kept Gray from allowing the blackness to drag him under.

A woman's scream.

Everything transpired in a split second. Gray swung his head in the direction of the sound, squinting into the sunlight toward the top of the dune, where a flash of molten metal pierced the brilliance of the sky . . . illuminating the person wielding the weapon.

"Bonnie! No!"

His warning came too late. The dirk spiraled from her hand, whistling through the air . . . and heading straight toward the chieftain.

Pinning the man, loincloth and all, to a tree, the knife quivering between his thighs.

Chapter 19

The silence that followed was so deafening, it was as if the world had stopped breathing.

Gray had little doubt that all eyes were riveted to the strategically lodged dirk; its precise placement having more effect at stopping the escalating hostilities than a bullet to the head.

He knew how easily that knife could have inflicted real damage, and how skilled was the woman who had thrown it, his scarred stomach testimony to that fact. Bonnie clearly hadn't intended to kill the man. Gray only hoped the chieftain recognized her benevolence. Otherwise violence would erupt there on the beach.

Gray held himself alert, expecting holy hell to rain down upon them at any moment. The booming laughter that erupted from the warrior a minute later took him completely off guard. He had anticipated a variety of reactions. Amusement had not been one of them.

In short order, the other tribe members chimed in, obviously waiting until it behooved them to utter a sound, as inappropriate laughter might very well result in a poison dart to the neck. Gray thought they sounded like a bunch of tree monkeys.

When the humor died down to a rumble, the chieftain plucked the knife from between his thighs and stared at it, a half grin curving his lips, an expression that appeared so unnatural that Gray figured smiling for this man was a rare occurrence.

The warrior's gaze rose to the solitary, unmoving figure at the top of the rise. Then he made a motion to his men. "Go," he ordered in Portuguese, pointing in Bonnie's direction. "Bring the girl to me."

Tension instantly returned to Gray. He leapt to his feet, his sole thought that of protecting Bonnie as he blocked the men's way. The natives immediately drew their weapons.

"No!" the leader barked. "Leave him." That command surprised Gray, considering that only moments before the warrior had been ready to disembowel him. Then the man added, "He is loved by Girl with Thundering Vengeance."

Gray gave only a second's consideration to the fact that he'd come within a heartbeat of being killed, thereby escaping the Grim Reaper yet again. Instead he watched the two men pass him and thought: *Girl with Thundering Vengeance?*

Good God, if that didn't beat all bloody hell. But the moniker fit Bonnie, damn if it didn't.

Amused, Gray's gaze followed the two warriors as they progressed up the dune. He hoped Bonnie wouldn't make any more foolish moves. These men were not the sort one threw food at or slugged with a shoe or threatened with a painful neutering.

The sun outlined her in all her heart-stopping perfection, standing above them like a goddess of glory and vengeance, her hair a flaming tumble around her. And for the first time in Gray's life he thanked God, a silent recital of gratitude for saving Bonnie and returning her safely to him.

She remained poised as the men approached her. Jack, on the other hand, took it upon himself to protect her, not comprehending, like most small dogs, that he weighed as much as a peanut and appeared as ferocious as a raging butterfly. The natives gave him not a second thought, which didn't sit well with Jack, who simply couldn't tolerate being ignored.

In a combination roll and slide, the puppy lunged at the men's heels as they escorted Bonnie down the rise, Jack's overly large paws often quagmired in the soft sand. He tumbled headlong down the last few feet, landing in a plump white heap against Gray's ankles. Gray scooped him up and got an excited lick when he was recognized.

Together they watched Girl with Thundering Vengeance glide past them, her head high, her bearing erect, and her mien utterly unflinching as she stopped in front of the leader, who assessed her every nuance. Gray had never been more proud of her.

The chieftain wasted no time in getting to the point. *"Sou o chamam Bem Corajoso e estão em minha ilha. Por quê trespassa aqui, ó vengeful um?"*

Bonnie glanced uncertainly over her shoulder at Gray. "What did he just say?"

The chief's dark eyes sliced Gray's way as well. The man grunted, which Gray took as a monosyllabic equivalent of *What did she just say?*

Gray replied, "She doesn't understand you."

The man pointed at Gray. "You. Here."

With Jack still tucked securely in his arms, Gray strode over to stand next to Bonnie, wanting only to gather her into his arms and hold her close. Until he believed he had lost her, he hadn't understood just how much she had come to mean to him. How very much he needed her.

She glanced sideways at him, a sweet smile touching her lips. "Hello," she murmured.

"Hello," Gray returned, drinking in her profile, that

sloped button nose, the smooth skin now lightly dusted with color from the intense sun, and those delicious lips he longed for, as if a single kiss could mean the difference between life and death.

The leader's inarticulate vocalization brought Gray's gaze around. He scowled at the man for the interruption before he realized what he was doing, or that his actions might result in his head adorning the top of a pike.

Instead of anger, the chief merely raised a black eyebrow, his expression communicating that he knew exactly what Gray was thinking.

One word, "Translate," ended the exchange and transported Gray back to the matter at hand.

Glad for a reason to return his attention to Bonnie, he said to her, "He wants me to translate what he's saying."

"Do ye think he's very mad that I threw my dirk at him?"

Gray wanted to laugh. "I think he probably appreciates that you didn't change him from a stud to a gelding. In fact, I suspect your display of skill has won his respect."

Her response was simple, straightforward, and it touched Gray all the way down to a place he didn't believe existed anymore, a level of caring he hadn't thought he possessed. "I couldn't allow him tae hurt ye."

For the first time in a long while, Gray couldn't find the right words to express what he felt, couldn't articulate how, in the middle of all this uncertainty, she could make him glad to be alive. Nor could he tell her of the anguish he had suffered when he had seen her go overboard, unable to help her, how tormented he'd been, and that he'd almost welcomed drowning when the ship had finally gone down.

If he knew what love was, Gray imagined this was it.

The thought yanked him mentally upright. Love? God forbid! He might admire Bonnie, respect her more than

he had respected any woman, find enjoyment in the
simplest things: her laugh, her smile, the way she said
his name.

But love? No, never that.

Fools and dreamers fell in love. Men who hadn't seen
what such an emotion could do to their lives fell in love.
People without an ounce of self-preservation fell in love.
And he was neither a fool, a dreamer, stupid, nor igno-
rant of the price one paid for unrequited love. His father
had suffered that fate for nearly forty years, and such
devotion had bought him misery and an early grave.
Gray would not let such a thing happen to him.

Impatient now, the warrior poked Gray's shoulder to
get his attention. "Tell." He gestured to Bonnie.

Without quite meeting Bonnie's eyes, Gray repeated
the man's words. "He says, 'I am the one they call Bem
Corajoso—Most Brave—and this is my island. Why do
you trespass here, oh, vengeful one?' "

"Vengeful one?" Bonnie slanted a brow, amused.

Gray wouldn't let himself get dragged under by the
twinkle in those blue eyes. "He calls you Girl with Thundering Vengeance."

She laughed; the sweet sound chimed through the
afternoon air, bringing an answering response in
Gray—and, unfortunately, in Bem Corajoso as well. The
bastard smiled at Bonnie in a purely masculine way,
much to Gray's mounting irritation. And Bonnie, devil
take her, actually smiled in returned!

Women! He'd never understand the perverse creatures.

The leader pointed at Bonnie and remarked to the
men beside him, *"Ó, vengeful um tem uma risada que faria
regular o rouxinol invejoso."*

"Did he call me vengeful one again?" Bonnie asked,
her amusement renewed.

Annoyed, Gray took a page from the warrior's book
and grunted in reply. He had no intention of telling
Bonnie that the man had just said she had a laugh that

would make even the nightingale envious. He'd take that information to the grave with him.

Damn it to hell! This was all they didn't need. They were now stranded on this benighted island with no rescue in sight, surrounded by savages—and bloody Most Brave had a look in his eye that Gray was coming to greatly dislike.

He had to find a way off this island, which seemed somewhat contradictory, considering the fact that he had been consumed with only one burning purpose day and night for weeks—*to get on this island!*

Gray realized with a start that a battery of eyes were fixed on him, making him wonder if he had just spoken his thoughts out loud.

"Are ye all right?" Bonnie queried, sounding concerned.

"Fine."

She hesitated, looking as if she didn't quite believe him, and then she gestured to the leader. "He asked you something."

Chagrined, Gray asked the man to repeat his question, and then for some sadistic reason, he went on to explain that a near-death experience, sun exposure, lack of food, and the very distinct possibility that his knees were about to give way were his reasons for the request, managing with uncharacteristic aplomb to completely alienate their not-so-gracious host.

"What did ye say tae him? He looks like a storm cloud."

Gray realized he wasn't handling the situation well. But it seemed some cruel joke to be spit out by the sea and land at the feet of this puling youth who had probably just that minute sprouted his first chin hairs.

With an expression that warned Gray to heed caution, Bem Corajoso repeated his request—or what the man termed a request, rather. It sounded more like an imperial command to Gray's ears.

"He wants us to join him in a feast. It seems we have

crashed upon his sandy shores on a high holy day."
Gray thought it prudent to leave out the part about the
tribute to Bonnie's bravery.

Such farrago would only swell her head anyway—
although Most Brave had made it quite clear that only
Bonnie's intervention and his respect for her skill had
saved them from being part of whatever religious sacrifices took place in this barbaric, uncharted land where
Gray doubted any law existed beside that of the chief
who, he imagined, yearned to sever Gray's intestines
from his body.

"A feast sounds lovely," Bonnie remarked, patently
unaware of the undercurrent swirling around her. "I'm
famished."

Gray frowned at her. "So glad you're viewing this
misadventure as a pleasant afternoon romp."

His comment effectively wiped any pleasure from her
face. "I'm not!"

"Doesn't look that way from where I'm standing."

"Would ye prefer I spat in the man's face?"

"You did it to me."

"This isn't the time tae be bringing up the past! I'm
trying tae keep us alive."

"Captain?" Gray vaguely heard someone call, but his
attention was focused solely on the vexing brat in front
of him.

"That's my job," he told her.

" 'Tis just like a man tae make such an idiotic statement!"

"Idiotic!"

"Captain?" the voice came again, a bit more urgently.

Bonnie rounded on Gray. "If ye hadn't noticed, we
are all but defenseless."

"I noticed." Damn, why did she have to be the logical
one? He knew all that. But the recognition wasn't
enough to stop the irrational thoughts running through
his head. Emotions warred inside him—damnably

uncomfortable emotions at that, foreign and bloody unnerving, and he wished to hell they'd go away.

Bonnie jammed her fists on her hips, which hiked up her already revealing shirt. "If ye are so observant, then why don't ye ken that we are making headway? Or is it that ye prefer tae die?"

Gray alternately fought off irritation and a fast case of escalating desire as his gaze slid downward to the deep *V* of skin visible at Bonnie's throat, four buttons having gone missing from his once pristine tailor-made shirt. He wondered if Bonnie realized how little she wore. He was fairly certain every man around them noticed.

Gray scowled. "We're in enough trouble here without you batting your eyelashes at this heathen," he pushed through his clenched teeth.

"Batting my—you're insane! I think that bash on the head I gave ye really muddled your wits!"

"Captain?"

The page went ignored again. "And I bloody well deserve another clobbering for not leaving you back in Scotland! God save me from waspish, know-it-all, knife-wielding females!" Gray felt like ripping his hair out, but not as much as he wished he could retract his words, especially after seeing the pain in Bonnie's eyes; it ravaged him.

"I wish ye had left me behind! I didn't want tae come with ye in the first place!"

Gray forgot all about the apology forming on his lips. "Now wait a damn minute. I—"

"Captain!"

As one, Bonnie and Gray spun around to face the person speaking: Prophet.

"What is it, man?" Gray bit out, angry at the interruption. He had been about to make a good point.

"Aren't you forgetting something?" He nodded toward the leader, promptly reminding Gray that his argument with Bonnie had just been witnessed by his entire crew and a group of hostile savages. Christ! Bonnie had a way of making him forget himself.

Dredging up what composure he had left, Gray turned to Bem Corajoso, choking on the apology he forced from his lips and repressing the urge to throttle the son of a bitch when he gave Gray an amused smirk.

The man then posed a question that took Gray off guard, caught up as he was in his black mood. So he was surprised how quickly he responded, though after the words left his mouth, he felt a bit dazed.

Later he knew he would tell himself that myriad reasons had caused him to say what he did, words he thought he'd never speak in his lifetime. Hunger. Ingesting too much saltwater. Anger-induced delirium. The sun in his eyes. Basic confusion. Mistaken translation.

Bonnie tapped him on the shoulder. "What did he say?"

Gray regarded her through eyes that had gone to tunnel vision. "He said we bicker like two people who have been mates for a hundred years."

"Mates?" she gasped, as if he'd just told her that he was in the habit of roasting babies every third Sunday.

"Horrible thought, isn't it?" Gray waited for her stinging retort but none was forthcoming.

Instead, Bonnie stared at him, her expression almost pained, as if . . . as if he had hurt her. But only if she cared about him would his comment have stung, and she didn't care about him. Did she?

"What did ye tell him . . . about us?"

Us. Was there such a thing? Gray wondered. And why did the thought of something other than the singular state in which he had lived in, a world that only consisted of words like *me, you,* and *them,* but never *us,* appeal to some untapped, heavily guarded place inside him. How could he have allowed this change to take place? Had he even recognized it?

And why did the subdued quality of Bonnie's voice gnaw at him? A belligerent, proud Bonnie he could deal with, but not a Bonnie who gazed at him with eyes that looked as if they had lost some of their faith, some of their trust. Not a Bonnie who suddenly appeared so very fragile. One tear . . . one damn tear would break him.

Perhaps that was what forced him to forgo a judicious reply to her question and seek that common ground where he could once more find steady footing beneath the barrage of her formidable temper.

"I said what any self-respecting man would say about a woman who nagged him unto death and drove him to the very brink of insanity. I told him you were my wife."

Chapter 20

"*Wife!*"

Bonnie was incredulous, but more than that she was furious with Gray, perhaps more than she needed to be and certainly more than the situation warranted. But being angry was better than the way she had felt when he had said how horrible being her mate would be. That had been an unexpected blow that hurt her more than it should have.

But what was worse was how she felt upon first hearing that word from his mouth. *Wife.* Glowing warmth had spread through her limbs like wildfire, and the realization that she actually liked the idea, even the tiniest bit, dashed her with ice-cold water.

Bonnie remembered when she'd seen Gray lying face-down on the beach. She had been so sure he was dead. Her soul had plummeted to the furthest depths of despair. Then he had stirred, and the world soared back to life.

She hadn't meant to be brave when she'd thrown her dirk at the warrior who had threatened Gray. All she had known was the need to save him. The repercussions of her actions had not mattered. A voice inside her had whispered that, without Gray, nothing would matter. But she could not confess such a thing, now or ever.

"Ye tell him the truth right this minute!" she demanded, standing toe to toe with her pretend husband, whose gaze drifted to her mouth, staring in a way that made swallowing difficult, that look at odds with the words he spoke.

"Trust me, I'd like nothing better than to retract such an ugly statement. Just saying the word *wife* makes me break out in hives. But unless you're prepared to let this savage have your body, you'd best learn to like me a great deal and attempt to act the devoted wife—as much as it may pain you to do so. Consider it practice for all the years you'll be spending with that caveman you intend to marry."

Bonnie ached to smack him—and then kiss him with all the passion she possessed. *You'd best learn to like me a great deal.* She already liked him far too much for her own peace of mind.

"But if you don't believe me, you are welcome to discover for yourself what he has in store for you. However, I feel duty bound to point out that that's not a piece of driftwood beneath his loincloth."

Bonnie's cheeks flamed at his coarse remark. Even so, she couldn't help darting a quick glance at Most Brave's manly attributes, discovering, to her horror, that Gray had not exaggerated. A hard-to-miss bulge strained against the material wrapped snugly around his hips.

"I'm the lesser of the two evils right now," he added tersely, bringing Bonnie's embarrassed gaze back to him. "You have nothing to fear from me. I wouldn't touch you if you begged me!"

The rest of their feud was cut off as Most Brave finally got fed up and shoved Gray's shoulder, nodding for him to move forward. Apparently they were to be guests at the feast whether they liked it or not.

In a less than loverlike way, Gray clamped his hand

possessively around her wrist and practically dragged her along behind him. Bonnie longed to kick him in his shin, but felt Most Brave's presence closely behind them, forcing her to seethe in silence.

Bonnie tried to concentrate on their surroundings to take her mind off the feel of Gray's large hand burning against her flesh, heat blossoming when he started stroking his thumb back and forth across the tender underside of her wrist.

She doubted he realized what he was doing, or at least she thought that was the case. He seemed completely oblivious to her, though he had slowed his pace somewhat, and his grip was no longer quite so painful.

And somewhere along the well-worn path they traversed, shaded beneath swaying palms and gently doused in the growing perfume of flowers, Gray's hand slipped down to clasp hers, his strong, lean fingers entwining with hers, saying all the things he couldn't, that he would protect her with his very life, that everything would be all right. Trust him.

Bonnie gently squeezed his hand, and when his gaze drifted to hers, a faintly puzzled expression in those beautiful silver eyes, she gave him a hesitant smile. She couldn't be sure, because he looked away, but she thought he had smiled in return. Just the thought of that smile blew a warm wind through her, taking away the fear . . . and some of the sting of Gray's earlier words.

Bonnie glanced around then, the scenery beckoning her eye. If they had to be stranded, they couldn't have found a more entrancing place to have been cast ashore.

The landscape was a moving artwork, rustling trees and shifting pink sands and a cool, sweet breeze bending the heads of flowers that captured the essence of a rainbow in a vibrant kaleidoscope.

All around the birds were singing as if a molten sunrise was cresting over the horizon. In the distance, clouds caressed verdant hills. And above them, gentle ribbons of watercolor swept the sky, like the effortless stroke of a painter's brush, a sight beyond imagination.

As they passed a wild explosion of spiked and barbed agave running riot in between the crevices of an out-cropping of rocks, Gray plucked a dainty bud and handed it to her. The gesture was so incredibly tender for a man who had been gruff and hot-tempered such a short while earlier. Bonnie tucked the flower behind her ear, soft petals stroking her temple.

So absorbed was she that she barely noticed time passing until, at last, they broke from the seclusion of the tall, fringed trees and came into a clearing that opened up into a surprisingly large village; one that, on first sight, appeared unexpectedly modern.

A long row of single-storied dwellings nestled close to one another, equipped with broad eaves and low-pitched roofs, bake sheds mottled and browned by the sun, and cylindrical chimneys reminiscent of a minia-ture minaret releasing thin streams of smoke, the air scented with the twigs and heather brought down from the hillsides. And on each door, testifying to the devout religious beliefs Most Brave had briefly spoken of, were crudely painted Immaculate Conceptions.

Towering in the distance behind the village was a hill facing the sea, a checkerboard of green and yellow fields borne right to the crest against the blue sky, only marred by crimson slashes that Gray told her were clay extrac-tions, the material used in their buildings. Dry stone dikes, like those in Scotland, divided the fields.

Bonnie had been wondering if any women inhabited the island, having seen nothing but men thus far. The idea of being the only female was more than a little daunting, more so after Gray's comment regarding Most Brave's desire for her.

Therefore, she was quite relieved to see an equal share of women working dutifully around the village, spreading wheat to dry on flat boulders or hanging newly harvested maize to dry on a cruciform framework under thatch, some preparing to mill the dried corn into flour. Not even the husks were wasted, but instead stuffed into flaxen satchels that resembled pillows and mattresses.

Absorbed, Bonnie nearly fell over a fat pig that stepped into her path. It squealed angrily at her, even took a few threatening steps toward her before the warrior chief barked out a single sharp command, sending the animal trotting off with a disgruntled stride.

The ruckus roused the villagers to the newcomers' arrival, bringing a pack of mocha-skinned natives swarming in a circle around them, speaking in voices of singing cadences and nasal vowels.

Older men, with leathery faces trundled up from the beach, long sticks slung across their wiry shoulders like the scales of justice, large, shining swordfish dangling down.

Bonnie was shuffled along amid a whirlwind of bodies. She didn't realize she had jammed herself into Gray's side until she felt his lips brush reassuringly against her ear and his low, deep voice whisper, "Don't worry. Everything will be all right."

A moment later, however, he tensed, the arm at her waist pulling her tighter against him as Most Brave moved in front of them, gesturing to her and barking out words she didn't understand. Gray's face hardened, and he wedged her slightly behind him, replying to the leader with a few guttural words and a negating slash of his hand through the air.

The warrior took several long strides forward. Gray broke away from her and matched the man step for step, escalating her panic as to what was about to transpire.

A hand clamped down on her shoulder then, startling her. "Ssh, lass. Calm yourself," came a familiar voice.

Prophet eased up beside her in a hobbling gate. Bonnie glimpsed the stained bandage around his leg, a memory flashing through her mind of him shoving her out of the way of a falling mast. Words of thanks were overridden by the sound of rising hostilities between Gray and the leader.

"What's going on between them, Prophet? What are they saying?"

"The chief wants you to go with the women to get cleaned up for the fiesta. Gray just told him you're not going anywhere without him, that you are his wife and you will stay beside your husband."

Bonnie waited for Prophet to make some comment about her new status as Gray's wife, yet he said nothing, which she appreciated.

She took in Gray's menacing stance and feared what might happen. While his staunch vow to protect her pleased Bonnie, she still wanted to berate him for his foolishness. Going with the women to bathe was not so important that he need challenge the warrior over it.

To her relief, the altercation subsided, and Gray returned to her side, looping his arm possessively about her waist, as if declaring she belonged to him, leaving Bonnie feeling distinctly like chattel instead of a cherished spouse.

"What happened?" she urged when Gray said nothing.

When he looked down at her, Bonnie was surprised to find the hint of a grin on his face and a heated, hungry expression in his eyes. *"We,* dear wife, are going to bathe."

Five women and two men accompanied Gray and Bonnie as they trekked to the highest island point, the view growing even more spectacular as they ascended.

To their left were the ripening fields of wheat, barley, and maize Bonnie had glimpsed earlier: dark, defining lines of dry stone walls sketching out rows. Stunning white butterflies flitted from dark barley spikes to shimmering maize, from myrtle grove to broom windbreak.

To their right, the rock face could hardly be seen through the dense covering of trees and bushes, euca-

lyptus, holly, and gnarled, twisted trunks of giant
heather. Even at this height, where the wind blew
straight from the Atlantic, she could smell the wafting
incense of pine. Where it came from, she could not
discern.

The villagers, she had noted earlier, appeared quite
content with their lives, moving about in the process of
their daily chores as if they didn't know or care that
another world existed outside their own.

Through translated conversation between Gray and
one of the women, Bonnie had discovered that the
island was entirely self-sustaining. They grew their own
grains and vegetables and even had animals. The girl
motioned to the chickens mingling among a small yet
plump herd of sheep. A short distance beyond were a
handful of black hens, which, according to Gray, served
a more important purpose beside food to the villagers.

"They're killed for the first meal in a new house,"
he explained. "The people believe they ward off death.
The carcass will be carried to each of the rooms and
then left in the maize loft, the pigsty, and the byre to
protect the human and animal occupants from the evil
eye. And if fever or skin disease befalls the inhabitants
later, then blood from the comb of another black hen
will be taken as a cure."

Bonnie would have preferred that story remain untold as it rang of superstition, causing her to wonder if
these people had other strange customs—ones she'd
prefer far less than bleeding black hens.

Upon reaching the top of the hill, Bonnie swiveled
in a slow circle, feeling as if she stood at the very pinnacle
of the universe. She could see for miles.

From their vantage point, she glimpsed the seabed
through the clear glassy water, sparkling in the late
afternoon sun, resplendent with spectacular submerged
colors. A thousand pounds of precious gems could not
demand such viridians and violet-ultramarines, azure
flowing into jade, cobalt to turquoise wreathed by

indigo, advancing in a brilliant serpentine blend to the shore.

Even at this distance, the dull thunder of surf reached Bonnie's ears, waves booming in mighty clashes and then fading, fusing one with the other into a musical composition.

A cloud covering coated the island from one end to the other, a tricky device, Bonnie now realized, enabling a person on shore to look out and see everything. But from the sea, the island would be hidden from view, as she knew from experience.

At that point, the little group diverged. The women headed down a set of rough-hewn steps carved into the side of a hill toward a pool of water that bubbled slightly around the edges and held a brown tinge to it.

"It's a *caldeira,*" Gray explained. "A crater filled with warm water, the product of some long-ago volcanic explosion, from which this island and all the surrounding islands eventually sprang."

Peering up into the handsome, rugged face that Bonnie thought she would never see again brought on a wave of delayed reaction to all that she and Gray had suffered, together and apart, as if her body and mind were telling her it was now acceptable to let out all that she had repressed thus far—the fear, the despair. Her knees buckled slightly beneath her.

Gray quickly took hold of her arms, his eyes filled with concern. "Are you all right?"

Bonnie dredged up her strength. "I'll be fine. I guess everything is beginning tae catch up with me."

"You've been through a lot." His thumb feathered across her cheek. "You'll feel better once you get in the water and relax."

Bonnie trembled from that tender caress, and the idea of easing into the water with Gray made a rush of anticipation sluice through her.

They followed the guards, who had remained with them, over the peak of the hill and partway down the other side. Along the twisting path, Bonnie noted boulders that had etchings carved into them, mostly religious symbols, which only drove home more fully the strength of the villagers' conviction in their faith. She stopped to study one rather intricate carving.

"They're like hieroglyphics," Gray remarked, pointing to a cluster of five objects. "These small shields are *quinas*. Each shield has five dots—or bezants, as they're known. In religious accounts, the *quinas* are meant to signify the five wounds Christ suffered on the Cross, and the dots represent the thirty pieces of silver for which Judas betrayed Christ—if you count the five dots in the middle twice—the logic of some zealot trying to divine meaning where there was none."

"And these?" Bonnie pointed to another group of etchings.

"That's an armillary sphere, depicting the celestial meridians, equators, tropics, and zodiac. In Columbus's day, people believed they could predict events, even cataclysmic events, by the way planets and stars aligned."

One of the guards waved a spear at them then, indicating that they were to move on. As they continued down the hill, a roaring sound filled Bonnie's ears.

Reaching a flat ledge, they pushed through a wealth of thick foliage. And there in front of them was the source of the sound, a pool of water three times the size of the one the women bathed in—and topped by the most incredible waterfall.

The men signaled them forward and then one spoke to Gray. "They said we have a half hour," he told her.

Bonnie longed to toss off her single piece of dirty attire but darted a wary glance at the warriors over Gray's shoulder. "Are they going tae stand there the whole time?"

"Not if I can help it." He winked at her and then snapped out a few words to the guards, who exchanged grins. A moment later, they disappeared beyond the dense foliage, leaving Bonnie and Gray in a world that, for the moment, was all their own.

"What did ye say tae them?"

He brushed a tendril of hair off her face, the light caress sending a quiver of yearning through Bonnie. "I told them we wanted privacy."

The way he said the words, husky and filled with secret promise, made Bonnie's heart beat in thick strokes. "Do ye think they'll come back?"

"I'm not inclined to care at this moment."

Neither was she, Bonnie thought, gazing into Gray's eyes. And as if he had seen into her heart and knew what she desired most, he drew her up hard against him and kissed her breathless, ravaging her lips until every fiber of her being ached with raw, wanton hunger.

How she had missed him. Every day that he had stayed away from her on the ship felt multiplied tenfold. Stubborn pride had kept her from going to him, but it would not keep her from him now. She realized that this, more than anything, was what she had been waiting for, to be in his arms again, to feel protected . . . loved.

"Bonnie," he murmured in a sensual rasp, peppering kisses along her jaw, down her throat, cupping her breasts with both hands. "I'm sorry . . . God, so sorry." The words began pouring out, words that said he had known the same torment as she. "You went overboard and, Christ, I thought I was going to die. I couldn't save you. Damn me, I couldn't."

"Ssh . . . no apologies." She nibbled the corner of his lip, wrapping her arms around his neck, craving nothing more than to get as close to him as possible. "It wasn't your fault."

"It was," he groaned, sounding caught between the twin demons of despair and desire. "I was the captain."

She sifted her fingers through his silky mane. "You're human first."

He made a wordless sound and yanked her shirt over her head, baring her body to his devouring gaze. Then he stripped out of his trousers and stood unabashed in front of her, fully aroused.

He lifted her then, and Bonnie wrapped her legs around his waist as he waded into the pool, his mouth fusing with hers as the water brushed her calves, and then her hips, up to her waist, the thundering of the waterfall no match for the roaring sound of her blood, pumping through her veins in hot rivulets.

The water made her body weightless, floating in a magical place created by Gray's mouth, his body, liquid making everything that much more slick, that much more erotic.

Gray's hands captured her waist, raising her so that her breasts were level with his mouth. Bonnie arched her back when he took her nipple in his mouth, her whole body tensing with the pleasure he lavished on her, filling her senses with a cornucopia of earthly delights.

She reached between them and wrapped her fingers around his engorged shaft. He released a guttural groan as she began to stroke him, loving the feel of silk over steel, needing him inside her with a desperation that bordered on painful.

She thrust her hips closer and slid her cleft over his sweet hardness, riding the heated length in the rhythm her body dictated, faster with every flick of his tongue on her nipple.

He cupped her buttocks, bringing her closer to the heat, increasing the pace and friction between their bodies. Her moans became wild, frenzied. Then he stopped the heavenly torture.

"No," she begged.

"Shh, little tiger." He wadded farther into the pool, a cascade of water pouring over Bonnie as he took them into the fury of the waterfall—and beyond.

The water raged around them, but only a mist touched her skin. She opened her eyes to discover that Gray had enclosed them in a glistening dream, away from prying eyes and worries. There, Gray resumed his erotic ministrations, quickly bringing her back to a fevered pitch as he rocked within the folds of her moist valley.

Bonnie clutched his shoulders, helpless to do any more than hang on as hot pleasure boiled within her, climbing to that bright spiraling place, the brink of climax. She wanted him inside her, to pulse around his shaft, not his fingers.

"Gray . . . please." She prayed he would not deny her as she took hold of his erection and positioned the hot, hard length against the secret spot that longed for him. He groaned and shook his head, grabbing hold of her wrist as the tip of his heat teased her silken sheath.

His jaw clenched in torment. "No, Bonnie . . . We can't."

"I must have ye . . . all of ye." She eased down on his shaft, dying in ecstasy as he filled her, a little bit, then a bit more.

"God." He dropped his forehead to her shoulder. "Don't do this to me, Bonnie. I can't. I won't."

"Why?" The word came out half cry, half protest. "Why won't ye give me all of yourself?"

"Because I can't, damn it! I won't be the other man! I can't have you and then give you up! Can't you see? Do you even understand what can happen here? A child, Bonnie. A baby. I won't have a bastard running around with my blood in its veins. I won't subject another human being to what I—" He cut himself off. "Just let me love you as best as I know how. Please, God . . . don't ask for more."

Bonnie closed her eyes, but nothing could stop the well of emotions inside her from overflowing, sending scalding tears down her cheeks.

"No, Bonnie . . . oh, God, don't." He sounded anguished, torn—and his pain only rent her soul that much more because she knew, in her woman's heart, that he cared for her, perhaps in the only way he knew how. "I'm a bastard, do you understand? A true bastard—damned and out of place and bloody unworthy."

"Don't say that!"

"My mother had a lover. Does that spell it out for you? She had lots of lovers, in fact. I don't know who I am. What I am. Where I belong. But, by Christ, what I do know is that I won't foist that label on anyone else. I won't drag anyone down into this fucking nomadic existence. I won't take from you something that I don't know how to give back. You have Ewan. You have a life. I don't have anything." His voice seemed to crack beneath a mighty weight as he repeated, "I don't have anything."

He turned from her then and plunged beneath the water, never hearing the words on her lips, words to tell him that she didn't want anything from him.

Except his love.

Chapter 21

Sunset was spreading between the two rugged head-lands as Bonnie emerged from one of the small dwellings, home to several of the unmarried females.

She no longer wore Gray's ripped shirt but was instead garbed in the native attire of soft animal skin, two separate pieces leaving an uncomfortably large portion of her body exposed. The top barely covered her breasts.

Although Bonnie had never considered herself the missish type, especially growing up with four brothers, she felt almost shy as she stepped out into the open in her new clothing. Her nervousness diminished as soon as she spotted Gray.

He sat away from the group, alone on the beach, the last rays of the dying sun coating his dark hair with streaks of red fire. Her heart clenched painfully at the sight of him. In the company of all these people, never had he appeared more alone.

A short distance from him, children splashed in the white-crested breaking waves, a few sitting in the sand as foam surged over their legs. They had spent the afternoon making sand ships, equipping them with masts and anchors compiled from branches and twigs and whatever debris was at hand.

Gray turned to look at the children as a burst of merriment rose into the air, his profile in silhouette against the backdrop of the setting sun, his expression poignant, a mental picture Bonnie doubted she'd ever forget.

He had said he didn't have anything to give her, yet he possessed everything she wanted and didn't know it. She had tried, but she couldn't get past the barrier he had erected.

Prophet had told her once that she could make things right for Gray, heal his wounds, but she had failed. Oh, how she had failed. While she had dwelt solely within the confines of her fantasy world, Gray had remained grounded in reality. She was betrothed to another man, bound by family honor to uphold her agreement, and should she and Gray survive and find a way back to their respective lives, she would never see him again. Unbidden, a painful thought popped into her head.

How can I live without him?

He glanced over his shoulder then and saw her standing there. A tentative smile lifted the corner of his lips, his expression endearingly boyish, asking if he was still welcome, which only made her feel like crying again. Hating him would have been so much easier, so much less complicated. But she had failed at even that.

He rose, dusting his hands off on his pants, still bare-chested, still beautiful. He remained where he was, looking uncertain. Bonnie could not resist, could not turn away as she knew she should for the protection of her own heart.

Instead, she headed toward him, knowing he couldn't help who or what he was, knowing she would not waste whatever time they had together dwelling on what couldn't be. There might not be any tomorrows for them, but there was now, and she would take it.

She stopped before him, unsure of what to say when

so many words longed to spill forth. He reached out and picked up a length of her hair, fanning it through his fingers, his expression tender.

"You look beautiful," he murmured.

Pleasure flushed her cheeks, leaving her unable to shake her newly discovered shyness. "I never thought I'd say this, but . . . I think I'd prefer a dress."

He chuckled low in his throat. "Fierce little Bonnie in a dress? What would people say?"

Bonnie didn't care what anyone would say. Where once she had been so touchy about anyone believing her anything but tough, self-reliant, not needing or wanting help, which somehow had equaled not allowing herself to be feminine, now she felt liberated by the same things, free to take pride in being a woman.

Gray's expression changed then, growing more somber as he said softly, "Would it be selfish of me to say that I wish no one else was here to see you looking like you do right now?"

Bonnie shook her head and whispered, "No."

She felt rooted to the spot as the sun began its final slide behind the horizon and torchlight gilded the night, casting Gray in shades of gold and bronze.

The enchantment was broken at Gray's low, fierce curse. "Damn." A scowl clouded his face as he glanced over her shoulder.

Bonnie followed his gaze and saw Most Brave striding toward them, his gaze raking her body with open lust. She had been so blinded by her fear for Gray, and then her anger, that she hadn't given much thought to the warrior's interest in her. Now she could think of little else.

Most Brave halted before them. The men exchanged a few words, then the warrior strode away. When Bonnie glanced up at Gray, she could see the strain around his eyes. "What did he say?"

"He wants you to sit next to him as a tribute to your bravery."

"And what did ye tell him?"

A hint of a mocking smile touched his lips as his gaze slid her way. "I told him we'd both be honored."

They sat in the sand within a circle of torches.

Had the outside world looked in upon the scene, it might have appeared like a simple celebration of faith and hospitality, but Bonnie did not delude herself as to her status. She, Gray, and his crew were captives, perhaps treated better than most and certainly freer, but that could change at a moment's notice.

The food flowed in seemingly endless supply as dish after dish was brought forth. Her stomach grumbled rather loudly, reminding her that she hadn't eaten in nearly two days.

Heaping platters of scarlet crabs, hot stone-baked bread, the swordfish the old men had brought up from the sea earlier that day, several flat baked cakes made of corn meal called *bolo de milho*, squid, *cracas*, a kind of oyster, and at least ten other foods were placed before them. No meat was served.

Into crudely fashioned goblets was poured the reddest wine Bonnie had ever seen, so deep in color, it appeared almost like blood, which in and of itself would have turned her away from drinking it even if the peculiar tang that wafted up to her hadn't. She made a face.

Gray chuckled when he saw her expression. "It's *vinho de cheiro,*" he told her. "Smell wine."

Bonnie wrinkled her nose. "What a perfect name. It smells terrible."

"It's rather potent as well, so it's probably best if you don't drink it."

She shot him a challenging look. "And are ye saying that I can't hold my liquor? My brothers and I make whiskey for a living. And that, too, is rather potent."

Gray knew that to be true. He distinctly recalled how

well the scotch had numbed his brain the night of Sarah Douglass's murderer.

The memory troubled him, so he shook it off. He had other things to concern himself with this night, like how he planned to get off the island. His quest to find the sacred heart was no longer as important as it had once been. Getting Bonnie and his crew out of here alive took precedence.

He had spotted a group of canoes down along the west side of the island on their way back from the water pool—after his ill-fated bath with Bonnie. Just thinking of those moments with her made him grow hot and cold in alternate bursts.

Jesus, he should have kept his hands off her. He had done so well on the ship, had shown restraint he didn't know he possessed, but the second she glanced up at him in their secluded paradise, safe, whole, unhurt, with eyes full of desire, reflecting the ache in him, Gray's control snapped, breaking his will and leaving him shaking with the force of his need.

And then he'd had to turn away, and doing so had been the hardest thing he'd ever done in his life. For once, he was being noble, a trait rarely associated with him. He'd never suspected nobility would slowly kill him, drive him crazy until the thought of madness seemed appealing.

But if he had allowed himself to slip inside Bonnie's gloved warmth, to take her wholly, completely—he didn't think he'd be able to walk away, and he had to walk away. He had no right to think of a life with her, no right to expect her to leave her fiancé, her brothers, her kin. Scotland. No right to think she'd want a bastard.

A sudden shout jerked Gray to attention, his hand automatically reaching for the knife he usually sheathed at his hip and coming away weaponless; he had been stripped by the sea of his defenses.

One of the warriors gesticulated wildly in his direction, the man's speech so rapid, Gray couldn't discern all the words—though a few stood out.

The ring, the ring, the man kept repeating. *Look at the ring!*

Then all eyes were fastened on him, and Gray looked down at his father's ring, the thick gold glinting wickedly in the light of one of the torches.

Unexpectedly, Most Brave leaned forward and seized Gray's hand. Gray fisted his other hand in an instinctive move to slug the bastard but found four spears aimed at him and Bonnie clinging to his arm, trying to tug his hand down.

With a muttered expletive, Gray allowed the man to wrench the ring from his finger. Only Bonnie's whispered words to remain calm kept him from violence.

The chieftain studied the ring, turning it over and over again, studying it at all angles while commenting on the insignia as a growing number of his men gathered around.

Then he glanced up sharply. *"Onde recebeu este?"* he demanded.

Gray had to refrain from telling the man it was none of his bloody business where he got the ring. Knowing Bonnie and his crew were depending on him to survive, he replied shortly, "It belonged to my father."

"Qual entre você é seu pai?" He pointed to Prophet.

"No—my father's dead." The words stung the part of Gray that had been left raw by his father's passing.

"O mal. Sorte má . . . Como o pássaro de demônio."

Evil, he called the ring. Bad luck . . . like the demon bird.

The demon bird, Gray's mind repeated.

Oh, Christ. Lady Beatrice. He had forgotten all about her. He had just believed she had survived, that those mighty wings had carried her wherever she needed to go.

"Where is the bird?" Gray demanded, already knowing the answer and wondering why the knowledge caused something to crumble inside him.

Somewhere along the line that stupid, ugly, goddamn loyal bird had become more than just a mockery of his mother and a symbol of things Gray wanted but could never have.

Most Brave's eyes held a malevolent cast as he replied, *"Matou."*

Killed.

"Carregou um animal pelo céu de noite como um specter de mal." The warrior made a graphic, thrusting gesture toward his chest with his knife. *"Lanceei a besta pelo coração."*

"Goddamn you!" Gray roared, shooting to his feet, his hands balling into fists at his sides. "It was no fucking evil specter. It was a damn bird. A damn bird!"

"Gray! Don't!" Bonnie jumped in front of him as Gray lunged toward the man who had killed his bird. The leader made not a single move, simply gazed up at Gray with an expression of immense satisfaction.

Gray tried to shove Bonnie out of the way, but she wouldn't budge. "Let it go . . . please," she begged, her words barely registering. Then she laid her hand gently against his cheek. "Gray."

Gray's gaze snapped to hers, tender blue eyes beseeching him to say no more, promising him a safe harbor for his grief if he only let go. Briefly, he closed his eyes, sucked in a deep breath . . . and then stepped back.

With the ease of a man who knew he was well protected, Most Brave rose and held up Gray's ring like a trophy. *"Manterei isto."*

Gray's jaw clenched. "Like hell you'll keep it."

The warrior ignored him. *"Irá bem com os outros um."*

A cold dart of anxiety spread through Gray at the man's claim. "You have another ring like that one?"

Most Brave nodded.

Gray shook his head. Impossible. He wouldn't believe

it. If another ring existed . . . then that might mean the gem existed as well.

He told himself to drop the subject, that the seditious prick was probably just baiting him. Gray's quest had ended when he nearly got Bonnie and his crew killed. He had failed, as he had failed too many times before.

But then he thought of Damien, of Silver Hills . . . of his father and what this dream had meant to him, and even as Gray glimpsed Prophet's wary expression, he still heard himself say, "I want to see this ring. Where is it?"

The chieftain regarded him for a long moment, and Gray suspected the man would reveal nothing. Instead, he shrugged and motioned for them to follow.

The parish church before them was tiny, single-celled, the façade wrought from basalt by some skilled but unschooled mason in the Portuguese baroque style, the craftsmanship fascinating in the same way an untrained concert pianist could be fascinating: genius despite lack of training. The church had been lovingly tended through hundreds of years of wind, water, and time's erosion.

They were ushered inside. Most of the furnishings were gone, except for the vintage altar and a primitive triptych over it, which Gray suspected harkened back to the time of Columbus.

One of the warriors came forward with a small, hand-made box with a cross crudely etched on the top. He opened it, revealing a yellowed piece of paper.

And a ring.

Wordlessly, Gray reached into the box and lifted out the ring. The gold gleamed as if it had just been polished. There was no doubt his ring and this ring were identical.

The magnitude of what was unfolding began to seep into Gray, freeing that last part of him that had truly believed his father had been duped, that he would forever be remembered as nothing but a dreamer, destined to lose in life no matter his best intentions.

Little pieces started falling into place, a correlation Gray hadn't made before, even though the obvious now seemed to have stood so clearly in front him. But of course the significance would pass by a man who had never been religious, who didn't believe an omnipotent god existed, a god of fairness, benevolence, one that would care about an illegitimate son or a dying man's last wish.

Gray read the words from the aged parchment: "There is only one Person in Jesus, and that Person is at the same time God and Man. His Heart, too, is Divine—it is the Heart of God."

The Sacred Heart of Jesus.

Slowly, Gray looked up. The men positioned in front of him parted, revealing what had been hidden, what he had been searching for.

Behind the altar, in an arched nave, stood the majestic figure of Jesus Christ, his head tilted downward to stare at the offering cupped in his palms.

A magnificent bloodred diamond.

Bonnie perched silently next to Prophet on the steps outside the little hutlike structure she and Gray were to share as husband and wife. She wasn't thinking about the long night ahead, of being so close to Gray and wanting to touch him but knowing she'd only cause distress instead of pleasure. Now her lone thought was of Gray's state of mind.

Where sand met sea, he roamed like a restless deity, moonlight streaking a path across the water, illuminating his frown and the heavy thoughts troubling him.

Bonnie was concerned. He seemed so distant, so remote since they'd left the church. She'd needed no translation to understand what had transpired. The glimmering gem had said it all. And what hadn't been said, Prophet had filled in.

"The islanders believe the stone is a divine gift from God, a glorious token meant for them to worship," he had told her on the way back to the village, repeating the story he had heard in the church. "They are convinced it holds mythical powers and will bring a lifetime of good fortune to those true at heart—and disaster to anyone whose intentions are not pure."

For some reason, the idea of the power the stone held seemed entirely believable to Bonnie. The natives had everything they wanted and appeared to be prospering.

"To keep in God's saving graces," Prophet continued, "they used to offer sacrifices."

That statement startled Bonnie from her contemplations about the stone. "What kind of sacrifices?"

Prophet hesitated, his expression uncomfortable, as if he had realized after the fact that he should have kept the information to himself. "It's probably best not to say."

Bonnie didn't intend to relent, even though a chill snaked down her spine at his words. "Ye mean human sacrifices?"

Prophet gave a brief nod, and the chill Bonnie felt turned into a sickening lump in her stomach.

"The jewel was stolen once, nearly four centuries ago, taken off the island by men the natives called *os demônios da mesma língua*—demons of the same tongue. Men who spoke the same language as the natives, but who didn't hold the same principles of religion. Pirates, or perhaps even Columbus and his sailors. They traveled between the islands and boldly seized whatever riches they found, even going so far as to take people as slaves."

"How did the jewel find its way back here then? Especially when the island is hidden by the mist?"

"I think someone on the initial voyage must have made a map. Cartographers were as necessary to voyages back then as the captain himself." Prophet scratched his fingers under his chin, a grimace showing his unhappiness over his heavily stubbled jaw. "As hard as it is to fathom the map surviving all these years, maybe Gray really had possessed the original."

Had possessed, Bonnie silently repeated. The map was gone now, disappeared in the scuffle in Lisbon after surviving who knows how many years before her interference. A piece of history lost forever because of her foolishness—and Gray had never said a word, never made her feel guilty for being the cause of his losing one of the few possessions bestowed upon him by his father. And she had never apologized for her role. She wished she had.

"Anyway," Prophet went on, "the chieftain spoke of another vessel returning years after the sacred heart was stolen. And with them was the jewel."

"But why would they return with it?"

"If the story holds true, the stone was ordered returned when Queen Isabella of Spain died. Isabella's daughter, known by most as Juana the Mad because of her frail mental state, was said to have secreted away the jewel after her mother's death, believing it cursed."

Cursed. Bonnie felt she was beginning to understand what being cursed truly entailed. Her eyes met Prophet's, and she knew the same thought ran through his mind.

"Juana fully believed her mother's fatal illness was the direct cause of the curse."

"It couldn't hold such power." *Could it?*

"We might not think so, but these people are very superstitious. During the years of the Holy Inquisition against Depraved Heresy—or the Spanish Inquisition, as it has become known—those who were not of *sangre limpia,* meaning of pure white Christian blood, were tortured and ritually burned at the stake, savage methods that carried far across the ocean. In their ignorance, people will murder for the sake of religion if they believe it is what has to be done to justify their ends.''

Prophet's words about sacrifices rang in Bonnie's ears. ''So Isabella's daughter had the sacred heart sent back in the hope of ridding herself of a curse?''

''More or less. Because of Juana's affliction, no one quite believed the story. They thought she had simply stolen the jewel off her dead mother's body and hidden it. For a girl who had everything, she had a habit of taking things that did not belong to her.

''And there was also the fact that her mother stood against Juana when she approached her father about marrying a man she loved but who he refused outright to consider. Juana took her mother's action as the worst of betrayals. There are some tales that even go so far as to say that Juana imbued the stone with its powers, that she had dabbled in witchcraft and cursed the stone, her way of striking back for having been denied her one true love.''

The story sounded not only fantastic but sad. ''What happened then?''

Prophet shrugged. ''No one knows. The ship bearing the stone never returned. What became of the fifty-seven men aboard is still a mystery.''

A mystery. Was that what she would become if she never got off this island? Bonnie wondered. Her family and friends never knowing what had happened to her, riddles and speculation forever shrouding her disappearance?

Yet the thought dimmed as her gaze strayed to Gray, standing alone down by the shore once again, his head bowed, the thickening night breeze teasing the ends of his hair. She was worried about him.

''He'll be all right,'' Prophet murmured, as if reading her mind. ''He always was too much of a thinker for his own good.''

''What's going tae happen tae us, Prophet?''

''We'll be just fine.'' But his words held forced optimism and his eyes conveyed a different story. "The captain will see to that."

Bonnie simply nodded. Yet as her gaze returned to Gray's solitary figure, she wondered who would be seeing to Gray while he was seeing to them.

Gray came to her as the moon peaked at its zenith in the sky and invisible ghouls invaded the stillness of the night, haunting the bay and the cliffs, the air stirring with diabolical cries.

Bonnie hugged herself, trying to keep from trembling, not wanting to reveal any weakness. She feared if she gave in to the terror, it would consume her.

Gray came to stand beside the bed, the light from the single, nearly extinguished torch casting exotic shadows on the contours of his face and splaying intriguing patterns across his bare chest.

Bonnie wanted him to lie with her, to hold her close and tell her again that everything would be all right. But she wouldn't ask, for to do so would seem too much like begging. She wanted Gray to need her simply and without remorse.

She closed her eyes as his knuckles swept down her cheek, the power of the emotions Gray invoked in her barely contained beneath one thin, easily shattered layer. Fear. Fear of losing him even though she'd never truly had him. All she had possessed was the illusion she'd built in her mind.

"Don't be afraid," he murmured, his fingers brushing down her throat in the lightest of caresses, his uncanny silver eyes plumbing the depths of her soul. "They're just *cagarros*—Mediterranean shearwaters." He had mistaken her trembling for fear of the strangely human-voiced birds whose sinister squawking cut right through her.

A sharp pang of awareness struck her then, reminding Bonnie of Lady Beatrice—and the look in Gray's eyes when he had discovered his beloved bird had been killed. A wild despair had simmered just below the surface, though outwardly he had given nothing away but anger. He would never have confessed it, but he had loved that bird.

He hadn't seen Lady Beatrice as ugly or predatory or a creature not meant to be tamed. What he had intended to be a mockery of his mother had, somewhere along the line, become very real.

But then, Gray had the wonderful ability to see below the surface, beneath outer beauty, beyond other people's preconceived notions.

Bonnie only wished he could see himself that clearly, see that he was not what his mother had made him or what society proclaimed him to be. But Gray's perception didn't extend to himself. He was blinded by his own self-loathing.

Another vision surfaced in Bonnie's mind, having lain dormant until this moment, when a connection had been discovered. She glanced over at Jack, asleep atop a mound of torn clothes Gray had scrounged from the wreckage, and Bonnie realized that she had found one small thing that might ease Gray's pain over the bird's death.

And so she said, "I believe Lady Beatrice saved Jack's life." The merit of that statement seemed not only possible but probable.

The pair had become friends over time. Lady Beatrice would swoop down from her perch to playfully taunt Jack, always remaining just far enough out of the puppy's jumping reach, occasionally stealing a toy or a piece of meat from Jack's bowl and emitting what seemed a chuckling caw as she soared skyward. Jack would retaliate by creeping up behind the bird when she came down from her nest for Gray's daily feeding, boldly plucking the bird's tail feathers.

They were indeed a pair, two animals who would never have coexisted under any other circumstances—

much like she and Gray, Bonnie thought. He was English and she was Scottish. Natural-born enemies, some would say, even today, after hostilities between the countries had long since died down. But taken out of their environment and thrown together, life had shown them that they had not been born enemies. They had been made that way.

The fingers that had been absently stroking her skin stopped abruptly, Gray's face clouding over. "What do you mean?"

"Look at Jack's shoulders. There are little puncture marks. I didn't know what they were when I first saw them. Now I believe they're from Lady Beatrice's claws."

Gray hesitated and then turned in Jack's direction, though he made no move forward. He simply stood there, and Bonnie wondered if she should have said anything. Perhaps he wanted no further reminders of the vulture he had saved from certain death on a swarming dock in India.

But then he padded across the floor and dropped to his haunches beside the pup, inspecting the tiny wounds, his expression lost in the shadows.

When he glanced up at her, Bonnie's breath caught in her throat at the gratitude reflected in his eyes. He was silently thanking her for telling him. She needed no words. That look would sustain her.

Slowly, he rose to his feet, the moment evaporating into something far more earthy. Elemental. Raw need battling conflict. Bonnie had never known Gray to be uncertain of himself, but he looked conflicted just then, his hands sliding into his trouser pockets as if he didn't know what else to do with them.

Abruptly, he turned away and headed for the door. "I'll sleep outside."

Bonnie sat up in bed. "Why?"

He stopped but would not look at her.

"Don't go." The words were so low, she wondered if she had spoken them at all. "Please, Gray."

"I can't stay, Bonnie. I just . . . can't."

"Just a few minutes . . . at least until I fall asleep."
She hadn't meant to ask, hadn't meant to give in to the
weakness, but she needed him, if only to feel his warmth
beside her, his breath fanning her hair, his solid presence lulling her worries into nonexistence.

A moment ticked past before he gave a single stiff
nod, his body tense, as if steeling himself for an unpleasant task. The realization pierced Bonnie like a mortal
wound.

She rolled to her side and squeezed her eyes tight.
"Go. Just get out of here."

A moment passed, then the door quietly opened and
clicked shut, sending Gray out into the night as silently
as he had come. Bonnie prayed no sound would betray
her, no noise reveal her silent sobbing. Only her pillow
would know the hot tears coursing down her cheeks.

Then the mattress sagged, a startled gasp dying on
her lips as a strong, solid arm curled about her waist,
pulling her close even as she resisted, a resistance that
withered as soon as Gray cradled her body next to his,
whispering words of sorrow and regret and desire in
her ear, yet never allowing himself to do more than
talk.

He was destined to remain still, to hold himself in
check when all about them faded into a shimmering
madness that neither their will nor the magnitude of
what they longed for could completely eradicate. Yet
they remained unmoving, not touching, two figures so
close but never more distant.

And as Bonnie drifted into an uneasy slumber, desire
and despair stayed with her, as did the chilling caw of
the *cagarros,* the sound like a harbinger of something
far more sinister taking place in the dead of night.

Chapter 22

"It's a fake."

Those were the first words Bonnie heard the next morning as she exited the cottage, waking to find Gray gone, only a faint indentation in the mattress to mark that he had ever been there at all.

She found him outside on the steps where she and Prophet had sat the night before watching him, absorbed in their own thoughts.

Now Gray and Prophet had their heads bent together, their conversation low as the village hummed with morning activity. The crew mingled about, not looking particularly like bereft castaways. Some flirted with the island women, who steadfastly avoided any contact; some explored their new surroundings; and others simply slept beneath the warm sun.

What a strange place they had found, Bonnie thought. They were captives, yet they roamed freely. But then, where were they to go? Where could they run? They were stranded in this place. Completely at the mercy of strangers whose customs they didn't understand and whose outward aspect seemed to hide something.

Bonnie started at a shrill sound that reminded her quite vividly of the *cagarros*. Their haunting cries had plagued her dreams, causing her to toss fitfully most of the night. Only Gray's soothing voice had warded off the demons.

Yet, remembering the way he had acted the night before, how he had wanted to escape into the night instead of remaining with her made Bonnie wonder if she had only imagined his calming words, the arms holding her tight, or the visions of a silver-eyed dream hunter who stalked the creatures stalking her and sent them scurrying into the shadows.

Bonnie shook off the thought and asked, "What's a fake?" which brought Gray and Prophet's gazes swinging over their shoulders.

Gray's face showed signs of fatigue, yet it also outlined his distress at having discovered her standing in the doorway. Clearly he had not wanted her to overhear his conversation with Prophet. Why?

"The diamond," he answered reluctantly. "It's not real."

Bonnie frowned. "I don't understand. Why would ye think it isn't real?"

"Probably because it's glass—or of the quality of glass, perhaps a lesser stone. The deception lies in its stunning, nearly authentic replication."

Gray stood, wrapping his hand around the wood column holding up the eaves that provided shelter from the sun, allowing Bonnie to glimpse the concern in his eyes.

She took a step toward him but faltered when she noted the way his grip tightened on the column, so acute his knuckles shone white, the same tension racking him as the night before when she'd asked him to hold her.

What had she done so horrible to push him away? Was it just that he could see the truth of her feelings for him in her eyes? She knew he wanted no part of love, no part of marriage.

No part, it seemed, of her.

Even Prophet glanced away when she looked at him. But she did not miss the sorrow in his eyes—or the hint of pity. Something splintered inside Bonnie: anger at Gray's aloofness and her own stupidity for falling in love with someone who could not or would not ever love her in return.

She swung away from them, back into the house. She went to slam the door, but a force far stronger held it open. She didn't need to look to know what that force was. She could sense every heated inch of Gray behind her. Her body trembling, she whirled around to face him.

His face was a study in fury, almost angrier than she. But what did he have to be upset about? He wasn't the one being rejected time and again.

"What the devil is the matter with you?" he asked tightly.

"Little ye care." God, how she hated the petulant quality of her voice.

She shoved past him, not sure where she was going, only knowing she had to get away, but he grabbed her arm and reeled her around.

"Don't run away from me, damn it."

"Why not? Ye do it tae me all the time." Sweet Lord, she had never expected this to happen to her, this falling, the endless, unstoppable descent.

His gaze darted sideways, reminding Bonnie of Prophet's presence, but she didn't care. What did it matter anymore? Did Gray think the man was blind? That he didn't recognize what was going on?

Bonnie tried to wrench free of his grip, but he would not let her go. "No one is trying to hide anything from you," he said. "If you'd give me a bloody minute, I'd explain."

Bonnie stared at him mutinously. "So explain."

He frowned, then let her go, driving his hands into his pockets, as if he couldn't believe he'd willingly touched her. Bonnie wished he'd find a shirt, cover up that chest she longed to smooth her palms over, the tropical rays having darkened his face and upper torso, making him look like a glorious god born of the sun.

"I knew the stone in the church was a fake as soon as I got a good look at it," he began. "The gem didn't have the right clarity or the same reflective characteristics of a diamond. I didn't think much of it at first because I figured the natives had made a duplicate after the stone was stolen to appease whatever god they bowed to. Then two things struck me.

"First, I realized that only a truly skilled artisan could have copied the real sacred heart to such perfection, and I doubt anyone here had that kind of expertise. And second, these people—whom I suspect are basically unchanged from their ancestors—don't strike me as the type to offer up a substitute to a god they believe needs human sacrifices to keep it mollified."

Bonnie processed all Gray's revelations and arrived at only one conclusion. "Are ye saying they don't know the stone isn't genuine?"

"Exactly."

"But how could they not know?"

"Nearly a decade passed between the time the stone was stolen and the time it was returned. I think the villagers saw something that looked like the diamond, had the same cuts, sparkled when held up to the light, and assumed it *was* the diamond, perhaps not comprehending two items could look similar but be the product of entirely different materials. At first glance, salt and sugar might appear to be the same thing when placed side by side. Only taste would distinguish the difference."

Bonnie shook her head, confused. "But Prophet told me that the men Queen Isabella's daughter sent to return the gem never made it tae the island."

"No, lass," Prophet quietly corrected. "I said the men never returned to Spain. I believe they did make it here.

They had a map and knew the perils awaiting them far better than we did, since they had traveled to the island once before."

"What do ye think happened tae them?" she asked, fearing she already knew the answer.

"I imagine they were killed," Gray said. "Knowing what I now know about these people, I doubt they looked upon the stone's return as a generous gesture, but rather as an opportunity to get revenge for its theft, and once they had the responsible party in front of them, they had no intention of letting the crime go unpunished."

"But these men weren't the ones who actually took the sacred heart."

"Doesn't matter. Guilt by association." Gray's gaze slid away from her and focused on the heavy jungle on the outskirts of the village. "I think one of the men, if not all of them, were sacrificed to *lugar que descansa.*"

"What's that?"

"The resting place," he replied, his words sending a spike of dread through Bonnie. "Although we have been allowed to roam freely, there is one place we've been warned to stay away from, a worshipping ground about a mile straight through the woods toward the opposite shore." He nodded in that direction. "From what I understand, it is a deep well of water that holds some sacred meaning to the villagers."

Bonnie wanted no further elaboration on the subject of sacred wells and sacrifices. "I still don't understand why anyone would make a copy of the diamond."

"Simple: someone wanted to retain the original." Gray faced her again. "Think of it; a genuine red diamond would have a value beyond measure. The villagers don't care about money or worldly possessions. Outsiders, however, would. And some people might not feel inclined to give a priceless gem back to a bunch of savages. In fact, I believe the ship's stopping here at all was merely an elaborate ruse: pretend to return the diamond but hand over a fake. Appease the queen's mad daughter while effectively camouflaging their true intent, which was most likely to sell the gem to the highest bidder.''

"But that would imply the entire crew knew of the duplicity, which seems impossible."

Gray shrugged. "Not so impossible. Greed is a highly motivating factor. On the other hand, it would have been too risky to let many people in on the plan. I suspect the captain and perhaps one or two trusted men organized the crime, and the rest of the crew would attest to the fact that they had returned the sacred heart to its rightful owner." He shrugged. "But I don't know. This is all conjecture on my part, things that seem to fit together."

"What do ye think happened tae the real sacred heart?"

"It could be hidden somewhere in Spain or Portugal or any of a million other places. Or perhaps it was aboard the ship and sank to the bottom of the ocean."

"What makes ye think the ship sank?"

"Maybe it didn't. Perhaps I was just thinking of my own ship." Bitterness laced his words, a harshness directed entirely at himself.

"But what if the ship didn't go down?"

Gray slanted a glance at her over his shoulder. "What's your point?"

"Well, what happened tae the real diamond, then?"

"If I knew that, then I could solve a four-hundred-year-old mystery, now couldn't I?" He spewed some of his acid in her direction this time.

"Fine. Forget I said anything."

"Let's do that."

"Now wait a second," Prophet said, having remained relatively closemouthed until that point. "I think Bonnie has brought up a valid point. What did happen to the gem?"

"Does it matter?" Gray mumbled.

"It does to me. I'd think it would matter to you as well, since you've come all this way for the damn thing. Aren't you the least bit curious?"

Gray rounded on Prophet. "The search for that fucking stone has cost men their lives and left us deserted in this godforsaken place," he said venomously. "Will finding it do us a damn bit of good now?" He made a wordless sound of disgust and then stalked away from them.

Prophet shook his head. "Boy's got more guilt on his shoulders than a body should have."

Once more, they watched Gray range toward the beach. This time, however, he disappeared from sight.

"What drives him?" Bonnie wondered aloud, as if knowing the answer to that riddle would make any difference, cause Gray to open up to her more.

"The lad has demons, my girl. Can't seem to shake them."

"I wish I understood him," she murmured, bowing her head, staring at her hands folded in her lap. "I wish . . . things were different."

Prophet slanted a glance at her from beneath his bushy brows. "How so?"

Bonnie shrugged lightly and said nothing. How could she explain something to Prophet that she didn't really understand herself? Describe emotions that were new and fragile and frightening? Tell him that she no longer felt like the girl who had been kidnapped from her home but a woman with needs and dreams? She had changed, but Gray hadn't. And now she had to learn to repress her feelings, contain her needs in much the same way Gray did.

"He doesn't trust easily," Prophet murmured.

Bonnie wondered if that was a gentle warning voiced in an effort to make her protect herself, or merely a statement of fact. Either way, the advice came too late. She had already learned how hard it was for Gray to trust.

She regretted how easily she had thrown away that trust, tossed it back in Gray's face when she'd taken his map and fled. She doubted she could ever find her way back to the tenuous place they had once been. And now he had given up on his dream and that, Bonnie realized, saddened her more than anything else.

She glanced at Prophet. "What do ye think happened tae the real diamond?"

"It was probably lost, as Gray said. Odd what a person will believe in. Mythical gems and ancient legends. In the light of day it's hard to imagine being part of something so elusive."

"Didn't ye believe in it? Even for a moment?"

He lifted his head and squinted into the distance, toward the horizon, where the sun gleamed off the water like a sheet of gold. "Aye," he confessed at length. "I did. I think . . . I still do."

Bonnie smiled faintly, heartened by Prophet's words, especially considering what she was about to put forth. "What would ye say if I told ye that I believe the sacred heart is still on this island?"

That got Prophet's full attention. "And what brings you to this conclusion?" He regarded her with a hint of gentle skepticism, the kind a benevolent father indulges a particularly wearisome child with.

"Well, it seems only logical that the real stone had tae be on the ship."

"And what makes it logical?"

"Because the captain of the ship had to have been the one who betrayed the queen's daughter."

"That seems a rather sweeping assumption."

"He was the only person who would've been entrusted with the stone. And he couldn't take the chance of not producing it upon his departure, in case Juana wanted tae see it or changed her mind at the last minute. Perhaps she didn't hand the gem over until moments before the ship was about tae depart. So I believe when the ship left port, the real sacred heart was on board."

"I see." Prophet nodded thoughtfully, though clearly not convinced of this sequence of events by any means. "If the diamond somehow made its way back to the island, it would be in the nave in the parish church, and we both know it isn't."

"And if it isn't in the church, and if it didn't go down at sea, that leaves only one place it could be."

"And where is that?"

"Hidden on the person who never intended tae return the sacred heart tae the villagers in the first place."

Prophet's expression changed from tolerant patience to keen awareness. "The captain, you mean?"

"Perhaps. Or maybe another person in the crew managed tae get his hands on it. Either way, there was only one gem, which means only one person could have had it in his possession. And since it's not in the church . . ."

"And if it didn't disappear with the ship . . ." Awareness clicked in Prophet's eyes, as if his train of thought had just gelled with the track Bonnie was taking.

"Then I think there is only one place the diamond could be. Where all those who were not pure of heart went."

Prophet's gaze collided with hers. "*Lugar que descansa.*"

"Aye." Bonnie nodded. "The resting place."

"You're out of your mind."

Gray's comment stung, but Bonnie had fortified herself for his reaction to what she knew would be a rather startling revelation, a claim that could only be proven true with investigation.

But the battle would not be an easy one, considering the mulish expression Gray wore. All things related to the sacred heart were now off-limits according to his dictate, but that didn't stop Bonnie.

Gray slanted an accusing glance at Prophet. "Why

did you foster this insane idea? Jesus, one would think you'd know better."

Prophet was entirely unaffected by the rebuke. "Perhaps because I don't find it quite as insane as you do. If you'd stop being so blasted pigheaded, you might see how clever Bonnie is to have figured this out."

"What, exactly, has she figured out? That some fool might have been sent to his death with the stone still on him? So now you think this ancient corpse is going to cough the bloody thing up because we 'figured this out.' If so, let me enlighten you.

"First of all, there would be no body remaining after all these years, most likely not even a skeleton, and secondly, does anyone know how deep the waters are around these islands? Some spots are over fifteen thousand fathoms deep. In layman's terms, that's more than nine thousand feet straight down. A nice little descent into hell. My bet is that the sacred well is a watery version of a bottomless pit. Somehow I don't picture these warriors pitching a person they wished eternally dead into water the depth of a fishpond."

Prophet merely scratched an itch and said, "So what's your point?"

Gray threw up his hands and stalked to the window. The sun was just setting on another day, and outside an evening of revelry was getting underway.

Bonnie's mind drifted back to that afternoon, when she had been informed that the young women of the tribe would be doing their ceremonial dance that evening and she was expected to join them. It had not been a request but a command, straight from Most Brave.

Gray didn't know about the dance. He had stayed away for hours. Long enough to make her worry. But she was glad he didn't know of the leader's dictate, for it would have only set off more tensions between two men who could barely tolerate each other. If dancing meant keeping the peace, she would dance.

To that end, she had spent a good part of the afternoon learning the serpentine movements and intricate rhythms of a dance that was not meant simply for entertainment, she soon discovered, but to be erotic as well. The intention was for God to favor the women with fertility.

An unexpected spurt of longing went through Bonnie upon learning that. A baby. What would it be like to have a child of her own? A little cooing bundle of sweet smells and soft skin and chubby rolls? Someone to love unconditionally and to love her that way in return?

A child, she thought—glancing up and catching sight of Gray in the shade of a palm tree, watching her with an intensity that made her breath lock in her throat— that was part of him, part of their union. A union, she realized with painful clarity, that would never take place. Bonnie had to force herself to look away. When next she glanced toward the palm tree, Gray was gone.

Bonnie closed out the memory and rose from the edge of the bed, padding to the opposite side of the room, absently fingering the soft petals of the flowers she had plucked that morning, thinking, for one silly moment, of presenting them to Gray, hoping, perhaps, to see him smile again.

"Gray's right," she murmured, not wanting to be the cause of strife between the two men. "It was a bad idea. Just forget I said anything."

"Forget it!" Prophet exclaimed, his tone stating that he was clearly unwilling to do any such thing. "We came all this way to find the stone; now I'm simply supposed to let it go?"

"You heard the lady," Gray said gruffly. "Forget it."

"Listen here, you selfish, brooding, arrogant, blind jackass, I'm sick unto death of that damn chip on your shoulder."

Bonnie swung around to gape at Prophet, having never heard the man raise his voice before. He had always struck her as the mildest of men. Now he looked furious.

"I loved your father, too," he went on, "and I'm not about to give up so easily on his dream. Damn it, man! I thought this time you'd get past this fear of failure you carry around with you, ready to throw an excuse out there any time something doesn't go your way."

"Leave off, damn you!" Gray warned, his face etched with menace, replacing the moody indifference he had stalked around with for days.

Instead of backing off, Prophet wore an expression that practically dared Gray to do something about it. "Maybe I was wrong about you all these years. Maybe you are—"

"Don't say it."

"—a coward."

Gray came away from the window like a shot, throwing a wild punch at Prophet, which Prophet ducked more nimbly than most men his age.

"Come on!" Gray shouted, waving Prophet on. "Hit me. I know you'd love to."

Prophet's fist clenched at his side, but he made no move toward Gray. "If a simple belt in the jaw would knock any sense into that thick skull of yours, I'd break my vow of nonviolence and beat you senseless. I would do just about anything if I thought it might heal the pain you carry around inside you, lad. I never had any children, but I love you like you were my own, as much as your own father did, and I can't stand to see what you put yourself through."

Bonnie watched all the anger deflate from Gray while another emotion twisted within him, an emotion he could not express, didn't know how to convey, and no man had been more tortured because of it.

Gray turned away and bowed his head. "I'm sorry . . . I . . ." He spread his hands in front of him, as if they could speak for him, but nothing came; the words were too difficult.

"I know, lad," Prophet murmured, stepping up behind Gray and laying a hand on his shoulder. "I know."

Gray raked a hand through his hair, his mane having grown even wilder in the weeks aboard the ship, the ends now trailing well below his shoulders, and his jaw darkened with stubble.

"Do you comprehend the seriousness of what you're proposing?" he asked Bonnie then, that silver gaze cutting her way. "We cannot simply go fishing in some sacred well for a diamond that—if it even existed in the first place—has to be long gone by now."

"But what if it isn't?" she asked, wanting Gray to renew his quest for the diamond, but not for any of the reasons she had given him. She knew that if he gave up on his dream now, he would never forgive himself.

For the love of his father, he had walked through fire. She couldn't allow him to abandon all the work he had done. And Bonnie suspected Prophet was prodding Gray for the same reason.

"If by some miracle we find the stone, what then?"

"We could return it tae the villagers." But even as Bonnie made the suggestion, she dismissed it, recalling the fate that had befallen the last group of people who had attempted to return the sacred heart. She shivered.

"Exactly," Gray said, witnessing her reaction.

"I say we try to escape," Prophet offered.

Gray treated him to a deadpan stare. "Oh, yes, that's simple. Let's just plunge into a dead pool, hunt for the stone, hoist it out, and then leave without even a fare-thee-well. That is a plan. I imagine you will now tell me you intend to part the sea like Moses and we can walk the thousand or so miles home?"

"I was thinking more along the lines of taking the canoes you said you spotted on the other side of the island."

"I see . . . and then what?"

"Well, then perhaps we can try to find our way back to the *Mary Celeste*. The ship wasn't that far from here."

Bonnie had completely forgotten about the brigantine they had seen shortly before the storm that had shipwrecked them had hit. She expected Gray to dismiss the idea out of hand, considering his mood; instead he surprised her.

"I've thought of that already. It won't work."

"Why?"

"Because that ship couldn't possibly have been real."

"Looked awfully real to me."

"We had to be experiencing some sort of hallucination."

Prophet lifted a bushy brow. "A shipload of people with the same hallucination? That seems a bit of a stretch." When Gray made no reply, Prophet threw up his hands. "Fine. We all hallucinated. But I don't hear any better suggestions coming from you."

"That's because I don't have a better suggestion," Gray grudgingly admitted. "As much as I'd prefer to disagree with you, fact is, there's no other way off this island except with those canoes. I guess we don't have any other choice, do we?" He glanced at Bonnie.

Bonnie met Gray's gaze, sensing that he wanted something from her. Her approval perhaps? Her agreement that this was their only option?

A very real fear suddenly burst to life within her, a realization that they might all die in this attempt to escape. But if they stayed on the island, they had no future. More than that, there was no guarantee that the natives would not kill them outright at some point. Tomorrow the celebration would end. What would happen then?

Breathing past the knot in her stomach, Bonnie softly replied, "I don't believe we do."

"Then I guess it's settled. Tonight, after the final celebration, we leave."

Chapter 23

They all tried to pretend nothing had changed, but the tension in the air was palpable as Gray, Bonnie, Prophet, and the rest of the crew joined the villagers that night for the final cap on the revelry.

Gray prayed he was the only one who sensed things were not the same, keeping a watchful eye on the warriors—most especially their leader, who sat on a large, flat rock directly across from Gray, the strong palm wine that had been served dribbling down the side of Most Brave's mouth as he stared unflinchingly at Bonnie, as he had been doing most of the night.

Gray had to tamp down the explosive rage churning inside him, a desire to wrap his hands around the man's throat and lift the whoreson bodily off the ground, images of the bastard choking to death on his own tongue tempering some of Gray's savagery.

Gray forced himself to remain still, drinking steadily of his wine to calm his volatility. Never had he felt more impotent, more powerless. He had caused all of this. He had put Bonnie in danger. Because of his damn visions of glory, they could all be killed.

The chieftain set aside his food and then clapped his hands. A group of women who had been sitting meekly on the ground behind him rose to their feet and headed for a circle that had been outlined with rocks. Beside Gray, Bonnie also rose.

He grabbed her wrist, seeing her wince at his unintentional roughness. He eased his hold. "Where are you going?"

"To dance." Her eyes gave nothing away, yet he could feel the wild racing of her pulse beneath his thumb.

Her words brought back the exotic scene he'd witnessed that afternoon, observing her from the shadows as she stood amid a group of women, her glorious hair swirling around her as she swayed to unheard music.

The need to touch her, hold her, bury himself deep inside her had nearly brought Gray to his knees. And when she looked up and saw him standing there, every muscle had tightened under the force of will he had to exert over himself to keep from sweeping her away and loving her in every way a man knew how to love a woman.

"No." He tugged her back down, not wanting any man to look at her, unable to share her in any way even as a voice asked him what right he had to tell her what she could and could not do. He was not her husband. Another man would be given that privilege. Still, Gray couldn't let go.

"I want tae dance. Please," she added in a whisper, her eyes pleading with him to release her, making something churn inside Gray, a wariness that could not be eased. "Please, Gray . . . Don't make this harder than it must be." She leaned forward and brushed her lips against his, and then extricated her arm from his grasp and hurried to join the other women.

Gray glanced across the fire, his gaze locking with the black eyes of the leader, a taunting gleam in the man's eyes as he snapped his fingers.

The heavy beat of a native drum began to pound out a dark rhythm, the sound reverberating in Gray's head as his gaze slid to Bonnie, who began to undulate, her eyes closed, her movements as natural as that of the other women.

Gray felt as if he watched from someplace far away, body and soul apart from each other, his heart beating in the same heavy tempo as the drum, his blood thickening in his veins, the world becoming one focus, one sphere of comprehension.

An odd heaviness settled over his body; everything was moving in slow motion. He held his glass out in front of him and the wine floated within his cup. Gray knew with the last bit of clarity he had left that he had been drugged.

His gaze lifted. *Bonnie,* he wanted to shout, but no sound issued from his mouth. No warning. He could only watch in horror and silent rage as the warriors howled their encouragement, calling for the women to move faster. Then the leader clapped again . . . and all the women were ordered to take off their tops.

Gray's head felt as if it weighed a hundred pounds as he pushed himself to his knees, reaching out for Bonnie, seeing the fear on her face, her arms clasped across her chest, shaking her head, refusing to undress.

"Leave her the hell alone!" Gray thought the bellow came out of his mouth, but he couldn't be sure. He couldn't find his center, his balance, as he tried to rise to his feet.

When he did, the ground seemed far away. He swayed, catching sight of the chief walking toward Bonnie, prying her hands from her chest, and when she resisted, backhanding her across the face, sending her spinning to her knees.

Gray lurched forward. "*No!*"

The man then grabbed the front of her top and yanked, rending the material and baring Bonnie's breasts to everyone. She scrambled away as Most Brave reached out to touch her. Voices soared around Gray, bodies—his men?—moving to help her, the warriors holding them at bay.

Things crashed at Gray's feet, he fell, struggled upright, his only thought to get to Bonnie, but he couldn't reach her. Dark laughter rang in his ears.

"Bonnie!" He saw her, those velvet blue eyes wide, fearing for him as she was being wrenched to her feet, trying to fight off the savage. Another slap made her stagger; only the man's hold on her arms kept her upright.

Gray surged forward . . . so close . . . so close. Then a hard object slammed into his stomach; another blow to his jaw rammed him facedown into the sand.

"No!" he heard Bonnie scream. "Leave him alone!"

Hands dragged him to his knees, his head dangling, blood trickling from the cut on his cheek. Fingers beneath his chin snapped Gray's head up.

"Watch me touch your woman."

Gray went wild, trying to yank his arms from the warriors that held him, earning him a punishing kick to his ribs, Bonnie's scream pierced him much more than any physical pain. Gray's head was lifted once more.

He blinked, trying to focus on Bonnie. She trembled before the warrior chief, but the bravery on her face was a knife to Gray's heart. Her eyes never wavered from his as Most Brave fondled her breasts, a single tear skimming down her cheek, a sight Gray would remember for the rest of his life.

Everything inside him broke into a million pieces as he bellowed his anguish. And for the first time in his entire life, Gray cried.

The warrior snorted in disgust and pushed Bonnie away when his attempts to arouse her failed. He blamed that failure on her, saying she was cold inside and that no man would want her, that even her own husband wouldn't touch her. He spat on the ground next to her and then spun on his heel, his people following him.

Bonnie sank to her knees, her hair cascading forward

to cover her nakedness and her shame. The tears flowed and she couldn't stop them as she hugged herself, rocking back and forth in the sand.

"Bonnie." The word was a tormented whisper.

She glanced up, saw his battered face, the blood, the utter despair in his eyes, and the pain seared her. She had caused this. She had incited the men by dancing, and Gray had been beaten because of her actions.

Prophet ran to help her, shedding his shirt and draping it around her, hovering in front of her to block her from view as she fixed herself.

The degradation she had suffered was forgotten as Gray's men lifted him from the ground. She rushed to him, shouldering one of the men to the side and wrapping her arm around his waist.

"Bonnie." He closed his eyes. "Sorry . . . so sorry . . . never forgive . . . myself."

"Don't," she murmured, pressing closer to his side, needing the comfort only he could give.

"He's been drugged," Prophet said, bringing Bonnie's gaze to him. "It was in his wine." He paused, unable to look at her. "Everything happened so fast. I should have—"

"It's over now," was all Bonnie could bring herself to say. She didn't want to think about it. She wanted to forget the savage's touch as if it had never happened.

Gray resisted as she attempted to help him. He was too proud to accept assistance from her, and she could see on his face that he could not get over what had just taken place. He wouldn't look at her, and her shame only deepened.

She stepped away and let his men lead him toward their little cottage while she walked behind. Gray fell back onto the bed, holding his head between his hands. The men departed silently. Prophet was the last one to go, laying a gentle hand on her shoulder before leaving Bonnie alone with Gray, despair closing in on her. She felt unclean and scared and more vulnerable than she'd ever felt in her life.

She slid slowly to the floor, wrapping her hands around her legs and burying her face in her knees, trying to will away the shock that threatened to engulf her, that wanted to take her away to a place inside herself. She could no longer fight so she let the numbness in, seeking forgetfulness within the dark corners of her mind.

Gray awoke in semidarkness, only the pink blur of dusk through the single window illuminating his surrounding.

Consciousness gradually surfaced, the heavy lethargy dissipating, his mind beginning to focus even as a multitude of images closed in on him. Wine, food, dancing, pain, torment . . . utter devastation.

Bonnie.

Oh, sweet God, Bonnie.

With a start, Gray sat upright, his heart racing, his palms sweating, consumed with the need to find her, save her. *Too late, damn you! Too late.*

And then he saw her. Curled up in front of the door, her knees drawn up to her chest, her hair in wild disarray around her, the fading light drifting across the nasty bruise on her cheek. He died that much more inside.

After all she had been through, he had done nothing to soothe her: not begged her forgiveness for failing her; not spoken a single word to tell her that she had been so strong, so brave, that she was the most beautiful woman he'd ever known.

Instead he had fallen into a drug-induced stupor when all he had wanted to do was pull her close and never let her go. He didn't deserve her—but God, how would he ever live without her when the time came?

Quietly, he rose to his feet, his ribs protesting, one

or two of them most likely broken. But the pain receded to dim obscurity as he walked toward Bonnie.

He stared down at her, his throat closing as a wave of anguish washed over him. He had brought her to this. All his stupid dreams and foolish notions. He should have left her back in Scotland. There she would have been safe.

He knelt beside her, wondering when it happened, when he had done the unthinkable and fallen hopelessly and completely in love with this brave Scottish lass. And in an instant of utter clarity, he knew the answer.

The first time he looked into those blue eyes.

He didn't care what he had to do; he would find a way to get her off the island. He would happily forfeit his own life if he could only save hers.

Gently, Gray slid his arms beneath her knees, ignoring the pain that slashed through his side as he rose. Her hair tumbled back, sweeping across his chest and arm, sending a sizzle of unadulterated desire sluicing through him. He swore viciously beneath his breath, seeing the full extent of the damage to her face.

Carefully, he laid her down on the bed, afraid of jarring her, waking her, seeing those eyes settle on him in accusation. Only now, when she could not see the true depths of his feelings for her could he allow himself the freedom to show it, to close his eyes and absorb her, praying he could get through another agonizing night of denying himself the only thing he wanted: her.

When he opened his eyes, he found Bonnie gazing up at him, sleepy-eyed and a bit wary. Unconsciously, he brushed his knuckles along her jaw. She flinched, and Gray cursed himself for his stupidity, for not being able to keep his hands off her.

Abruptly, he straightened, sliding his hands into his pockets. "I'm sorry . . . I didn't mean to wake you."

She said nothing, only stared at him with eyes like a frightened doe, leaving him frozen in fear and need. When a single tear slipped down her cheek, he bowed his head and sank to his knees, wishing the natives had killed him. Hell would be so much easier than facing that lone tear.

He shut his eyes tight when her fingers slid into his hair. She whispered his name with a voice like a nightingale, calling him from the darkness.

His entire body shuddered as she traced a path down his neck, over his shoulder, outlining the muscles in his arms, before reaching his hand, tentatively entwining her fingers with his—and he held on as though his entire life depended on that simple touch.

A force that would not be denied drew him forward. He wrapped his arms around her and laid his forehead on her stomach, all the while telling himself to get out, that he shouldn't stay there, his fist clenching and unclenching with restraint as Bonnie smoothed her hands over his hair as if . . . as if he was the one to be soothed and not her.

"It wasn't your fault." Four softly spoken words that tore through Gray's barriers, ripping away any sense of what was right or wrong, what he wanted and what he shouldn't have. His mind, his soul, his world had become Bonnie.

And his hunger would no longer be held in check.

With a groan, he gave in to the yearning inside him, cupping her face between his hands and kissing her with all the fierce passion only Bonnie could call forth, a love so strong it could make him break his vow.

He kissed her eyes, her nose, her chin, feather-light caresses over her bruised jaw, whispering words of apology, of heartbreak, uttering promises in the heat of the forbidden, forcing him to surrender to a fate stronger than he could deny.

Through the roaring of his blood, Gray heard Bonnie whimper and stopped abruptly, realizing with stunning self-loathing that he had acted no better than that savage bastard, inflicting himself upon her when she was vulnerable.

He reared back. "Jesus . . . I'm sorry. I . . ." He tried to move away, but Bonnie caught his face between her hands.

"Please, Gray . . . I need you. Don't deny me again. I—I couldn't bear it."

"But I thought . . ." He pressed his forehead against hers. "I don't want to leave you, but I don't want to hurt you, Bonnie. I've hurt you enough."

"Ye'd hurt me more if ye left me now. I want ye tae take away his touch."

His touch. Gray's body tensed as if a whip had just lashed across his back, agony welling up in him. "I didn't stop him . . . I didn't . . ." He bowed his head. "God help me."

"Make me forget," she whispered in his ear, gently kissing his neck. "Make me forget everything but you. I need ye inside me, possessing me, wiping away the hurt with your body."

Gray lifted his head and stared down into her eyes, eyes that would haunt him all his days and beyond. And when she raised her mouth to his, he knew that whatever happened, tomorrow could be damned.

Bonnie's eyelids drifted shut as Gray's mouth closed over hers, a surge of pleasure flying through her that only Gray's touch could evoke. She savored each glide of his lips, each silky-sweet thrust of his tongue. Unlike his first kiss, this one was tempered with restraint, lingering, hot. Mouths suffused, breaths mingling, moans intertwining.

Bonnie realized with sudden, vivid clarity that she had spent her life either looking back or looking forward, but rarely living in the moment. Now, with each breath they took, their lives hanging in the balance minute by minute, the only thing that mattered was the here and now.

A soft sigh of rapture escaped her lips as Gray's mouth skimmed along the column of her throat, his voice husky and low as he told her how beautiful she was, how desirable, that he would make everything right again, obliterate the hurt, the fear, the pain—and Bonnie had no doubt he would. She drowned in the heated weight of him, the long, hard length of his body encompassing her.

He rolled to his back, and Bonnie found herself on top of him, his molten gaze intent on her face. "If you want me to stop, I will. You're in control, Bonnie."

His words touched her all the way to her soul. Her Gray, so fierce, so determined, so much the warrior was, in this, a gentleman—the gentleman he claimed never to be. To be in control of this man was a delicious prospect that made her chest heavy and her lungs tight. How she had dreamed of this moment.

Her legs spread over his hips. She pressed deep against his long, hard shaft. The memories of the things he had done to her, how he had swept that heated length along the slick, wet petals where her desire culminated made her want to rub back and forth across it, to unsheathe its silky length and stroke her moist valley along hot steel.

Clothes resisted her; she wanted to feel only Gray's skin against her. She removed her shirt, sliding the material off her shoulders. It puddled at her hips, baring herself to Gray as if she bared her very soul.

His gaze never wavered from her face as he took the shirt and tossed it to the floor. Then he slipped a small section of her hair between his fingers and began to tease the ends over her thigh, along her stomach, and then gently, almost reverently, stroking the silky tip over her nipples.

Hot pleasure poured through Bonnie. She arched her back, feeling wanton, stopping Gray's playful exploration as she took his hand and boldly placed it over her breast. She needed him to touch her there, take away the shame another man had foisted upon her with brutality.

The first sweep of his thumb across her aching peak

made her thighs clench, throbbing where their bodies met. She rocked against Gray's arousal, a sheen of sweat beginning to spread across his chest.

She lay her hands against his shoulders, sinking into the endless depths of his eyes as long-denied passion blossomed between them. "Taste me."

He knew what she wanted and needed no other encouragement. He sat up and bent her back over his arm, taking her nipple into his mouth, each gentle tug sending a dart of liquid warmth to the core of her, her nails lightly scoring his chest as he caressed her.

Her moans grew frantic, her fists clenching the bedsheets as he suckled her, giving each breast equal attention. She felt drugged, dazed, completely lost in pleasure—and she wanted to remain that way.

He cupped her buttocks, cradling her tightly against his erection. She clutched at the buttons of his trousers, tearing at them in a frenzy to free him, wanting to wrap her hands around that smooth satin.

He groaned as she made her first tentative contact. He was as perfectly made there as he was everywhere else. Mesmerized, she stroked him, a bead of moisture appearing on the hooded tip. She wanted to taste him.

She scooted back and leaned down. He stopped her. "You'll kill me," was all he said before taking her down to her back, coming over her, his tongue flicking one pink nub, then the other, before scoring a wet path down her stomach . . . to the very heat of her, where his mouth took up once more.

The first glide of his tongue nearly brought her off the bed. So sinful, so wicked. "Oh, yes," she moaned, her breath coming in little pants. He slid his arms beneath her thighs, pulling her tighter to his mouth. Then his large, warm hands slid up her sides, returning to her breasts, taking her nipples between his thumb and forefinger, rolling gently while his mouth worked magic between her slick folds. "Gray . . . Oh, God."

"Yes, love . . . let me feel it."

Bonnie spiked back against the bed as her climax tore through her, each pulse dragged from someplace deep inside her, light spiraling behind her eyes as she reached heaven in Gray's arms.

He eased a finger into her and then another. She squirmed against the sensation. "You're so tight." He pulled his fingers out. "I can't," he said, more to himself then her. "I'll hurt you."

The tears were unexpected after the joy he had just given her. "Why?" Her voice broke. "Why can't you love me?"

"No, sweetheart. Don't." Keeping his weight on his forearms, he moved over her, kissing her chin, her cheek. "This has nothing to do with not desiring you." He kissed away her tears.

"Please don't be honorable," she whispered, stirring against him. "Don't tell me about Ewan or what I want or don't want or about making mistakes." She slid her hand between their bodies and found him, still aroused. She wriggled her hips and eased his tip into her waiting warmth. He groaned and clenched his jaw. "For once, tell me how ye feel. If not with words, then with your body. But if ye care nothing for me, then please . . . just go, say no words. I don't want anything ye won't freely give and I don't want more from ye than ye have within ye tae share. My virginity is my gift, the only thing, other than my love, that I can give to one man—and this I give to you and ask nothing in return."

Emotions choked Gray, emotions that he had walled up years before. "No woman has every honored me as you just have. It humbles me, Bonnie . . . It humbles me in ways I never thought possible. And though I don't deserve you . . . God help me, I want you." Then he kissed her, hard, taking her hands in his, lacing them above her head. "I love you," he murmured, the words drowned out as he entered her in one swift, rending stroke, ending his battle, the war he had waged against himself, branding her as his own from this moment forward . . . no matter what came between them.

He drove into her with the force of a storm, whipping Bonnie's breath away, eradicating every thought and fulfilling every fantasy she'd ever possessed. The tender lover was gone. In his place was a man as fierce as thunder, demanding every ounce of her, allowing her no place to hide, no choice but to relinquish everything she had promised with words and without. Her body. Her heart.

Her very soul.

But as Gray took her to that bright, magical place yet again, Bonnie knew the one thing she wanted he couldn't give.

Tomorrow.

Chapter 24

They came at dawn, while Bonnie and Gray slept, dragging Gray from bed to the sound of her screams.

"No!" She scrambled after him to be thrust back by one of the warriors. "Leave him alone!"

"Don't, Bonnie!" Gray's eyes warned her to stop. "Let them take me. . . . Find Prophet and get out of here."

Bonnie shook her head wildly. "No. I won't leave you!"

One of the savages pointed to the bed, and all eyes swerved to the sheets, where a dark stain proclaimed what had transpired between them during the deepest part of the night.

Gray's dark laughter brought Bonnie's head snapping up. "He won't touch you now." An edge of barren triumph pierced his words. "You're not a virgin anymore."

A horrible thought crossed Bonnie's mind, which seemed to only be confirmed by the slightly crazed look in Gray's eyes. He had given her what she had wanted, taken her virginity, loved her until she could only feel skin against skin, the pleasure a rainbow prism inside her. And in the offering, he had sacrificed his own life to save hers.

He had known. Dear sweet God, he had known that Most Brave would take her, force himself upon her, and Gray had battled everything inside him that told him to leave her untouched.

While Bonnie's heart expanded with love for what he had done, it also tore irreparably with the fact that he hadn't truly wanted to make love to her. He had done so because he had to.

Then Most Brave spoke. "You get stone from well. Then"—he pointed at Bonnie—"she watch you die."

Bonnie gaped in shock at the hackneyed English that poured from the man's mouth.

"You slimy bastard," Gray hissed. "You knew all along what we were saying. You fucking goddamn piece of shit!"

His insults garnered him a punishing blow to his stomach that doubled him over with a groan. Then they dragged him out, shoving Bonnie behind him.

As she stumbled along in the sand and into the heavy undergrowth rimming the village, Bonnie pleaded with Most Brave. "I'll do anything. Please, I beg ye, don't kill him." The leader ignored her, continuing to push her along without even looking at her. She moved directly in his path and took hold of his arm. "Ye want me. Take me!"

The warrior's eyes blazed fire, and in the next instant, his hand swung out, the devastating blow sending Bonnie flying into the sand.

Before she could even focus, she was hauled to her feet and forced to go on, branches tearing at her shirt and face as they walked for what seemed like an eternity. As they broke through the trees, one final shove sent her stumbling to the edge of a dark blue pool of water.

When she glanced up, she saw Gray being yanked upright between two huge savages, one eye swollen shut, telling Bonnie with agonizing clarity that the men had beaten him further. On his knees between them, his head dangled toward the ground.

"Gray," she said in a raw voice, wanting to touch him, help him.

As if the effort was pure agony, he slowly raised his head and looked at her. He mouthed something. *I love you,* she thought but couldn't be sure. Nothing seemed real, least of all this moment, or the words that rifled through the air.

"No one ever survive test of sacred well." Most Brave motioned to Gray. "You go, find stone. Come back without"—he jerked Bonnie to her feet and pressed a knife to her throat—"she die. Come back with, then only you die."

Bonnie struggled to speak, but the blade's edge pressed harder against her neck. She met Gray's eyes across the pool of water. She tried to shake her head, tell him not to go, but nothing could get past her lips.

"It'll be all right," he said, nearly falling forward as the men hoisted him to his feet and abruptly let go.

"In!" Most Brave ordered him. "Now!"

The man's hand on Bonnie's arm grew punishing when Gray did not move fast enough. She winced.

"Let her alone and I'll go in."

"No!" a voice shouted, riveting everyone's attention as Prophet shouldered his way forward. A swift, hard kick to his side from one of the warriors brought him to the ground, gasping for air. He shook his head and tried to speak. "I'll . . . go. Leave him. He's . . . injured."

"Damn you, Prophet! Stay out of this."

Prophet glanced up, and for the first time, Bonnie could see his age, how vulnerable he truly was. Even though Gray was injured, his strength far outmatched Prophet's, and they both knew it.

"I love you, boy. Like you were my own. Let me go. You have something to live for."

Most Brave barked out a command then, and Prophet was seized. Then he thrust a finger at Gray. "Go!"

Gray stepped up to the edge of the water, and Bonnie willed back the tears. She'd always thought bravery had come naturally to her, but she realized then, that until that moment, she had never truly been tested.

In the next instant, Gray plunged into the water, disappearing beneath the glassy surface as if he had never existed.

Bonnie shoved Most Brave away, not caring if he killed her. With a dark laugh, he let her go, and she dropped to her knees beside the pool, trying to find Gray beneath the rippling water but seeing nothing but her own reflection gazing back at her—and the tears she finally allowed to flow freely.

They had to drag Bonnie away from the water when fifteen minutes passed without Gray's return. *"He isn't dead!"* she had cried. But no one had listened.

The angry rumblings of Gray's crew grew in proportion, saying no man could survive beneath the water that long. The bloody bastards had murdered their captain.

Wildly, Bonnie tore at her captor's hands, kicking and screaming as she looked over her shoulder, calling madly for Gray, waiting for a body to emerge from the water and seeing nothing but utter stillness as the pool disappeared from sight.

Toward the end, the warriors had to carry her. Grief had taken away every ounce of fight. Gray had been her anchor, the only thing that had seen her through this ordeal. Now he was gone and she couldn't go on without him.

As rough hands thrust her into the little cottage that she and Gray had shared, bolting the door behind her, Bonnie collapsed to the floor, praying she'd close her eyes and never wake up again.

* * *

The rumbling jolted Bonnie in the middle of the night, a sound like the unearthly beating of drums, mingling with her dreams of *cagarros* hidden in the trees, surrounding her, screeching out their sinister cries as they waited to swoop.

With a start, she sat up, her body covered in sweat, her mind disoriented, thoughts tumbling one on top of the next. She wondered if she still dwelt within the numbing embrace of sleep or if she was truly awake. Neither way brought peace. She now lived the nightmare, and there was no place to hide.

The rumbling came again, but this time she recognized that this was no dream. Beneath her, the ground shook, sending her startled gaze flying madly about in the darkness as the walls began to creak and vibrate.

The first timber crashed down right beside her, propelling Bonnie to her feet. She stumbled in the direction of the door, her heart pounding so hard she thought it would explode. Dear God, what was happening?

She reached for the door a moment before it flew open, the wind sending the heavy wood crashing against the wall. A dark figure loomed in the threshold.

A muffled scream died on Bonnie's lips as the figure reached for her. She thrashed at the arms that sought to capture her. She would kill herself before she let the warrior chief take her to his bed.

A hand grabbed her and hauled her out into the night as the world began to rock beneath her feet. "Ssh, lass. It's all right."

"Prophet?"

"Aye."

Madness erupted around them then, and Prophet tugged her away, no one even noticing them as the islanders ran from their homes, dropping to the ground in the middle of the village and chanting in rising hysteria.

"O deus de demônio esteve deixa frouxo!"

"What are they saying?" she cried as Prophet barked out orders to the crew.

"The demon god has been let loose." He forced her to the side as a lone warrior ran toward them, brandishing a spear aimed straight at Bonnie. The weapon arced through the air, slicing across Prophet's arm.

The men grappled in the darkness, sending Bonnie scrambling back as they crashed next to her, Prophet's bulk pinning Most Brave to the ground as the first mate's fist slammed across the leader's jaw with the resounding crack of bone against bone.

Prophet wrenched her to her feet, Most Brave either unconscious or dead on the ground. "We have to get out of here. Fast."

"What's happening?" The earth shuddered violently beneath her, the acrid smell of smoke filling the air. She coughed as a vaporous cloud crept in around them.

"Volcano." The single word froze everything inside Bonnie. "We have to get to the canoes."

Amid the confusion and noise, Bonnie suddenly remembered the puppy. "I have tae get Jack!"

Her gaze swung to the cottage to find Jack trapped inside, a large beam having fallen in front of the opening, blocking his way.

Bonnie jerked from Prophet's grasp, hearing his curse as she raced back to the little house. She scooped up Jack a second before another beam fell, landing directly in the spot in which the puppy had been only a second before. Bonnie hugged the dog tightly to her.

Prophet reached her then. "Come on!"

They began to run, pounding through the thick undergrowth, trying to find their way in the darkness. She stumbled several times, Prophet sweeping her up, refusing to let go of her hand as he pulled her along behind him, trees toppling down helter-skelter around them.

And then Bonnie saw the beast. The red eye of the

volcano, a lava flow spewing forth from one of the *caldeiras,* sending rock shooting hundreds of feet into the sky, the air filled with the roaring sound of the quake and the sharp thud of the stones hurtling madly toward the ground.

"Keep under the trees!" Prophet shouted over the desperate keening of the wind, long lengths of palm breaking off and hitting them, the sand swirling up to choke them along with the first hint of ash.

A huge explosion ripped through the ground, the tremors sending both of them hurtling headlong into the sand, Jack spilling out of her arms and disappearing completely in the next instant. Prophet dragged her upright before she had time to draw breath.

"Prophet!" He seemed not to hear her, lost as he was in the fight for their lives. "Stop!"

Sharply, he turned. "We must keep going! We're almost there!"

"Jack—" Another ear-splitting noise whipped away the rest of her words. No time for explanations. She had to find Jack.

Bonnie dashed in the direction she'd last seen the puppy, calling wildly, unable to hear, barely able to see, despair and a sense that all was lost nearly bringing her to her knees.

Smoke made her throat raw, leaving her powerless to scream as a towering figure suddenly loomed before her. Without a second thought, she slammed her foot into his midsection, doubling him over as she reeled around to flee in the other direction.

An arm like a steel band snaked around her waist, wrenching her back, nearly driving the breath from her lungs. She fought wildly, desperately.

"Goddamn it, Bonnie!"

Bonnie went stock-still. That voice. It couldn't be. She swung around . . . and found herself staring up into a face she thought she'd never see again.

Her throat closed as she threw her arms tightly around

Gray's neck as life disintegrated around them. Something squirming against her chest drew Bonnie back. The pup yapped at her.

"Jack! Oh, ye saved him!" Bonnie wanted to ask Gray a million questions, but Prophet plowed in behind them, about to take a swing at Gray until recognition swept over him.

"Thank God!"

"Let's get the hell out of here!" Gray twined his fingers in Bonnie's, and together they fought their way through the underbrush.

They were going in circles, Bonnie was sure of it. Everything looked the same. Dear Lord, they wouldn't make it. The night engulfed them. They were lost. They had to be. They had been running forever with no shoreline, no canoes, nothing in front of them but endless trees and the sound of the earth fracturing in their ears.

Then, as if God had heard her pleas, the roar changed to the palpable boom of surf pounding against the shore. A moment later, they came out on the beach.

"There!" Gray pointed to a group of long, indistinct shapes.

"The canoes!"

They dashed forward just as dark figures emerged from the tree line. Bonnie froze in fear, certain the warriors had found them.

"It's the crew!" Prophet crowed triumphantly.

They plunged the canoes out into the foaming sea, the tremors making the ocean rise, sending waves driving into each other, the force of the undertow sucking the canoes outward, cresting on waves that nearly dashed them back into the beach.

Only the men's fierce, back-breaking rowing kept them moving away from the island, spray soaking them all to the bone. Bonnie held on for dear life, knowing the battle was far from over. The ocean had become its own beast, and the night would be a long one.

Gripping the sides of the canoe, she glanced over her shoulder toward the island. Lava blanketed out in all directions like a rapidly spreading disease, destroying everything in its path, a canopy of orange and red shooting long fingers of color into the sky as the Isle of the Mist disappeared forever.

The heat was what roused Bonnie, the sun blasting down on her, the gentle rocking of the canoe bringing everything back with vivid clarity.

They had barely survived the raging swells of the sea, the men fighting the storm all night, the beast beginning to subside as a sliver of sunrise jutted over the horizon. And when the battle had been won, exhaustion overcame everyone like a numbing pall, pulling them down into a dreamless sleep.

Gray pressed tightly against her side, the small width of the canoe not giving them much room to maneuver, but Bonnie didn't care. She wanted him close. Just having him alive, warm and vibrant and whole, lessened the fear of what was to become of them now as they drifted in the middle of the ocean with no food or water, no way to even catch any of the life-sustaining fish just out of their reach.

Before sleep had lured them beneath a dark blanket of temporary forgetfulness, Bonnie had asked Gray one question: how had he survived underwater all that time?

"An underground cavern," he explained. "There are tunnels, a network of them, created from other volcanic explosions, I imagine." He glanced toward the island, a small, glowing blip in the distance where lava and ash still consumed everything in its reach. "Or perhaps the island truly was the gateway to Atlantis. Guess we'll never know."

He faced her again. "I believed I was going to die. I was prepared for it. Then, moments before I thought my lungs would burst, I saw a hole and swam through it into a cavern. I stayed there. I don't know how long. I waited—thinking about you, praying you'd be all right until I could come for you."

Bonnie gently laid her palm against his face. "When ye didn't surface . . ." Emotion closed her throat.

"I know," he murmured, brushing a tender kiss across her lips. "It's over now."

But both of them understood their ordeal wasn't over. Neither spoke about the future, about what would happen next, whether they were destined to die now, after all they'd been through together, the trials they'd overcome. Such an end seemed ignoble, hugely unfair in light of the walls they had scaled. They had beaten so much more than death.

But, Bonnie thought, as her limbs grew heavy once more, the strain of rising to see what faced them was too enormous a task; if she must die, then there was no place she'd rather be than in Gray's arms.

Three days later Bonnie had accepted her death as inevitable.

She was surprised she wasn't more frightened. The fragile nature of human mortality, of life coming to an end, had always scared her, more so after her father died.

Seeing her father lying there on his bed, clothed in his best tartan, had felt surreal. To a ten-year-old, death had appeared as sleep, as if her father would awaken at any moment, smiling when he saw his daughter, opening his arms for Bonnie to fling herself into them.

But that never happened, and death's finality had rung darkly within Bonnie from that moment forward.

Now, however, she felt at peace, light swirling around her, voices calling her. She recognized the voices and smiled. No, she thought in some distant place in her mind, it would not be so bad.

"For the love of God, man! Throw the Jacob's ladder over the side and be bloody quick about it!"

The harshness of the voice jarred her, making her frown and try to turn away from the noise, but she couldn't move; her limbs were weighted down.

"Bonnie! Oh, sweet Jesus, Bonnie."

Aidan? The name spiraled dizzily through her head.

Bonnie moaned as hands touched her legs, her skin burned from the sun, though Gray had try to protect her body from exposure as best he could.

He jerked beside her, his voice nearly unrecognizable. "Goddamn you! Be careful with her!"

Then she was being lifted, carted from one set of hands to another, hoisted up into the air as if she were ascending into heaven. The motion stopped abruptly, and Aidan spoke again, but this time with such venom that Bonnie flinched.

"Look what ye've done tae her, ye bloody bastard! If she dies, I swear, ye'll wish we had hanged ye!"

"If she dies," came Gray's raspy voice, edged with despair, "you won't have to kill me . . . I'll do the honor myself."

Chapter 25

Gray came down with malaria.

No one thought he would survive the week, let alone the entire voyage, especially since the return trip to Scotland had been delayed by an additional ten days due to rough seas and fighting westerly winds.

Bonnie didn't remember most of the trip, only snippets, tintypes in her mind of her brother hovering over her or someone struggling to feed her, cold cloths being applied to her face and a mound of blankets piled on top of her.

Visions of Gray had haunted her, of seeing him dive beneath the dark water of the sacred well never to resurface. The nightmare would jerk her awake time and again, panting, sweating, an unvoiced scream on her lips.

It wasn't until they were into the last leg of the journey home that Bonnie finally felt well enough to sit up and eat her first meal unassisted.

She had been severely dehydrated, the ship's doctor had told her. Another day or two and she would have died. Thank goodness she hadn't been burned all that badly or it could have been much worse, he said. She had tried to tell them that Gray had saved her from that fate, but no one would listen to her.

She had wanted to see Gray, but her brother had deftly evaded her questions about him. The more close lipped Aidan became, the more Bonnie's concern grew, until finally she had stumbled out of the cabin calling Gray's name, slapping her brother's hands away when he attempted to take her back to her bed.

She had found Gray in the dank and dirty hold, being kept prisoner, an ankle chained and bolted to the floor as if he could make a bid for freedom lying there with his chest hardly rising and falling, a sickly sweat glistening over his upper torso, still wearing his torn trousers.

Bonnie had thought he was dead when she first saw him, his pallor ashen, his eyelids barely fluttering when she sank down beside him and stroked his cheek.

Her brother had tried to tear her away from him, telling her that he was very ill, as if she couldn't see that for herself, couldn't see how very close she was to losing him.

Bonnie had turned on Aidan then, a red haze of savage anger blinding her the same way it had that day she had taken her dirk to Gray. She seized her brother's knife, ripping it from its sheath before he knew what she was doing and thrusting it toward him.

"Bring him up this very minute, or by God, I'll skewer ye where ye stand!"

Aidan had gaped at her in shock. "Ye don't know what you're saying. The fever must still be upon ye. I saved ye from this bastard. Don't ye remember?"

Bonnie's hysteria rose, the pain at witnessing how horribly Gray had been treated tearing her to shreds. "How could ye do this tae him? If he dies . . ." A sob lodged in her throat.

A fierce scowl crossed Aidan's face. "Why do ye care if he dies? The man stole ye from your kin. We've been scourin' the seas lookin' for ye, spread out in every direction. Ye were near tae dead yourself when I found ye. Had we not stopped in Lisbon and heard about a sailor who was nearly beaten tae death by a hulking Englishman, we might never have traveled as far as we did. The map the man handed over was the only clue we had."

Bonnie barely registered the fact that her brother now possessed the map. "Did the slimy toad tell ye that he tried tae rape me? If Gray hadn't found me . . ."

The tears running down her cheeks pulled Bonnie from that terrible day back to the present. She glanced down at Gray, calm and still on the bed after a night of thrashing about, a night Bonnie had spent praying.

Her maid, Alpen, poked her head in the room. "How is he today, miss?"

"A little better," Bonnie replied wearily.

She'd barely slept in the nearly two weeks she'd been home and she was thankful to have Alpen. Bonnie didn't know what she would have done without the kindly older woman who had been her only ally against her brothers, giving her a shoulder to cry on when they had proven difficult.

Aidan had been determined to lock Gray with the rest of his crew in the rat-infested dungeon that hadn't been used for more than forty years.

"I want him in a bedroom in the castle," Bonnie insisted vehemently, prepared to go to any length to keep Gray near her. "Post a guard if ye must, but he will be here."

Her brother reluctantly capitulated to her demands, returning Selwyn to guard duty, and this time the man had no intention of allowing Bonnie to elude him as she had once before. He stood outside the door like a sentinel.

What anyone thought Gray could do in his condition was beyond Bonnie's comprehension. Even if he should awaken and attempt to escape, the only way out would be through the window, and the drop of nearly fifty feet to the ground below would deter even the most stouthearted.

But her brother was more determined than ever to see Gray hanged this time, to pay for a crime Bonnie knew he had not committed. No amount of talking on her part would convince Aidan otherwise.

He had ranged the length of the library in long, angry strides as he carried on about her duty to her family, to their dead father, her solemn vow to uphold his request. He would not yield to her foolishness. At no time had he asked her what she wanted, what she wished for her own life. Bonnie wondered if her happiness meant anything to Aidan. She had always thought it did. She no longer felt such conviction.

Abruptly, he had stopped ranting, regarding her for a long moment before striding purposely toward her, coming to stand directly in front of her, his eyes searching her face. "What is this man tae ye, Bonnie?"

My lover, my friend, the man of my heart, she longed to say, but such words would be pointless. They would not save her from marrying Ewan, and they would not make Gray love her. "He doesn't deserve tae die," she said. "He's not a murderer, Aidan."

"You're daft, girl," he scoffed. "Ye saw him with your own two eyes."

"I never saw him kill Sarah. The man I've come to know would never have done such a thing."

He waved a dismissive hand at her. "The bastard has muddled your mind."

"My mind has never been clearer. Don't ye see that he could have killed me at any time? But he didn't."

Her brother chose to ignore the truth staring him in the face. "Ye were half dead when we found ye."

Bonnie had had this argument with her brother countless times since her return and he still did not hear her. She wondered if he ever would.

"What would it hurt ye tae dig a bit deeper?" she

asked. "Tae search around and ask more questions? What good will it do ye if ye hang an innocent man?"

Aidan's jaw tightened. "Even if he didn't kill Sarah, the whoreson kidnapped ye, and that alone is a hanging offense."

"I forgive him."

Aidan's frown sharpened into an angry scowl. "Did he touch ye, Bonnie? Force himself on ye?"

Bonnie almost laughed with despair and regret. Gray? Force himself on her? Never. How many times had she wished he had been less noble? Even now she wanted him with a fervor that was hard to contain. She suspected she would always want him.

"No, he didn't force himself on me."

"Are ye carryin' his child?" Aidan demanded, lowering his voice to a discreet level, as if worried someone might overhear his sister's shame. "Is that why ye protect him so?"

The question took Bonnie aback, not because of its unexpectedness but because she had wanted so desperately to be carrying Gray's babe, to have something of him that she could love if she could not have him.

She bowed her head, tears threatening. "No, I'm not carrying his child." Her monthly had come the week before and she had sobbed with the loss.

Heartbreak overwhelmed her, and she could stay not a moment longer. She fled the room and had not seen her brother since. He had kept his distance. As she had. Once again, her family had left her little choice. She would have to find a way to free Gray herself.

This time, however, the task would be much more difficult. Between Selwyn and the extra guards her brother had stationed around the castle, attempting to escape undetected would be a mammoth feat. As well, she had Gray's crew to consider. They were locked up in another section of the castle, a fortress much harder to break.

One plan presented itself, an idea that depended on

things Gray had told her during their time together. Bonnie only prayed God would give her the necessary time to pull it off. It would mean asking Ewan to delay their wedding once more. She didn't look forward to the meeting.

"His fever is down today," Alpen remarked, bringing Bonnie back to the present as the maid-turned-nurse pressed the back of her hand to Gray's forehead. "Aye, he's definitely cooler. I think all your tender care has pulled the lad through."

Bonnie hoped that was so. "I need more quinine," she said, speaking of the medicine the doctor had recommended for Gray's treatment. "Can ye send someone tae get more?"

Alpen frowned slightly. "What happened tae the last bottle?"

"I dropped it by accident." Bonnie moved next to Alpen and opened her palm for the maid to get a glimpse of the small bottle, still full, in her hand.

Bonnie darted an anxious glance at the door standing ajar, knowing Selwyn was just beyond, ears attuned to report back anything suspicious to her brother.

Bonnie's gaze met Alpen's, endeavoring to convey with her eyes what she could not say. Alpen, God bless her, quickly understood that Bonnie needed no more quinine, but something far more important instead.

Alpen nodded. "I will dispatch a boy tae the apothecary immediately." She made sure to speak loud enough for Selwyn to catch it.

"Thank you." Cautiously, Bonnie pressed the sealed envelope into Alpen's hand, who then slipped it into her apron pocket. The expression in Alpen's eyes said that she prayed Bonnie knew what she was doing.

Then her maid departed. Now only time would tell if Bonnie's plan would work.

She sank down onto the bed beside Gray. He was quiet, no longer thrashing and moaning as if his very soul were being pulled from his body.

The first week, when he had been in the throes of delirium, had been the worst. Every demon that dwelt within his soul had come out to torment him. The only way she could calm him was by lying down beside him.

For hours she would listen to his ramblings, hearing the heartbreak of his life, memories of a painful childhood, of a mother who didn't love him, ripped between two worlds by the cruelest word a parent could call a child: *bastard.*

From the depths of the darkness Gray dwelt in those two weeks, he revealed himself to her, the fear he had lived with, the self-loathing, the rejection. It all spilled out during those long hours when she didn't know if he'd make it through the night, laboring for each breath until Bonnie felt her own lungs would explode as she matched his rhythm, trying, through some madness, to force another inhalation, another exhalation.

At last he had overcome the worst of it, or so she hoped. He had lost weight and his face showed hollows that had not been there before. But Bonnie was heartened by the fact that he had woken up that morning, a smile filtering across his lips when he looked at her, and she felt certain he was on the mend.

At lunch, she had managed to get some food into him. He had whispered her name and stroked his knuckles across her cheek before his eyelids had fluttered shut, pulled down into a healing sleep.

Now she could only wait . . . and pray.

"You're late."

Bonnie stood in the great hall of Belraine, the Cameron stronghold for over two hundred years, and stared dispassionately at her husband-to-be, unable to call forth even the smallest amount of regard for him. He seemed different somehow, or perhaps it was only she who had changed.

With a stiff stride that told her he was displeased that

she had not been prompt, he met her in the middle of the hall. Bonnie glimpsed the large portrait of Ewan's mother hanging over the fireplace in the dining hall. The woman's eyes seemed to follow her every move.

Belraine had always left Bonnie cold. The vaulted ceilings never held any laughter. The tapestries were severe-looking, depicting war scenes, and the tables were barren of anything that would make the castle feel more like a home. It was evident that there had been no woman's touch to lift the harshness of the place in many years.

Ewan's mother, gossips whispered, had never forgiven her father for losing the land that had been in their possession for six generations, property that should have been passed down to her sons. She died an embittered woman.

Ewan, though formidable, had never seemed bitter to Bonnie, merely uncompromising, authoritarian, far too sure of himself. But he was laird and held much responsibility, so she had dismissed those traits as part of his position.

But now, seeing the way he regarded her, Bonnie thought she glimpsed something akin to hatred in his eyes. She knew he was still angry with her, though he did not know the full extent of her entanglement with Gray, that she had actually gone to his cell with the intention of releasing him on that night so long ago.

Her brothers had remained surprisingly closemouthed on the issue, but Ewan had pressured her for answers, more concerned with what had transpired between she and Gray than with her general welfare. His verbal attacks became more pronounced with each day that she put off their wedding.

That was the reason she had come today, to ask him for more time. She harbored no illusions that things would go well. She was glad to have Alpen along, and relieved to know her letter was safely gone.

Ewan stopped before her and regarded his pocket

watch once more; it was missing the fob sporting the clan crest of five swords tied together with a ribbon. "It's half past the hour. Ye were supposed tae be here at four sharp."

"I was detained," was all the answer Bonnie intended to give.

Ewan's features hardened. "Nursing that murdering bastard, ye mean?" When she made no reply, he locked a hand around her upper arm and yanked her down the hall toward his office. "Stay here!" he barked to Alpen when her maid made to follow them.

Bonnie darted a glance over her shoulder and gave Alpen a reassuring nod, even though inside she worried about what was to come.

Ewan's fingers dug into her arm, but Bonnie said nothing. She knew he wanted her to whimper, to punish her for some unnamed slight. She would not give him the satisfaction.

Once through the office door, he gave her a slight shove and slammed the door behind them. Bonnie tried not to show her fear, but the way Ewan looked at her made her stomach knot with unease.

She forced her chin up and met his cruelly appraising regard squarely. "I've come tae ask for more time."

He pushed away from the door and stalked toward her. Bonnie chided herself to stand firm, but she couldn't help the half step back she took before she stopped herself.

When Ewan stood in front of her, he leaned down and said tersely, "No." Then he startled her by snaking an arm behind her back and roughly hauling her against his chest. "I've been more than fair with ye. That murderer has been getting all your attention and I've received no reward for my patience, not even a single kiss from my betrothed, and I'm not a happy man, my sweet." His voice dropped to a growled warning. "In fact, I'm quite put out at this moment. What are we tae do about that?"

Bonnie's first impulse was to lever her hands between them and pry him off. Having him so close, feeling the sickening hardness of his sex pressing against her belly made her stomach heave.

But she knew if she let her anger show, he would only place more demands on her, and she needed him to remain benevolent. For Gray's sake, she could not take the chance of angering Ewan. If he forced her hand, she might find herself wedded before the day was out.

Swallowing her revulsion, Bonnie forced a falsely sweet smile on her face. "If it's a kiss ye desire, my lord, it's a kiss ye shall have."

Then she lifted up on tiptoe and lightly touched her lips to his, hoping her acquiescence would dispel his anger. Instead, his arms tightened around her, crushing her to his chest as his mouth moved brutally over hers, driving her back until she felt the edge of his desk against the back of her thighs.

She struggled wildly, trying to cry out at his savagery, but the sound was covered by his mouth and his harsh grunts as he ground his hips against her, one hand roughly squeezing her buttocks and the other hand sliding up her side to cover her breast.

He would take her without her consent, rape her. She knew it as surely as she knew the mistake she had made in giving him even the smallest encouragement.

As he pushed between her legs, bending her back over the desk, she caught his tongue between her teeth and bit down as hard as she could, tasting his blood in her mouth, his howl of pain echoing throughout the cavernous room.

When she released his tongue, he leapt back, his face a mask of rage. He lifted his hand to strike her, and Bonnie cringed in expectation of the blow. But it never landed. His arm remained suspended in midair, even though everything about him screamed that he wanted to kill her.

A rapid knock sounded at the door. "My lady?" Alpen called out. Bonnie could hear the thread of panic in her maid's voice.

"Tell her you're fine," Ewan ordered through clenched teeth.

Bonnie strove to control her breathing, her entire body shaking over what had almost happened. "Everything's all right, Alpen. I'll be out in a moment."

Ewan eyed her malevolently, making no attempt to hide his feelings. " 'Twas a very bad thing ye did, my girl . . . a very bad thing indeed."

"I'm sorry. I didn't mean tae hurt ye, but . . . ye frightened me." Bonnie hated the lie. She had wanted to hurt him and only wished she had done worse, but she held her tongue. She had no other choice.

As she suspected, he placed the blame for his actions on her shoulders. "Had ye not kept me waiting all these years, taunting me with your body, begging a man tae be tamin' ye, ye wouldn't have been treated so harshly. Ye brought it on yourself. All the more reason we should be wed immediately—before I take what is mine and the hell with the vows."

The thought of Ewan on top of her, doing to her what Gray had done made bile rise in Bonnie's throat. She could never willingly submit to his pawing. Though she could not have Gray, being with another man would feel too much a betrayal.

"I'm only asking for a few more days, my lord. Ye've been patient this long. Please," she added, loathe to beg, but willing to do so for Gray's sake.

His gaze raked her body and his eyes held no warmth when they met hers, telling her clearly she would pay for the grief she'd done him this day.

"Ye have till Sunday, but not a day more. And then ye will be my wife, Bonnie MacTavish. As God is my witness."

* * *

Gray heard the bedroom door open and pretended he was asleep. Selwyn liked to check on him, hoping, Gray suspected, to find him awake, all the better to hasten along his execution. Gray did not need the facts of his current prisoner's status explained to him. His circumstances were patently obvious.

As soon as he was well, he would be dead.

He thought it rather ironic to be nursed back to health for the sole purpose of being killed. But his demise from illness would certainly ruin his executioners' enjoyment. They had been waiting so long to see him meet his final reward, as violently as possible.

Gray figured Selwyn was in as big a hurry as Bonnie's brothers to see him dangling by his neck, since Gray had not endeared himself to the man.

As if to expedite the process, the giant would come in and jab Gray in the side to see if he'd get a reaction. Since the bastard always poked his bruised ribs, it was difficult for Gray to keep his moan of pain behind his teeth.

He had succeeded rather admirably thus far. But since the last poking session was only a short while earlier and his ribs still ached, Gray wasn't sure if he'd make it this time.

But as soon as the door closed and the breeze carried that faint hint of heather, Gray knew it was not Selwyn who had come to see him. It was Bonnie.

But being with her was its own torture, each gentle stroke of the cloth across his head, each sweetly whispered word that he get well and wake up, each tender brush of her lips against his before she departed was slowly and irrevocably killing him.

For two days he had wanted to speak to her, but words eluded him. He had failed every test placed before him. Moreover, he had failed her. He was a coward, just as she had once called him, because he couldn't face her, couldn't tell her how much he loved her.

The moment she sank down on the bed, her thigh pressed to his, he felt more pain than Selwyn could ever inflict on him. If only sickness had taken him, Gray thought. If only she had let him remain behind his comfortable barrier.

"Come tae me, my love," she crooned like an angel, making Gray wonder if she knew he was awake, saw through his pretense. The beckoning quality of her voice made him want to give up his charade and enjoy whatever time he had left with her.

Too soon. Too damn soon. He just wanted a little more time. He wouldn't ask for anything else if only he could have these last few hours with her.

"Aye, but ye are a handsome lad, and quite a charmer, too." Her low, breathy voice caused every muscle in Gray's body to contract. "Never have I seen such beautiful brown eyes."

That remark brought Gray up short. Brown eyes? A sudden surge of jealousy swept through him as he realized Bonnie was not talking to him.

"My eyes are gray, damn you!" Despite his best efforts, he could no longer remain quiet.

But when he opened his eyes, blinking away the blurry haze, he realized he had made quite an ass of himself, for the only other male in the room . . . was Jack, who proceeded to vault from Bonnie's arms and pounce on Gray's stomach with enough force to expel the air from his lungs.

"Jack!" Bonnie exclaimed, trying to recapture the wriggling puppy as it slathered its tongue exuberantly over Gray's face. She finally managed to scoop up the dog, much to Gray's relief. He had visions of being smothered in slobber.

Quickly, she placed Jack on the floor, and then the next thing Gray knew, Bonnie's warm lips were pressing sweetly against his. The contact immediately sent a hot flood of desire surging through him, and though he suspected Bonnie only meant the kiss the way Jack did, as an exuberant welcome back to the land of the living, Gray wanted much more.

He drew Bonnie down on top of him. She gave no resistance, but instead melted into him in a way no other woman ever had. Never had it felt so good to be alive, to feel the intoxicating warmth of her body against his, his blood racing through his veins as he ravaged her mouth like a man who had long been denied the only thing he needed to survive.

"Gray," she murmured between kisses. "Oh, thank God."

Gray couldn't think beyond the need that poured through him. For so long he had denied himself and Bonnie. What a terrible time to discover he didn't want to deny himself any longer.

She wore a dress. His Bonnie. Never had he been more thankful. He rolled her over onto her back and gripped the hem, slowly raising the material, skimming his hands along the silky length of her calf, up her thigh, his hands delving beneath to cup her buttocks.

"Selwyn," she murmured, reminding him of the guard just outside the door even as she moved against him, her fingers bunching in his hair, sweet moans issuing from her lips as he mouthed her nipple through the fabric of her dress. He felt frenzied, wanting to shove inside her and stay there, make her forget his fate and himself forget that this time she could not come with him.

"The devil with Selwyn." If the man entered now, for ill or not, Gray would strangle the life from the bastard.

"But . . . you're sick."

"So heal me."

Gray unbuttoned his breeches, and without another word, slid fully into her slick, waiting warmth, feeling her tighten around him, pulling him into her body.

"I love ye," she whispered, the words spilling out as he thrust into her, dying with sentiments he could never return, to leave her in this world with a love he could not share. It would be heartless, so he showed her his love the only way he knew how: with his body.

He wrapped his arms beneath her legs to bring her tighter against him, needing to get as deep as possible, striving to touch whatever part of her he could, perhaps wishing, in his wild need, that he could plant his child inside her.

He lifted her higher, his hands groping for the buttons on her bodice, pulling the material free, groaning as his mouth latched on to one ripe, rose-colored nipple, feeling her hot sheath contract as he suckled, drawing the peak higher in his mouth, pounding into her with the fury of a storm until ... sweet Jesus, she pulsed around him, drenching him with her honey, letting him sink into her very soul, his own climax searing through him.

Reality came back all too soon. Gray cursed himself for being ten times the fool as he slowly eased out of Bonnie and rolled to his side. He should have left her alone. She deserved better, so much better.

As if sensing his withdrawal, she righted her bodice and resumed her position on the edge of the bed, darting anxious glances at the door.

"I'm sorry," he murmured, wishing he could stay with her, hold her, make things right.

She stared down at her hands, and he felt like the worst bastard God had put on this planet. All he ever did was hurt her when all he wanted to do was love her.

She withdrew something from the drawer of the bedside table. "This is for you." She took his hand and placed the familiar object in his palm.

It was his map.

"I don't understand. How did you get this?"

She glanced up, tears brimming in her eyes, the sight

wrenching Gray's heart from his chest. "It doesn't matter. I just wanted ye tae have it back."

Then she leaned over and brushed a poignant, bittersweet kiss across his mouth, a sob breaking in her throat as she pulled away, bounding to her feet and dashing from the room, leaving Gray to listen to the sound of his world crumbling around him.

Chapter 26

Today she was to be married.

This moment had always seemed surreal to Bonnie. She knew the day would come but she had never been able to envision it. Perhaps she had simply believed that if she wished hard enough, things would change.

But they hadn't, and misery seeped into her bones. Nothing she did could shake it, least of all sitting in her bedchamber preparing for a wedding she prayed would never take place.

So she'd stolen out of the castle when no one was looking and come to the spot she had seen in her mind a thousand times but had never returned to since the day Sarah Douglass was found dead.

The alleyway behind the tavern.

She didn't really know what she was doing, what she expected to find. But nightmares had haunted her these past few days, visions of this place beckoning her back— ever since she had left Gray's room in tears.

She had not been back to see him since. She acted the coward, sending Alpen to feed him, to report to

her on how he was doing, trying not to see the pity in
the older woman's eyes.

Gray was recovering, up and walking about, Alpen
said. Eating heartily once more. Asking about her. Bonnie blotted that out, concentrating instead on the fact
that his strength was returning.

She should have been heartened by this news, but
she could not summon the emotions she should now
that Gray's health was returning. She just wasn't ready
to let go, to never see him again. To be another man's
wife.

Bonnie laid her hand over her womb, shivering in
remembrance of the way Gray had loved her, the fury in
each fevered stroke, the all-consuming passion. Perhaps
this time he had planted his babe inside her. Sweet
merciful God . . . how she hoped so.

Bonnie shook herself from the memories and concentrated on the present, glancing around the dirty alleyway, her eyes briefly lighting on the spot where Sarah
had once lain, cold, blood pooling around her.

No traces of blood remained, yet an aura clung to
the place, as if Sarah's soul had been entrenched in
that spot, her spirit yearning for justice. And that was
what Bonnie wanted, what brought her here today. Justice.

Not just for Sarah, but for Gray as well. Even if her
plan worked—and Bonnie prayed it did though time
was quickly running out—she knew the charge of murder would enshroud Gray all his days. He had risked
death to salvage his name, his honor. She couldn't let
that be for naught.

A sudden noise made Bonnie jump, her heart skip-
ping a beat as she whirled around to see who had
entered the alleyway. She exhaled in a rush when she
saw that it was only a ragman, rummaging around for
bits of food and whatever else he could find in the refuse
pile outside the tavern. Yet she couldn't quite dismiss
the fact that she was alone with the man.

He glanced up then and caught sight of her, his startled, wary expression telling her that he had not realized she was there. Bonnie recognized this man, had seen him once or twice before, knew he was a loner, always scurrying away when anyone got too close.

"Wait!" she called out when he made to leave.

He darted a frightened look over his shoulder, seeing her closing in on him, his gaze swinging from her to the end of the alleyway, perhaps wondering about making a dash for it before she got too close.

"I won't hurt ye," she vowed as she neared. With every step, he seemed to shrink, as if falling into himself in an effort to be as small and inconspicuous as possible.

"I weren't doin' nothin', mistress," he said, the whites of his eyes standing out starkly in his dirt-streaked face. "I were just wantin' a wee bite tae eat."

Bonnie's heart went out to the man. Clearly he was just scrapping by. She dug into her pocket and retrieved a few coins. "Here, take this."

"Oh, no, mistress. Ye canna be givin' an old beggar yer money. Wouldn't be right."

"Please . . . I want ye tae take it."

Reluctantly, he held out a wizened hand, and Bonnie deposited the coins in his palm. A glimmer of something caught the corner of her eye, then disappeared. But, when the man pocketed the coins, she saw what it was, an incongruous object on a poverty-stricken man.

A gold watch fob.

Without thinking, Bonnie reached for it, wanting to take a closer look, but the beggar backed away, fear in his eyes.

"May I?" she asked.

The man hesitated and then extracted the dull, battered pocket watch—with its gleaming fob, a clan crest she well recognized emblazoned on it.

"Where did ye get this?"

"I didn't steal it, if that's what ye be thinkin'."

"I know ye didn't steal it." The fob burned a hole in

Bonnie's palm, her mind shifting back to the day in Belraine when Ewan had ranted about her being late. His fob had been missing. "Did ye buy this fob?"

"Nay, mistress," he said, so low Bonnie could barely hear him. "I found it."

An ugly suspicion began to burn in Bonnie's brain. "Where?"

The man swallowed and darted an anxious glance about the alleyway. "I should say no more."

"Are ye afraid?"

He began to ring his hands and shuffle his feet nervously. "Aye, mistress."

"Why?"

"Because . . . people will talk."

"What people?"

He swallowed. "All o' them. They'll say 'twere me who done the deed—an' I didn't do nothin' wrong. I swear it!"

Cold suspicion crept up Bonnie's spine. "What will they say ye did?"

His murky brown eyes flashed away from her, toward the crates at the back of the alley. "It were just lyin' there," he said in a thin, strained voice. "Next tae her."

The words froze Bonnie's insides. "Sarah Douglass? Is that who ye mean?"

Panicked eyes flew back to hers. "I didn't mean tae take it," he rushed out. " 'Twas just so shiny an' sittin' on the ground pretty as ye please. I shoulda known 'twere evil when the mon come back lookin' for it. Furious he was. Ragin' an' a-swearin' enough tae call forth Lucifer from the pits o' Hades. He woulda kilt me had he seen me, I know. He will now. He'll come after me an' slit me throat, too!"

Without warning, he shoved Bonnie to the ground and raced away down the alley. "No! Don't go! Come back!" But he was gone, taking his information with him, the proof she needed to clear Gray's name.

And yet, when she glanced down at the fob he'd left

behind in his mad flight, she knew she had the one
piece of evidence that would cast the light of suspicion
on the man who had to be the real killer.

The man she was about to marry.

A bone-deep trembling shook Bonnie's limbs when
she realized the impact of her discovery. No one would
have ever suspected Ewan. Not the laird of a mighty
clan. Yet what could have compelled him to kill Sarah?
That part made no sense. He barely knew her.

How she longed to confront him, demand that he
tell her how his fob piece came to be laying in the alley
next to Sarah's body. But what did she expect? That he
would admit he was the murderer? Not likely.

No, her only choice was to show her brothers her
discovery. Together they would face Ewan.

As Bonnie dusted herself off and rose a bit shakily to
her feet, she realized the cold piece of metal clasped
in her palm had the power to change lives, to right a
terrible wrong.

Yet a disturbing thought gnawed at her: without the
ragman, she had no way to prove the fob had been
found in the alleyway. Aidan might very well think she
had fabricated the whole story to get out of marrying
Ewan, or simply to save Gray from the noose.

Bonnie knew then that she had to find the beggar
and plead with him to tell his story. She would have to
assure him that no harm would come to him and offer
him Aidan's protection.

Her deliberations halted when she heard the noise
again, the soft, barely audible scuff of feet. Bonnie's
head came up, her senses alert, her mind whirring with
the realization that the beggar had returned.

She whirled around, a smile of gratitude wreathing
her face. But the smile quickly died when she saw that
it was not the beggar who stood only a scant foot away,
but a towering man . . . with eyes of the palest blue. And
those eyes blazed into hers with deadly menace, stating
clearly that if she made a sound, her life would be forfeit.

"Where is he?" the stranger demanded in a low, rough voice.

Bonnie forced herself to breathe. "W-where is who?"

He leaned down close to her face and said with barely suppressed anger, "My brother."

"Has anyone ever told you that you smell like a barrel full of rotten eggs?" The jibe earned Gray a forceful pound in the back from a hand the size of a shovel. He found his balance at the last moment, saving himself from another face-first slam into the floor. He shot a glare at his guard. "You should be glad I'm handcuffed; otherwise I'd beat your ass up and down this hallway."

Selwyn snorted derisively and treated Gray to another vibrating shove that rammed his shoulder into the wall. Pain ricocheted down his side. Before he had a moment to recuperate, the giant seized him by his collar and heaved him forward again.

Gray had a number of choice words he would have enjoyed hurling at the bastard, but if he wanted to live long enough to enjoy the one outing he was allowed each day, it would behoove him to keep his comments behind his teeth—while he still had them.

Nevertheless, he couldn't contain one last colorful remark, "I hope you choke on your tongue," which garnered him a meaty fist to his midsection, the air knocked from his lungs in a whoosh.

Gray doubled over, nausea roiling up inside him as he collapsed to the floor, his head pressed against cold stone as he labored to catch his breath.

A voice drawled, "Not a very sporting attitude, old man. The lad's all but defenseless. Why don't you pick on someone your own size?"

The next thing Gray heard was a cracking thud and a grunt; then the earth shook with the impact of Selwyn dropping to the ground beside him in an unconscious and very ugly heap.

Only one person Gray knew could have felled this Goliath.

"Need any help, brother?"

With a pitiful moan, Gray eased back on his haunches and stared up at the last person he expected to see, knowing his expression was too pained to look confused. "Damien."

His brother quirked a brow. "I see you did not heed my advice and stay out of trouble."

Gray attempted a grin but knew it appeared more like a grimace. "And I believe I told you that trouble was my middle name. I take after my older brother, after all."

"Smart ass." Damien clasped Gray's hand and hefted him to his feet.

"Another trait we share."

"Are you all right?"

"I could be better." He rubbed his aching stomach.

"You look like shit."

"How kind of you to notice," Gray murmured dryly. "May I ask what you're doing here?"

Damien, always impeccably attired, even in the midst of potential anarchy, dusted a speck of lint from his sleeve. "That sounds suspiciously ungracious, brother. But since you're clearly not up to snuff, I will outline the obvious. I'm here to save your ass. No need to thank me. Seeing your humiliation is reward enough."

"And might I ask how you knew my ass needed saving? I had yet to unleash my full wrath on that fat slug." He cast a disgusted look at a still-unconscious Selwyn.

Damien quirked an amused eyebrow. "Your full wrath? I shiver to think of it. But enough idle chitchat. I will tell you everything as soon as we get the hell out of here. I'm a shade indisposed—bloody Scottish weather—and couldn't possibly fight more than ten or fifteen men, tops. So it's best not to dally. Follow me."

Without another word, Gray followed his brother, completely baffled as to how Damien knew he was in trouble, though the man had always been damn uncanny. When they were children, every time Gray hid, Damien located him before five minutes had passed. Gray could have buried himself underground and his older brother would have sniffed him out. Gray was convinced Damien possessed some bloody second sight. Unnerving, it was.

What was perhaps more unnerving was how his sibling seemed to know his way around the castle, ducking through a hidden doorway, slipping down a dark, narrow corridor until finally reaching the end and carefully easing open a cleverly disguised stone portal that groaned with the heavy scrape of rock against rock.

Once outside, they quickly blended into the woods, the foliage thick enough to adequately cover their stealthy departure.

"Keep moving," Damien urged. "The guard will awaken any minute and sound the alarm."

Gray could feel the affect his illness had had on him. His chest heaved with the exertion of running and his legs felt as if they would give out at any moment. If Damien hadn't chosen that moment to stop, Gray might very well have collapsed.

Breathing hard, he sank his hands onto his knees and endeavored to catch his breath, perspiration trickling down his back even though the day was cloud-covered. Damien, the sod, hadn't even broken a sweat, nor did he look the slightest bit winded. The rotter had always been in deuced good shape.

"You could . . . at least pretend to be . . . tired," Gray said between breaths.

"If it would make you feel any better, I'm tired on the inside."

Gray straightened, feeling as if every limb was cramped or about to spasm, and returned his brother's long-perfected dry smile.

"I have two horses tied about a mile away," Damien informed him. "Do you think you can make it that far?"

Gray had no intention of telling his brother he couldn't make it, though he had his doubts. "Of course."

"Good; then let's go." Damien began to move away, but Gray took hold of his arm.

"I have to get my men."

"Obviously you think me dim-witted. Your men were saved first, thanks to the help of a robust matron named Alpen and a bit of muscle on my part to overtake the single guard. The castle is replete with hidden passageways. While I came for you, Alpen was guiding your crew out. We are to reconnoiter at the designated meeting place in an hour. So hustle, my man. This is no time for naps. I'd rather be home to dine with my wife this evening instead of having a tedious scuffle with a bunch of sapheaded Scots. Now, if you please." Damien waved a hand ahead of him.

Gray gaped at him. "Did you just say . . . *wife?*"

"I see your hearing is still sharp. And yes, I did say wife. Married three months now, and bloody blissful, I might add. And as a newlywed, I'm in a particular hurry to take up where I left off nibbling on my darling wife's neck. So, once again . . . if you please." When Gray still didn't budge, Damien gave him an impatient look. "Must I carry you? Or could there be something about 'let's go' you don't understand?"

Gray glanced over his shoulder. He could just make out the dim outline of the castle. Everything had happened so fast, so unexpectedly, that he hadn't had a moment to think. Perhaps that had been a good thing, because if he had, he probably wouldn't have left.

He wanted to see Bonnie, just one last time. He knew he shouldn't, that it was better this way, quicker, cleaner, to sever all ties. He was a complication that Bonnie didn't need. Yet logic seemed to have deserted him.

"Something wrong, brother?" Damien inquired.

"No . . . I'm just . . ." *What? In love with a girl whose brothers want to kill me? Going to miss her sweet face? Think about her even though I know she's better off without me?*

"Could your hesitation have something to do with a petite Scottish lass with intriguing blue eyes?"

Gray snapped to attention. "You've seen Bonnie?"

"Is that her name? Hmm. Seems rather fitting."

"Where is she? Is she all right? Did she say anything about me?"

Damien reared his head back and slanted a dark brow at him. "Good Lord, man, I never thought the day would come. This is positively priceless."

"What the blazes are you talking about?"

"Why, the fact that you've been whipped, my boy. Head over arse for a female. A goner. I'll be damned."

Gray snorted. "Not bloody likely."

A broad grin split Damien's face. "You're in love with her."

"I'm not in love with her," Gray steadfastly maintained, his teeth aching from the lie.

"Could have fooled me. I've seen that look before, my good fellow. And you, dear boy, are hopelessly ensnared. Trust me, running away from it won't do a damn bit of good. I tried. Once the lovebug bites you in the ass, you're pretty well done in for."

"Don't be stupid."

Damien shook his head, clearly amused at Gray's expense. "You certainly are fighting it, aren't you? What, are you worried the girl doesn't love you in return? Or are you simply stupefied that you've met your match? Deuced hard to believe a woman fell for you." He shrugged. "I guess there is someone out there for everyone. Even you."

Gray searched for a biting comeback—snappy retorts were de rigueur between himself and his brother, after all—but hell and damnation, he could think of not one bloody thing to say that didn't sound suspiciously like he wanted to avoid the subject.

Damien chuckled. "A feisty little spitfire you've got there, brother. Didn't seem to appreciate my coming alone to rescue my defenseless sibling. Thought I should have brought an army or something. Marched in here and promptly waged war. Wanted to drag out the queen's dragoons. Scream bloody murder. Clearly the girl doesn't know who she is dealing with. It's patently obvious that the famed adventures of the Sinclair clan haven't reached this far north."

Gray's brain took a moment to return to a functioning state. "Are you saying Bonnie brought you here?"

"I believe I answered that. She's a clever girl, and I rather admire her. Never expected to find the female version of you in this backward country. But damn if she isn't just as stubborn, cockeyed, and misguided as you. Bursting with bloody nobility." Damien shook his head and heaved a sigh. "Now, what is all this rot about saving me from losing our beloved ancestral home? I hope you didn't nearly get yourself killed on some hare-brained scheme. I might very well have to kill you myself if that was the case."

"How the hell do you know what I was doing?"

"I'd rather like to say I was an oracle, thereby retaining that shiny aura of mystery that once clung so tenaciously to me in my heyday, sending people fleeing for their lives instead of having every bloody person think I'm a veritable saint, a misunderstood sheep—due to my wife's campaign to completely eradicate any hint of the hell-born devil I once was. But alas, should Eden get wind of today's escapade, she would have my hide—and I do so want to keep in the darling girl's good graces. Ain't too fond of the couch, you see. So, to answer your question—Bonnie told me."

Gray scowled. "And how would she know? I never told her."

"Seems you still have that terrible propensity to talk in your sleep, or in this case, during your delirium. Confessed quite a bit, from what I understand."

"So glad to know you two were having a nice chat while I was here getting beaten," Gray muttered, disgruntled, and more than a little bit curious about what else he might have said in his sleep.

Damien stared blandly at him. "Please. I punched you harder when we were lads than that overdeveloped grunt did today. By the by, that girl of yours is rather exceptional. Think I'm going to like her. Can't wait to introduce her to Eden. I suspect they'll become boon companions."

"Don't hold your breath. Bonnie's getting married." The words left a rancid taste in Gray's mouth.

"Ah, yes. That's right. Married. Today, as a matter of fact."

Gray felt as if a steel rod had just been rammed through his head. "Today! What do you mean today?"

"Meaning not yesterday or tomorrow. Does 'today' have a different connotation in your world?"

Gray raked an agitated hand through his hair and scowled off in the direction of the castle. "I can't bloody believe it. She's marrying the bastard." Did their time together mean nothing to Bonnie? Was that why she had not come back to see him after that last time in his room? When he had pressed her body down into the mattress and loved her with all the pent-up emotion inside him, trying to tell her with actions what he couldn't say with words?

"Does it matter if she's getting married?" Damien inquired. "If I recall, you don't love her. So why should it make a difference?"

"Because it does," Gray snapped.

"I see. Here is where I imagine you are going to tell me we must save her from a life of drudgery and unhappiness, correct?"

"No."

"No? Dear brother, you are turning me inside out. Care to explain why we won't be going after the lady in question? Seems the thing to do at this juncture."

"Because."

"Ah, now there's an electrifying answer that makes complete sense. I see everything clearly now."

"You don't understand."

"Care to enlighten me, then? I've been told I'm a rather good listener."

Gray felt as if his insides had been scooped out, leaving him completely hollow. All his life he had thought himself empty, barren of feelings, but never had he known emptiness as he experienced at that moment. Bonnie would be marrying another man.

He didn't care anymore about concealing the truth. What did it matter now? The ugliness he had kept hidden was what sent Bonnie away from him, that self-imposed wall Gray had imprisoned himself with all these years. He wanted to speak the truth now, like confessing a sin, revealing a black stain.

"I'm not good enough for her."

Damien quirked a brow. "Excuse me? How could you possibly not be good enough? You're a Sinclair, my boy."

"That's the point. I'm not a Sinclair."

"Not a Sinclair? What folderol is this? Do you mean I mercilessly tormented you as a child and you weren't even my brother?"

Gray swung around. "This is serious, damn you! I'm not your brother. Do you understand? I'm a bastard, mother's by-blow. She told me so years ago."

Damien blinked . . . and then threw back his head and roared with laughter. "You always were a gullible clod."

Gray stalked away, not sure where he was going, just needing to head somewhere, anywhere. "I'm glad you find this so amusing. I'm sorry I told you. I shouldn't expect you to understand."

Damien caught up with him. "Now that's hitting below the belt. And besides, surely you, of all people, should know you can't believe any of Mother's tripe. The woman takes cruelty to a whole new level."

Gray stopped abruptly and faced his brother. "Did she ever tell you that you were a bastard?"

"Countless times."

"I mean, illegitimate."

"Well . . . no, but—"

"Thought so." Gray continued walking.

Damien clutched Gray's shoulder, grinding him to a halt, his amused expression gone. "Come on, Gray. You have to know by now that Mother revels in causing a furor. Her world would crumble to dust if she wasn't making someone miserable. I've finally learned to accept it. Who knows how she was treated as a child? Maybe this type of malicious behavior is all she understands."

Damien could tell his brother was not entirely convinced by his argument. Damn mother to hell! The woman was a blight on humanity.

"Gray, listen to me; you are my brother, you will always be my brother, and there isn't anyone in this world who is going to convince me to believe otherwise."

"But what if I truly am another man's son?"

"It wouldn't make a damn anthill's worth of difference to me. Blood alone is not what makes us brothers. It's knowing it in here." Damien tapped his chest. "In your heart. That's the only place it will ever matter to me or Nick. And together, brother, we will shake the very pillars of heaven. Now," he said brusquely, "shall we step back into the lion's den and carry away the bride-to-be? You know how much I enjoy a good brawl."

Chapter 27

Bonnie had exhausted every lead to find the ragman.

For nearly two hours she had searched the alleyways, querying the vagrants who haunted such places, obtaining leads that went nowhere.

What made her task all the more difficult was that people were looking for her. A young girl of about fifteen had spotted her and told her so. After all, only an hour remained before Bonnie was supposed to get married—to a man who could very well be a murderer.

From that point on, Bonnie had tried to remain as inconspicuous as possible, but time was quickly running out. She needed the beggar's help if she wanted to confront Ewan. Without the man, it would merely be her word against Ewan's.

Determined to keep trying, Bonnie resumed her inquiries. But a few minutes later she halted in her tracks when a commotion caught her attention. She gasped. Her brother's men were heading in her direction!

Quickly, she ducked into an alley and slipped between two crates, kneeling down. Cautiously, she peered around the edge of the crate. A guard was not more than ten feet away! He was speaking to the girl who had warned Bonnie that they were looking for her.

Bonnie jammed her back against the wall when the man suddenly glanced down the alleyway, her heart thumping in heavy, painful strokes. Would he come this way? Would he take her back to her brother? Back to Ewan? What would happen then? Oh, if only she had more time!

Two words, "Escaped murderer," drifted to her ears, telling her that she was not the target they sought.

Relief flooded Bonnie, but not for herself. For Gray. His brother had managed to free him. She had been so worried, unable to believe the towering man who had frightened her half to death would be able to sneak through the castle undetected, even if she did tell him about the secret passageways. As well, there was Selwyn to contend with.

But clearly the man who had introduced himself as Damien Sinclair had far greater skills than she had given him credit for.

She had wanted to go with him when he left to help his brother, but she had forced herself to remain where she was. Seeing Gray again would only make things that much harder, one more memory to keep her heart from mending. She could at least do this one last thing for him—prove his innocence so he could truly be free.

The guard finally departed, and Bonnie slipped from her hiding place, moving warily along the alleyway, expecting someone to spring out at her at any moment. She peered around the corner of the building and saw the men moving away. She closed her eyes and sagged in relief, saying a silent prayer for Gray's safety.

She emerged from the alley, trying to remain in the shadows as best she could. She had only taken a dozen steps when a hand took hold of her arm. Bonnie swung around, ready to lash out at whatever devil awaited her, but it was only the girl the guard had been speaking to.

"I knew ye were back there, miss. Saw ye dash away, but I didn't tell no one. Figured ye must have had yourself a good reason tae be keepin' outta sight."

Bonnie gathered her breath and stilled her heart, managing a weak, "Thank you."

"I think ye should know, miss, that there be a murderer about. The prisoner has escaped. So I warn ye tae tend tae yourself carefully."

"Did they say anything else about the, er, prisoner?"

"Mighty baffled, they are, as tae how the man got away. They say he was helped, but don't nobody knows by who. He just up an' vanished."

Bonnie could only hope Gray and Damien were long gone by now.

"Now heed me words, miss. The man's a dangerous one, he is. Keep an eye about ye."

"I will—and thank you again."

The girl bobbed her head.

Bonnie started to go, intent on resuming her search for the beggar, but then hesitated. On impulse, she turned back to the girl, deciding to take a chance and ask her if she had seen the man Bonnie was looking for. Bonnie gave the best description she could and felt the first seed of true hope burgeon inside her when the girl nodded her head.

"Aye, miss. I think I know the man ye be speakin' of. Old Angus. 'Tis a quiet sort, he is, given tae roamin' alone. Keeps tae himself mostly."

"Do ye have any idea where I might find him?"

"Well, he sometimes stays at the old Duggan place. 'Tis fallin' down an' full of mice." The girl made a face. "Not fit for a body, if ye ken my meanin'. But Angus don't seem tae care."

"Where is this place?"

"Just a short ways outside of town. I'll show ye."

* * *

Bonnie's heart sank as soon as she came upon the ramshackle cottage on the outskirts of the village, its walls crumbling, the roof caved in, several rodents scurrying over the rotted steps.

The girl hadn't been exaggerating when she said the place was run down. It was completely uninhabitable. How could Angus possibly stay here?

It would be foolish of her to walk up those rickety steps and take a chance stepping inside, not knowing what might collapse about her. Besides, not a single sound came from inside, and she had called Angus's name several times. The house looked deserted. Bonnie sighed. Clearly, this was another dead end. But she might as well take a quick peek inside since she was here.

Squaring her shoulders, she headed carefully up the steps, the wood creaking ominously beneath her, a little field mouse scampering over her shoe nearly causing her to lose her balance and tumble back.

"Relax," she chided herself.

Her hand trembled slightly as she reached for the knob that hung from the door at an angle. It came away in her fingers at the first pull.

Using her hand, Bonnie eased the door open a few inches, glimpsing broken furniture, cobwebs, and a thick layer of dust on the floor.

"Hello?" No reply met Bonnie's ears.

An air of disuse clung to the place, yet she spotted a single battered tin plate sitting on a rough-hewn table, half-eaten food on it, revealing that someone had recently been there.

Wretchedly disappointed, Bonnie turned away, deciding not to waste anymore time here. Time was a commodity too short in supply to waste. She was about to head down the stairs when she heard the creak of wood.

Heart hammering in her ears, Bonnie swung around,

expecting to see Angus standing there, wariness and
suspicion etched in every crevice of his world-weary face.
But she was alone; nothing had changed.

Then the sound came again.

Swallowing, Bonnie returned to the door, her breath
coming in short pants, her palms growing clammy as
she eased open the door the rest of the way, the hinges
screaming in torment. Then, as if greased, the portal
swung freely, revealing a gruesome sight.

Sprawled out in the middle of the floor, blood oozing
from a gash at the side of his head, was the man she
had come looking for: Angus.

Terror held Bonnie immobile for a moment, but concern quickly won over fear and she rushed to Angus's
side, kneeling down beside him. "Angus?" He didn't
move. She shook him lightly. "Angus, please wake up."

Then a floorboard groaned . . . directly behind her.

"I'm afraid that will be impossible. I've killed him."

Panic sluiced through Bonnie in a startling jolt, propelling her to her feet. She stumbled back over the
broken pieces of furniture, knocking the tin plate to
the floor, nearly falling as she swung around to stare
into the eyes of Angus's murderer.

"Where the hell is she?"

Gray was frantic. It seemed as if he and Damien had
been searching for Bonnie for days instead of a few
hours, always managing to stay out of the reach of the
MacTavish clansmen who poured through the town like
kilted ants. But the danger was inconsequential to finding Bonnie.

More than once Gray had nearly said the hell with
hanging back in the shadows and instead grabbing
someone by the scruff of the neck and rattling loose
some answers. But each time he tried, Damien's hand
clamped down on his shoulder, hauling him back.

"Be patient, man. We'll find her."

Gray prayed to God his brother was right. He could not rid himself of the escalating sense that something was wrong, that Bonnie was in trouble and needed him. If anything happened to her . . .

"Now there's a suspicious-looking character," Damien said, gesturing to a man loitering in the shadows across the street.

Gray's jaw tightened as he stared at the man Damien referred to. "I know him."

"You do?"

Gray nodded. "He was at my farce of a trial."

A keenly felt volatility arose in Gray as he remembered what had transpired that day, how his hands had itched to strangle the son of a bitch, a sensation that stirred to life again.

"Well, if my instincts are right—and they are rarely wrong—I think he's up to something."

Gray agreed. The shifty bastard clearly had a purpose, but the townsfolk were too busy rallying themselves together for their manhunt to pay any attention.

When their target suddenly hastened toward the wooded area at the edge of town, casting a glance over his shoulder to see if anyone was following before disappearing from sight, Gray felt in his gut that this trail would lead him to Bonnie.

"Let's go," he said, blending into the thicket.

"Right behind you, brother."

A knot of fear settled in Bonnie's stomach as she stared in horror at the man standing not more than fifteen feet from her, his face lit with an evil smile, a smile that conveyed she would not be leaving this place alive.

He took a step toward her, and Bonnie quickly skirted around to the other side of the table, her gaze flying about, looking for another way out. But there was only one: the door.

And a murderer stood between her and freedom.

"Ye look as if ye've seen the devil, lass."

"I have." The words came out a raw whisper.

He tsk-tsked. "Ye needn't be so surprised. I thought ye had it all figured out in the alleyway."

The blood drained from Bonnie's face. "Ye were watching me?"

"Aye, I could have killed ye in the same spot where I slit that other bitch's throat. Would've been fitting in my opinion. But then that stranger showed up and ye left with him, which brought ye a few hours' reprieve. Now ye've crawled intae my web. How very obliging of ye."

"Why are ye doing this?"

"Ye weren't my prey. I was there for this scum." He spat toward Angus's prone, lifeless form. "I knew he had found the fob; it broke off during Sarah's struggle for her life. Such a shame that women are so weak. She never had a chance." He shook his head in mock sorrow. "I heard someone coming down the alley and had no time tae retrieve the fob. How fortuitous for me that ye convicted the Englishman of my crime."

"But why did ye kill Angus now? He must have had the fob all this time."

"Aye, I imagine he did, but it didn't much concern me because you and the Englishman had disappeared. I figured ye were dead, and no one seemed tae be thinking about Sarah and her untimely death anymore." The ominous slit of a smile he had worn thus far melted away, to be replaced by an expression considerably more sinister. "But then ye had tae go and return, and I couldn't have old Angus confessing what he knew in one of his drunken stupors. He had tae be taken care of. But then he up and disappeared. I think ye drew him out of hiding."

"Me?" Bonnie could not bear the thought of being the reason for Angus's death.

"I suspect he might have been trying tae get up the

nerve tae speak tae ye about what he knew of Sarah's murder. He didn't just appear in the alleyway today. He followed ye—and I followed him. But, thankfully for me, the man has always been a spineless little squint. Ran off on ye—but left the fob. That was his mistake. Now, it appears it's going tae be the cause of your unfortunate, fatal accident.'' From behind his back, he produced a wicked-looking knife. ''They'll say that Angus killed ye, and then, stricken with remorse for his actions, he killed himself.''

Bonnie's chest constricted, her lungs unable to get enough air. She had to force herself to breathe past the fear building to blinding proportions. ''No one will believe that.''

''I think they will. Angus was never quite right in the head. The townsfolk will use their limited imaginations and assume it was Angus who killed Sarah and not the Englishman. Somehow you discovered what he'd done, so he had tae kill you, too. A few whispered words bandied about will get people headed in the wrong direction. It did with that English bastard. Your clan was whipped intae quite a frenzy. Bunch of idiots,'' he taunted with a laughing sneer.

Bonnie could not believe what she was hearing. But she had no time to digest his sickening revelations as he began to stalk her, his stride unhurried and purposeful. He knew he didn't have to rush. No one would find them or even hear her should she scream.

''Come now, lass. Don't make this harder than it has tae be. Your death has been fated for a long while now. If things had gone the way they were supposed tae, ye would already be dead.''

Bonnie backed away as he advanced, keeping the table between them, hoping to draw him around to the opposite side—farther away from the door.

''Why are ye doing this?''

''You're a MacTavish. That's crime enough.''

''But our clans have made peace.''

"Peace?" he snorted derisively, the word sounding like a curse on his tongue. "There is no peace. Ye and your kin are a bunch of thieving bastards. Ye took what rightfully belonged tae my family."

Bonnie stared at him in disbelief. "This is about the land?"

His eyes narrowed to slits, madness shining brightly in their depths. "Did ye think ye would get away with it? That ye could steal frcm us?" His voice rose with each word.

"We didn't steal!" Bonnie retorted, moving ever closer to the door. "That land was won fairly."

"Fairly!" he raged, his face mottled. "Ye stole it and ye know it!"

Methodically, he tracked her every move. Her only hope was to run as fast as she could toward the door and pray her legs would not give way.

Her blood roared in her ears as she continued to back away. Then, unexpectedly, he lunged for her. Bonnie screamed and flew toward the door. He grabbed her hair, yanking her back. She slammed into him. Frantically, she clawed at the hand tangled in her hair. Then she rammed her elbow back into his stomach.

He grunted in pain and momentarily loosened his grip on her hair. Bonnie wasted not a moment, and bolted for the door. No knob! She clawed her nails around the edge and slung the portal back . . . barreling straight into another body.

Instinctively, she opened her mouth to scream, but a hand clamped down, muffling the sound. "Ssh, lass. No one is going tae hurt ye."

Wild-eyed, Bonnie glanced up, the familiar voice momentarily suspending her struggle.

"Let's go back inside now."

Bonnie shook her head, trying to rip his hand away.

He ignored her, giving her a less-than-gentle shove before entering swiftly and closing the door behind him, situating Bonnie squarely between the two men.

Sean Cameron . . . and the newest arrival.

Her bridegroom.

"I counted two of the bastards."

Gray barely heard his brother, his body and mind consumed with a need for action. They had circled around behind the rundown shack, barely able to see through the single dirty window to the gathering inside.

The moment Gray caught a glimpse of Bonnie on the other side of the room, saw her pale, frightened face, fear twisted through him like a knife.

Gray didn't realize he had started for the front door until Damien grabbed hold of him. "Think, man!" he said in a low, fierce voice. "If you act rash, you might get yourself and Bonnie killed. We have to draw them out."

Gray knew Damien was right, but he couldn't think straight. God, he had only told her one time how he felt, and that had been in the heat of passion. He had to tell her what was in his heart, his soul, let her look into his eyes and know this was forever. He had to say the words.

"If anything happens to her . . ."

Damien squeezed Gray's shoulder. "I know, brother . . . I know."

"I'm sorry it had tae come this, my dear," Ewan said without sincerity, shaking his head. "I had hoped tae kill ye on our wedding night: an unexpected fall down the stairs at Belraine or an accidental ingestion of poison. Alas, things have not worked out the way I planned." He turned a malevolent glare on his cousin. "Because this stupid fool mucked everything up— *again.*"

Sean glared at his cousin with something akin to hatred. "I didn't ruin anything! How was I tae know that cow Sarah would overhear our conversation about killing your bride?"

"If ye had kept a tighter rein on the stupid bitch like I told ye tae, she wouldn't have been snooping where she didn't belong," Ewan hissed in return.

"Well, she's no longer an issue. I killed her like ye told me tae do."

Aye, and ye left my bloody fob behind for that old beggar tae find."

"I didn't leave it behind! The damn girl grabbed hold of it. I didn't know it was missing until I went to return the watch tae your room."

Bonnie gaped at Ewan, feeling as if the world had been cut from beneath her feet. "Ye told him tae kill Sarah?" Until that moment, she had thought Sean had murdered Sarah on his own whim, but Bonnie realized now that Sean had never done anything on his own. He had always been Ewan's puppet.

Ewan affected a detached expression. "I couldn't have her telling ye of our plan, now could I? I don't think ye would have married me if ye knew ye wouldn't survive the wedding night." A salacious smile curved his lips, his gaze raking her body. "Though I would have made your last night alive a pleasurable one, sweet, I assure ye."

Bile rose in Bonnie's throat. "You're sick."

His jaw clenched, his fingers tightening into fists at his sides. "No, I'm very smart, and I'll tell ye why. For years I hated my grandfather for losing our land, cursed him to everlasting hell for his bungling. But then I discovered a way tae not only get Cameron land back, but tae strike at the very heart of the MacTavishes for cheating us out of our property. I would marry you."

Bonnie was staggered by the loathing that resided in Ewan, masked so effortlessly all these years. "And how would that get your land back? It belongs tae my family, not me alone."

"Ah, but that was your bride price, my girl. Didn't ye

know? Your brother, Aidan, dowered that land to ye, and as your husband, it would be mine, back in the hands of the person it rightfully belonged to at long last. There'll be no feud tae further deplete my funds, and best of all, the precious daughter of a thieving swine will be dead. No one the wiser. So ye see, I'm smarter than ye think.''

"Ye'll get nothing! I'll never marry ye."

"And there ye'd be wrong again. Ye'll still marry me."

"You're insane!"

"If ye don't, I'll have your brothers and half your clan massacred before they know what hit them. Shortly there will be a church full of people gathered to celebrate the coming together of our two clans. All the people ye love under one tidy roof. Think of the bloodbath that will take place if ye don't do as your told. If ye behave yourself, I promise tae make your death as painless as possible."

Horror took Bonnie in its grip. She was being left no way out. Either she married Ewan or her kin would die. "Ye have tae promise me that ye won't harm my family."

"Once I have my land back, your family can burn in hell for all I care. Now"—he measured the word— "come over here and give your husband-tae-be a kiss— and mark my words, should ye try another move like ye did at Belraine, ye will be very, *very* sorry." He regarded her with a smug half grin that said he had won. But there was one way she could thwart him, the only option open to her.

"No."

"What do ye mean, no? I said tae come here . . . *now!*"

"I'll marry ye because I have tae, but I won't let ye paw me. Ye'll not touch me."

A red flush of anger scorched Ewan's neck and cheeks. "Get over here, damn ye!"

Inside, Bonnie trembled, but she held her ground. "No."

Ewan took a threatening step toward her, but Sean

grabbed his arm. "We haven't the time for this. Just get tae the church, man!"

Ewan glared at her, his jaw clenching and unclenching. Bonnie didn't think he would relent, but then he barked, "Let's go."

Sean seized Bonnie by her hair and thrust her forward into Ewan's arms. He leaned close to her ear and hissed, "Ye'll be sorry for your defiance, I promise ye." Then he shackled her wrist in his ruthless grip and dragged her to the door, Sean behind them.

They had just descended the steps when a flash of movement caught Bonnie's eye. Then an ear-splitting bellow thundered into the sky as a body hurtled full out toward Sean, ramming him in the stomach, the air audibly knocked from him as the two figures flew off the porch, crashing with a heavy thud over the other side, out of sight.

Bonnie was whipped around as Ewan positioned her in front of him, his arm hooking around her neck, applying pressure so that her breath came out in gasps.

"Let her go," came a dark voice, full of black venom, another body emerging from the side of the house, tall, powerful . . . and dangerous.

"Gray," she whispered, her eyes locking with his.

"Stay where ye are!" Ewan bit out fiercely, his hold growing more punishing on Bonnie's neck. She dug her nails into his forearm, struggling to pry him away. "I'll kill her!" he vowed.

"Harm a single hair on her head and hell won't be far enough for you to go to get away from me," Gray said menacingly, taking a step forward.

"Stay back, damn ye!" He raised his arm. In his hand was a gun . . . the barrel pointed at Gray's heart.

Bonnie could feel the frenzy in Ewan, a cornered dog wildly seeking a way to escape. He would do anything to get free . . . anything . . . even kill Gray in front of her eyes.

"Tell him!" Ewan ordered. "Tell him to stay back or your dead!"

"Gray . . . please don't. Just let me go."

"Let you go?" Gray shook his head. "That's not possible. I once foolishly thought that I could, that a stone would bring me happiness, bring me freedom, but it was you who did that. My father told me when he placed that ring in my hand that someday I'd find what I was searching for. Well, I've found it—and it's you, Bonnie. It's you. You saved me . . . so many times, in so many ways. Now nothing will keep me from saving you. I want to be your hero, the man of your dreams. Your everything."

Bonnie's eyes blurred with tears. "Ye already are," she whispered in an agonized voice.

Then Ewan's arm tightened, choking her. He backed away, looking around frantically as they edged closer to the woods.

Gray kept on coming. "You'll never get away. Let her go."

Ewan suddenly stopped, a burning oath on his lip. "You're dead, ye bastard," he hissed. To Bonnie, he sneered, "Watch your lover die."

And in the next instance, he fired the gun.

Bonnie screamed as the bullet ripped through Gray's chest, sending him spinning to the ground, a stain of blood seeping through his shirt.

"No! Dear God, no! Gray!" She struggled wildly against the hands that gripped her. "Let me go!"

Damien barreled forward then, a sound like a war cry on his lips. Ewan raised the pistol again, but Bonnie bit down on his arm. He yowled, the bullet flying wildly into the air. He threw her to the side and aimed the gun again. Damien dove to the ground, rolling quickly, the bullet driving into the earth in the spot he had just been.

Bonnie scrambled on her hands and knees toward Gray, taking his head into her lap. "Gray . . . Gray . . ." She brushed the hair back from his face, her tears dropping onto his shirt, mingling with his blood. "Oh, please don't die . . . please . . . I need you."

His eyelids fluttered, and then those beautiful silver eyes gazed up at her. A half cry, half laugh broke from her lips. "Bonnie . . ."

"Bitch! Ye've ruined everything!"

The raving bellow jolted Bonnie, her head swinging around to find the gun leveled on her.

"Now ye'll die." Ewan cocked the hammer.

Gray lifted his head. "Behind you," he rasped in a pained voice.

"That ploy won't save her. Say good-bye tae your true love . . ."

Bonnie closed her eyes and held on to Gray, but the next sound she heard was not a bullet but a heavy *thwap* followed by a grunt.

Her eyes flew open to find Ewan unconscious on the ground . . . and Prophet's beaming face regarding them over the top of a bush, a thick tree branch in his hands. Then a whole group of familiar faces appeared from amid the foliage—Gray's crew and Alpen.

Gray grinned weakly at Prophet. "I thought . . . you told me . . . you abstained from violence."

Prophet shrugged and returned Gray's smile. "Someone once told me that a simple clubbing over the head was the most effective means of incapacitating someone. Thought I'd take his advice."

Gray chuckled and then winced in pain. "Damn . . . that hurts."

"Lie still," Bonnie ordered, gently probing his injury.

He tugged at a lock of her hair. "Lean down, I have to . . . tell you something."

"Hush. Save your strength."

"No, I have to tell you . . . something. It can't wait . . . any longer."

Bonnie cupped his cheek. "What, my love . . . what do ye have tae say?"

"Something I should have said . . . a long time ago. I love you, Bonnie . . . I love you."

Epilogue

"And that, my dear grandchildren, is the story of the brave and fearless treasure hunter."

"But wait, Grandpa!" Liam protested, leaping from Gray's lap. "You didn't tell us what happened to everyone."

"Oh." Gray scratched his cheek. "Well, they all lived happily ever after, of course."

"But what about the bad man?" Maggie asked, staring up at him with wide eyes, full of admiration. "Did Prophet kill him?"

Gray ruffled her hair. "No, moppet, just gave him a good headache."

"Did they hang the man for being so mean?" Liam persisted. "Feed him to the sharks? Make him go to bed without supper like Mama does to me and Mags when we're bad—though she always does come with a tray a little while later. Did they do that, Grandpa? Did they?"

Gray felt the first niggling of worry that perhaps he had gone a shade overboard with his tale. Visions of an angry Bonnie berating him for giving the children nightmares flashed through his head.

And then his worry became reality when he heard a voice say in a displeased tone, "Aye, husband, what did happen?"

Gray swallowed. Lord, he was done for now.

Sheepishly, he rose from his chair and turned on his heel like a prisoner about to face execution. However, it wasn't just his wife he found behind him, but his whole family: his brothers, Bonnie's brothers, their wives, his four daughters, their husbands—all looking damnably amused.

But Gray couldn't concern himself with them. He had to soothe his wife, and judging from her expression, he suspected he and the dog would be sharing quarters.

He gave Bonnie a chagrined smile. "Hello, love. How's dinner coming?"

She cut him off at the pass, knowing him too well to be fooled. "Never mind dinner. Are ye brangling these bairns again with your fanciful tales, husband? After I specifically told ye not to?"

"Well, I . . ." Gray frowned and admitted gruffly, "You told me to keep them occupied."

"Aye, with a game of tag or marbles."

Liam scooted around the couch and hastened over to his grandmother, tipping his head back and blinking up at her with big eyes that never failed to melt Bonnie. Gray knew he was in for it now.

"You mean none of what Gramps told us was true, Grandma?"

Bonnie knelt down beside Liam and brushed a lock of unruly hair from his face. "Oh, my sweet baby, didn't I tell ye that your grandfather was a good storyteller?"

"You mean you didn't throw a knife and pin a savage to a tree?"

"Throw a knife?" Bonnie shot a sharp glance at Gray, frowned at him quite expertly, having been doing it for nearly thirty years, and then returned her attention to her grandson. "No, love, I didn't throw a knife at a savage."

"And Grandpa didn't almost die of malaria?" Maggie asked, peering at Bonnie over the top of the chair.

"Malaria!" That earned Gray another glare. "No, your grandfather never had malaria."

Gray looked for the nearest exit as Liam dug his grave a bit deeper.

"And he wasn't accused of murder and he didn't steal you away from Uncle Aidan and take you to a lost island and solve a four-hundred-year-old mystery either?"

Bonnie gaped. "Steal me? A lost island?"

"And Uncle Damien never came to save him?"

Damien barked with laughter at that. "Save him? I think I walloped your grandfather in the head one too many times when we were lads and it has affected his mind."

Gray scowled at his brother, who wrapped an arm around his wife's waist, looking entirely too smug—as did Nicholas, whose wife, Sheridan, stifled a laugh behind her hand.

"Come here, my doves." Bonnie beckoned both children to her side. "Now, your grandfather didn't mean any harm. His special gift has always been his ability tae sweep a person away into adventures of the heart." She glanced up at Gray, a hint of tenderness in her eyes as she added, "He takes after his father."

Gray smiled, knowing then that everything would be all right.

He rubbed his hands together. "Well, I'm famished. Let's eat!"

His foibles forgiven, the group rumbled their assent and headed into the dining hall. Gray, however, hung back.

"Bonnie."

She turned and gave him a quizzical glance. Gray said nothing, just looked up. He stood beneath the mistletoe.

She shook her head. "Oh, no, husband. Ye'll not win me over that quickly."

Gray simply smiled. "Come here, love."

She looked as if she might protest, but then she sighed at her fate and glided toward him, still as beautiful today as she had been all those years ago when he had fallen in love with her.

When she stood before him, gazing up at him with those incredible blue eyes, Gray knew that in Bonnie he had found what had eluded him all his life. She was his safe harbor.

His jewel beyond price.

He kissed her with all the love he had in his heart, and then, hand in hand, they went to join the celebration. Christmas was a night made for miracles, after all.

Behind them, the Christmas tree twinkled and the fire blazed in the hearth. For those who believed in miracles, should they look upon the Nativity scene on the mantel, they just might think they saw a perfect red diamond cradled in the hands of Jesus.

ABOUT THE AUTHOR

MELANIE GEORGE lives in New Jersey with her teenage son and two small dogs. When she is not writing, she is trying to restore her hundred-year-old house. Her award-winning books for Kensington include: HANDSOME DEVIL, DEVIL MAY CARE, LIKE NO OTHER, and DANGEROUS TO LOVE. She looks forward to the release of her first contemporary novel, THE MATING GAME, in the spring of 2002. Melanie loves hearing from readers. You can visit her at: *www.melaniegeorge.com*

Romantic Suspense from

Lisa Jackson